THE TEMPLE
OF THE
THREE WHISPERS

BOOK EIGHT:

PRIESTESS OF RUIN

BRIAN HARMON

The Temple of the Three Whispers
Book Eight: Priestess of Ruin

Copyright © 2025 Brian Harmon
Published by Brian Harmon
Cover Image and Design by Brian Harmon

ISBN- 978-1-945559-36-5

Don't miss these other great books by Brian Harmon!

The Temple of the Blind series:

The Box (Book I)
Gilbert House (Book II)
The Temple of the Blind (Book III)
Road Beneath The Wood (Book IV)
Secret of the Labyrinth (Book V)
The Judgment of the Sentinels (Book VI)

The Temple of the Three Whispers series:

The Lady of Cedric's Cove (Book I)
Circles in Hermes' Footsteps (Book II)
Misplaced in Mysteria (Book III)
The Denselands (Book IV)
The Impassible Wall (Book V)
The City Beyond Memory (Book VI)
The Keeper's Dollhouse (Book VII)
Priestess of Ruin (Book VIII)
The Temple of the Three Whispers (Book IX)
Whispers in the Murk (Book X)

The Rushed series:

Rushed (Book 1)
Rushed: The Unseen (Book 2)
Rushed: Something Wicked (Book 3)
Rushed: Hedge Lake (Book 4)
Rushed: A Matter of Time (Book 5)
Rushed: All Fun and Games (Book 6)
Rushed: Something Wickeder (Book 7)
Rushed: Evancurt (Book 8)
Rushed: Relic (Book 9)

Hands of the Architects trilogy:

Spirit Ears and Prophet Sight (Book 1)
Pretty Faces and Peculiar Places (Book 2)
Broken Clocks and Amber Threads (Book 3)

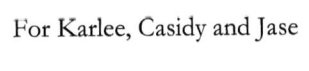

For Karlee, Casidy and Jase

Chapter 1

Awareness blossomed from nothingness. An awareness of darkness. Of cold. Of silence. An awareness of raw existence. Of consciousness where there had before been none. Of birth. Of awakening. Awareness of a duty to the faceless creators and to the Keeper of the Cycle to whom they pledged their great work. Awareness…and a somewhat troubling realization that he had gained this awareness much too soon.

He knew nothing until this very moment. His mind was brand knew, blank but for his basic programming, his memory utterly empty. But memories were only the data gathered from experiences. The core data was already there. Therefore, he understood what he was, why he existed. He was a tool of the Keeper, a means to an end, a vital gear in the ever-turning machinery that kept the universe going. And he understood what he *wasn't*. He wasn't a man. He wasn't human. He had no name, no identity, no *life*. He was something else, something both less and more. Most of all, he understood what he was here to do. His job. His *purpose* for existing.

But understanding was different from experiencing. That part of his artificial mind was an enormous void in which now floated a handful of curious seconds filled with darkness and silence and preprogrammed understandings and ponderings about how the timing was wrong and the clock inside him wasn't aligned with the world outside.

And it was no small difference. He wasn't supposed to be awake for quite some time yet. Even for one such as him, for whom time mattered little.

There must be a reason for it. But he couldn't think of one.

He needed more data.

He could sense the stoneworks chamber around him. His body and mind were still attached to it. Everything was working as expected. He could feel the other two wombs nearby. They were still dark and undisturbed, both without and within. They showed no sign of waking any time soon.

He stood there in the ancient nesting chamber, surrounded by cold stone, feeling the energy of the stoneworks pass around and through him, contemplating what this meant. It wasn't an error. It couldn't be. Because the Faceless Ones' designs tolerated no such concept. Because the *Keeper's* designs tolerated no such concept. It was impossible for any calculations to be off, for any malfunctions to occur. And yet here he was, perplexingly operational considerably ahead of schedule.

His first few days passed like this, his empty mind pondering how and why he might arrive at his destination unaligned with the proper time. Might it have something to do with the flaws of the universes? Those were one of the few unpredictable factors in the design. But even that seemed unlikely. The only *realistic* reason was that he was meant to awaken early from the start, meaning that he wasn't early at all and it was instead his clock that was programed to be misaligned at this point in his journey. Yet, he couldn't fathom why that would be the case. He had a single purpose and awakening early would make no difference to that purpose. It would only take him longer to do it.

And what would be the point in withholding data from him? For maximum efficiency, he should already have all the details of his mission preprogrammed into him. And as far as he was able to discern, he did, in fact, have that information. He was simply activated far too early.

Once he was finally convinced that no further data could be gathered without moving from this spot, he disconnected himself, exited his stone womb and stepped out into the open expanse of the nesting chamber.

The other two remained inactive. They weren't asleep, exactly. In fact, they weren't yet even alive. Little more than cargo, really. And they would stay like that. It wasn't his job to awaken them and their programming was irrelevant to him anyway. They served different purposes, were destined for different stone-works. Yet given his own unexpected modifications, he naturally wondered if perhaps they had been altered in some way as well. But even if he had the means of examining them, they had nothing to do with his duty here. They were meant for very different destinations.

With no knowledge to be gained, he dismissed them and began walking. He had no need for any light. The layout of the nesting chamber and the path leading out was programed into his brain along with his purpose. He knew exactly where his feet were at any given instant in relation to his surroundings. He knew exactly how far he was going, how many steps it would take him, how long it would be.

The only thing he didn't know was what sort of world he'd awakened to.

Not yet.

It took three days to reach the end of his passage and step out into the latest universe crafted by the Keeper's Architects, but that mattered little. He could have walked for years, if necessary. He didn't tire. He didn't hunger or thirst. He was an artificial being, after all, capable of surviving where living humans couldn't. To him, it was but a stroll through the darkness. He didn't even perceive time the same way the living would. To him, time was only data.

When he reached the end of the path, the Faceless Ones' devices worked flawlessly. The way back was permanently sealed. The way forward was thrown open.

The sun was blinding.

The weather was stifling.

He was surrounded by huge trees stretching up into a clear, blue sky. There was a light breeze that did little to cut through the afternoon heat. And there was an abundance of green both above and below.

It should have been beautiful, but the air smelled of smoke and was foul with the distressing sounds of distant screams.

He stood there for some time, a few minutes, a blink of an

eye to one such as him, processing everything, contemplating this new information stored in his infantile memory. He made notes of the weather and the terrain. He logged information about the creatures hidden among the towering trees around him. Small, flittering, flying things covered in feathers. Small, furry things scurrying through the branches and curled up in their dens. And so many tiny, crawling things in the dirt and the grass and the leaves. He didn't need to see them. He was able to detect things humans couldn't, with senses they didn't possess and wouldn't be able to understand.

Once he'd logged all the data he could find, he turned his attention to that distant commotion and began walking.

Curiosity was a part of his programming. It was one of the ways he would emulate the biological creatures he was modeled after, better to blend in, to go unnoticed, to stay out of humanity's business. Less risk that way, both for himself and for them. It would be unfortunate, after all, for him to interfere in any significant way. That wasn't why he was here. But his curiosity was also a useful tool for collecting data in real time, for learning. Because the more he learned about these creatures the Keeper valued so much, the more he understood them, the better he was going to be able to walk unnoticed among them until the time came for him to fulfill his ultimate duty.

But curiosity also sometimes led to very unpleasant things.

He followed the sounds of the screams until they fell quiet, then he followed the plumes of smoke rising above the forest canopy until, finally, he stepped out of the forest and onto a scene of bloodshed and destruction.

The remains of primitive wooden buildings atop artificial mounds of earth were smoldering. A small field of simple crops had been trampled and the ground was littered with broken tools, firewood, crushed baskets and scraps of food and animal bones and hides. Bloody bodies lay everywhere. Both men and women lay slaughtered in the dirt. Little ones, too, incapable of fighting back. Not one survivor remained.

He stood there. studying the scene, processing it all. This wasn't a mere skirmish. There was nothing left. The entire village was massacred, wiped from the face of the earth, altogether erased from history.

This was an *extermination*.

He wasn't prepared for such cruelty.

He felt his curiosity melt into a menagerie of other feelings. Sadness and despair. Anger and regret. Disgust. Things the Faceless Ones knew a human would feel when stumbling upon such a scene.

He didn't care for these feelings. He didn't want them. What happened here was not his business, and yet he found himself almost overwhelmed by these primitive emotions.

It was his first glimpse of mankind and already he was witnessing the aftermath of violent battle.

What kind of world had he awakened to?

His first impression of humanity was war. And it would be far from his last.

Chapter 2

The Priestess of Ruin sat upon her throne of decayed treasures, a fearsome silhouette against the churning, blood-tinged sky stretched over the littered wasteland behind her. Here, deep within these most decrepit depths of the universe's inevitable decay, she lingered for untold ages, waiting and pondering and scheming against the so-called Keeper and the endlessly spinning wheels of his great and *boring* mechanizations.

But mostly, she *watched*.

She watched a great many things, all the time, all at once. Time, after all, meant nothing to one such as her. It didn't flow like a river, unheeding, unstoppable, not when you had the power to reach out and seize it whenever you liked. For her, time was much more like pages in a book. She could flip through it as she pleased, forward or backward, skipping around, studying whatever interested her, word by word, moment by moment, examining all the gritty, gory, *dirty* details.

The filth of the world never failed to entertain her. If there was one thing humans were good at, it was deceit and betrayal. Lies. Cruelty. Selfishness. Injustice. The awful things people did to one another was like an endless symphony played especially for her enjoyment. She could always find someone doing something nasty to someone else, every day, every hour, every *moment*.

In *this* moment, she was watching the Faceless Ones' newly born puppet as he set off through the wilderness, his poor, virgin eyes already tainted by the ugly, inherent truth of humankind. A new toy for her to play with... Such possibilities... And yet the Keeper of the Stoneworks would have planned for that, just as he always planned for everything. (So *boring*.) She wouldn't be able to destroy the puppet. Nor would it be possible to corrupt it in any significant way. If she did, then it would inevitably be that it served no purpose from the start and was only there to distract her. The Keeper's aptitude for anticipating every possibility was beyond even *her* ability to comprehend. The best she could do was watch the silly toy wander this poisoned world, seeing with its own artificial eyes the horrors of these delightfully depraved creatures known as humans. And that was precisely what she'd do. Maybe she'd give him a little nudge now and then, point him toward the most awful things he could experience. Who was to say what might happen? With enough time, even a tool of the Faceless Ones might lose faith in the cycle.

And the Priestess of Ruin was nothing if not patient. She had plenty to keep her entertained. Her gaze was infinite. In this same moment that she watched the puppet, she watched a great many other things, as well. Again and again, she watched the countless, ever-waging wars that raged across the Keeper's most recent world, endlessly, repeatedly, and all at once, ever amused by the follies of mankind, ever amazed at the endless cruelties they seemed so adept at inventing. Not merely the bloodshed of the battles themselves, but every horrible act committed in the name of those pointless wars.

And at the same time, she watched the future-shaping events that occurred within the nearest of the Faceless Ones' gatehouses, as the Keeper's first six crawled through its stone guts in the final hours of the old Mother's long life.

And so too was her gazed fixed on the present, on today's twelve, and the havoc she was bringing to everything within the storm-drenched depths of the City Beyond Memory. A darkness was gathering there, she knew. A raw, chaotic miasma hung thick in the turbulent atmosphere, heralding a new and unprecedented end on the horizon, a cycle like none that had come before it.

Alone beneath her bloody sky, deep in the heart of the twisted wastelands of the Ruin where no one, living nor dead nor otherwise, had ever ventured, a smile touched her ancient lips and a wicked laugh echoed across the baked landscape.

It had been many ages since she'd had this much fun.

How long could the Keeper's infallible redundancies keep up with her chaotic meddling? How did he plan to put back the pieces she'd already taken off the board? How would he *unbreak* all the shattered gears she'd left strewn throughout the Temple of the Three Whispers?

It wasn't that she didn't think he could do it. On the contrary, she knew that he would. He had everything all planned out, a thousand steps ahead of her. That wasn't why she did the things she did. The fun was in watching *how* he did it, the lengths to which he would go just to keep his great machine running.

But there were only so many broken pieces he could hold together. At some point, it was going to be impossible even for *him* to plan around everything. At some point he was going to have to change the outcome. He was going to have to move on to plan B.

This was going to be *her* time. She'd scattered all the pieces he'd placed upon his game board. She'd even stolen several of them away from him completely. Two were here with her now, trapped beneath the red sky over which she held dominion. And a third she'd cast out into the endless void, unlikely to find his way back. His playthings were now *her* playthings. And she intended to enjoy them to her heart's content while she waited for his machine to crumble.

She was going to beat the Keeper this time. She could feel it. But it wasn't the idea of winning that excited her. It was the thought of seeing what he would do *then*.

That was what thrilled her. What was he going to do next? How far would he go to protect the cycle? What would he sacrifice to ensure one more world?

And what kind of world might he settle for? It wouldn't be the first time he chose a rotten one over an unsustainable one, after all.

And the Black World was full of so many fun and wondrously twisted things...

Her lips curled into a wicked smile as she rose to her feet and strolled naked across the barren landscape, her long curls trailing behind her as she gracefully stepped around the countless spoiled artifacts and ruined treasures that littered these rotten lands. Watching always entertained her, but what she really wanted was to play. And there were new toys waiting here in the Ruin for her to play with.

"So much fun…" she hissed, her voice rolling across the barren earth like a peal of distant thunder.

Chapter 3

Violet crept through the broken stones that littered the floor, her heart pounding with terrified anticipation. It didn't make sense. She peered up at that eerie red sky that was somehow hanging above her even though there should be no sky up there at all. She was inside one of the towers near the heart of the city. She might have become more than a little lost these past few hours since the other one fell silent, but she knew well enough that she couldn't be anywhere near the top of it. There were countless floors of stone stacked above her.

And how could everything look so old and ruined when the entire City Beyond Memory was built to be ageless? It had existed throughout countless cycles, remaining as pristine as the day the final stone was laid.

(*Ruin infects everything eventually. It will even spread across this city in the end. There will be no stopping it. The door must be opened before it can destroy all that we built.*)

The other one's dire warning…

Was that what was happening? Was she too late?

No… That didn't feel quite right. This felt like something different. It was like the portals she and Corey had encountered. A *pocket*. Merely mimicking the space around it. But this one was more complex than any they'd explored. She'd never seen anything like that bloody sky. And as she squinted up at it again, she realized there was something flying around up there. It wasn't a bird. Birds didn't warble like that, in and out of view like something from a flawed piece of CGI. That was something entirely different. And probably something very dangerous.

This whole situation was bad. The pockets she and Corey

found were all accessible through fixed portals. To exit, they only needed to retrace their steps and walk back out the way they came in. But there was no portal here. She was brought here by that frightful red glow.

It was the same color as that alien sky above, she realized. The same terrible aura. Almost as if this strange world were *alive*, as if it had taken it upon itself to reach across the boundaries and gulp her down like some otherworldly predator.

(*Something sinister is stalking you. The path I've shown you in this time has grown too dangerous. I've steered you off it in hopes that you might slip past, but it hasn't worked. Ruin is nipping at your heels as we speak.*)

Was that what this was? Had the Ruin caught her? Would it be impossible to escape, then? Was she stuck here? Forever?

Even if there did turn out to be a portal here somewhere, how would she even go about finding it? She had none of Corey's intel on this location to narrow it down. She had no equipment, even if any of their data *had* ever consistently led them to a portal. Her cell phone was dead, and even if it wasn't, it wouldn't help her find her way between two locations that both lacked any kind of cell service.

She could see in this place. That sky was the color of blood, but it was at least a *daytime* sky. She could see as far as these crumbling walls allowed her, meaning she could also see that there were no dangerous creatures lurking in here with her, crouched in the darkness, just waiting for her to stumble across it. But that was literally the only advantage in this situation.

She glanced back the way she came, to the pool of water she'd splashed through in her futile desperation to escape the red glow. But there wasn't a drop left. Everything was dry and baked and dusty. Even if something monstrous didn't show up to eat her, was there any water to be found in this world? It wasn't as if she had any supplies. If it turned out that she was trapped here, she could only hope to last about three days with nothing to drink.

But maybe it was premature of her to think she had any chance of lasting that long.

This room was easily twice the size of a sports stadium. It

was no wonder she couldn't see across it with her flashlight when she first broke the surface of the water. And just like before everything changed, every surface was made of that same smooth, gray stone. But there was a layer of dust and grime settled over everything. And the only sound was the eerie howling of a dry, hot wind. The walls were all cracked and crumbling, but even the most broken parts were still too high to see over. Strangely, however, she couldn't see any other walls sticking up behind these surrounding her. This was a labyrinth. There should have been walls *everywhere*. And what about all those other towers surrounding this one. Why was there nothing but that same red sky in every direction she looked? Was this all there was? Was this the only structure left standing? Was there anywhere for her to even go?

There were two doorways leading out of the room, one on either side, facing each other. She was making her way toward the closer of the two, anxious to see what might be waiting on the other side of it. But getting to it wasn't going to be easy. The floor was littered with broken stones ranging from scattered gravel to chunks the size of railcars.

It didn't even make sense. Where was the rest of it? Even if there was only one floor above her, wouldn't it have collapsed straight down, filling this entire chamber with rubble? The more she looked at it, the more it looked like something someone sketched out for the grand scene in some graphics-heavy blockbuster movie, the set of the final showdown, perhaps. The sort of place the Avengers might throw down with the next big villain.

But that was the sort of thing they'd seen while exploring portals, after all. Once, in a quiet Ohio town, they entered a portal under an old, covered footbridge and found that half of it was simply gone, with no structural supports whatsoever to hold what was left of it up. It was defying gravity, following its own physics.

It was a cool find. They took several pictures of it, but beyond the bisected bridge, they were unable to find anything else. Wandering more than a hundred feet or so away resulted in them just ending up back in the real world, looking at a *whole* bridge.

Corey simply declared it an anomaly. A fluke. There were probably millions of such places out there, little overlapping spaces that nobody ever noticed because almost nothing changed. It was what made it so hard to distinguish them from the real world.

She stopped and listened. Did she hear a noise just now? Or was it only that wind again? It was hard to be sure. She was so jumpy…

Where was the other one? She warned her she needed to conserve her energy, but wasn't this reason enough to get her lazy ancient ass out of bed and lend a hand? Shouldn't this qualify as an emergency?

She continued forward, slowly, gingerly tiptoeing through the rubble, raking aside the small debris with each step to make space for her foot. She needed to be careful not to step on anything sharp. She couldn't afford to injure herself. And there was no sign of her boots. They didn't travel to this ruined version of the labyrinth with her. They were probably back in that *other* room, at the bottom of that monster-infested pool.

Every few seconds, she was sure to look *upward*, too, keeping an eye on those warbling bird-like things circling around in the sky, making sure they weren't getting lower, circling, preparing to swoop down on her. There were three of them up there now, after all. Were they gathering like vultures, just waiting for her to die?

Things just kept getting worse and worse, it seemed. Maybe she wasn't as good at this stuff as she thought she was.

Her dad was probably right. She should've gone to college and applied herself to leading one of his company's project groups. She wouldn't be in this mess if she'd gone that route. But she made her choice and he respected her decision. She probably wouldn't have minded the work. They did some pretty cool stuff there. It was the other stuff that she didn't care about. Meetings. Deadlines. Team projects. As the sole heirs to their fathers' business, she and Corey would've ended up running the whole thing one day. And the politics of big business…all that stuff with investors and lawyers and accountants…employees and taxes and contracts and waste management and conservation concerns and ethical policies and all the rest… It all just sounded like an absolute nightmare. It always had.

She stopped walking, her thoughts scattering, a shiver racing down her spine.

That definitely wasn't her imagination. She heard something. It was carried on the wind, a faint but unmistakable sort of moan, like something that might have been at home on a Halloween haunted house soundtrack.

Something was out there.

Somewhere beyond those crumbling walls…in whatever unknown grounds surrounded this ruined chamber…

God, she wished Corey were here. He was so much braver than she was.

She took a shaky breath and continued onward, creeping ever closer to that open doorway ahead of her. She was hugging the wall, staying close to it, hoping it would make her less noticeable to any and all things here. The doorway, on the other hand, was closer to where the water's edge was. Therefore, from this angle, she couldn't see very far into it. But there appeared to be a corridor leading away. Like in this room, there was no ceiling in there, but at least the narrower space should provide a little better protection than this wide-open emptiness.

But she wasn't going to be able to keep to the walls for long. The corners of the chamber were more intact than the inner walls, but the floor there was also more littered with rubble. She'd have to clamber over it in her stockinged feet to keep that sense of safety. And if she slipped and broke a toe or something, she certainly wasn't going to be any better able to defend herself in the event of an attack.

She scanned the gaping sky looming over the tops of the walls across the rubble-strewn chamber. There were even more of those bird-things now, but they appeared to still be high up in the sky, taking no notice of her that she could tell.

She crept farther out into the room, cutting the corner, urging herself to move a little faster in spite of the increased debris underfoot. But she was only about halfway there when she heard that strange and unsettling moaning sound again, much louder this time. Much *closer*.

She looked back toward the wall she'd been keeping to and felt her stomach drop at the sight of something black and shadowy rising up into view beyond it, blotting out more and more of the sky as she stood watching, enormous beyond describing. Like a living *mountain*.

"Oh shit…"

Chapter 4

Gina wiped at her tears again. They wouldn't stop falling. Keith was gone. And there was nothing she could do to stop it. She just...stood there...*useless*.

He was so nice to her, too. Even when they first met, back on that boat, he never treated her with anything other than kindness, unlike so many people she'd known. He didn't doubt her when she told him she could sense things. He didn't judge her. If anything, he acted impressed, as if what she could do were some kind of talent instead of the hateful curse it had always been.

Was it her fault? Was she supposed to have been able to do something for him? She didn't think she had that kind of power, but what did she really know about any of it? What if the goddess sent her here to save him and she failed?

Or maybe she was only being selfish right now, searching for reasons to blame herself, making it about her while someone else was suffering so much more.

She glanced back at Nicole. She was keeping pace behind her, her watery gaze aimed at some thoughtful nothing somewhere beyond the floor ahead of her. There were tears on her cheeks and none of that feisty spirit she'd possessed up until now. She wasn't even really pointing the light forward. It was sort of half-heartedly illuminating their feet, which of course didn't matter since the one leading the way right now could basically see in the dark. But she looked so different like this. So...*broken*.

It was worrisome. She had no experience with this sort of thing. She didn't understand people very well. She scarcely understood her own mind, much less how someone else's mind worked. But she understood that something very profound had happened. Something very painful. Something very meaningful.

She kept thinking of how those two talked to each other on the boat and back in the Denselands before they were separated. Nicole had been nothing but nice to her, but she was downright *mean* to Keith. From the moment they met ("What the fuck are *you* doing here?") almost right up to the moment they were separated ("I never *needed* you! Can't you get that through your fucking skull?") she was practically *hostile* toward him. Andrea told her they used to date, so she understood that there was bound to be some strained feelings. And she certainly had never had any experience with romantic relationships, so what did she know? But still it seemed so…disproportionate. Nicole even told her that he was a nice guy, that she shouldn't judge him based on how she acted toward him. (*We have a history. Things got sort of messy. I've got some pretty big feelings about the whole thing, I guess. But he's not a bad guy in any way, I promise.*) And she was right. He'd been very kind to both her and Andrea. He wasn't even really mean to Nicole except in response to something she said to him.

But she supposed she simply *couldn't* understand it if she didn't know the first thing about dating someone. Maybe that was just the way it was. Maybe breaking up just made people like that. She'd probably never know what it was like.

What she *did* understand, however, was regret. Failure. Missed opportunities. And though she was no expert on love and loss, she expected that Nicole was feeling a *lot* of that sort of stuff right now. Because *she* was feeling a lot of it and she was too late to do anything but witness the tragic finale.

She didn't know what to do to make anything better. She didn't think there *was* anything she could do. And that was heartbreaking. Nicole had taken such good care of her. She'd looked after her as much as Andrea, as if she were anything more than a stranger who showed up out of nowhere with wild stories about being sent by a goddess. And how many times had she saved her life now? She owed this woman so much more than this unhelpful silence.

All she could do was return the favor. She'd keep her safe.

She'd stay by her side. She'd make sure nothing harmed her while she was heartbroken and vulnerable.

Except...*could she?*

It wasn't as if she were simply on a leisurely stroll. She was leading her back to the glass labyrinth, with no idea what might be awaiting them there.

That monster was gone now, at least. She still didn't understand what happened back there, how she was able to do such a thing, but she was certain it was dead. (Or...as dead as something that was never alive in the first place could be...she supposed...) She could still feel the burn on her side where it left her its painful goodbye gift. A final act of hateful malice before it winked out of existence, she supposed. But even without that thing, she knew that the glass labyrinth was a dangerous place. What would it even be like for someone who wasn't like her? Would Nicole even be able to tell the difference? Or would the experience be too much for anyone else to handle?

She never really made any progress while she was in there. She was too concerned about staying away from the thing with too many mouths. But she *did* sense something ominous about that place. There were areas farther out from where she wandered that felt wrong, that felt dangerous in ways she couldn't fully comprehend.

What if all she managed to do was get Nicole killed, too?

She felt sick to her stomach with worry. Could she really do this? She was finding it harder and harder to believe that she was strong enough to do whatever the goddess sent her here to do.

Distracted, and with no real need of it, she didn't notice for a moment that the light had faded. Everything had gone dark around her.

She stopped and looked back.

Nicole had slumped down to the floor and was hugging her knees, the flashlight pointed uselessly at her dirty sneakers. Her pretty face was pinched into a miserable expression.

"Oh no..." she breathed under her breath as she hurried back and knelt beside her.

"I don't understand," she said in a voice that was nothing

like the confident woman she'd traveled across worlds with. This voice was as soft as her own, little more than a pitiful squeak, full of grief.

"I don't either," was all she could think to reply with. She wasn't used to consoling people. She didn't know the first thing about it. What would help? And what would only make the situation worse?

Seeing the tears fall down Nicole's face made tears of her own well up in her eyes. It was like being back in that awful grief room again, overwhelmed by these suffocating emotions, except this time the pain was real. She wasn't going to be able to just walk away and leave it behind. She was going to carry this with her everywhere she went, for a long time, she was sure. Maybe for the rest of her natural life.

"Why does it have to be like this?" she wept, her face contorted with misery, her tears flowing faster. "I don't understand." Great, shaking sobs bubbled up, overwhelming her. "I don't understand anything!"

How did things end up like this? She couldn't help wondering if it was her fault. If she hadn't lost track of Nicole back on those rain-drenched streets, would Keith still be alive? What happened after she ran off into the storm?

"*I'm so confused!*" bawled Nicole. Her face was turning red. She was clutching at her legs with all her might, as if holding on for dear life. "*What's wrong with me?*"

Gina didn't know what to say, so she did what Nicole had done for her so many times on this journey. She reached out and hugged her.

And for a long time, she remained like that.

Chapter 5

"He's right there," whispered Olivia, her nails biting into his arm again as she crowded closer to him.

Wayne's heart was racing. "Who?" he asked. "Where?" But these weren't questions he needed to ask. Who else would give her such a fright at a time like this? "He" could only be the scarecrow man in his bloody hound-skin suit. And he could see for himself that her flashlight was fixed on the passage directly in front of him.

He could almost see it, too. A shadowy shape hunched in the darkness just beyond the reach of their lights.

He stepped in front of her, determined to shield her, no matter what happened next.

But...what was going to happen next? What was the monster doing? Why would it just be crouched in the darkness there, watching them? Was it simply waiting to see how close they'd get to it? That didn't seem right. That was the behavior of an ambush predator, the kind of thing that struck swiftly and killed without hesitation. The scarecrow man liked to *play* with his prey. He'd always made sure to let them see him first. He wanted to scare them as much as possible. And they clearly already knew something was there. What was he waiting for?

He was bent forward, thrusting his light into that darkness, trying to see, but now he straightened up, his body tensing.

Where were his bugs?

Was that it? Was he merely biding his time, waiting for his nasty little minions? Were they on their way back to him right now, weaving their way through the labyrinth's impossible tangle of passageways?

He hated this place. Why did it have to be a labyrinth?

Olivia was pulling at the tail of his shirt, urging him to back away. He took a step back, but he couldn't decide if fleeing was the right option. Right now, at least they knew where he was, his eyes were fixed on that shadowy shape. If they fled, there was no knowing where he might turn up next.

But as he watched, the shadow in the darkness lurched closer, taking shape in the gloom at the end of his flashlight's reach. It was just as they last saw it, a mangled corpse of a hound, twisted into something upright and unspeakably awful, those square jaws gaping open, thorny tongue dangling.

He could smell it now. Rancid. Foul. Grotesque.

He spread his feet apart, clenched his teeth and balled up his fists, prepared to hold his ground, determined to defend his fiancée, regardless of what may happen to him.

But the scarecrow man didn't attack. Those rotting remains seemed to settle toward the floor a little, hunching, almost squatting there. It had no eyes, of course, because hounds had no eyes, and yet he knew that this monster was staring at them, watching their every move.

"What do you want now?" demanded Wayne. Behind him, he felt Olivia crowding closer to him, pressing her face against the tattered and bloodied back of his shirt. He was very much aware of the pain there, a constant sort of burning, more like a sunburn than cuts and scratches. It was a constant reminder of all the hell they'd already been through, and uncomfortable enough that he'd all but forgotten about the punctures from those killing vines and his gashed knee from way back in Gutler's Weep. Only the painful gouge in his shoulder measured up. But it wasn't all that bad. It could have been much worse. And compared to his concern for his fiancée, it was as inconsequential as a paper cut. It wouldn't stop him from protecting her. "We don't have the thorn anymore. It's gone. Used up. So fuck off!"

He didn't think the monster would answer him. He expected it to simply launch itself into an attack, but he was wrong. In that same, hideous voice that seemed to have been pieced together from garbled grunts and burbles, the beast in the darkness spoke up: "Not gone."

"What?" He frowned. Not gone? What was the creep talking about? Of course the thorn was gone. They'd lost it.

Hadn't they?

"Still there," said the scarecrow man in that repulsive mimicry of human speech that Wayne was increasingly aware was merely a clever manipulation of creaking bones, squelching flesh and grinding scales. "Inside," it croaked, its words gurgling and bubbling like a sucking chest wound, making his stomach sour. "In *her*."

"What's it talking about?" whispered Olivia.

"I can still take it," the monster seemed to decide. "When I'm ready. When I'm done playing."

He didn't take his eyes off the murderous monster, but he crouched a little, steadying himself in preparation for it to lunge at him. He wouldn't let it lay a hand on Olivia. He didn't care how many times he'd have to die to protect her.

"And there are so many things to play with in this wonderful place." The monster leaned forward, that grotesque, thorny tongue wriggling into the light, bloody and swollen and foul. "For instance..." it burbled in that perversion of a voice, "...where did the other girl go?"

He felt his heart sink at the thought of this monster setting its sights on poor Andrea. "That's none of your fucking business," he growled.

Olivia was tugging at his shirt, urging him to flee, but he was reluctant to turn his back on this thing and run. It felt like a trap, like it was waiting for them to do just that. He didn't want to be this close, but at least he could see it. He wasn't wondering where it might pop up next, if it might be crouched just around the next corner, ready to lash out with those stolen scales and grind off his face.

"She was different," gargled the scarecrow man. "She smelled like death. She's walked among the beautiful ones."

Beautiful ones... He used that phrase back in Gutler's Weep. It seemed as if that was what he called the dead. (*If I pulled out your still-beating heart right now, you'd be one of the beautiful ones forev-*

er.) And wasn't that precisely what Andrea was doing when she entered those murk passages? Walking among the dead?

"You are *way* too into dead shit," he informed the creep. "You know that, right? Like, that's not even *remotely* normal."

Olivia's tugs were more urgent now. She wanted to run. But he still didn't quite dare. He was increasingly sure that the scarecrow man was waiting for them to make the first move.

The gurgling and grinding noises of the monster in the shadows became something like a grotesque laugh. "Death *is* the normal," it replied. "Death is eternal. Everlasting. Peaceful. *Life* is the anomaly. Temporary. Finite. Messy. Painful and full of fear and uncertainty. Life consumes and degrades. Life pollutes. Life is competitive and greedy. Life only exists to make death greater."

"And now you're a philosopher?"

"*Wayne...*" squeaked Olivia.

He reached behind his back and squeezed her hand. He wasn't ignoring her. He could feel the tenseness in her. She was sensing something. Her psychic alarm was going off. Something scary was going to happen here. They *needed* to be moving. But they couldn't flee just yet. Somehow he simply *knew* that would be a mistake. They needed to wait.

But for what?

The scarecrow man planted those dangling claws on the floor and leaned forward, the hound's bloody head emerging from the gloom into the glare of the light, a gruesome mask painted in shadows and gore. "The living are not beautiful. They are only fragile. They exist only to be broken. You'll see it, too. In time."

Wayne shook his head. "Not likely, freakshow."

Again, the monster laughed in its broken and disjointed voice.

He gave Olivia's hand another squeeze, attempting to reassure her, but they were almost out of time. The monster leaned farther into the light, one foot came forward, its dislocated claws splayed across the stone, still glistening with oozing blood.

"I'll show you," promised the scarecrow man. "You'll see."

"Go now," said an oddly familiar voice from somewhere behind the monster.

The scarecrow man twisted its foul body around, its stolen claws outstretched. "Who's there?"

Wayne didn't hesitate. Gripping Olivia's hand for dear life, he turned and fled into the darkness of the labyrinth.

"Was that Erin?" gasped Olivia.

He had no idea. He couldn't remember exactly what her voice sounded like. He only knew that this one sounded somehow familiar. And he didn't care *who* it was. That was the distraction they needed, their only chance of making it more than a few steps before the monster ran them down and tore them to pieces.

A great, gurgling howl exploded from somewhere behind them. It didn't sound like merely the scarecrow man venting his frustration. Something was happening back there. Was Erin able to physically attack that thing? Was she restraining it somehow?

He didn't dare look back. He couldn't risk slowing down. This was very likely the only chance they were going to get.

The passage branched to the left. He didn't wait to see if Olivia had any feelings about it. They needed to get out of that thing's line of sight. The more turns they took the better. What they needed was to get lost as quickly as possible.

He turned left again at the next intersection, then right at the next. Right again. Left. Right. Right. Left. As quickly as his legs would carry him without letting go of Olivia's hand.

The next intersection came into view and he immediately set his gaze on the passage to the right, taking no time to think.

"This way."

He jolted to a stop and shined his light to the left, panting.

"What's wrong?" gasped Olivia as she peered around him to see what he was staring at.

"Did you not hear that?"

"Hear what?"

Clearly, she did not. But she heard the voice that called out from behind the scarecrow man, the one that commanded them to, "Go now." What was the difference? Was there more than one ghost following them around in this darkness?

Another of those monstrous howls echoed through the stone corridors, much closer than it should have been.

He was still chasing them, probably getting closer with each passing second.

He didn't waste any more time considering the options. He set off to the left, following the voice.

The path was curving farther to the left. That could be good. It could help them stay out of the thing's line of sight. Maybe it would miss them and go a different way.

"I've got a bad feeling!" gasped Olivia.

He cursed under his breath. They didn't have *time* for one of her bad feelings. They needed to be much farther away before they were going to have time for bad feelings. But he couldn't let it slow him down. She was probably just feeling the scarecrow man getting closer. They needed to keep moving, keep turning, keep getting themselves more and more lost. That was all.

But the passage straightened out and revealed nothing more than a wall blocking their path.

A dead end? *Now?*

He slammed his fist against the stone, frustrated. What the hell? The voice told him to go this way!

Olivia cried out for him, her nails digging into his arm, her light thrust back into the darkness behind them.

He turned and stepped in front of her, facing the oncoming horror.

Was this all there was? Was this the end of the road for them? After all they'd been through, was death the only thing that awaited them in this damned labyrinth?

The scarecrow man's morbid abomination lumbered into view.

It looked...disheveled? One of those dislocated claws was missing. There was a patch of broken scales in the razored hide that wasn't there before. It kind of looked as if it had been hit by a truck on its way here.

"Wayne..." whimpered Olivia.

"It's okay," he assured her, knowing damned well that it

was no such thing. What the hell were they supposed to do now?

"Death stirs in your presence..." gurgled the monstrosity as it crept closer. "Gains power... Form... Substance... Like nothing I've seen before..." It rose up, bristling, flexing those deadly scales. "Intriguing..."

"I don't understand any of your crazy," he informed the thing.

As he watched, the monster's head seemed to detach itself from its shoulders and float forward, twisting and rotating to one side, an eerily inquisitive sort of gesture, but entirely horrific. That disgusting tongue rolled and flopped as it turned, obeying gravity while the rest of its remains obeyed the whims of their morbid puppeteer.

"What are you?" growled the scarecrow man.

Before Wayne could react, the stone beneath his feet dropped. The ceiling came rushing down at them, pushing them even as they found themselves falling.

Then, in almost the same instant, it slammed to a stop and they struck the floor. Pain shot up through the knee he hurt way back in Gutler's Weep as well as the gouge in his shoulder as he was forced down onto all fours. And behind him, he heard Olivia let out a great, startled yelp.

"Are you okay?" he gasped, shining his light back at her.

"I think so..." she replied in a breathless sort of squeak as she plucked her dropped flashlight off the floor. She sat up and brushed her hair back from her face, her pretty eyes wide and afraid. "What happened?"

Relieved that she didn't appear harmed, he turned his light forward again. "We've moved," he replied.

She shined her light up at the stone above them, then back at the dead end that still blocked the way behind her. "Moved *where?*"

"Down." Just like back in that first passageway, when the labyrinth swallowed up Keith and Corey in a single instant, the entire dead-end they were standing in had suddenly dropped into a lower passage.

The scarecrow man was no longer blocking the path. He

was still in the corridor above, possibly fuming over having lost his playthings just when things were getting good. With any luck he'd never be able to find them again, but somehow he doubted it.

Ahead of them, a new passage had taken the previous one's place, one that didn't look like any other passage he'd yet seen. It wasn't smooth and featureless. Instead, there were strange grooves etched into all four surfaces, creating bizarre, spiraling patterns that seemed to flow into the mysterious darkness ahead.

"Come," sighed the whispering voice from somewhere in that darkness. "Find me."

Chapter 6

A raw and suffocating panic was gripping Brandy's heart as she fumbled with the broken flashlight in the all-consuming darkness.

It wasn't fair. Why would it choose *now* of all times to break? She didn't have time for this! She needed to *see*! Albert was hurt! She couldn't help him if she couldn't see!

Her body felt cold and numb, as if she were submerged in ice water. She couldn't seem to seize control of herself.

Then Albert pulled her close and kissed her.

Surprised and distracted, her heart seemed to stutter in her chest. It was such a familiar and natural sensation that for a second there she almost thought everything was okay, that her world wasn't really at its end.

But everything was not okay.

Was it only the overwhelming panic playing tricks on her, or did she taste blood on his lips?

"Listen to me," he whispered, his breath warm against her face as he spoke. His voice was even. Calm. Patient. But *tense*. She could hear the quiver in it as he fought back the pain in order to speak to her. "We don't need the light."

"Of course we do!" she cried. "We can't read the book without the light!"

"Yes, we can. I did it before."

"What?"

"Take it. Believe."

A great, terrified sob escaped her. She didn't understand. What was he going on about? Was he delusional? She clutched the book against her chest. She couldn't even *see* it in this darkness, much less *read* it.

"Magic," he sighed. "It's real. You know it is."

Magic. The very sound of the word made her angry. Magic was supposed to be wondrous and happy and cheerful and whimsical. But it wasn't any of those things. It was *dirty*. It was shameful and vulgar and perverse. Magic took something beautiful between her and him and turned it into little more than an instrument for conjuring spells. She *hated* magic.

And yet, what else did she have in this dreadful moment?

"Believe in it," grunted Albert.

Believe in it. Right. Like this was all just some silly fairy tale. Like she could just turn off the terror that was gripping her heart and play the pervert's ridiculous games. She didn't sign up to be a sex witch. She signed up for a lovely honeymoon at a beautiful resort. She signed up for spending time with her new husband, not grieving over him!

She closed her eyes and tried to calm her ragged breathing. Magic *was* real. She'd seen it work so many times now. It showed her the truth in people again and again, truths she was able to *use* to help them escape that hotel. It revealed hidden passageways. It had transported her to Albert's side across countless black miles of that awful forest. But could it really fix *this*? Didn't the pervert tell them that they couldn't make drastic changes. They couldn't make someone drop dead or conjure stacks of cash at their feet, so why should she be able to suddenly heal a life-threatening wound? That didn't make sense.

She unclenched her grip on the book and looked down at it, her chest still hitching. As she expected, she could see nothing. She couldn't see the paper in front of her face, much less make out what was written on it.

"Did it before..." breathed Albert. "When we were separated... It's real... Just have to try..."

He was really able to do it? Read a book without any light?

No... Not just *any* book. *This* book. The pervert's *spellbook*. The same book that didn't get wet after they jumped in the river. The same book that kept translating itself from that bizarre gibberish into legible passages.

She took another ragged breath and tried to calm herself.

Believe in it, he said... Belief tended to come after proof, not before. Belief without proof was merely faith, and faith could be easily misguided. Wasn't that precisely how cult leaders manipulated their followers?

No. This wasn't helping. She needed to clear her mind of all this doubt and negativity. She needed to empty it *completely*. Start with a clean slate and open her mind as wide as possible. She needed to literally *make room* for what was written in these pages. Because she was suddenly very certain that if she let herself think *anything*, her doubt would wash away the words and leave her with no chance of saving him.

She sniffed back her tears, flushed her mind of all thought and stared at the darkness before her.

It was right there. She saw it before the flashlight broke. She was reading the first paragraph of it, her heart leaping with hope.

First, there was that vulgar bullshit about coursing blood powering both hearts and cocks, like anyone in need of this stuff had time for the creep's disgusting deep thoughts on the subject. But then it said that other thing. Something about stitches, wasn't it?

(*Emotional magic can be as effective as stitches.*)

That was it! It was right here!

...somewhere...

She pictured those words in her mind, just as she read them before everything went dark.

Please, she thought, begging and pleading with whoever or whatever received these kinds of prayers in a world like this. *Please let this work.*

She squeezed her eyes closed and tried to clear her mind.

Albert was still there, she could hear him breathing. It was soft, shallow. She wasn't even sure he was still conscious, but he was still with her. For the moment at least.

Again, she wiped away the tears in her eyes and focused on the passage in front of her. She could see nothing in this God-forsaken darkness!

And yet...

Emotional magic. *Sexual* magic. Healing and stimulation.

These words just came to her. Did she remember them? She didn't think she was able to read much of it before the light broke. Certainly not enough to understand what to do.

She sniffled and focused on the page again.

The act of lovemaking. Two bodies becoming one. Physically *and* emotionally. And *magically*.

A part of her wanted to curse at the pervert for wasting her time with more of his filthy attempts at poetry, but another part of her realized that it wasn't what this was.

When two bodies become one during the sacred act of lovemaking, especially when the two combined are of a very close emotional bond, the merging can, under certain circumstances, go far beyond mere penetration. Two can literally become one, both physically and metaphysically.

She blinked down into the darkness, her thoughts racing. That wasn't *reading*, exactly... But she most certainly gathered that information from the page. It was as if the book gave her the information, sort of like asking a computer to read an article aloud for you. Except it seemed to deliver the information directly into her head.

Using sexual energy, two could become one. Two people *sharing* a single body...

She tossed the book aside and grasped Albert's face between her hands. "Hey!" she gasped, then kissed him. "Please still be with me!"

"I'm here," he groaned, weak but aware.

"I know what to do. Just stay with me for a minute."

"Sure..."

"Just trust me," she said, unfastening his shorts and yanking them down.

"Wha...?" he grunted.

They caught on his shoes, so she pried them off as well, tossing it all aside. She stood up and stripped off her own shorts, kicking off one of her shoes in the process. Then she perched herself atop him, straddling his hips.

Two needed to become one. She needed to take him inside her so that they became one form, one body, but then she needed to take it further than that. She needed to *merge* with him on an emotional and mental level. That, alone, wasn't going to be anything new for them. They did that all the time. Lovemaking wasn't simply about physical pleasure with them, after all. It was a bond. It was how their hearts touched, she sometimes thought. This was like that. She needed to feel like that. She needed to get to that point.

But he wasn't exactly running on all six cylinders… He was badly injured. His body was weakening. He wasn't going to simply *rise to the occasion*, as it were. He was only human. And he was losing a lot of blood.

This should have been the end of it. Her last shot at saving him stamped out before she could even begin. And yet she found that she knew exactly what to do.

She reached down between her thighs and took hold of that part of him. It was a gentle touch, a subtle motion, little more than a caress. But it made him shudder beneath her, revealing that it worked. In an instant, he was ready for her.

It wasn't the touch. It was the *intention* behind the touch. It was her will passing into him, her desire. Her *love*.

"What's happening?" he gasped.

"Relax," she sighed. "Breathe. Focus on staying with me."

It was such a strange sensation, easing herself down onto him as if this were any other romantic moment while her heart pounded with fright and the overwhelming smell of his blood filled her nose. She was terrified of what might come next, and yet her solution to this problem was to hop on and take a ride? It felt so wrong! And yet she knew that it was the only way. If she *didn't* do this, she was going to lose him forever. He was going to *die*.

Her hips moving up and down, their bodies falling into that familiar, lovely rhythm, she opened her eyes into the darkness and looked down at him, fixing his gaze with her own, even though she remained blind.

Her Albert. Her husband. Her best friend and one true love. Her soulmate.

She took him inside her and let the familiar emotions fill her quivering body.

She lifted her face and closed her eyes, letting the memories of all the wonderful moments just like this one flow back to her, letting those feelings warm her body.

When she looked back down, she realized she could see something new. There was a mark drawn through his chest, glowing like a burning ember in the darkness. That was where the spike had entered his body. That was where the injury was located, where the damage had been done. It was deep. *Frightfully* deep...

(*You can see the truth in people.*)

Was that what this was? The truth in Albert? Was she actually looking at a visual representation of the pain he was feeling right now? Was this a psychic visualization of the wound that was killing him?

Whatever the reasoning behind it, that was her target. That was what she was looking for. She needed to focus all this pent-up energy on that point. But she wasn't quite there yet...

She stripped away her shirt and yanked his up, then she leaned forward, pressing her skin against his. Nothing between them, just as it should be. And all the while, her hips never stopped moving, her sexual momentum never slowing.

She could feel it building. Like a sip of hot coffee on a cold morning, warming her from the inside out, spreading up and out from deep in her belly.

She was almost there... That earth-trembling feeling that she knew so well... She was right on the brink of it... She wanted it so much...

But she wanted something else much *more*.

She focused on that mark burning inside her mind, grasping at it with all her might. She could feel it herself now, sharp and aching, deep in her chest, physically painful, but also something *not* physical. An unpleasant sort of *wrongness*. A terrible sensation of dreadful inevitability. A grim, looming truth.

Death.

She was sensing death. It was hovering over him, slowly closing its black arms around him.

But she wouldn't let him go.

She *refused*.

She reached out with some inner part of herself that she didn't know was there and grasped the burning mark, squeezing it with all the strength she could muster.

The pain in her chest flared as if someone had just plunged a knife into it. She grunted and clenched her teeth against it.

At the same time, Albert cried out and arched his back.

She was hurting him!

But she knew she couldn't stop. She had to be strong.

She focused on that warmth inside her, clinging to it, desperate to not let it fade, and she funneled it into the mark.

This was the important part of the spell, after all. This was why they needed to become one. That injury was too much for him to survive. She needed to take some of it away from him. They needed to *share* the wound.

When two became one, they split the malady. One mortal wound could be turned into two superficial ones.

But this was no simple feat.

The pain was excruciating. She cried out. She wasn't going to last. She couldn't take it. But if she let go now, she'd never save him! She had to bear it! No matter what!

Then it was fading. That burning mark melted into the darkness. That feeling of something dreadful looming over her dissipated like morning fog.

She took a shaky breath and clutched at her chest. There was a wound there, just beneath her sternum. She was bleeding. But it didn't hurt nearly as much as it did a moment ago.

It didn't hurt nearly enough to matter more than the other pressing matter.

Albert wasn't moving. He was lying there beneath her. Was he breathing? She couldn't tell through her own labored panting. Her heart was still pounding with the exertion of it all.

Was she too late? Was it all for nothing?

"Albert?" she whispered, terrified of the thought of never hearing his voice again.

He didn't answer her.

Instead, his hands grasped the sides of her head, surprising her. Before she could utter a sigh of relief, he was kissing her. *Intensely.*

She was confused. Did this mean he was okay? Did she do it?

He wouldn't stop kissing her so that she could ask him. And she didn't want him to stop. She kissed him back, eager, almost *hungry* for him, pressing into him, meeting his intense energy. She wasn't sure she'd ever wanted anything so badly as she wanted this right now. She could feel his lips, his tongue...

And that other part of him...

"*Mmph!*" she exclaimed, her eyes flashing wide with surprise in the darkness.

Before she knew what was happening, he rolled her onto her back and thrust himself deep inside her.

The pitch-black world around her seemed to shudder as an intense, almost *electric* sensation washed through her body.

Again, she cried out, her voice echoing through the labyrinth, this time not with pain or anguish, but intense, sensual bliss.

Chapter 7

Andrea groaned as she spiraled up from the murky depths of a deep and heavy sleep, her mind sluggish, unable to comprehend why she was so cold and uncomfortable.

She tried opening her eyes, but everything was all blurry. She felt strange. Heavy.

This wasn't her bed...or any bed for that matter... It was hard and cold and lumpy... Things were poking her...

She rubbed at her eyes. It was coming back to her. The Denselands. Erin. The murk-infested passageways. Olivia telling her that something wasn't right.

Did something happen?

She opened her eyes again to find that she was back in her own apartment. Or...what was left of it? It looked like a tornado had ripped through it. The roof was torn off. The walls were stripped away, the bare studs jutting upward like the ribs of some long-dead titan. The furniture was overturned and thrown around, broken to pieces, litter and rubble and debris strewn everywhere. Everything was ruined. And all of Nicole's photographs...scattered everywhere...

She looked down at a dirty and tattered picture of the six of them together. Her and Nicole. Olivia and Wayne. Brandy and Albert. Their faces all faded and discolored, the paper warped and brittle. The sight stirred a number of stinging emotions within her. Her friends. Her home. Her life. Ruined and aging. She felt tears welling up in her eyes and squeezed them shut, forcing them back.

No. This wasn't right. It wasn't real. It couldn't be real. It was like something out of a nightmare. She looked up at the sky looming above her. That wasn't her sky. It had never looked like that, all red and boiling with unnatural clouds, casting a sickly, blood-tinged light over everything. This had to be some kind of trick, one of those pocket dimensions Gina told them about, perhaps, like the one the barely-there dragged Nicole into. Was this another of Glum's traps?

She needed to get out of here. A dreadful panic was starting to stir within her. What sort of new horror was this?

And where were her clothes? She sat up, covering herself as she realized that she was naked again, just like in all those dreams about the temple. And just like that strange experience beneath the ghostly cemetery.

The more aware she became, the worse everything was. She was lying naked and unconscious on the filthy floor of her ruined apartment in some kind of apocalyptic nightmare. And now that her eyes were wide open, she realized that there were strange things flying around in that boiling sky, things that warbled in and out of view in a queer sort of way that made her feel oddly queasy when she tried to follow them.

She attempted to get to her feet, only to stagger and fall as an intense dizziness washed over her. Was something wrong with her? Had she been drugged?

She closed her eyes and tried to steady herself.

What happened, anyway? She recalled walking through those murk-infested corridors... Then Olivia's psychic alarm started going off... (*Something's not right. We shouldn't have come this way.*) Everything escalated so quickly. It was all a blur. Had they chosen a bad path? Should they have gone the other way? Was it *her* fault? (*We have to get out of here. Now.*) But it was too late. That strange, darkling thing... It was on her in an instant, enveloping her, *swallowing* her. Everything went black. She didn't even have time to scream.

It was that awful impostor. She was saying all those creepy things inside her head.

(*Gonna get ya...*)

But how did she end up here, under this horrid red sky? And where did her clothes go? She opened her eyes and looked down at herself. Her arms and legs were still covered in dried mud from that reeking chamber. It had worked its way up her shorts and under her shirt, even down her collar, so that little more than what was covered by her socks and undergarments remained even remotely clean. It didn't look like she was merely caught in some kind of delusion, like back in that awful, endless apartment building. It looked like someone had physically removed her clothes and taken them before leaving her here.

She took a shuddering breath and tried again to stand. That strange dizziness lingered, but this time she managed to straighten herself up and stumble toward what was left of the window.

She had to be careful. She was barefoot and there was debris and broken glass everywhere. One wrong step and she could end up with a nail sticking out the top of her foot. She crept slowly, testing each step, just like all those times she was moving around blind in the frightful darkness of the gouging station and the all-consuming black of the murk.

"Olivia?" she called out, not daring to raise her voice much above a whisper. "Wayne?" Where did they go? Were they still safe? Or did the shadow thing get them, too? Were they also here somewhere, separated and lost? "Erin? Are *you* still here?" She turned and looked behind her, a shiver creeping up her back as only an awful howl of wind replied, groaning and moaning through the broken walls. "Please tell me you're still here," she whimpered, her voice little more than a scared croak quickly swallowed in the wind. Why did she keep ending up alone like this? She hated being alone!

She reached the window and leaned against the frame, careful to keep her hand clear of the broken glass. She felt tired, as if she'd struggled up a sheer cliff instead of crossing the ruins of her living room. She was having trouble catching her breath. She closed her eyes again and steadied herself. She didn't even feel this weird after Erin made her that strong drink. What was wrong with her? Again, she wondered if she'd been drugged or poisoned somehow. She wished she could remember how she came to be here.

I can do this, she told herself. *I'm strong enough. I can handle it.*

She took a long, slow breath, willing her heart to ease.

She *could* do this... Five years ago she proved she was stronger than she knew. She was braver than anyone had ever given her credit for.

But when she opened her eyes, it was just in time to see something tall and dark darting past on the other side of the window, mere inches from her face.

She twirled around and pressed her back to the remains of the wall, her hands clasped over her mouth, her heart hammering with fright.

What was that? It didn't look like a *person*. It was too dark, almost black, like a shadow. And it was much too tall. She *definitely* didn't imagine it. Did it see her? Where did it go?

She felt another wave of dizziness wash over her. Her knees threatened to buckle under her weight. She didn't know what to do. There was something out there. Something big. Something *fast*. And there was nothing to *keep* it there. There was no glass. There was no *roof!* The entire wall above the window was gone! She needed to run, but where was there to go?

She turned her head, her hands still pressed to her mouth, and peered out at the street beyond. Everything appeared to be in ruins out there. Did the whole world look like this? Was there anywhere safe left? She didn't understand what she was seeing. What happened here?

She scanned what was left of the room around her, searching for something to use to defend herself. A broken chair leg, perhaps? A piece of splintered lumber? A loose pipe? *Anything?* But there was nothing that looked like she could wield it effectively.

Something scratched at the bricks just outside, nearly wrenching a startled cry from her.

She needed to get control of herself. She couldn't let herself scream. She couldn't let them know she was here.

She crept sideways, tiptoeing through the rubble, away from the window, keeping as close to the walls as the debris allowed. There were knives in the kitchen. Big ones. Nicole's mom bought all sorts of kitchen stuff for them when they first moved in, saying it wasn't a home without a fully stocked kitchen.

She raked her foot across some tattered cloth on the floor that might have once been one of Nicole's blankets and eased her foot down on the filthy carpet.

One step at a time. Quickly…but not careless… Watch out for broken glass and splinters.

She reached out with her other foot to rake more of the ruined blanket aside.

Then something grabbed her elbow.

She twirled around, a strangled squeak of a cry escaping her as she tried to scurry away from whatever horror was attacking her, stumbling and tripping over the debris in the process.

But nothing was there. She was still alone in these tattered shambles of her home.

It made no sense. She was certain she didn't just imagine it. She could still feel the sensation of a hand closing around her elbow.

Boo… chuckled the impostor's awful voice right in her ear.

She took a step backward, surprised, and tripped over the remains of one of the broken dining room chairs. A sharp pain shot through her butt and the back of her arm, wrenching a painful scream from her before she could stop it.

Something beyond the battered walls screamed back at her. The sound of it was so terrible it wrenched a second cry from her, this one of sheer terror, and *several* somethings responded. They seemed to be coming from every direction, hideous, half-human, almost *mocking* shrieks, unnerving, like something out of a horror movie.

Now you've done it, giggled that awful voice as something gave a loud bang somewhere beyond those broken walls.

She needed to go. Now! But when she tried getting to her feet, something broke beneath her with a loud snap.

Outside, something responded with another shriek and a crash that sent bolts of icy terror up her spine.

They're coming to get you!

Chapter 8

Everett watched as the flames ate through the paper walls of his dollhouse prison, spreading rapidly, surrounding him.

"Yeah, I can see we're in trouble," he replied to the panicked message that Alice sent screaming through his consciousness.

As the blackened paper shriveled into ash and peeled away, it revealed more and more layers of burning paper behind it, stretching as far as he could see in every direction. It was odd, like watching a book burn, page after page curling and crumbling and flaking away in the searing blaze, but all around him, deeper and deeper.

Fire spread across the ceiling, revealing the same endless layers of paper stretching ever upward above him.

If the floor was like that, too—and he knew it was because he could already see it beginning to catch—then what was going to happen when he fell through it into that same hellish inferno below?

(Forever falling... Forever burning...)

He cringed at the awful thought. "Yeah, let's not do that."

And yet what option did they have? There was no elevator car to escape into. The door he entered through was a blazing tunnel. There was nothing else here, no way out. And it was getting smaller with every blistering second.

(Afraid!)

He clutched the doll against him, trying his best to shield her from the fluttering embers that were beginning to rain down around them. "It's okay. We're not quite cooked yet."

But it was getting harder to see any other outcome.

So much for being the one in control here. Was he *ever* in control? Did he ever have any chance of thinking his way out of this mess? Or was this just like that stone labyrinth? An unsolvable puzzle with no way out?

Or maybe it was the Priestess of Ruin. That shadowy figure waving cheerfully as the elevator doors slid closed. Did *she* take his control away? Did she break the Keeper's rules and set the dollhouse on fire?

The flames had almost entirely enveloped the ceiling and were creeping across the floor now. Ash and embers were falling all around him. It was getting harder to breathe.

He took another step backward, then glanced over his shoulder at the open elevator shaft waiting back there. If he wasn't careful, he'd kill himself before the fire had its chance.

(Fall down.)

He coughed and shielded his face. "Yeah, I know." But the elevator shaft was the only thing *not* currently ablaze. If he didn't think of something soon, he'd be forced to choose between burning alive or leaping to his death.

(Fall. Jump.)

"That's probably the preferable one, yeah."

(Up. Down. Back and forth.)

He coughed again and took another step back. He was right on the edge now. It was getting harder to think, making it difficult to wrap his head around this bit of weirdness. Up and down? Back and forth? What was she talking about? Was she trying to tell him how to get out of this mess? Or was she just panicking, the same as him?

(Hurry!)

His eyes were burning. It was getting harder to see. He turned and leaned into the elevator shaft, hoping the smoke would rise up it, allowing him a breath of fresh air.

(Afraid!)

"I know you are!" he coughed. "I'm working on it!"

But he didn't know what else he could do. He stood there, staring straight down the bottomless shaft.

Up and down.

Back and forth.

Upside down and backward.

"Wait…"

If up was down and everything was inside out…maybe the way back up to where he started…

(Fall down.)

"Fall down…" he breathed. Let go. Take the leap. "Like Alice tumbling down the rabbit hole, but backward, right? Out of Wonderland and back to the real world."

The heat was beginning to burn his exposed skin. Time was running out. But he needed to make sure he did this right. This wasn't just passing through a doorway. This was leaping bodily from this entire backward universe. He needed to make sure he understood what he meant to do or he might not survive this.

He needed to picture the stone labyrinth. The *right-side-up* labyrinth. The one where Violet and Andrea and Wayne and Olivia were wandering right now, all of them probably wondering what happened to him.

(Rabbit hole…)

Yes… Just like the rabbit hole. A portal of his own making. A door that would take him away from here, not just into another version of it.

As the crowding flames licked at his heels, he braced himself and stepped into the empty shaft, plummeting into the darkness below.

Chapter 9

Erin stood motionless in the darkness, frightened, her heart pounding, her hands pressed against her face, as if confirming for some reason that she was real. What was this place? How did she get here? And why couldn't she see anything?

What was going on?

"It's normal to be confused," she whispered to herself. The words were strangely alien, but at the same time somehow comforting. It was her own words, she understood, spoken from somewhere deep down in the depths of her confounded mind. She was telling herself that this was what was expected to happen...though she couldn't for the life of her understand how this was anything close to normal.

Slowly, she slid her hands down her body, past her chin and her neck, over her chest, to her lean belly, to her hips, to her thighs. She was still wearing the silvery dress she bought in order to slip into that lovely woman's wedding, yet that felt like so long ago for some reason... That hot, sunny day... That tranquil lake...

And after dark, something else... Something *monstrous*...

(*Where is it?*)

An awful shiver ran through her body. She remembered something terrible looming over her, something with far too many limbs and mouths.

(*Gone. Somewhere you'll never reach it.*)

There was pain. *Terrible* pain, like she'd never experienced before. And then everything became so confusing. There were fragmented memories floating around in her head, like bits of wreckage strewn across the ocean floor. A pale train speeding *doing its best to tell you what's there.*)

Something was slowly drifting up from the depths of her sluggish memory, piecing itself together, forming something that she could vaguely understand.

She remembered the young woman with the bright red hair and piercings. It was like a hazy, mostly forgotten dream, but it was real. She took that woman somewhere…somewhere that wasn't quite spiritual but also not the same as where she was now… Somewhere in between… Somewhere she could be alive like this…physical…*human*…but still somehow retain her knowledge of the other side. She was able to explain these things to her…tell her about the Murk and her curious power to interact with it…about hidden, shadowy passages like this one…

There was so much she couldn't understand while she was in this temporary imitation of her old body. Everything she knew about this place came from that other version of her, the one that was dead and gone, the one she was when she *wasn't* physical, when she was whatever she was when she was on the other side of the veil. But she understood *enough*, she realized. She understood that she needed to cross this black passage. And she understood that she needed to be extremely careful.

This was a passage where the physical and the spiritual overlapped and intertwined. But unlike other passages, this one was impassible to transient spirits like her. Only in this form would she be able to pass through here and reach wherever it was she wanted to go beyond it.

But there were dangers here. That uneasiness she felt wasn't merely a side-effect of the confusion and disorientation of returning to a physical form. She brought herself here with a grim warning embedded in her thoughts.

Places where the murk bled through were dangerous to those rare few who could sense it. And the closer to other side one was, the more dangerous it became. To one such as her, who was already passed on and only a visitor, it was far more perilous. She was going to have to be extra careful.

Because sometimes *other things* bled through as well…

She stopped moving. Her body—or whatever this thing was

that looked and felt like her body but was really only some kind of *vivid dream* of the body she once had—had gone ice cold. She didn't dare move a muscle, didn't dare so much as *blink*. Whatever passed for her heart was pounding. She held her non-existent breath. And her blind eyes were wide with a sudden and gripping terror.

It wasn't a conscious thought. It wasn't something she heard or felt in the darkness. It was a reflex. An *instinct*. She simply possessed a very sudden and utterly crippling understanding that something was near her.

Something *dreadful.*

There were no words in her mind to describe what she knew was here. No one alive could comprehend it, not even one only emulating life such as she was. Neither alive nor dead, nor even one of those dreadful *unnatural* things that sometimes drifted into the other two worlds. It was something else altogether. Something that only existed in the darkest depths of the farthest reaches of the spirit realm, scarcely seen by mortal souls. It didn't manifest itself here. It wasn't created. It wasn't born. It wasn't here until a moment ago and yet it didn't arrive. It was simply here with her. And right now she was in terrible danger. If she let it notice her, it would be the end for her. Not merely her life, but her very *soul* would be gone.

She stood there, terrified beyond words, waiting, anticipating the worst. She could almost picture the thing. A grotesque, indescribable mass of everything and nothing all at once, sloughing its way toward her, seemingly taking up the entire passage.

To the part of her that was mimicking a living brain, it was apparent that there was no way out for her, no chance that it wouldn't discover her here. But somehow the greater spiritual part of her understood that things like size and distance and speed and proximity weren't consistent across all existence. They might as well be two strangers blindly wandering the vast dunes of the Sahara for all that those things mattered.

But only as long as it didn't notice her.

She was going to have to remain still and be patient.

Desperate to escape the suffocating terror, she searched her mind for something else to focus on and found her thoughts drifting back to Breastbroke. To those iron gates. And to those silenced screaming wheels...

Chapter 26

The more strings Corey attached, the more he glimpsed the countless corridors of the City Beyond Memory and the more details about things he shouldn't know seeped into his mind.

Something bad had happened to Gina and Nicole. He didn't just suspect it now. He was certain of it. He could feel the overwhelming sorrow and regret that was overwhelming them. And he didn't like it at all.

Someone was gone. Someone had actually *died* in this place.

But who?

He could still feel Wayne and Olivia out there somewhere. They'd recently had a bad scare, and they were worried about someone they lost track of, but he didn't feel any of that suffocating grief that he felt from the girls elsewhere in the labyrinth. Whatever happened, it wasn't the same kind of traumatic. It felt more like when he lost track of Violet back in the Denselands. That sensation of fear and regret and helplessness.

And then there was Albert and Brandy. They, too, had recently had a scare, but then there was an enormous surge of really intense *sexy* emotions that seemed to wash everything else away. It had to be the sex magic they described way back on the carriage ride from the hotel. The first time he heard about it, he was curious, but not in some pervy way like Violet would probably accuse him. He was merely intrigued. How did sex magic work? What could it to? He was fairly sure anyone would be curious about that sort of thing. But what he felt while touching these stone contacts was far more overwhelming than he would have ever expected. What kind of spell had they cast? What were they really capable of?

But as curious as it was, it couldn't hold his attention right now.

His thoughts kept circling back to Gina and Nicole, to that awful feeling of loss and regret and tragic parting...

(*The Keeper plans for every contingency, not just the good ones. He makes the hard choices.*)

Who was it? Who had they lost?

Gina and Nicole. Wayne and Olivia. Albert and Brandy. Counting himself and Austin, that was eight of them accounted for. But where were the other four? He couldn't find any of them.

And one of them was Violet!.

He didn't like those odds.

Not one bit.

Chapter 27

Violet screamed.

Something much too large and much to ice-cold to be a hand was clenched around her thigh, as strong as a machine, pulling her. Sharp claws were biting into her skin, tearing at her as she struggled to kick free.

She thrust her arms out in an attempt to grip the stone, wedging herself in place in a desperate attempt to fight the thing off, but it was a wasted effort. In a single, agonizing instant, she was *ripped* from her hiding place as if she were nothing more than a ragdoll caught in the churning teeth of some mighty machine, her fragile body yielding to the immovable stone, bending and breaking and tearing and snapping

There was so much pain. More pain than she'd ever felt before. Something was broken, but in the torturous chaos she wasn't sure whether it was her arm or her shoulder or her collarbone or her ribs or even all of them at once. Everything was all blurred together into a single sheet of blinding agony. Every motion sent torturous shockwaves through her battered body. And her suffering wouldn't end! She was dragged through the broken stones and into the blood-tinged light, then yanked up off the ground by something hulking and hairy and snarling.

This was how she was going to die, she understood, the realization blooming inside her and spreading across her terrified brain like a bruise as she felt herself swinging around in the devil's monstrous grasp, broken bones twisting and grinding inside her battered body

Then, bizarrely, she found herself airborne, *thrown* like some discarded toy.

She struck the hard ground with a horrible, agonizing jolt. She bounced. She rolled. Everything was a tortuous blur as she tumbled down the rocky slope, her body enveloped in unspeakable pain.

She wasn't going to survive this. There was no way she wasn't broken beyond repair, no way she could push through this kind of suffering. Her journey was over.

She'd failed.

As she skidded to a stop, facedown and trembling in the dry, cracked earth, the taste of dirt and blood filling her mouth, her thoughts somehow landed on Corey.

She never found Corey…

She never saw him again…never had the chance to tell him what happened to her back on the shadow road…never got to tell him about those hound monsters…never even said goodbye…

But as she blinked back the dust and the tears, it occurred to her that she could see again. That eerie red glow was back. The monstrous thing eclipsing that bloody sky was gone.

And she was no longer in the ruined labyrinth. The stone floors and walls had vanished. She was lying on bare earth at the base of a rocky hill.

Stranger still, even the bulk of the pain was inconceivably gone. She pushed herself up off the ground, and looked down at her body, at the scratches and scrapes that covered her exposed arms and legs from her tumble down that hillside, but there was no sign of the injuries she suffered when that devil thing tore her from her hiding place. Nothing seemed broken. Inside, her body was unharmed. It was as if nothing leading up to the painful slide down that hill ever happened. Even that taste of blood in her mouth wasn't what it seemed to be. She wasn't bleeding inside somewhere. She bit her tongue.

"What in the actual hell?" she grunted, looking around at the barren landscape that stretched as far as she could see in every direction, a lifeless, blood-tinged wasteland dotted with strange, white stalks that jutted out of the earth like great, porous bones.

Ruin.

"You…" she gasped as she struggled back to her feet. The other one, who merely told her to prepare herself and then abandoned her to those…*things*…

Ruin has always existed. It's a crucial component of a living world. A necessary evil in the struggle to maintain balance across all universes and slow the inevitable decay of age.

"*Now* you want to chat?"

Like all realms, it has its own rules, its own dimensions. It is limitless. Infinite. And yet it defies infinity itself because it grows with each passing cycle. And as a result it is far more *in your time than it was in mine.*

What the hell was the other one going on about? There were different sizes of infinity? She seemed to recall something from back in her school days about infinity as a number being smaller or larger depending on what you did with it. Infinity plus two was bigger than infinity plus one, but wasn't the end result always just…*infinity*?

Or was that not how it worked? She might have been remembering it wrong. She was never that good with math.

I have very little power in the Ruin, explained the other one. *I can't protect you there. I can only warn you of the danger you are in. And only while* she *is looking away.*

She spat onto the ground, trying to rid herself of that taste of dirt and blood. "Who's 'she?'"

The Priestess of Ruin. Bringer of Darkness. Harbinger of Ends. Goddess of Decay.

"She sounds like a real peach," she grumbled, rubbing at her skinned elbows. That tumble really hurt, but compared to that torturous experience she imagined a moment ago, she didn't feel like complaining. She turned around, scanning her surroundings. The ground was bathed in that eerie red light, but otherwise it looked like the same kind of terrain she saw back in the Wood. Were those strange, ivory-colored stalks *night trees*? Did those trunks have *bones* inside them?

She's taken advantage of my weakness to spirit you to her realm, where I can do even less to protect you. But that doesn't make you defenseless. You are stronger than you know. And death cannot take you here. The very composition of this reality is connected to your presence on a primordial level. Existence flows around you like a stone in a stream, averting itself far easier than eroding its way through you.

"What the hell does *that* mean?" She didn't understand any of this. It sounded like some kind of metaphorical self-help nonsense!

And yet she reached up without thinking and hugged herself, recalling the awful, agonizing pain she felt when that thing seized her and tore her from that too-small hole, snapping her bones like fragile twigs in the process. That never happened. It couldn't have happened because she was still here, still whole, still *alive*.

A hallucination?

Or something far more complex than that?

She is coming. Run.

She turned around, her gaze darting across the baren landscape, instinctively searching for some sign of an ominous figure approaching, but whatever was coming would be nothing so simple as a shape on the horizon.

Didn't the other one just refer to this thing as a *goddess?*

Keep moving. Keep fighting. Endure. Survive.

"That's not helpful!" she shouted, terrified. She didn't need encouragement. She needed a rescue team!

But the other one had already fallen silent again. And she was becoming aware of a strange, heavy feeling descending over her in the bloody glow of that evil sky. Something was approaching. Something both awesome and dreadful, that filled her with primal and absolute fear.

She couldn't decide which direction this awful feeling was coming from, so she simply ran, ignoring the sharp pains in the soles of her unprotected feet, desperate to get as far from this place as possible before it arrived.

But she couldn't outrun a god.

She could feel it, like a fog settling over everything, all around her, everywhere at once, all-encompassing. There was nowhere for her to run and yet what else could she do but run? Terror kept her legs moving, even when the rocks bit into the tender flesh of her feet.

A desperate scream escaped her as shadows seemed to boil up from the earth all around her, strange, amorphous shapes like bubbling tar that uttered horrid, unnatural voices that seemed to come not from around her as she ran, but from deep within her own head, like the voice of the other one, but without a shred of warmth or gentleness. These voices wormed their way through her mind like parasites burrowing through her brain, warping her thoughts and perceptions until the bloody wasteland around her was twisted into a macabre landscape of distorted colors and shapes.

She blinked hard, trying to clear her vision. But she felt as if she were falling as much as she was running, as if she were careening wildly down a steep hill, barely keeping to her feet.

Then the ground simply wasn't there.

She fell.

She screamed.

Then she struck the earth with a bone-jarring impact that sent pain shooting through her shoulder and knocked the wind from her.

When she looked up, she was lying on a broken stretch of deserted asphalt, surrounded by the skeletal remains of dead trees and the crumbling husks of long-abandoned buildings looming beyond them in the distance.

She rolled onto her back, still trying to catch her breath, still waiting for the pain in her shoulder to recede. She was still in the Ruin, still beneath that sickly red sky. But this didn't look like either the temple *or* the Wood. It looked like her world. Or what was left of it, anyway…

Endure…

She blinked back her tears and watched one of those strange flying things with the warbling trails pass high above her. Endure? That was her advice? Endure *what*, exactly?

She realized as she lay there that she could hear a troubling sound carried on the wind. Someone, somewhere, was *screaming.*

Who was that? Who else could be in this poisoned world with her? And what could make someone scream like that? It sounded as if they were being *tortured*.

Was it a person? Or was it only another trick of the Priestess' Ruin? It was a terrible sound, distorted by the wind until it was difficult to tell with any certainty. And yet there was something about the sound that triggered her instincts, setting her on edge, making her want to find the source of it, to help whoever was making that noise.

She couldn't ignore it. She needed to figure out where it was coming from.

But as she rolled onto her side so that she could sit up, she saw them.

There were four of them crawling from the ditch, moving toward her. They looked sort of like pigs. But not the cutesy kind they kept on farms. Wild pigs. *Boars.* And yet they were no such simple thing. Longer back legs than front legs, with far too many tusks bristling from their twisted jaws, drooping ears that dragged the ground in tatters. And no visible eyes.

"Oh shit," she gasped, her heart in her stomach.

She scrambled to her feet, but they were much faster. They were on her in an instant, driving her back to the ground before she could take a single step, those vicious tusks piercing and gouging and tearing into her, ripping her apart while she screamed in futile, desperate terror.

Chapter 28

Nicole held onto Gina as if she were clinging to a life raft in the open ocean, as if she'd sink and drown if she lost her grip. And that was precisely how it felt. Gina was real. Gina was her friend, her only companion in this dark and lonely place. Everything else was cold stone and darkness and uncertainty and heartache.

Every time she thought she was in control, she'd see Keith's face in her mind and the pain and regret would start all over again.

She couldn't stop thinking about last time, about how they lost Wayne much the same way, only to have him returned to them, alive and well (if slightly damaged). She wanted so badly for that to happen again, but she didn't dare to hope. She couldn't bear the disappointment. And somehow, she felt as if she *knew* it wouldn't happen again. In fact, it felt as if she should have known it was going to happen all along, as if she were a fool to ever think it would end any other way…as if she'd been through this a million times before and should have known better…

"I'm going fucking crazy," she muttered under her breath. Her poor brain must be exhausted and running on fumes. It was a wonder she wasn't raving mad.

"What?" asked Gina.

"Nothing." And it *was* nothing. She was physically and emotionally drained. A few more hours of this shit and she'd probably be spouting all sorts of insane nonsense. "I'm sorry."

"Why?"

"You saved my life back there, and now I'm just dead

weight."

"You need time," she replied. "I understand."

She squeezed her tighter. "You're sweet. But I know I'm dragging you down." The poor girl might as well be shackled to a boulder for all the good she was doing her. She was *literally holding her here.*

"I really don't mind."

She reached up and wiped at her eyes and nose. "Your step-sisters were fucking idiots not to want you in their family," she decided.

"There's a really hot, half-naked woman cuddling me like a teddy bear right now," she replied in that same, sleepy tone. "My stepsisters can go fuck themselves."

This caught her by surprise. A great snort of a laugh escaped her, forcing her to cover her face. "Oh my god…" She rolled onto her back, wiping at her eyes and nose again. "I wasn't expecting that from you."

Gina sat up and brushed her long hair out of her face and Nicole stared up at her. It wasn't as soft and silky as it was when they first met. It was messy and tousled, and no wonder given all they'd been through.

Her own hair was a mess, too, she knew. That shower she took back on the boat helped, but she doubted anyone would be able to tell. And they were still filthy and covered in those gross, black smears where that last monster…sort of exploded, she guessed? She definitely didn't have the bandwidth to process any of *that* bullshit.

She sniffled and wiped at her eyes again. "I kind of forgot you were into girls. Sorry I keep shoving my tits in your face."

"I don't mind." She leaned forward, her small face full of worry. "Are you okay?"

"No," she replied immediately. "But yeah." She lay there, staring up at the passage's stone ceiling, a sickly aching deep in her chest. "But no."

"I get it," Gina assured her.

Again, she reached up and covered her face. This was achieving nothing, she knew. They should be up and moving.

They'd never find the others if they just lay here. And yet the very thought of getting to her feet and just carrying on like nothing happened felt wrong.

Was she just being selfish? Did she even have a right to feel this much pain? She treated Keith so badly. She was the last person who deserved to mourn him. And now she was being a burden to poor Gina, too.

What was wrong with her?

Why was she like this?

She lowered her hands and stared up at the ceiling of the passage again. Gray stone as far as she could see. Just like the last one. Albert called it a temple, but that wasn't what these places were. Nothing was worshipped here.

This was a *tomb.*

Nothing more.

"Why did you do it?" she asked.

Gina blinked down at her, confused.

"The first time, I mean. When Ada gave you that first job. Why did you trust her? Why didn't you just…run away and never look back?"

She was still sitting there, looking down at her, her hair still pooled over her lap. "I guess I kind of did. At first. I mean, I didn't really know what was going on. I thought it was just a dream. I ignored it. Because dreams are just dreams. I was just happy to have any dream that wasn't a nightmare."

Nicole reached out and squeezed her hand.

"Then it became a recurring dream. But it wasn't a bad recurring dream. It was just her, standing there in that bright white place that I couldn't ever quite remember in the morning. She was beautiful and she was kind and she was comforting. But every night the dream was a little longer. And then she started telling me I was supposed to go to Cakwetak. She kept showing me that tower. And that was a little scary. I didn't want to go to the tower in Cakwetak. I didn't want anything to do with it. I could just tell, even from the dream, that there was something wrong with that place. But she kept telling me I was supposed to go there. And that if I went there, I'd finally find the thing I most wanted." She shifted her weight, uncomfortable. "I'd never had anything like that happen before. I wasn't sure what it meant. I just kept ignoring it and ignoring it, hoping it would go away. After a while, I even tried not sleeping. But that doesn't work, of course."

"So eventually you caved in and went," she surmised.

"I thought I'd go crazy if I didn't. I was living and working in a little town in Illinois at the time, on my own, away from everyone who never wanted me around, just trying to live my life. But I was barely getting by. And losing sleep didn't help anything. I think people thought I was on drugs or something. So I just got up one day and went."

"And everything worked out okay?"

"Eventually. I was terrified of the place when I first drove up. I actually turned around and started home. But I went back. Because I knew the dreams would just keep coming. That place was a nightmare wrapped in normal lives. I'd never felt such a concentration of dark and monstrous things in one place before. It was like standing at the gates of hell. But I walked in. I didn't even know what I was supposed to do. I walked up to the receptionist and just told her my name. Next thing I knew, I was standing in front of one of the Twelve Teeth. Janon Tane. He told me when I'd start and handed me an envelope full of money to get me started." She brushed back her hair again and met her gaze. "So I moved to Cakwetak. There was even a number tucked in with the money for an apartment nearby. They took care of everything. And as a bonus, I got to draw for a living. Not a bad deal. But it never made that place any less scary. Every single day was terrifying."

"Was it worth it?" asked Nicole. "When it was all over, were you glad you listened?"

"Yes." She didn't waste time pondering the question. She knew the answer. "While I was there, I at least had a real life. I had meaningful work and money and a nice home. And I met some of my favorite people in the whole world because of that place. That's why when the goddess called on me again, I didn't hesitate." She gave a timid attempt at a smile that Nicole, for one, found positively adorable. "And now I've met even more favorite people."

Nicole sat up and hugged her.

"Not just because you're hot, though," Gina clarified. "Or half naked."

Nicole gave another snort of a laugh and squeezed her tighter. "You're one of my favorite people, too. If I ever meet those stepsisters of yours, I'm kicking their asses."

"Okay."

Chapter 29

Wayne stopped walking. He couldn't say exactly why. Nothing had changed. He was still in the same stone corridor with those same strange, squiggly carvings all over every surface. And yet in spite of that, it felt as if something had happened.

"You okay?" whispered Olivia, her grip tightening on his arm.

"Yeah," he replied, although the truth was that he didn't really know if he was okay or not. He felt strangely disoriented, as if he'd fallen asleep for a second there and missed something. He glanced back, trying to wrap his head around what felt off, but everything was just as it was supposed to be. At least, as far as he was able to tell...

He continued forward, his eyes peeled for unseen dangers in the looming darkness.

With no idea where they were or even what they were supposed to be looking for, this felt like some kind of cruel punishment. It reminded him of that tunnel of horrors he was forced to pass through back in the first temple, where all sorts of terrifying things scurried just beyond the reach of his light and lurked in the shadows in the corners of his eyes.

(*The things in this tunnel are imaginary as long as you don't prove them otherwise.*)

He shivered at the very memory of the Sentinel Queen's eerie warning that night. And for the next few hours he found himself traversing a waking nightmare, knowing that the moment he let his guard down the imagined terrors would become real and tear him limb from limb. And the things in that tunnel didn't go easy on him. They made themselves known. They whispered to him. They made footsteps in the silence. They screamed without warning. They rushed up behind him. They cried out his name.

He had nightmares about that road for months after returning.

In the Temple of the Blind, he had a goal. At first he was following Albert and his box full of clues, his *map*, searching for the meaning behind all the madness. Then he was searching for Olivia, determined to rescue her from the depths of that black Wood. And once that was done, it was his goal was to catch up to Albert and the girls. He focused on those expectations. He made them his mission. But what was his goal in here? He still didn't know what they were looking for. Another of those towers? Like the one where they fought the Caggo and ignited the inferno deep in the temple's belly? Or another City of the Blind, where another half-breed sentinel waited to point the way? Or would it be something completely different this time?

He wished someone would just tell him what he was supposed to do in this infernal darkness.

Again, he glanced back. That feeling that something had changed was still lingering with him. He didn't like it. "Does it still feel safe down here?"

"I think so," replied Olivia. "I mean, I feel kind of uneasy, but that might just be me. I'm starting to get *really* afraid of the dark. If we ever get home, I think I'm going to buy nightlights for every outlet in our apartment."

"No arguments from me," he grumbled.

"But I'm definitely not feeling any kind of panic or dread. Not even when I think about going back the way we came."

He nodded. That was a good sign. But it didn't explain why he suddenly felt as if something around them had changed. Did they pass into a different area of the labyrinth? Had they finally left the murk passages behind, perhaps?

He continued onward, his thoughts churning. He wished he understood this place. He hated not knowing what was going on. It was so frustrating!

Again, he heard the mysterious whisper of a voice, but it was softer than it was before, too faint to make out what it said.

Were they getting farther away from it? He thought they were moving *toward* it.

Were they still going the right direction? It wasn't as if they'd turned around. Maybe the passage was circling back the way they came?

Ahead of them, a fork appeared in the path. They could veer left or they could veer right. And as they drew closer, he saw that both passages contained a second fork a short distance beyond that, doubling the choices to four. Two paths continued on straight ahead, more or less, while the other two set off toward the left and right.

So many choices. So little odds of doing it right.

He stopped where the path first split and shined his light both ways, studying them, but of course they all looked identical. And that voice didn't give him any clues, no matter how hard he listened.

"Anything?" he tried, raising an eyebrow at Olivia.

She shook her head. "Everything feels the same down here. I don't know if there's just nothing here or if something's making it harder for me to sense things."

"Let's hope it's the first one." With no clues to help him decide, he chose left, then left again, hoping that deviating from the path they'd been following all this time might at least take them somewhere new.

But his light only revealed the same stone walls and strange etchings as he pushed onward.

He cocked his head to one side, listening. Did he just hear that voice again? The faintest of murmurs over their shuffling footsteps?

No. That was probably just his imagination. It was *too* soft. Too short.

The more he thought about it, the less he thought that it must be Erin. It simply didn't make sense. She'd proved herself more than capable of communicating. She had the power to physically *shove* him into that killing vine. Why would she suddenly be too weak to make her voice heard? And why would she only speak to *him*?

He kept thinking about what Andrea said about a *different* voice inside her head. Someone she called the Priestess of Ruin, who may have been the very same entity that Maeve warned them about. Was *that* who was calling out to him right now? And if so, why? And should he dare trust anything the voice told him? According to Andrea, she was some kind of ancient god and might have been meddling with all of them from the very beginning.

"Those weird patterns are breaking up," observed Olivia.

He glanced around and realized that she was right. Those squiggly etchings in the stone were unraveling themselves and growing fainter. There were fewer patterns than there were before.

"What do you think *that* means?"

But of course he had no idea. He didn't know what it meant when they appeared, much less when they went away again. Were they important? Were they supposed to tell them something? Did they have a purpose of some kind? Corey referred to this whole place as a sort of *machine*. Did they have something to do with that?

"Beware the prisoner."

He turned and looked behind him, frowning. That was definitely the voice again. A faint whisper, loud enough that it could have been right in his ear, but still strangely distant. But what did it mean? What prisoner?

"You okay?" asked Olivia.

He nodded. Maybe he misheard it. It was so soft, after all. He let the words circle through his head as he continued forward, trying to decide if it should mean anything to him.

Holding tight to Olivia, determined to keep her safe no matter what crossed their path in this stubborn darkness, he pushed onward, watching those etched lines as they thinned out, unraveling from those squiggly shapes and growing shallower and fainter, slowly disappearing, one by one.

He couldn't be sure if they traveled a hundred feet or a hundred *yards* before they faded away completely, but he was confident it was somewhere in that range. Then the labyrinth was as it was before, smooth and clean and flawless, without so much as a crack after all the endless ages it had stood here.

He didn't know if this constituted an improvement over their situation or if they should be concerned, so he remained on guard, pretty much as he'd been all night.

Their flashlights revealed that the path before them was beginning to slant downward now.

Was that right? Were they *supposed* to be going down?

He was probably overthinking it. After all, how much did their *choices* really affect anything? It felt more like they were being *herded* through the labyrinth, forcefully guided, kept on track.

They were like the scarecrow man's morbid toys, mere puppets at the ends of the Keeper's strings.

All they could do was wait to see what the little monster threw them at next.

Chapter 30

"Why did only *some* of our shit move with us?" asked Brandy.

It was a good question. The flashlight and the book were both there when they came back to their senses, along with most of their clothes, but Brandy's shirt and one of his shoes didn't make the trip with them. Was it only the stuff closest to them? He couldn't fully remember what happened back there. He was in a lot of pain and losing blood. And then the rating switched to "mature" in an instant. He wasn't even sure how he managed it in his condition. It was like his body reacted automatically to her touch, as if all this sex magic business had trained him on an instinctual level. It all escalated so quickly he couldn't even keep up. His shoe and her shirt could have flown anywhere during all of that.

He'd discarded his remaining shoe and gave his bloodied tee shirt to Brandy, leaving him in just his shorts and socks. And his underwear. He still had those, too, at least. Unlike Brandy, who hadn't had hers since all this nonsense started.

The chamber they somehow found themselves in was about twice the size of a football field, with those stone columns scattered throughout it in a strange sort of concentric oval pattern. This was probably something he wouldn't have noticed if not for the psychic snapshot he perceived of it when he first woke up. It was too big and their sole flashlight was too limited to allow him to see far enough to make sense of it otherwise.

That same psychic snapshot also revealed that the claustrophobic corridors of the labyrinth surrounded them on all sides and also below and above, far too complex for him to grasp a definite path leading anywhere of any significance. What he *could* see was that the three doorways leading out of this chamber all led into separate areas of the labyrinth for as far as he was able to sense.

In other words, it wasn't really helpful at all beyond giving him a quick view of this one mostly empty space. But at least it saved them the time it would've taken to circle the room in search of a way out, he supposed.

"I really liked that shirt, too..."

"Sorry."

"It's fine. What about you? Are you going to be okay without your shoes?"

He looked down at his socks. "We didn't have shoes the first time," he reminded her.

"I know. And I still have fucking calluses."

She wasn't wrong. It was nice having shoes up until now. Last time they'd all complained of sore feet along the way and for days after. But it wasn't like he had any choice. "I'll be fine," he assured her. "I'm just glad you still have yours."

"Just tell me if you need to stop and rest. Don't push yourself too hard."

"Sure." Ahead of them, the wall and the passage leading out appeared from the darkness, just as he knew it would. This psychic awareness thing was pretty handy, he supposed. When he was able to use it, anyway.

Everything that happened back there... He kept playing it over in his mind. For obvious reasons, of course...but not *just* because of that. It was intense. It was sexy. It was *beautiful*. But it was also, he was fairly sure, an entirely new level of emotional magic. It wasn't just *one* thing, for starters. First, Brandy was able to read the book even though it was too dark to see, just as he was able to do back in the Denselands while they were still separated. But then she was able to make him...well...*ready to go*...despite his pain and weakened physical state. That was kind of weird. Was *that* in the book as well? Or did she just sort of instinctually know what to do?

She was able to heal him. Mostly. Something about splitting

the wound between them. He didn't like the idea that she now had a matching one, but that was how she did it, it seemed, and it *was* better for them both to have a minor injury than for one of them to have a mortal one. Still, he hated that she had to hurt herself in order to save him, no matter how minor.

But that wasn't the end of it. They teleported again. Or…something like teleporting, he guessed. They ended up in a completely different chamber of the labyrinth. He could sense no sign of the anxiety room in any of the surrounding areas. Which was yet another thing. He was able to get that psychic map of the area, which before now had usually required him to consciously redirect his sexual energy, taking all that pent up sexuality and funneling it into a mental picture of his environment rather than releasing it into an orgasm. But he didn't recall even thinking about that. It was less like what they did at Shanzer's party and much more like what happened to them in the sex room. He felt as if he'd lost all earthly control and was driven by blind lust, eagerly rushing from one climax to the next. According to Shanzer, that would waste their sexual energy, but they did all those things regardless. He even fixed the broken flashlight! How much emotional energy did they generate back there? And how much of it did they *spend*? What were the limits of this so-called sex magic? And what else could they do with it?

The passage ahead of them continued straight for about two hundred yards, he knew. Already the room they came from had been swallowed back into the gloom. At the far end, there was an adjacent passage running left and right. To the right would be two more intersections, but those were all dead ends. They wanted to go left. And then straight through the next three intersecting passages. After that the path would fork and they'd probably want to go right. That was the path that continued beyond the limit of his view back there and the one most likely to lead them somewhere the soonest.

He'd already forgotten the layout beyond the other two passages leading out of that room, recalling only that the paths leading from those were more complex than these. And now that he was thinking about it, it seemed like even the way back was growing fuzzy, almost as if his brain were automatically dumping what he no longer needed to remember. Was it that he was psychically supercharged by what happened back there, allowing him to retain selective information more efficiently? Or did the sexual magic also give him some kind of memory boost, almost like plugging an external memory device into a computer?

Was all of this in the book? Or should he start taking notes?

This was all so fascinating. They'd discovered actual magic. They'd *performed* actual magic. If it was possible to do the things they'd done since Shanzer sent them on their way, then there was no limit to what might be possible. This could be the answer to all his questions. It could be the answer to all the world's greatest mysteries. It was the sort of power that could make all their wildest dreams come true. And yet he found himself reminded again and again of just what such power might cost. He almost died back there, after all. He *would have died*, if Brandy hadn't managed that spell. And the spell itself... It was *dangerous*. It didn't simply heal him. Instead, it took half his physical damage and transferred it to her. The more he thought about it, the clearer it became to him that if the wound had been any deeper, that spell might only have ended up killing them both! That was a pretty big detail they were missing! What kind of cost might other spells come with? What hidden dangers were there to be found in the shaman's book of mysteries?

And magical drawbacks were hardly the most pressing of their concerns right now.

There was Dolly to worry about.

Why the hell was *she* here? And *how*?

He remembered the way she simply stepped out of the statues, her skin and clothes and even her eyes the exact shade and texture, as if she'd been one of them all along. And the way Brandy obviously couldn't hear or see her...

(*That girl is nothing like she appears to be. She's an incredibly powerful* witch. *And she's immensely* evil.)

The last time he encountered her was while he was in the clutches of the psychic predator, inside that protective mental construct Shanzer somehow created to shield him from it. He was only a voice on the phone, but she seemed as real as he was. She was perched on his lap, teasing him, making obscene propositions as casually as she breathed. But that was *outside* the city walls. How could she reach him here?

Unless some part of her never left his head...

"Aren't you clever?" she whispered into his ear.

He jumped and twirled around, his arm thrust out to protect his bride.

"What's wrong?" gasped Brandy.

What indeed? If she was asking him that, she clearly didn't hear the voice, despite the fact that it seemed to come from that side of him and was plenty loud enough to have been heard from no farther away than she was. Yet he very much doubted it was only his imagination.

"Did you see something?" pressed Brandy, frightened.

He shook his head. "Just... Spooked I guess..."

She's dangerous and cruel, he recalled Lucianna warning them. *She lies as naturally as she breathes. The terrible things she's done has earned her a rightful eternity in a place far worse than any hell you could imagine.*

"Don't lie to me."

He glanced over and saw that she was pointedly staring at him.

Right. Psychic. The truth in people. He'd always had a hard time keeping secrets from her. It wasn't really a problem in their daily lives since he had nothing to hide from her, but she always knew when he was planning a surprise. She almost always guessed her birthday and Christmas presents. And considering the supercharge that last romp gave his own psychic abilities, hers were almost certainly heightened as well, meaning he literally couldn't lie to her right now.

"Sorry," he amended. "I mean I don't really know. *Maybe* I'm just spooked. Maybe not. But there's nothing here right now."

This was a proper truth. She was satisfied with it. She didn't press the matter further, but instead leaned a little closer and scanned the surrounding darkness with those wide, pretty eyes.

(She can't resist the urge to cause trouble. She can't help herself. If she sees an opportunity to do someone harm, she'll seize it.)

He gripped her hand tighter and continued forward. He'd been dismissing it as a trick of his mind. He was in a lot of pain and losing a lot of blood. It wasn't impossible that he could have hallucinated a stone Dolly in that desperate moment. But that voice just now was worrisome. If she was really here, really interfering in some way, then she was likely going to be trouble. It was too dangerous to keep it a secret. "We may have a problem, though," he confessed.

Chapter 31

Andrea couldn't stop screaming.

She knew the things outside were coming. There was no way they didn't hear her. They'd probably be swarming from miles around. But she couldn't stop. The pain was unbearable. There was so much blood. And it was clearly broken. Her foot was turned at an unnatural angle. It was like stepping into a bear trap. And she couldn't pry it open! She gripped at the bloody steel, but she didn't have the strength. And every little movement was *agonizing.*

She didn't know what to do. She couldn't get away. Her mind was a chaotic storm of blinding pain and overwhelming terror. She couldn't breathe. She closed her eyes and tried to push past it, but she could feel herself blacking out.

Aren't you being a little dramatic?

When she opened her eyes, the blood was gone. There was no steel trap. There were no broken bones. Instead, her foot was caught in loop of old wire dangling down from what was left of the ceiling.

"What...?" No. That wasn't what happened. There was no way she simply scared herself and *imagined* that. She saw the blood with her own eyes. She felt every second of excruciating pain. She could still vividly *see* the metal buried in her skin, the blood pooling around her broken foot. It hurt *so much.*

Still blinking back tears, she looked down at herself. In all the pain and panic, she'd lost control of her bladder. She was sitting in a puddle of warm urine, the smell of it wafting up around her.

"You're so gross," Stella's voice whispered into her ear.

She cried out, startled and turned to look behind her. That wasn't in her head. That was someone speaking to her. But there was no one there. The ruined hallway was just as it was when she walked through it. She was alone.

In fact, she was *very* alone. Even the things outside had gone silent for some reason. The only sound was the occasional soft howl of the wind blowing over the broken walls.

But that made no sense. She sniffed and wiped at her nose with the back of her hand. *Why* did they go quiet? Where did they go? What were they doing?

Her legs were still shaking and the wound in her knee was throbbing, but she needed to get up. She needed to be moving before they came back. She reached out and grasped the door frame to steady herself, her eyes still wide open, watching for any more unseen danger. She just needed to stay alert and get to her feet.

But before she could move, she felt something wriggling across the top of her foot.

She jumped and yanked her leg back, but she was still tangled in that loose wire.

She needed to calm down. She was on edge, jumping at every little thing. She was going to step on another nail if she didn't watch what she was doing. She took a deep breath and let it out slowly. Then she reached down to untangle her foot from the wire.

Except…it wasn't a wire.

She blinked down at it confused. It looked like some kind of black vine.

No… That wasn't right. She was *sure* it was a wire last time she looked…

But as she grabbed hold of it, it suddenly tightened around her ankle. She uttered yet another terrified scream as something dragged her into the shadowy bathroom, which was no longer a bathroom at all. It was suddenly very big and very dark.

She was being dragged blind across what felt like bare earth. Rocks bit into her back and butt, clawing at her bare skin, wrenching fresh screams from her.

What was happening? And *why*? She didn't understand any of this!

She reached out for something to grab onto, but there was nothing.

Then there was a blinding flash on either side of her. Towering flames belched from the earth. An intense heat washed over her. An explosion? Did a gas main blow? Everything was happening so fast, her poor mind could barely keep up.

But even as she struggled to yank her foot free, she realized that she was back on the burning mountain again, just as it was five years ago.

And the thing that was wrapped around her ankle was no vine.

It was a night tree.

Not one of the sad, sickly ones from the Denselands. This was the night tree from the night they came here, healthy and enormous and writhing in the undulating firelight like some tentacled deep-sea monstrosity.

It dragged her to its trunk and then lifted her up into its coiling branches as if she weighed nothing. In an instant, those awful limbs wrapped themselves around her waist, encircled her arms and legs and slithered around her neck, cutting off her screams.

She could feel those tiny, piercing teeth biting into her skin everywhere they tightened.

She already knew she wasn't going to be able to escape. She wasn't strong enough. And she was all alone.

Are you though?

She couldn't breathe. Her vision blurred and doubled.

Something was walking around out there. It was upright like a person, but it wasn't one. It was dark, like the murk, featureless and ever shifting. She somehow knew that it wasn't human. And it wasn't one of the things that were lurking outside that ruined version of her apartment, either. This was something altogether different.

And even as she felt herself blacking out, she found that she was even more frightened of that figure than she was of the tree that was killing her right now.

You're never alone, breathed the impostor as everything went black. *Never.*

Chapter 32

Everett wasn't sure when the empty void turned into a concrete shaft. Nor could he remember exactly when the rope ladder turned into a steel one. And yet he was most definitely making his way up through what looked like some kind of vertical industrial-type tunnel, not entirely unlike the places he saw inside that frightful gouging station.

He wasn't even entirely sure how it was that he knew what this shaft looked like, considering he was still without his flashlight and therefore climbing through absolute darkness. But he found that he could picture everything around him inside his head. Did that mean it was another manifestation of his own imagination, perhaps? Like everything else he encountered on the other side of the void? Or did this all have something to do with the way Alice somehow changed from a doll to a rope ladder and then into this steel ladder? Was this shaft *her* creation? Was *she* the shaft?

She definitely wasn't gone. He could still sense her inside his head, urging him to keep climbing.

But where was she taking him?

All he knew for certain was that he hadn't made it back to the City Beyond Memory yet. That place had no ladders or concrete. Everything was that smooth, gray stone. This was either another steppingstone on his way back to the right-side-up world or she was leading him somewhere entirely new.

Chapter 33

The saw blades were still there in the old sawmill, great, toothy disks, long rusted and rising out of the invading weeds and brush like the forgotten bones of a slain giant.

Once upon a time, Erin knew that those would have been shiny and new and sharp enough to eat through any tree it was fed. When this place was in full operation, those would have been spinning at high speeds, making a deafening racket that probably carried for miles, meaning that they were literally "silenced screaming wheels."

She still didn't understand why the antlered old creep didn't just call it the Breastbroke Sawmill and hand her the address, but whatever... She was here now. And as much as she didn't want to, she supposed it was time for her to get to work.

She made her way through the crumbling building and out the back. She wished she'd packed some more practical clothes. Denim shorts, tee shirt and sneakers were fine casual wear for exploring urban areas, but she wasn't properly prepared for a nature walk. She'd rather be wearing jeans and boots. At this rate, she was going to end up getting snakebit. Or at the very least she'd end up covered in poison ivy and ticks.

She glanced back the way she came. Those stupid clues started with the gate and pointed her at the saw blades. If Horatio expected her to actually find anything in this wilderness, then she was going to need an exact path to follow. She wasn't exactly the nature type, after all. She was far more likely to get lost than to find anything hidden out here. So unless the antlered weirdo was massively overestimating her, it stood to reason that she should probably continue in a straight line following those first two clues, which was going to lead her deeper into the forest. That would make the most sense, she thought. It wasn't like this thorn thing was going to just be lying on the side of the road somewhere.

It became immediately apparent that this wasn't going to be a simple stroll through the woods. The trees and brush were dense and thorny back here, with no sign of a clear path she could follow. There was no road leading back this way. There wasn't even a game trail that she could make out.

She was going to scratch her legs all to hell. She just knew it.

But as soon as she ventured down the hill and deeper into those trees behind the sawmill, the thorns quickly became the least of her worries. She began to feel strangely and intensely uneasy. It wasn't merely the deep shade and the drop in temperature, she was sure. It felt as if she were being watched.

Something passed overhead, casting a darting shadow across the mottled sunlight on the forest floor. Was that only a bird? Or was it one of those *other* things she'd been seeing. It was difficult to tell the difference sometimes, even when her vision wasn't being obscured by a dense forest canopy.

Reality wasn't what it used to be, it seemed. And she longed for the simpler days when her biggest worry was where her next paycheck would come from.

She pushed her way through the brush, hissing when the briars cut into her bare legs and arms, groaning with disgust when cobwebs smacked her in the face, and nearly jumping out of her skin when a rabbit bolted from her path.

She wasn't cut out for nature, she decided. Her place was up on stage, playing her music and singing and being ogled by men who were either drunk or getting that way. It might not be the most glamourous of lives, but it was a lot less *itchy*, that was for sure.

The mosquitoes had found her, it seemed.

As she stopped to slap at one on her leg, she looked back the way she came, her mind still strangely uneasy, and caught a glimpse of what looked like someone disappearing behind a dense patch of crowded evergreens.

Cursing under her breath, she picked up her pace, gritting her teeth against the slapping branches and stinging thorns.

She wasn't sure which scenario would be worse. Should she hope it was just some local poking around the sawmill grounds? In her experience, human beings were usually more dangerous than the shadowy things that made themselves known since her visit to the Elysium Fog. It would be just her luck to stumble across some psycho serial killer out here. But she was also quite sure that those things she kept glimpsing had the potential to be *very* dangerous. She wasn't exactly the helpless maiden. She could hold her own against a few horny drunks in a bar parking lot. She might have a better chance defending herself against a modern day Jack the Ripper than whatever *other things* might be lurking out here.

At the bottom of the hill was a narrow gully running left to right. With the sawmill behind her, her best bet was to cross it and climb the next hill, keeping in line with the gate where she started. But was she still going in a straight line? It was hard to be sure while weaving through the trees and the brush. And she'd lost sight of the sawmill within minutes of setting off down the hill.

Again, she looked back. There was no sign of whoever or whatever she saw back there, but that uneasy feeling was still with her. Something didn't feel right. Her instincts were telling her to get out of this forest. But if she gave in and ran back to her car, she was sure she'd only be delaying the inevitable.

She stumbled over a root and cursed. She needed to pay more attention to where she was placing her feet. It wouldn't do her any good to figure out where those hidden eyes were watching her from if she stepped in an old post hole or tread on an angry rattlesnake.

She made her way up the hill, her attention focused on the rocky terrain and those damned briars that kept scratching at her exposed skin. Once she reached the top and the terrain leveled out again, she leaned against the trunk of a tree and waited to catch her breath.

She wasn't used to this much physical activity. Maybe she

should start jogging or something.

Again, she looked back the way she came, out over that shady gully, and tried to decide if those were only the shadows of swaying branches or something more solid creeping in and out of view.

Why did this place feel so unpleasant? Why was she so anxious? She used to like nature. She loved visiting the various parks near her bookings and eating her lunch in the open air. But then again, she supposed a park was different from a wild forest. She slapped at another mosquito and then scratched at a bite that was starting to itch on her cheek.

Nature was best in little, neatly groomed increments, she decided. The snakes and bears could *have* the real nature.

A loud caw surprised her and she looked up into the trees above her. Immediately, every other thought was washed out of her brain.

Just like that day she drove into the city of Crump, the branches overhead were filled with crows. Hundreds of them, each and every one staring down at her, watching her.

And something about them filled her with a sudden and overwhelming dread.

Chapter 34

The world never seemed to get any better. Not really. Austin had traveled a great deal of it in his many years, after all. He'd seen far more of it with his own two eyes than any mortal man ever had, and had recorded every detail of it in his vast memory banks. And throughout it all, there had *always* been war. Somewhere on this planet, at any given time, people were perpetually killing each other. And if they weren't killing each other they were abusing each other, using each other, taking advantage of each other or otherwise victimizing each other.

He couldn't understand how such beings managed to even survive this long, much less be of any kind of cosmic importance to one such as the Keeper. It was unfathomable that the universe be put through so much for the purpose of a species that seemed utterly determined to destroy itself.

There were peaceful places scattered here and there, places where the days passed and little ever happened. But that peace was only a shallow illusion. It had always astounded him how much vileness could be found hiding just beneath the surface in such places, how much raw potential for greed and indifference and cruelty the men and women in this world contained within them, filled to overflowing with prejudices and intolerance, always looking down on others, judging them, criticizing them behind their phony smiles.

Had human beings always been like this? So full of intolerance and bigotry? He couldn't comprehend why the Keeper would care anything about keeping such a species alive for the duration of a single cycle, much less ferry them from one incarnation of the universe to the next throughout the cycle's entire existence.

Was there something about them that he couldn't comprehend? Some hidden potential that only the wisest beings in the cosmos were capable of recognizing?

He wasn't one of these creatures. He possessed knowledge and understandings that they didn't have. As a tool of the Keeper, he was born with an awareness of the cycle, of the Faceless Ones and of the universes that came before. He knew of all the significant worlds that existed unseen beyond earth's whisper-thin boundaries and all the ways to enter them. He knew about the spectrum and how to navigate it. He knew of the Three Powers and the core realms of the natural, the supernatural and the unnatural they signified. And he knew about the other god-like entities that prowled the world undetected by mortal senses. He was even aware of all the things that went on undetected right beneath those oblivious human noses, catastrophic breaks in the boundaries between worlds, intrusions from the supernatural and unnatural realms, fluctuations in the psychic void, even changes to the timeline. He knew a great many things, and still mankind remained a perpetual mystery to him throughout his agonizingly long existence.

But it wasn't his job to understand. And it wasn't his job to question these things. It was his job to wait. It was his job to make his way to the second gatehouse when the time came. It was his job to be the bootup disk, as Corey had described it, for the next stage of the Keeper's grand machine.

He stared at his bag of books lying just out of reach. Unfeeling though they were, his fingers itched to hold one of them again, to dive one more time into the fiction, into the fantasy. It was precisely these kinds of befuddling ponderings that had always made him want to retreat into those made-up worlds. When left too long to reflect on this seemingly rotten race of selfish beings, he always found his thoughts circling around like this, questioning things he had no business questioning, fuming over the perceived importance of creatures who didn't even value their *own* importance.

The real world was an unfortunate place.

It was ironic really. In stories, characters like him always yearned to be real boys, yet he was a made-up person trapped in the real world desperately longing to be a fairy tale.

Chapter 35

Violet wasn't sure how long she lay there screaming before she realized that the boar-things were no longer there and that she wasn't, in fact, being eaten alive.

She was curled up into a ball, shielding herself, sobbing and wailing and screaming for help, unable to catch her breath. But the monsters were gone. She was still unharmed, except for those scratches and bruises she received when she fell down that rocky hillside. And her bruised shoulder from when she fell and landed on that old stretch of highway.

(*Death cannot take you here. The very composition of this reality is connected to your presence on a primordial level. Existence flows around you like a stone in a stream, averting itself far easier than eroding its way through you.*)

Still gripped by the sheer terror of the experience, she wiped at her face and sat up, unable to understand it. Death couldn't take her? She couldn't die? But she could experience the agony of those deaths?

Was this a blessing or a curse?

And where was she now?

The ruined city was gone, as was the skeletal forest before it and the crumbling labyrinth walls before that. She was lying on a dusty floor inside some kind of structure. Everything was dark except for a line of filthy, dingy windows on one side, that horrible, bloody light filtering through the grime.

She was shaking too much to trust standing on her feet, so she pushed herself up onto her hands and knees and crawled toward that meager crimson light.

Her feet still hurt from running through that rocky forest, as did her skinned knees and palms. Her whole body felt bruised. Somehow *those* little injuries remained with her, but there was no evidence of those awful hog creatures or that monstrous devil-thing. She wondered what the difference was. Who decided what she kept and what never happened?

She reached the windows and rose to her feet, gripping the dirty sill to steady herself. Then she raked her hand through the thick dust. It didn't help much. The outside was just as filthy as the inside, probably more so. But she could see that she was staring down at a deserted city street from the second floor of one of a number of businesses.

And it wasn't just any street. This was her hometown. This was Tunipet, Missouri's Main Street.

Why would she be here? And why was it bathed in bloody Ruin?

"That's not real..." she muttered to herself. It couldn't be. Tunipet was on the other side of countless miles of the Wood. This was another illusion, like everything else here. When she first arrived, she found that same bloody sky looming overhead, even though the Ruin presented itself as the same room she'd just left in the temple. If she were really still inside the labyrinth, she wouldn't have been able to see the sky. Her scant knowledge of the city's layout was enough to know that there were still countless floors above them. This was the same. If she looked closely, she could see the difference.

There were no other buildings visible *behind* the storefronts across the street. There should be more roofs back there. She should be able to see the church steeple from here. And the water tower. Instead, it was as if this red mockery ended at the back walls of those stores.

This wasn't Tunipet. It was just a crude copy.

(*The very composition of this reality is connected to your presence on a primordial level.*)

She doubted that she could understand the full meaning of those words the other one spoke to her, but if this world was connected to her, then perhaps that was why all these different ruined places looked familiar. This was obviously another world, not so different from the pocket dimensions she and Corey had explored. Except those places were small and localized. They mirrored the space around them. This was more like the Wood. It was huge. And perhaps its physical appearance mirrored *her* instead of the world around it.

That would sort of make some sense, she supposed. Or at least put it into a context that she could understand a little better.

She turned and squinted into the darkness of the room behind her. She seemed to be alone here, but she very much doubted that it would remain that way.

"Okay…" she breathed. "So what do I do now?"

You die.

A hard shiver ran through her. "What?" she gasped.

Over and over again.

She pressed her back against the windowsill, her green eyes wide with fright.

Forever.

"You're not her." It sounded like the other one. It spoke through her head in her own voice like the other one. But this wasn't the other one.

No. I'm not.

"You're her. The Priestess of Ruin."

I am.

"What do you want with me?" She could hear the terrified tremble in her voice as she spoke and she hated it. But fear was stronger than pride. It cut far deeper, making her legs tremble again, taking her breath away, making her feel faint.

She reached for her pocket, for the flashlight she tucked away there when she found herself beneath that boiling red sky.

Nothing much, replied that awful mockery of the other one. *Only to watch while you…* The voice seemed to fade away inside her head, as if the speaker had simply wandered off. But then it completed the sentence not inside her head at all, but right into her ear: "…suffer."

She screamed and darted from the window, her heart freshly racing. That wasn't her imagination. Someone was right there. She felt the breath on her ear, the presence of someone standing right behind her. And yet no one could have been behind her. She was standing with her back to the window. There was no room for someone back there.

But that awful voice was still ringing in her head, giggling like a giddy, spoiled child.

She needed to get out of here, but where could she go? She wasn't merely trapped inside this building. She was trapped inside this *whole world*.

"Two little birdies caught in my cage..." sang a girlish voice that seemed to drift eerily through the room with no origin.

What did that mean? Two little birdies? Was someone else here, too? She hadn't seen anyone.

But she found her thoughts drawn back to the moments before those boar-things attacked her. She thought she heard someone screaming...

"How many feathers can I pluck before they stop screaming?"

"This bitch is seriously psycho," muttered Violet. She was still trying to fumble the flashlight out of her pocket, but her hands were trembling and she was too afraid to stand still. She needed to flee this place. She fumbled through the darkness, trying to find the door. It had to be at the very back of the room if she couldn't see it. But as she moved deeper into that heavy darkness, she felt more and more as if something were wrong with this space. She felt eyes on her, and not just those of the so-called Priestess of Ruin. Something else was here. Something dangerous.

Better watch out, giggled the sadistic goddess from somewhere inside her head again.

She finally caught sight of the door, a mere rectangle of slightly darker shadow hidden in the gloom, and she ran for it, desperate to flee this awful space.

But something caught her foot and she fell.

Too late!

She rolled over and struggled to pull her leg free, but something was wrapped around her ankle, squeezing her, gripping with incredible strength.

Terror filled her. She didn't want to go through that torture again. She couldn't take it. She'd go crazy! She sat up and grasped at her ankle in the dark, but the thing her hands found was squishy and slimy, wrenching a fresh scream from her. She snatched her hands back, revolted.

What the hell *was* that?

The world seemed to swim in and out of focus. She couldn't breathe. Panic was overwhelming her. Something was groping at the back of her shirt. Something cold and wet brushed her cheek. And the thing around her ankle was slithering higher, creeping up her calf toward her thigh, wrapping itself around more of her leg.

She kicked at it, but it only squeezed tighter.

"Let me go!" she cried. She needed to free herself. She needed to run away. But she couldn't shake the thing off.

Something dreadful was slithering up the back of her shirt. Another was curling around her bare thigh.

She had to get out of here!

She grabbed at the thing around her ankle, but she couldn't get a grip. It was too slick. All she ended up with was two handfuls of foul slime.

Then something had her wrist.

She was entangled!

"We're gonna have so much fun together," hissed that awful voice in her ear as those foul, slimy things tightened around her and began pulling.

She tried to scream, but she couldn't draw a breath. She was being strangled.

And yet, even in her terror, she managed to realize that she wasn't being strangled quickly enough. Whatever had her was pulling her in several different directions, stretching each of her limbs. She felt her joints pop and her tendons stretch. She was going to be pulled into *pieces*!

"So. Much. *Fun*."

There was blinding pain and a terrible, wet tearing sound.

Chapter 36

Gina cast her psychic gaze out across the surrounding corridors again. When she ran after the thing with too many mouths, she left the vicinity of the glass labyrinth, but she could still feel its strange energy nearby. She just needed to weave her way back through the tangle of passages to where she left it. But the twisted layout was making it difficult. And so was that strange distortion that limited her visibility. It still seemed to be originating from the stone itself.

What was this stuff? It looked and felt like ordinary gray stone, but it was no such thing. It had curious properties, like nothing she'd ever encountered before. The longer she was here, the more certain she was of it.

"By the way," said Nicole. "What happened to Brandy and Albert? I don't remember anything after we reached the gate."

She glanced back, surprised. "Nothing?"

"I remember we found the gate. Inside that cave. And I was distracted by something. I turned and looked around while you were all discussing that circle... Then that Hotdog freak was there."

"He came back?" She recalled the goddess assuring them that Hochog was dead, but warning them that they hadn't seen the last of him. (*What walked away and remains out there is only an empty husk. Only Goar Nangup remains.*) Those words frightened her then and they frightened her now. (*What comes back will be different and in many ways more dangerous.*)

"It's his fault everything went to shit back there," confirmed Nicole.

She glanced back the way they came, nervous.

"He's gone now," she assured her. "Pretty sure he can't hurt anyone else. Not until he gets a new nutjob follower, anyway."

"That's good."

"Anyway, yeah. Hotdog Creep jumped me in the cave and next thing I knew I was in here, all alone."

Gina considered this. So it was Hochog and his nightmare god who made her behave so strangely. And it sounded like they used her to sneak into the city. They were trying to sabotage the cycle. Did that mean that Nicole was a key part of that? The goddess *did* say she had a role to play, in spite of the fact that she had no psychic abilities to speak of.

"So what happened, anyway?"

"We never noticed anything on the other side of the wall. You were still there when we turned around. We went through the gate together. All four of us. But after that, you were acting weird. Really quiet. We thought you were just tired. But then you ran out into the storm and disappeared."

"Storm?"

"Everything inside the wall is caught in a permanent, violent storm."

She glanced at the stone above their heads. "I didn't even know there was an outside. All I've seen is…*this*."

"Albert says the entire city is another temple. He called it the Temple of the Three Whispers."

"That sounds right. He likes naming things."

"That's what Brandy said."

"A storm…" she sighed, pondering it.

"A really big one. Lightning and thunder. Lots of rain. Really hard to see or hear anything. It even clouded over the psychic part of my mind. That was how we lost you so fast. It was impossible to follow you once you were out in it."

"I guess that explains why I woke up soaking wet…"

"Probably. We were all really worried about you."

"Sorry. All I remember is waking up alone in the labyrinth and Hotdog Creep was stalking me like some kind of zombie terminator. If it wasn't for Keith—" But her voice cut off at this. "He saved me," she finished in a much softer tone.

"I'm the one who should be sorry. I never sensed anything. You kept saying something was wrong. You kept looking back, like something was following us. But I couldn't see it. I still don't know why."

"It wasn't your fault. It wasn't even Hotdog anymore. It was that *god* of his. Fucking *Goar Nangup*. He was wearing Hotdog's corpse like a costume. I got up close and personal with him while he had me knocked out for a while and let me tell you that thing would've given H. P. Lovecraft a permanent hard-on." She hugged herself against a hard shiver. "Fucking *nightmare fuel*."

"That sounds awful," she replied. And more than that, it sounded *familiar*. That was what her entire life had been like, after all. Maddeningly terrifying things that seemed to seep right into her mind until it was impossible to even feel like she could hide…

Humans had the potential to be monsters. She'd seen it time and time again. But even the worst people paled in comparison to the truest horrors that lurked unseen in the shadows of the universe.

She pushed these thoughts from her mind. It wasn't going to do her any favors to start thinking about things like this and frighten herself. She needed to stay brave for Nicole.

Besides, they were finally getting close to the glass labyrinth. She could feel it just beyond this next passage.

Except…this wasn't the way she came. Unable to recall the exact route she took, relying on her limited psychic awareness, she'd taken a wrong turn. This was somewhere different. But it didn't matter. She didn't need to be in the same place to cross over again. There were lots of cracks between the two. And she was fairly sure that even using the same crack to cross back over wouldn't ensure that she went back to the same point she left from. Things outside the so-called "real" world didn't follow the same rules.

But would Nicole be able to slip through the cracks the same way she'd done? That was the real question. Taking her back to where the glass broke wasn't an option. And not merely because she wasn't confident she could find the spot again. It wasn't there anymore. In her fear, she couldn't remember it very clearly, but she was fairly sure that the glass only remained broken for an instant, just long enough for the thing with too many mouths to cross over. Then the gaping hole was just gone. It was as if the labyrinth were able to heal itself.

Only those cracks remained. And Nicole wouldn't be able to see them. What if she crossed over, only to arrive alone on the other side and unable to get back to the same place she left her?

And what about the monstrous entity that broke the glass?

(*There's another... Something far stronger than a mere spirit, something I can't see. I think it's been with you for some time, possibly since the first doorway, watching you, biding its time, but it's able to cloud itself from my sight somehow.*)

She felt an anxious knot forming deep inside her belly as she drew closer to the unnatural energy of that glass boundary. With all that happened, chasing that monster, protecting Nicole from it, that strange explosion she used to get rid of it... And of course poor Keith... Well, she'd kind of forgotten about it.

(*It seems to attract unwanted things. And it delights in your misfortune.*)

Something even the goddess didn't understand... And she'd felt its power for herself. It showed itself to her specifically so that she'd know what she was up against. It played with her. It even *kissed* her.

A true goddess...

Something ancient and dark and immensely powerful beyond her comprehension...

This was the sort of fear that used to paralyze her when she was growing up, that used to make her cry, that used to make it impossible to do anything else. But she wasn't a child anymore. And she didn't have the luxury of letting fear still her feet.

"So what happened after that?" wondered Nicole. "How'd you get separated?"

She felt a pang of guilt in her heart. She didn't want to confess that she basically "ditched" them, as her roommates back in Cakwetak would've said. "We were separated when I found the glass labyrinth," she said instead. "Last I saw them, they were fine. And they were still together."

"That's good. Hopefully they still are."

"I hope so, too." If anything happened to them, she wasn't sure she could bear the guilt. But she couldn't help feeling as if those two didn't need her help staying safe. There was something about that magic they used. It felt...*significant*.

She reached the end of the corridor and walked up to the wall waiting for her. Without letting go of Nicole's hand, she reached out and placed her other palm against it, feeling the energy that radiated there.

"What's going on?" whispered Nicole.

"This is it. The glass labyrinth."

She was quiet for a moment, uncertain. Then, in that same whisper: "I don't see any glass."

"I know."

Nicole could only see the stone. Because that was all there was. The glass was an illusion, little more than a metaphor concocted by her own strange mind. She doubted if she'd be able to see anything different even from the other side.

She cast her psychic gaze left and right, scanning the overlapping surfaces.

Something to the right?

Her left hand still pressed to the wall, she walked in that direction, studying the stone while the glass beyond unraveled from the darkness, revealing itself to her inner eye little by little.

Ten yards... Twenty... Thirty... There was something there. Just a glimmer. A glint. A flicker in the warbling illusion of warped glass. She was getting better at spotting the cracks, she realized, able to recognize the anomaly from a greater distance. But that distance was still greatly distorted. She was approaching that flickering something more slowly than she was walking, moving much faster through the stone than she was moving alongside the glass.

Then she stopped. All at once, she was there.

A familiar refraction, a spectrum of non-light both sparkling and darkling in that maddening contrast that only her inner sight could detect.

She squeezed Nicole's hand. "Right here."

"*What's* right there?"

Gina turned and took her other hand, squeezing it around the flashlight. "I'm not sure what's going to happen next," she explained. "I can't really describe it. But there's another labyrinth on the other side of this wall that we need to get into. I'm not sure how this all works and I'm afraid I might lose you if I do it wrong."

She blinked down at her, confused. "Okay. Well... I mean, I trust you. Just tell me what to do."

She felt a pang in her heart. She trusted her... She wasn't sure if that made it easier or harder. What if she messed up and stranded her here all alone? What if she lost her forever? What if she ended up being responsible for her not making it home?

But standing here wasn't an option, either. The longer she delayed, the more she felt the glass labyrinth pulling her. Whatever the reason for her being here, she was only going to find it on the other side.

"I think..." she began, hesitating. "Maybe close your eyes. Try not to think too much about anything. For me, it was like...I just let go and let it happen. Does that make sense?"

Nicole nodded. "I think so."

"Good. I really hope this works."

"I trust you," she said again, closing her eyes.

"Try to move with me when I move. Stay with me, no matter what you might feel."

She nodded again.

Gina took a deep breath and closed her eyes. She *really* hoped this worked...

For a moment, she did nothing. She focused on the crack, pushing everything else from her mind except the feel of Nicole's hands in her own.

Please, goddess... she thought.

Then she stepped backward, pulling Nicole with her.

In an instant she was on the other side. She was once again surrounded by that strange, warped glass, revealing corridor after corridor of the surrounding area looming beyond. Just like last time, she felt weirdly disheveled again. Her skirt felt twisted and one of her sandals was loose. But none of that mattered. What mattered was Nicole.

She was still gripping her hands! She was still with her! "We did it," she sighed, relieved. She let go of her and turned around, opening her eyes.

Nothing had changed. Every surface was still the same smooth and featureless stone. But she already knew that. She could feel it when she was here the first time.

"That felt weird," said Nicole.

"Yeah. It's like that."

When she looked over at her, she was standing there, frowning, staring down at her feet. "My shoe ate my sock," she sighed in the most pitiful voice she'd ever heard.

Gina looked down to see that she was right. Only one sock was still visible.

When she looked up at her face, tears were welling up in her eyes again.

"It's okay," she said, quickly. "I can help. Don't cry." She dropped to one knee and grasped her shoe. "Here. Hold onto me."

A soft sob escaped Nicole.

"Don't cry. I'll fix it." But when she looked up, she wasn't crying. She was laughing.

"I'm sorry," she sighed, wiping at her eyes. Then she knelt down and hugged her again. "Thank you. I know I'm a mess."

"It's okay. I don't mind. Really."

And she truly didn't mind. It felt nice. Not just being hugged, but to actually get used to being hugged...

"I still don't see any glass," muttered Nicole.

"I know."

Chapter 37

Olivia sat on the cold floor of the gently sloping passage, her cheek pressed against Wayne's chest, clinging to him, listening to his breathing and his heartbeat. Her legs were sore and her feet were aching. She couldn't remember the last time they took a break.

The passage they were following had continued downward for a long time, and when they finally arrived here at the bottom, it was only to find the way forward flooded. If they didn't want to retrace their steps all the way back up that hill, they were going to have to get wet again. And since neither of them were particularly excited about going for a swim, they decided it was time to take a well-deserved breather.

"It's not *still*, like the pools in the first temple," Wayne observed.

"Neither was that giant *toilet* you got us flushed down," she reminded him.

"True," he chuckled. He was tired, too. She could tell. They'd both been going almost nonstop since they arrived in the Denselands. They took a much needed rest in those sandstone ruins after he woke up from those nasty killing vines, and another after they crawled out of the water in that weird alien nature preserve, and again after Andrea found them, but that was about it. Right now, she'd give anything to be back on that train, in their own private room. She wanted nothing more than to just crawl into a nice warm bed and sleep for *days*.

A nice, hot bath sounded amazing, too. But that was definitely *not* what was in store for them. That water looked *cold*. And scary. She couldn't even see how deep it was. What if it just kept getting deeper and deeper until it completely submerged? How could they be sure there'd even be a way out? There was no way she was brave enough to trust something like that. She'd panic and drown within a few seconds. She still wasn't over those despicable never-children trying to drown her in that fairy forest. Even now, the very memory of that awful ordeal made her nuzzle against Wayne's chest, pressing herself as close to him as possible.

Yet she found that she simply knew the way forward wasn't blocked. If it were, then her psychic alarm would be telling her not to continue forward. As it was, however, she wasn't feeling any particular aversion to going either forward or backward. Neither option was presenting her with that feeling of looming dread. Instead, there was simply a much more subtle feeling that forward was *better*.

Even her own psychic brain wouldn't cut her any slack, it seemed.

"The first time, most of the pools inside the temple were completely still," Wayne recalled. "Like mirrors. Like nothing had ever disturbed them. I remember thinking there was something *crazy* creepy about it."

She knew exactly what he was talking about. She'd felt it, too. Those pools had seemed bottomless. Shining their lights down into them was so eerie. Nothing but darkness down there. It was far too easy to imagine something terrible staring up at them from those mysterious depths.

"The water was never flowing until we reached the City of the Blind. The fountain we found the Sentinel Queen bathing in was moving. So the water *was* flowing. There was a source somewhere under it all."

She wondered how deep those pools had to be that the water flowing in and out to maintain that level didn't make the surface move at all? And what kinds of similar bottomless pools might be waiting for them in *this* labyrinth? Again, her gaze drifted to the water ahead of them. It almost *lapped* at the stone, like tiny little waves against the shore. It didn't have any kind of debris in it, no dirt or sand. It didn't even make any bubbles. It appeared utterly clean, just like the surfaces of the stone around them.

She could smell it, too. It was an earthy sort of dankness, but not quite like anything she smelled before. There was a distinct quality about it that she couldn't identify, something that no water in her own world had ever smelled like, probably. Precisely *because* this wasn't her world. The minerals in it were probably completely different. If there were any minerals in it at all.

If she weren't so weary, she might've smiled a little at the realization that she was thinking about these places the way Albert did. She was analyzing the details, making hypotheses... She'd never really understood why he was so hung up on the temple. Personally, she just wanted to forget that it existed most of the time. Her memories of that place were too frightening to hold onto like that. And it wasn't as if he'd waltzed through the whole thing unscathed. He broke his arm down there. He hallucinated a violent, agonizing death. He believed, just as she did, that Wayne and Andrea both died. He even thought that he lost Brandy for a short while there. Why did he want to spend so much time existing in that world? But she supposed there was something to be said about all those unanswerable questions. For the right mindset. For the right person.

"We should just get this over with," groaned Wayne, his body tensing as he prepared to stand.

Olivia tightened her grip on him and pressed herself even closer, holding him in place. "Mm-mm."

He tightened his grip on her in return. The feel of those strong arms never failed to make her feel comforted, no matter what might be going through her head.

"Not yet," she insisted, her voice muffled against his chest.

"Okay," he breathed, relaxing again. He wouldn't pressure her. He never did. He was wonderful like that.

She remained that way for a while, clinging to him, her face pressed against him, desperate to keep him as close as possible. She was so terrified of losing him again. Next time could be the last, after all. There were no guarantees in life. And there were only so many second chances. It felt like her luck must be running awfully thin by now.

And yet, the scarecrow man was proof enough that moving forward wasn't the only way to speed headlong toward danger. If that supernatural psychopath found a way to follow them, then staying on one place could be just as fatal as rushing blindly ahead.

With a regretful sigh, she pressed herself against him once more, holding him as tightly as she could for a moment, then she let go and stood up.

As soon as he was on his feet, she grabbed his arm again and held on.

"This is going to be really unpleasant," he grumbled.

She replied with a sound that was something between a whine and a whimper. She really didn't want to do this. But the sooner they crossed this probably very unpleasant pool of water, the sooner they could begin to dry off. That was the best she was going to get as far as motivation went.

"Want me to go first?" he offered. "See how deep it gets?"

She gave her head a hard shake and gripped his arm even tighter. "Don't you dare!" she grumbled.

"Okay. Just throwing it out there."

It actually gave her heart a little jumpstart to even hear him suggest it.

When this was over, she might have to make him take some more time off, just so she could spend a whole day clinging to him like this. She needed all the assurance she could get that he wasn't going anywhere.

"Ready?"

She sighed. It was a deep sigh, a long sigh, drawing out the feel of his shirt against her face. Then she pulled away and turned to face the frigid pool standing in their path. The longer they hesitated, the worse it was probably going to be. She even managed to give him a little tug, leading the way, as it were.

She wasn't even fully dry from their *last* swim. Her shirt and khakis were dry enough, but her socks and undergarments were still a little damp and giving her a chill. She didn't want to have to start over. It felt like torture.

Her foot dipped beneath the surface and the water rushed in, freshly soaking her sock, the cold sucking her breath away.

This was going to be miserable.

Chapter 38

Brandy looked back the way they came, uneasy. As if they didn't have enough problems already, now they had that spooky skank, Dolly, to worry about? She should've wrung that slut's neck when they found her hiding under the covers in the pervert's gaudy guest room. She was starting to *really* hate that woman.

"Shanzer used her like some kind of psychic link to facilitate the room he made to protect me from the psychic predator. It was weird, like the plot of some lame television show or something. But it must've worked, because I didn't end up with my mind eaten. She said he put her in some kind of sleep state similar to what I was in and used her to reach me. I keep wondering if maybe it had something to do with that crazy cat lady's dream world."

"He just called me up on a phone," she recalled. There was no room. There was no Dolly. But then again, there also wasn't a psychic predator. That was wherever *he* was. She was all alone in that darkness, in no need of a psychic safe room inside her head.

"That was how he talked to me, too. I was sitting in an armchair, holding a handset while something was clawing at the space from outside. But Dolly was *there*. Like, physically in the room with me. I could feel her."

"Could you now?"

"What?"

"Feel her?"

"No!" He glanced back, flustered. "I mean, *yeah*. But not like *that*."

She could tell he was lying again, but she didn't press the

matter. She could see the truth in him, *all* the truth, not just some of it, so she also knew he didn't do anything inappropriate. He wouldn't do that to her, not even in some kind of dreamlike mind vault. Especially with a certifiable psychopath like Dolly. And she really didn't want to start a fight so soon after such an awful scare. But she reserved the right to be jealous. He was her husband. And that creepy slut was all over him back in the pervert's gross mansion.

"Shanzer kept insisting that the connection worked better if she was as close to me as possible. No matter how many times I pushed her away," he quickly added.

She looked back over her shoulder again. She didn't like the idea of that witch stalking them.

"I don't think she's here in the temple," he went on. "Not physically. I think the real Dolly is probably still back in our world with Shanzer. Instead, I feel like she did something when she was inside that room with me. Left some part of herself in my mind, you know? Just to screw with us." He reached up and scratched at his belly. He did the same thing after they left the guest room, she recalled. The same spot where that little bitch had her cheek lying when she lifted the covers. Was it only his subconscious memory of her there, or was there a deeper connection of some sort? It wasn't hard to imagine that the little bitch had somehow tagged him while he was sleeping, probably on the pervert's orders, even.

"So she's just running around loose inside your head?"

"I guess so. Some kind of psychic attachment, maybe?"

"Then how was she able to break the flashlight?"

"I don't know. But it proves she's more than just a harmless hallucination. She might be capable of hurting us."

"How the fuck are we supposed to protect ourselves from something like *that*?"

"Good question. I'm not sure." He glanced down at the light. "I'm not even sure how I fixed it. I can't even remember what I did now."

Brandy didn't care how he fixed it. She was only glad it was working again. She wanted to be able to see in case that witch showed up. She was enough trouble back in the skeevy mansion where the pervert could keep her reined in. But he wasn't here. The bitch was off her leash. And far worse, she was somehow inside his brain. She might as well be a ghost. What sort of mischief could she cause like that?

"'The human mind is infinitely larger and more complex than most people are capable of ever imagining,'" said Albert. "'Inside every living person exists a unique multitude of existence, an entire multiverse unto itself, capable of extraordinary things, limited by little more than tragic ignorance and blatant stupidity bred by generations of closed-mindedness and intentionally misdirected beliefs. Very few even scratch the surface of their true potential anymore. But those who do can achieve god-like things.'"

Brandy squinted at him, confused. "Why are you talking like that?"

He glanced back at her. "Shanzer's book," he explained. "I was reading."

She looked down at the square bulge in his back pocket.

"I know. Weird, right? I figured if it was possible to read the book in the *dark*, then why should I even need to take it out."

He had a point, she supposed. She'd experienced the whole "magic reading in the dark" trick herself. Unable to see the words on the page, her mind simply fed her what was written in it as if she remembered it. It was the only thing that allowed her to save his life back there.

"He goes into his pervy poetry stuff again after that," he added. "Comparing what's in our heads to what's in a vagina. I'm..." He made a face at something she couldn't see. "Yeah...I'm not gonna repeat any of that. It's...unnecessary."

"Fucking pervert," she growled.

"Yeah." He shook his head. "Anyway, it seems like he's saying that our thoughts have the potential to be tangible. Not just to us, but to others, too." He glanced back at her again. "Like when we first used it to escape the psychic predator, how it felt like we were together, even though we didn't end up in the same place."

"When we took 'long distance relationship' to the next level," she said, nodding. She remembered it just fine. It was such an intense feeling that she couldn't understand why he wasn't with her when she woke up. It was simply too *real* to have only been her imagination.

"Not gonna lie. It's pretty scary to think that it can be that hard to tell the difference between what's real and what's not."

"No shit. It means that bitch might as well be right in front of you." It seemed to her that the little psycho could do anything she wanted to him and there was nothing she'd be able to do about it. Could she wrap her nasty little hands around his throat and strangle him to death right in front of her eyes? It was a deeply helpless and unsettling thought. And it pissed her off.

"I mean, I guess it's not so different from, like, schizophrenia or something," he reasoned. "Maybe people who struggle with reality are actually perfectly sane but just caught up in *this* sort of stuff."

"That'd suck." But she could definitely imagine such a scenario. If she didn't have Albert that first night six years ago to confirm it all, she probably would've thought *she'd* gone insane.

Ahead of them, another passage appeared. Albert shined his light down one way, then the other, frowning. "I'm still getting little flashes of my surroundings, but not like before. And what I'm getting isn't really very helpful. All I can see is that it's a maze. Like I don't already know that."

She turned and looked back the way they came, uneasy. Unlike him, she was supposed to be aware of any *people* around her, but while she was fully aware of Albert to the point that she could tell how honest he was being with her as if it were written on his face, she could sense no one else at all. If that witch really was haunting him like some kind of psychic poltergeist, then whatever form she was in didn't count as human, which was a rather terrifying thought.

What was the little bitch up to? What was she planning? Was she really trying to break the cycle? How would something like that benefit her? And most of all, how were they supposed to protect themselves from an enemy *inside his fucking mind?*

Still bloody from head to toe, Albert continued straight ahead and she followed, clinging to his hand, determined not to let anything, witch or otherwise, separate them again.

Chapter 39

Again, Andrea struggled up from the depths of sleep, her throat sore, her head pounding, her body aching. What happened? Where was she?

But then it all came rushing back to her. The night tree! She was dangling from its coiling branches, slowly strangling to death. She could still feel those unnatural tendrils wrapped around her body, lumpy and cold and strangely hard, preventing her from moving. Her eyes flashed open and she gasped for air.

She could breathe again…

Things were different. The burning mountain was gone. The sky was once again that sickly shade of red. She stared up at one of those strange, bird-like things with the not-right wings and the odd, warbling streamers trailing behind them, her mind racing. How did she get here? What was going on?

She tried to pull her arm free and found that those weren't toothy, coiling night tree branches holding her, but instead heavy *chains.* They were wrapped around her the same way, as if those alien limbs had simply transformed into steel links, but instead of dragging her up into that man-eating medusa-like monstrosity, she was chained to a concrete wall, hanging there like some perversion of a crucifix, her arms and legs spread wide, leaving her unable to even cover herself.

What was happening to her? Just like the trap that she remembered snapping closed on her foot, the night tree and its effects were simply gone. She could no longer feel the burning teeth marks, only bruises from these unyielding chains.

She didn't know what was real anymore!

But as she glanced around, she began to realize where she

was. These walls were familiar. Crumbling concrete. Crude graffiti. Litter strewn across the ground. She couldn't see a single tree, but she knew without any doubt that this was the forest behind her parents' house.

"No…" she breathed. "No, no, no, no, no…" She couldn't be here. Not now. Not *alone*. Not after she learned its grisly secret.

These were the walls of Gilbert House. The Gilbert House that existed in the *real* world, the one that was only a set of meaningless walls hidden away in the forest just outside the city limits. She was *inside* those empty walls, meaning the *real* Gilbert House was just beneath her feet, in a secret basement accessible only through the hidden cellar door, with its impossible five stories sitting atop it in another world where monsters roamed the endless darkness and dead bodies lay undiscovered.

She tried to free herself, straining against her bindings as a frightened sob escaped her. It was all pointless, of course. She was only bruising herself more. If she wasn't strong enough to break free of those branches, she certainly wasn't going to be able to snap any of these chains. She knew this. And yet what else could she do but try?

Something moved in the corner of her eye and she snapped her head toward it, her heart leaping.

It was the thing she saw through the gaping hole in her bedroom wall. Or…*one* of them, anyway. It stepped out from around the corner. Dark and thin, impossibly tall, even hunched over as it was. Those terrible, blazing eyes shined back at her through the tangles of its filthy, matted hair.

The terror that welled up inside her as she met those evil eyes was overwhelming. Her body felt like a lead weight hanging there, helpless and so desperately vulnerable. Something hot and vile bubbled through her guts and a numbing sort of static seemed to fill her mind. She wanted to scream, but her throat was locked.

Then the thing opened its deformed mouth and let out one of those wailing shrieks and the world seemed to pulse with darkness as her very consciousness wavered. Stars danced before her eyes and her body shook with fear.

She yanked at the chains, desperate to be free, but it was futile.

It was moving toward her now, its crooked legs bending at odd angles, pivoting in unnatural ways. Its feet were too big, with too many toes that were each long and crooked and dug into the earth with each step. Those horrible tangles of fingers were splayed out before it, knotted and gnarled and twisted, but each one ending in a sharp, hooked claw.

As she struggled, she caught sight of another pair of eyes shining at her from the other direction. A second creature was already moving toward her, this one crawling across the ground as if attempting to sneak up on her.

Then a third leapt up onto the wall directly above her and shrieked down at her. This time, her throat opened for her and she let out a terrible scream.

The world swam out of focus as the blood rushed from her face. She stared up through a blur of tears as those claws lashed out, tearing into her tender skin.

Another awful shriek sounded from below her, accompanied by a searing pain in her belly and an awful, agonizing shifting sort of feeling deep inside her.

Excruciating pain followed her down into a spiraling emptiness that she could only assume was the cold, vast depths of death.

Chapter 40

Everett stopped climbing.

Alice didn't tell him to stop. He found that he simply knew that he'd reached the top of the shaft.

Gripping the steel rung with one hand, he reached up with the other, imagining a lever hovering just overhead. Sure enough, his fingers brushed against cold, rusty metal. A door of some sort. He gripped it, finding that he even knew exactly which way to turn it. There was a great grinding noise, a heavy clank, a groan, and then he was pushing it up and open.

He still couldn't see anything. Everything was just as pitch-black as the shaft. But he could tell that there was a much larger space up there. He could picture the floor stretching out in every direction, but no walls or ceiling. And the space was entirely and eerily empty.

Uncertain, he climbed up out of the shaft and then eased the door back down again. (Or was it a hatch? Was that the right word for a door that opened upward instead of sideways? Or was a hatch just a different type of door, regardless of which way it opened? He should look that up sometime.) The second he let go, it slammed back down into place and vanished. It wasn't just that he couldn't see it or that there was no handle on this side to open it again. He simply understood that it was no longer there. And neither was the shaft below it. Whatever mysterious and quite possibly *imaginary* means he'd just used to reach this space had ceased to exist in an instant, not merely *as if* it were never there, but entirely *because* it was never there…even though that made no sense whatsoever.

He knelt there, pondering the feeling, his hand sliding over the surface of the floor where there should have at least been a gap or a seam or *something*. But there was nothing except cold, unyielding concrete.

"Weird," he muttered, and left it at that. There was no reason to keep fussing over something that was no longer there. Especially when the thing that had vanished had only led back the way he came and he had no interest in returning there. He needed to be focused on moving forward.

But which way was forward?

He went to prop himself up on his hands so that he could stand and felt his fingers brush something soft in the darkness. He wrapped his fingers around it and found it to be Alice. She was back in her doll form again.

He picked her up and cradled her in the crook of his arm as he stood. Then he turned in a circle, trying to make out something in this utter darkness. But of course he couldn't see anything. There was no light. Not so much as a faint glow. And if there were any fairy mushrooms or smudges or spirit things for him to see, then they, too, were hidden in this oppressive darkness because nothing showed itself to him, not even in his mind. Inside his head, where his fruitful imagination revealed all the weird things he saw, there was only a vast, flat floor stretched out forever in all directions.

"I give up," he said after a moment. "Where are we?"

Then he frowned at the word that materialized inside his head.

"Limbo?" He turned around again, letting the word simmer in his thoughts. "What, like *purgatory*? That kind of Limbo?"

No. That wasn't right. This had nothing to do with the spirit world or religion or anything like that.

"More like an in-between place..." he muttered thoughtfully. Like when they talked about *processes* being caught in limbo. This was a sort of stopover. The bad news was that they hadn't made it back to the City Beyond Memory yet. But the good news was that they were no longer in the void. Better still, they were on the *right* side of the void. The *right side up* side of the void. They were making progress. "Okay," he said, nodding. "Got it.

But what do we do now?"

Alice didn't answer him this time.

For a moment, he frowned into this empty silence, wondering what might be wrong. Then he realized that it was like when he first began talking to her. She wasn't suddenly rendered unable to communicate. She wasn't being coy. She simply didn't have the answer. She didn't know.

"Okay," he said again, giving her a gentle squeeze. It wasn't as if anyone ever promised that navigating the mind-bending realms that blended the boundaries between the physical and the imaginary beyond the borders of reality was going to be easy. This was brand-new territory. He was learning as he went. And so was she, it seemed.

Wandering aimlessly didn't seem like it was going to get him anywhere, but neither did just standing here, so he picked a direction at random and started walking.

It was strange. Everything was eerily silent here. Even his footsteps felt muted. There was no wind, no echoes, only the background noises inside his own ears. He was able to hear himself just fine when he was talking to Alice, so it wasn't as if there were anything wrong with his ears and there was no kind of weird, sound-dampening quality to the atmosphere or anything. (Was that a thing? It seemed like it would be a thing.) Was it simply that there was nothing here for the sound to bounce off of? Was this how sound naturally behaved in an utterly empty world with no wind?

He wished he understood these things a little better. But wishing had never accomplished much in his life. He'd done much better getting off his butt and going to find the things he wanted.

And that was what he was going to keep doing. He set off through the darkness, blind and deaf and completely ignorant of this new place he'd found himself in.

He hoped something interesting happened sooner than later.

Chapter 41

Erin didn't dare move a muscle. It was *right there*. Right in front of her face.

It wasn't something she could see, nor hear, nor feel. She didn't precisely even *sense* it, like some kind of psychic intuition. It was something else, something *spiritual*, she thought, a thing from her *other* existence, beyond the veil. She simply *knew* that this monster was right in front of her. And it was unspeakably terrible.

She stood motionless, her eyes still wide open with fright, still holding her breath, not daring to make the slightest sound.

How long had she been standing like this? How long since she'd blinked? How long had she been holding her breath? Was there a limit? Did she even need air anymore? It had never really crossed her mind to test it. Or was it something else? Was time standing still? Or was she frozen in place, at the mercy of the unthinkable thing looming before her? Already caught in its petrifying gaze?

Fear wormed its way through her every nerve and wrapped itself around her, threatening to suffocate her. Why would she come to a place like this? Did she really do it on purpose? Did she understand what she was doing when she decided to manifest and walk through this nightmare corridor? Or had she made a fatal mistake? What was she thinking, trusting this job to her *mortal* self?

She didn't even understand what was happening right now. It made no earthly sense. Why hadn't it attacked her? Could it not see her when she stood still? And why wouldn't it just go away? Why was it just...*lingering* there? Was it sensing her? Was it *toying* with her?

She wasn't sure why, but for some reason it reminded her of those crows she encountered behind Breastbroke... It gave her the same deep-down feeling of unease, as if she were staring into the gaping maw of some inconceivable truth buried in the very fabric of her DNA. She could almost hear that awful cawing as she stood there, waiting for it to move along.

Just like back then, she found herself wondering if she would ever be able to leave this unpleasant place.

Chapter 42

Corey sat there for a moment, pondering these new feelings, curious.

Now Gina and Nicole had disappeared from the temple's labyrinth.

Where had they gone? And *how*? That was *six* people missing now, and yet there was nowhere for anyone to go.

The wall surrounding the city prevented anyone from leaving. The only way to enter was through one of the three gates with the Whispers. And that was a one-way trip. There was no keyhole on this side of the wall, meaning there was no way out and therefore nowhere for anyone to go. The only way for them to return home, he somehow found that he knew, was to open the doorway at the top of the central tower. And he would have known if someone had done that.

The only explanations he could come up with were that they were either dead—which he refused to believe—or they'd stumbled through some kind of gateway. This place probably contained at least a few pocket dimensions. Perhaps even tons of them. That was probably the best case scenario, but even that was worrisome. After all, he and Violet had seen their fair share of dangerous and downright inhospitable pockets. What kinds of horror shows might be lurking on the other side of a portal here in *this* eternally dark place?

And by now it was very clear to him that several *other* entities had managed to slip through the moment the way was opened. The thing that attacked Austin was only one of several. He couldn't really sense them like he did the people. They were difficult to track. Elusive. Probably things having to do with spirits and the unnatural and all those psychic abilities that were going around.

Whatever they were, he was certain they were dangerous. He wished there were some way for him to communicate with everyone, to let them know what he knew. Information was power, after all. He understood that better than anyone. The more you knew, the better you were prepared for anything this weird world threw at you. Even made-up information could be useful in its own way, he firmly believed. Imagination was more than just a child's plaything, after all. It was a tool. An asset. It helped one to think outside the box and around corners.

He plucked another string from the organized coils on the floor around him and studied it. Six missing persons, one of whom he was certain was now dead...

"That crazy cat lady said there were twelve of us," Albert told them way back on that otherworldly carriage ride, meaning that half of them had now vanished from his sight.

And then Brandy added, "She also said two of us wouldn't come home."

That wasn't good. He didn't care for those odds at all. That was a one-in-six chance of ending up on the wrong side of the grass.

He supposed one could look at it another way, though. If Albert and Brandy's "crazy cat lady" knew that exactly two wouldn't make it, then that meant ten of them *would* make it, regardless of whatever might happen down here. But he didn't care for that particular perspective. That would mean accepting those two deaths, which felt like trading those two lives for the other ten. It shouldn't be that way.

But he also couldn't change the fact that someone seemed to have already fallen...

He glanced over at Austin. *He* never intended to leave this place. And he didn't even technically count as a person, did he? He was some kind of ancient android. Maybe the two who were meant to fall had already fallen and there would be no more losses.

He lifted the string and wrapped it around the spike where

it belonged. That kind of thinking just wasn't helpful. First of all, he still didn't know *who* they'd lost. What if it was Violet? He didn't want *anyone* to die, but he wasn't sure he'd even *want* to go home without *her.*

And for that matter, just how did *he* fit into that equation? He'd nearly forgotten about that fun detail. This job was going to prevent him from leaving this room until the door was opened. If this place was going to come tumbling down like the last one, then the odds of him finding his way out before it happened were nearly non-existent.

(*There's no 'one percent' about it.*)

Again, he glanced back at Austin. That would be three of them… That math didn't add up. Did that mean he *would* find his way out? Or did Austin not count because he wasn't really alive? But if Austin didn't count, then who was the twelfth person? There were only eleven of them.

This was confusing.

"You'll *never* finish in time at this rate," Austin reminded him, sounding exasperated.

"I'll be fine," he assured the rude, obnoxious junk pile as he plucked another string from the floor.

(He wouldn't lie. If he *had* to choose someone to kick the bucket first, it'd be the unpleasant robot guy.)

He reached up to wind the string around its matching contact, but stopped, distracted.

That wasn't right. It was supposed to go over here on the next one, wasn't it?

He frowned. No. The first one was right. But something seemed off. Why was he confused? This stuff was literally hard-wired into his genetic memory. He shouldn't be able to make mistakes, not even briefly.

He reached out and wound the string around the spike. This was right. He didn't know why it felt wrong for a second there. He must've let himself get distracted, thinking about all that death stuff and worrying about Violet.

He reminded himself that Violet was a perfectly capable woman, plenty strong enough to take care of herself.

He was sure she'd be fine.

Chapter 43

Violet screamed and sat up, her heart thundering in her chest, her green eyes wide and wild with terror. She was hyperventilating.

Once again, the pain was gone. She was unharmed. She still had all her arms and legs. All she brought with her was the perfectly vivid *memories* of her brutal death, which was quite enough to give her nightmares for months, she was sure.

She looked down at her open palms, dazed, and realized she was wrong. She was left with only those terrible memories and two hands covered in viscus slime...

She turned and vomited what little remained of the lovely breakfast Lucianna packed for them onto the floor.

Why was this happening to her? She couldn't understand it. If the sentinels and the Keeper knew all that they claimed to know, how could they allow something like this to happen? It made no sense. It was beyond cruel. It was *sadistic*.

She had to get out of here.

Coughing and gasping for breath, she clambered to her feet and stumbled. The sky above was still the color of blood, meaning that it wasn't over. It wasn't going to end. That monstrous bitch was going to keep coming after her, keep sending those *things* to torture her. She couldn't afford to sit around waiting for one of them to show up again. Her only chance was to run, to stay ahead of it as long as possible.

She tripped and grabbed onto something cold and hard. Another wave of nausea rolled over her and she had to close her eyes. When it passed and she looked up, she saw that she was kneeling on a grave, clinging to a weathered headstone.

"Oh shit," she panted, exhausted. She looked around and found that she was surrounded by gravestones. They stretched for as far as she could see in every direction.

This couldn't be good. What now? Zombies? Ghouls? Vampires?

She turned all the way around, scanning every stone, every ominous shadow, convinced that there must be something lurking out there, just waiting to murder her.

(*How many feathers can I pluck before they stop screaming?*)

She shuddered at the memory of those awful words.

The Priestess of Ruin, the other one called her. And the Bringer of Darkness. Harbinger of Ends. And the Goddess of Decay. What manner of hellish horror was she? It sounded like she was *playing* with her, the way she giggled and taunted her while those slimy tentacle things dismembered her...like some sick child handed the power of a god.

Her eyes open for the next foul surprise, she set off across the vast cemetery, her heart still pounding with fright.

What was she supposed to do?

Endure.

She let out a frustrated growl. "Seriously? Is that all you have to say? Because it's *not helping!*"

I'm not able to help here. All I can do is encourage you to endure.

She cursed under her breath and looked back over her shoulder, making sure nothing was chasing after her.

Endure, she said again. *It won't be long now.*

"Won't be long until *what?*" Until she was killed for real? Until she went utterly mad?

But once again the voice inside her head had fallen silent.

"Thanks a lot!" she huffed. What the hell was the point in having an ancient supernatural being inside your head if she was completely useless in an emergency? She helped her get away from the Everett-thing and those storm drafts, but she couldn't just take the wheel and get her the hell out of *this* mess?

It was all so frustrating!

And was there no end to this damned cemetery? There was no sign of any roads or fences. Nor were there any buildings.

There weren't even any trees. It was as if she'd fallen into an entire world that was nothing but one big boneyard.

She wanted to say that this couldn't be all there was, but the truth was that she knew better. Places like these weren't real. The other one already told her that it was connected to her. Everything she'd seen so far had been places she'd been. Recently. Even now, as she ran past the endless stones, she realized that she recognized it. Sort of. She'd never seen a cemetery this size, but didn't this sort of look like just a supersized version of the old cemetery near Corey's family's property back in Tunipet? She drove past it only the day before Gina's phone call sent them off on this bizarre adventure. It was as if someone had taken a picture of the little plot and then copied and pasted it over and over again, stretching it on and on and on.

"Fun!" whispered that awful voice in her ear.

She screamed and twirled around, startled, but there was no one there. She was alone in the endless field of stones.

A familiar giggle drifted from somewhere to her left and she turned again.

Ready to play some more? asked a voice inside her head.

She clasped her hands over her ears as if she really thought that would do any good and turned around again, searching. "Leave me alone!"

What did she want from her? Why was she torturing her like this? What did she do to deserve this nightmare? She couldn't understand it.

"Did I make you cry?"

Again, she twirled around. Again, no one was there.

"I like making tough girls cry."

Where was she? Why couldn't she see her? Was she hiding behind one of the stones? Somehow she doubted it. This was the kind of monster who didn't have to hide, the kind that was only seen when it wanted to be seen.

"The toughest ones always break the hardest."

Again, she turned. Still, there was no sign of her phantom tormenter. "What do you want?" she demanded, her voice cracking. "Why won't you leave me alone?"

Because I like the way you suffer, replied the Priestess of Ruin inside her head.

Again, Violet cried out and covered her ears. "Leave me alone!" She stumbled backward, trying to shake the psychic intruder from her thoughts.

Her foot slipped.

She fell into a hole and landed on her back, the wind knocked out of her, stars dancing before her eyes.

Where did this come from? There weren't any holes in the ground. She would've seen it while searching for the origin of that mocking voice.

But as she blinked up at the rectangle of red sky above her, she realized that this wasn't just a hole. It was an open grave.

"Oh god!" she gasped. No. She didn't like this at all. Still gasping for breath, she scrambled to her feet, but the grave was too deep. She couldn't reach the tops of the dirt walls. She was trapped.

As she stared up, shadowy silhouettes appeared. They walked up and peered down at her, each one familiar. That was clearly her father's figure. And her mother. And that looked like Albert and Brandy on the other side. And there was Corey! She'd recognize that great, pudgy build anywhere!

"Help me!" she shouted, reaching up for him.

But to her horror, he only reached out over the hole with a shovelful of dirt and dropped it on her.

She turned away, shielding her eyes, but instead of feeling it strike the back of her head, she heard the awful thump of it falling onto wood.

She was no longer standing. She was lying on her back, staring up at the underside of a wooden lid.

"No-no-no-no-no!" she cried, thrusting her hands up, trying to push it open. But it wouldn't budge.

Shovelful after shovelful of dirt thudded against the other side of it.

"*Let me out!*" she screamed, terrified. "*Don't do this! Please!*"

"You said to leave you alone," chuckled the Priestess of Ruin, her voice seemingly inside the horrible box with her. "You can't get more alone than this."

Violet screamed. She pounded against the wooden lid.

She'd never felt such overwhelming panic before. It was suffocating.

"SOMEBODY HELP ME!"

But no one could hear her.

Chapter 44

"So you called this place 'glass' because your crazy psychic vision lets you see through it like glass," said Nicole, sweeping her light across the same gray stone surfaces she'd been seeing since she woke up on this side of the impassible wall. She could see no difference between this area and the one they supposedly just left. It was all exactly the same. "I mean, that makes sense. I can kind of see how that would work."

"It's complicated," said Gina in her same, sleepy voice. "It's hard to describe to other people."

"I can imagine." It was a matter of simply having access to one of your senses and trying to describe it to someone who didn't. She'd worked with deaf children as part of her special education degree, so the concept of comprehension barriers wasn't exactly new to her. But it was kind of strange being on the flipside of things.

"Is your sock okay?"

"What? Oh." She looked down at her foot, distracted. "Yeah. It's fine." Then she gave a tired laugh. "I'm sorry. Don't worry about me. I'm kind of a mess right now, but I'm okay. Really."

"Let me know if you need to stop."

"Sure."

She watched Gina as she walked. She was still clinging to her, gripping her hand, not daring to let go. She felt bad for worrying her.

She felt bad for a lot of things...

"So..." she began. She wasn't sure what to say. It was hard keeping her thoughts together. But she didn't like how heavy the silence felt whenever they weren't talking. "Can you describe what you're seeing?"

"Not very well," she replied. "It's a lot like the other labyrinth, really. Just a maze. But not. It's kind of..." She trailed off, looking for the right word.

"Crinkled?"

"Yeah. Crinkled."

Everything was crinkled. It was starting to feel as if God had grown sick of the world and just wadded it up and threw the whole fucking thing away.

And why not, really? The world was full of pain and misery and cruelty. It was full of disappointment and heartache. It was the kind of world where good people died for no good reason...

She stared down at Gina's small hand, clinging so tightly to her own. No. That wasn't fair. There was a lot more to the world than just the bad. But most of that felt so far away right now.

How was she supposed to just keep pressing on like this? Keith *just* died in her arms. You didn't simply get up and keep walking when someone died. The world was supposed to stop. People needed to grieve. They needed *time*. They needed to go home and cry into their pillows and wallow in all their regrets. *Tomorrow* they could get up and take a few shaky steps. The next day they could try taking a few more. But to just...*keep going*...like nothing ever happened?

And he didn't just die. He died *because of her*. He died because he ran into that evil meadow to rescue her. It was her fault. *All of it* was her fault. Everything that happened was because of her, because she was stupid or because she was weak or because she was an insufferable bitch. Or maybe just because she didn't deserve any better...

What did you do when it was your fault? How long was long enough when you were the one to blame?

And yet she just stood up and walked away. She left him there. As if she had any right to leave this godforsaken darkness in his place.

She felt as if she were going mad.

Gina stopped walking and squeezed her hand a little tighter.

"Don't let go of me," she said.

"What? Why w——?" She was going to ask why she would ever let go, but she didn't get the chance. Gina looked up at the ceiling and then... Well, she wasn't sure *what* happened next. It wasn't the same sort of sensation as when Andrea used the leaf. There was no lurching of her stomach, no shifting of gravity, no vertigo or disorientation. And yet something had suddenly and most certainly changed. She hadn't been paying close enough attention to tell whether the layout around her was different, and even if she had been, she couldn't see far enough in this gloom to be likely to tell the difference, and yet she felt strangely as if they'd both moved.

A strange sort of shudder passed through her, subtle, but at the same time weirdly intense, like a slow-moving electrical shock passing from her feet all the way up to the top of her head, accompanied by an odd sense of surrealness that left her feeling as if nothing in this place was real.

Then, as quickly as it came over her, it was gone.

"Are you okay?" worried Gina.

She blinked down at her, confused. Then, very slowly, she replied, "Yes?"

For a moment, they stood there like that as Gina tried to decide if she was really okay. Then she seemed to be satisfied. She turned and looked ahead of them, those sleepy eyes peering through the darkness into whatever world revealed itself to her. "The glass labyrinth doesn't work the same as the stone labyrinth. It's not light that it warps. There is no light. Instead, the imperfections in the glass distort reality."

Nicole blinked at her, struggling to keep up. "Okay," was all she could think to say.

Gina turned and looked back the way they came.

Or...*was* that the way they came? She still had the strangest feeling that they weren't in the same place they were a moment ago.

"I didn't notice before..." she muttered.

Nicole frowned at her. "What?"

Again, she turned, this time scanning whatever mysteries

were hidden behind the walls. "I was too scared. Too concerned about staying away from that monster. I never saw that there were more layers." She turned and faced the other way, her gaze sliding up and down, back and forth, those dark eyes wide in the gloom, but also strangely distant, oddly blind. "I never would've found my way through like that."

"Am I...supposed to be following along? Because you lost me a while back. Sorry."

She shook her head, distracted. "No. This is my job. Why I'm here. There's something only I can do." She gave her hand a firm squeeze and started walking again. "Don't get separated from me. I can't guarantee I'll be able to find you. And I really don't want to lose you again."

"I'll do my best," Nicole promised. And she *would* do her best. She only hoped that her best would be good enough. Because right now she was having trouble believing she was good for anything.

"Why are you so much trouble?"

She tugged Gina to a stop and looked back the way they came.

"What's wrong?"

"I don't...?" She stared into the darkness back there, confused. That memory just now... She almost believed she heard his voice again. But that was... "I'm losing my fucking mind..." she muttered.

"Are you okay?"

"Yeah. I'm..." She faced forward again. "I'm fine. Sorry."

"You sure?"

"I'm okay," she insisted. But the fact was that she suddenly felt very weary. Maybe everything they'd been through was all catching up to her at once. "Keep going. Don't let me slow you down."

Clearly unconvinced, Gina turned her attention on the path ahead and continued onward, into the endless darkness, exploring the glass labyrinth that only she could see.

Chapter 45

Somehow, it wasn't as bad as Olivia thought it was going to be. It turned out that the floor leveled out a short distance beyond the edge of the water. The entire pool was only about a foot and a half deep, not even enough to submerge her knees.

But her footsteps kept splashing the water up her legs so that even her butt was starting to get wet.

Still, she didn't dare to complain. It could be much worse. And it probably still *would* be before it was over. It seemed highly unlikely that a little wading was going to be all the labyrinth planned to throw at them.

She kept sweeping her light over the water ahead of them, expecting to glimpse something moving. *That* was more like what she expected to find down here.

Wayne stopped walking and tilted his head, listening.

"Voices again?" she whispered.

But he shook his head. "Don't know. I'm not even sure I *heard* something so much as…*felt* something?"

She shined her light downward again, concerned. It was so easy to imagine something horrible slithering around their feet in this darkness. Slimy eels. Bloodthirsty leeches. Ravenous piranhas. But all of them magnified by the horrors of the temple like those dreadful hounds.

"Not in the water," he assured her. "In the *floor*. Like how sometimes when big trucks rumble by you can *feel* it more than *hear* it? It was like a vibration in the stone."

Vibrations? What did *that* mean? She didn't remember anything *vibrating* in the last temple. Unless you counted when the whole place started exploding or falling apart.

She stood there, unmoving, listening, feeling, but there was nothing. Not a sound, not a rumble, not even a splash.

"Gone now…" he breathed. "Maybe just my imagination."

Or it could not be his imagination at all. She shined her light back the way they came, uneasy. But her psychic alarm still hadn't gone off. There was no sense of dread, imminent or otherwise, only that very subtle feeling that she should continue moving forward.

Again, he started walking. Again, she kept pace with him, still clinging to his arm.

She didn't know why there was a partially submerged passage inside the labyrinth, but she didn't waste time wondering about it. She also didn't know why there were bottomless pools in the first temple. She didn't know why there were hounds or sex rooms or huge chambers filled with reeking mud. She didn't know a great many things, so what did another thing matter? To be honest, she was starting to feel somewhat numb to the whole thing. She was so tired of it all, so ready to be done and back home in her warm, cozy bed, snuggling with her wonderful fiancé.

She hoped everyone else was still okay, wherever they were. Andrea. Corey and Keith. Everett.

She was so relieved when Andrea told them that she knew Everett and that she arrived at the city wall with him. She practically felt sick every time she thought about him, worried that he may have never left the stone road's sandstone city. It not only made her feel better about him, but also bolstered her faith that all their friends were capable enough of finding their way back from this dreary nightmare.

"There it was again," said Wayne.

She shined her light down at her submerged feet. "I felt it too that time." It felt like a miniature earthquake beneath her feet. He was right. It *did* remind her of those felt-more-than-heard rumbles that trucks sometimes made when they passed on the road outside their apartment.

But what was it? It wasn't as if there were a freeway nearby. There should be no machinery of any sort in a stone labyrinth in the middle of the Wood.

They pushed forward, making their way through the cold water. The passage ahead seemed to be curving to the left.

"Water seems more agitated the farther we go," observed Wayne.

"You sure it's not just us splashing around in it?"

"It's hard to tell," he agreed. "Might just be our own waves bouncing back at us. But I feel like it's getting choppier, you know?"

She couldn't tell the difference one way or the other.

Again, he stopped. "Did you see that?"

"See what?"

"There was a light just now."

Another of those strange rumbles seemed to pass through the stone beneath them. She shined her light down at her feet, then back the way they came, then forward again. She still wanted to know what that was, but she was distracted by the idea of a light up ahead. Another flashlight in the dark? One of their lost friends?

She realized she was pulling at Wayne, trying to go faster, excited by the idea of finding someone, and had to calm herself. She didn't know what might be up there. It could be some kind of monster for all they knew. Or a trap. Or nothing at all. She didn't see any light herself, after all. Maybe he only imagined it?

Then she saw it for herself, a faint flicker from beyond the still-curving corridor. "What *is* that?" she whispered.

She felt his grip tighten around her arm. His body was turned slightly, his shoulder and hip pushed forward, ready to protect her as he continued on.

Her heart was pounding again. She hated this never-ending fear. She didn't know how much more she could take.

Was it only her natural instincts in the face of the unknown, or was her psychic alarm beginning to sound? She couldn't tell the difference.

Flickers and flashes of lights just beyond their sight...

Ominous rumbles beneath their feet...

And was that a low growl she just heard over the splashing

of their feet?

She held her breath, convinced that something terrifying was going to spring into view any second.

Then Wayne stopped again, his head cocked, his expression twisted with bewilderment. "Is that thunder and lightning?"

She blinked up at him, confused. Thunder and lightning? A storm? Inside the labyrinth? In the middle of a weatherless forest? How did that make any sense?

Again, they pushed forward. She still felt uneasy. Her nerves remained tightly wound, ready to turn and flee at the slightest sign of danger. But she found that she was more curious than afraid now. She wanted to know *why* there was thunder and lightning inside a stone temple? Was there some sort of electrical generator in the next room? Were there doorways to living worlds in here somewhere? Was it some sort of electricity-spewing monster? The equivalent of a giant electric eel?

Finally, the passage straightened up again. The opening was straight ahead. A near-constant flicker of lightning strobed beyond it, broken by occasional bursts of blinding light accompanied by great blasts of thunder that became exponentially louder as they approached the end of the passage. And now she could hear a steady drone of heavy rain pouring down as well.

"That's new," said Wayne, raising his voice to be heard over the din of the unexpected tempest.

She supposed that answered the question of just where all this water was coming from. Whatever area was beyond that opening was clearly flooded.

Was it even safe to keep going forward? Or would they be struck dead by lightning the moment they attempted to step out of the passage and into the raging storm?

She searched her mind for warnings, but it was difficult to define precisely what she was feeling. There was no shortage of that awful dread, but it also still felt like they were supposed to be continuing forward.

Which was it? What were they supposed to do? How could she keep them safe?

She felt the rain well before they reached the end of the

passage. It blew in on stiff gusts of wind, cold and stinging.

She shielded her face with her arm and peered out into the chaos beyond the doorway. The space there was wide open. It was difficult to see, but she didn't think it was another chamber. It seemed like she was looking at whatever world existed *outside* the temple. Just like how half the first temple existed deep in the earth beneath Briar Hills and half in the Wood, inside that burning mountain, this second temple seemed to exist half in the Denselands and half in whatever storm-ravaged world this was.

For some reason, she recalled the constant wind that blew across the Denselands. Nadia said it always blew toward the impassible wall. Was this where all that wind eventually came? Did it somehow cross the barrier and build into this storm?

She frowned at herself. What an odd thought. Why would she even consider something like that? That wasn't the sort of thing she wasted time thinking about. She was far more concerned with questions like, "What kinds of monsters might be hiding out there?" and, "How can I keep my fiancé from being fried by lightning?" and maybe even a little, "What's all that electricity going to do to my hair?" (Because that was just who she was and she had no intention of apologizing for it.) And yet, something felt significant about that random train of thought, about the connection between the wind in the Denselands and the storm over the City Beyond Memory.

Was someone speaking to her? Deep inside her mind, like the way the Sentinel Queen spoke to her that night five years ago? Someone like Erin, perhaps?

Or maybe she was just tired and overthinking everything.

They finally reached the doorway and leaned out into the pouring rain, squinting up at the churning, lightning-filled sky above.

They were definitely outside. But she already knew that. Ordinary intuition? Psychic abilities? Or alien thoughts inside her brain?

She pushed away the thoughts and focused on the space in front of them. There were better things to worry about. Like how there was a lightning storm above them and eighteen inches of water below them. Wasn't that, like, the first rule of electrical safety?

"It really is a city," shouted Wayne.

He was right. She could see the outlines of towering structures all around them, illuminated in brief flashes by the lightning. There was a tall, skyscraper-like structure directly across from them, with what looked like the rooftop of a shorter structure connecting it with the one they were looking out from. There appeared to be a ledge on either side, allowing the rain to collect and pour over. And in the center of the flooded rooftop was a circle of stone columns holding up a slab, on which more stone columns held up another slab, and so on. Creating a strange, tiered tower stretching up into that violent, churning sky.

But that was no spring rain out there. She was already dripping wet merely from the wind blowing the rain into the passage.

A bolt of lightning struck the stone tower, a blinding flash, accompanied by a deafening explosion of thunder that wrenched a startled scream from her and made Wayne turn and shield her.

"Yeah, fuck that!" shouted Wayne, pulling her away from the dangerous area.

But she resisted him and pointed across the rooftop. She wasn't sure exactly how she noticed it. Only the brightest flashes of lightning illuminated the space enough to reveal it. Another doorway. She could feel the psychic part of her brain pulling her toward it.

That was where they needed to go.

"You sure?" asked Wayne, his voice barely reaching her even as close as he was.

She nodded. She was. Though she had no idea why.

Another bolt of lightning struck, its crash of thunder loud enough to make her ears ring, and she buried her face against his shirt.

She could even smell the burning ozone in the air.

Again, was this safe?

Wayne was leaning out into the storm again, shielding his face from the rain and squinting up at the strange tower. She looked up at him, saw his lips moving, but a rumble of thunder drowned him out. And yet, somehow she found that she under-stood him anyway. He was commenting on the two lightning bolts that had already struck the tower, on the fact that lightning was supposed to hit the tallest object around.

Did that tower act like a lightning rod, drawing it away?

Which would be safer, she wondered, keeping as far from it as possible or as close to it as possible?

He looked down at her, uncertain.

"We have to," she shouted over the storm, though she still had no idea how she knew this.

He didn't question her. He never did. He simply nodded and then looked out into that pouring rain. She could see him preparing himself. His shoulders raised. His muscles tensed. He took a deep breath and sort of swelled. If he were a beast, he would have bristled. Then he slipped his arm all the way around her and pulled her close, determined to shield her from as much of the rain as possible.

He was such a gentleman like that.

But despite his best efforts, this was going to be extremely unpleasant. That rain was cold. The wind was harsh. And that lightning was terrifying. Her psychic alarm was telling her this would be no romantic stroll through a summer shower.

"Ready?" he asked her.

She nodded. She was as ready as she was going to get.

They both braced themselves. Then they rushed out into the storm.

It was good that he was holding onto her, because she was practically blinded the moment they stepped from the passage. The wind whipped the rain in every direction, making it impossi-ble to see. And it was so cold! Why was it so cold?

She clenched her jaw against the discomfort and pushed onward, keeping pace with Wayne.

It would be over soon. They just needed to cross this roof-top. That was all. It wasn't even that far.

Another bolt struck the tower with another ear-splitting boom that shook the very ground beneath her, wrenching a scream from her.

It felt like the world around her was filled with crackling static, but no electricity rushed up her legs and stopped the pounding of her heart, so she supposed she couldn't really complain.

She pushed onward, clinging to Wayne's shirt for dear life.

It would be over soon, she told herself again.

And yet, something felt off.

The doorway on the other side was still calling to that psychic part of her mind, urging her onward, showing her the way…but why was her psychic alarm only growing more frantic? Shouldn't this be the worst of it? Was she missing something?

A terrible certainty abruptly seized her, like a great, shuddering stutter in her heart.

She turned around, wrenching herself from Wayne's grip and then dug her heels against the stone and shoved him backward with all her strength.

She heard him cry out, surprised.

Then something slammed against her.

Everything went dark for a second. The chaos around her seemed to go out of focus. A pain spread across her back. She felt herself tumbling. Water rushed up at her, splashing across her face and up her nose.

She pushed herself up onto her hands and knees, coughing and gagging, the breath knocked from her lungs.

What happened?

What hit her?

And where was Wayne?

She couldn't see. She couldn't hear.

She thrust her arms out, searching for him, but she couldn't feel him anywhere, either.

Where did he go? She had to find him!

But as she sat up, still wheezing for breath, her psychic alarm rang out like a deafening bell.

She blinked up at the strange tower as another bolt of lightning struck it.

Something was there. Something not quite visible through the rain and the haze. Something enormous and monstrous and dreadful.

And it was reaching out for her with terrible hands.

Chapter 46

Albert's light fell on the elongated form of another sentinel statue standing in the path ahead of him.

"Oh good," grumbled Brandy. "It's Long Dong Silver again. The fuck does he want this time?"

It was a good question. He hadn't seen all that many of these guys this time around. There was the one back in the carriage house. And the one standing in the river, of course. Besides those two, though, there were only the ones in the warning chambers leading to the emotion rooms. Back in the first temple, they were all over the place, often miming out hints and warnings about the choices that lay ahead.

But then again, thinking back on it, those were all there *before* they reached the Sentinel Queen's City of the Blind, in the area that was designed to prevent intruders. There were no sentinels in the labyrinth beyond. Maybe that was the difference. This temple was way out in the middle of the Denselands. It didn't need such security, and so it was *all* labyrinth. And the trials they were supposed to endure, like the emotion rooms and jumping into the river to escape the storm-dwellers on the hostile surface, were scattered throughout.

If that were the case, then what was this guy trying to tell them? Because he was clearly saying *something*. Instead of standing there with his feet together and hands down at his sides like a good, attentive soldier, he was standing in the middle of the passage with his arms stretched out to the sides and legs slightly apart and bent, as if just starting to take a step, and he was all the way up on those elongated toes. It almost looked like he was dancing, though he couldn't wrap his head around why.

He walked up to it and studied the curious pose.

"Is he doing yoga?" asked Brandy, her light sliding along its outstretched arms. "I'm not into yoga. Can you imagine me trying to do Downward Dog with *you* around? I wouldn't last two seconds."

He glanced over at her, an eyebrow raised. "Dito, princess."

Her lips spread into that mischievous smirk again and she bit her lip. "Yeah."

"Seriously though," he sighed, staring up at that blank face. "They only pose when they're trying to say something. Is it a warning? Or a hint?" He walked around it, studying every detail. "What are you telling me to do?"

The flashlight beam dropped to the statue's obscene genitals. "Air out your dick, looks like."

"With *you* around?" he replied without looking at her. "I wouldn't last two seconds."

This made her laugh. "Fair enough."

Albert turned and peered down the passageway behind the sentinel. It was facing them as they approached, as if it knew they'd be coming from that direction, meaning that if it was telling them anything, it would probably relate to something farther ahead.

"Are we supposed to keep going?" wondered Brandy. "Or turn back?"

He was already continuing onward, squinting into the darkness ahead.

"Of course we keep going," she grumbled, hurrying after him. "Why do I bother asking?"

"We won't know what he was trying to tell us until we see what's waiting for us. We can still turn back if it doesn't look good. But if we avoid *everything* we'll never get out of this labyrinth." Because he was sure they weren't looking for an exit. They were looking for something hidden in this darkness. Like the tower in the first temple, where they confronted the Caggo.

"Whatever you say," she muttered, grabbing his hand again.

"We'll be fine," he assured her.

"Liar," said a voice that wasn't Brandy's.

Albert stopped and looked back. "What?"

"I didn't say anything," said Brandy.

"I called you a liar," said Dolly.

He cursed and pulled Brandy closer, his heart racing. She was back? What was she up to this time? Did she come to break their flashlight again?

"What is it?" worried Brandy. She was pressing herself closer to him, swinging the flashlight back and forth, trying to see what had him so on edge.

"You're going to get her killed down here."

Where was she? He couldn't tell where the voice was coming from. Was she hiding just out of sight? Or was her voice only inside his head? He couldn't tell the difference.

"Is it *her* again?" whispered Brandy.

"It's only a matter of time," promised Dolly. "You'll see."

"Leave us alone," he shouted into the darkness.

The witch's laughter echoed in response from somewhere in the distance. It faded to nothing as he listened to it.

What the hell was her problem? Why was she so determined to mess with them? Did she actually *want* them to fail? Did she want the cycle to end? How would that benefit her in any way?

"Where is she?" whispered Brandy.

"Gone, I think..." But not for good, he was certain.

"What did she say to you?"

"Nothing." He pulled her closer, hugging her. Suddenly, the fact that she was covered in blood was bothering him. It felt like a vision of events to come.

(*You're going to get her killed down here.*)

He gritted his teeth and continued onward, his arm still around her. "Trying to mess with my head. Make me doubt myself. Basic, everyday movie villain crap."

Brandy shuddered. "I should've smothered that whore with a pillow the second I found her in bed with you."

He scowled at her. "Don't start saying it like you walked in on us. You were there too. She was in bed with *us*. I'm not giving *you* a hard time about fooling around with some creepy witch."

"That's because it was *your dick* in her hand!"

"*I* didn't put it there. She's a literal witch. She probably has a box of them in her closet."

This caught her off guard. A bark of a laugh escaped her.

"Seriously," he grumbled. "That was *not* my idea of a good time. That woman makes my skin crawl. It was like waking up with a snake in my sheets. And now she's in my *head* like some kind of psychic stalker."

Brandy looked back the way they came again. "I mean, Lucianna said she was much older than she looked. She's probably some gross, shriveled up old hag under there."

"Probably." It definitely wouldn't surprise him. Regardless of what she looked like, she was clearly a monster. But he wasn't going to have the luxury of steering clear of her.

What was she up to? He couldn't wrap his head around why she'd want to sabotage them like this.

Ahead of them, the passage opened up. There was some kind of chamber. A moment later, as they drew closer, another sentinel emerged from the darkness, identical to the last one, its impossibly long arms outstretched. Its legs slightly apart and bent, as if just starting to take a step.

But what did it mean?

The walls parted, the chamber growing larger with each step he took, revealing a great, cavernous space ahead of them.

Directly behind the second sentinel, the floor began sloping downward, sinking into the shadowy darkness ahead.

"I have a bad feeling about this," sighed Brandy.

Chapter 47

Andrea sat up with a desperate gasp, her hands probing at her face and belly where she felt those things tearing into her with their strange tangles of deadly claws. She half-scooted and half-crawled across the floor, a manic sort of combination of whimpering and panting escaping her with each rapid breath she took. She'd never felt so utterly terrified before. Her brain was a chaotic storm of wordless screams and palpable panic that set every nerve in her body alight. So sure was she that she must still be in the clutches of those horrid abominations that she couldn't grasp why she couldn't see them anymore. They were already on her, attacking her, *killing her*, so where were they? Which direction would they come from next? She didn't want to be hurt anymore! She couldn't stand it! *Why wouldn't someone help her?*

She backed herself up against the wall, still hyperventilating, cowering from her invisible assailants. Her arms were raised to shield her face, her knees drawn up, her body pulled tight and small, cringing in anticipation of the next agonizing attack.

She wasn't sure how long she remained like that, gasping and crying and shivering, before it finally occurred to her that she was no longer in those horrific ruins, no longer chained to the wall, no longer surrounded by monsters.

This was somewhere new.

And the pain from those awful, gnarled claws had vanished. Her face wasn't torn. Her belly wasn't ripped open. All of her insides were still inside her where they belonged. Just like the crushing jaws of that steel trap she stepped in and the strangling, biting tendrils of that groping night tree, it was all just *gone*, as if it never happened, as if it were all inside her head.

Was she going insane?

Slowly, she lowered her arms and peered out at her surroundings. That eerie red sky was gone. Everything was dark. The floor beneath her bare butt and feet felt like naked concrete. Was she in some kind of garage? Or maybe a basement?

She wiped at her eyes and sat up straighter, struggling to see anything in the darkness.

There was a faint hint of light some distance to her left. A way out?

She tried to stand, but grimaced at the pain in her knee where the nail had pierced her. She grasped at it, wincing at the feel of the wound and dried blood there. That one was still real. And something about realizing this was oddly comforting. It was a constant. A single spark of sanity among the madness. Something, perhaps, that she could cling to in whatever nightmare trap she'd fallen into, simply knowing that there was some reality mixed in with the fantasy. She might be able to use that. Like an anchor keeping her from drifting farther from reality. Or a lifeline, perhaps.

Again, she tried to stand, this time careful to favor that knee as she rose, and managed to get her feet under her.

There was that dull pain in the arch of her foot, too, she realized. Where she stepped on something sharp. And she could feel the bruises where she fell over that broken chair. That was all around the same time, in that messed-up version of her and Nicole's apartment. That must've been real. Or at least real enough to have caused her those particular injuries. She refused to accept that her home had been destroyed like that, not in *any* reality. It was just a cruel trick. But it was a trick full of very real broken furniture, shattered glass and dangerously sharp nails.

Her eyes wide open for dangers lurking in this unfamiliar darkness, she crept toward the light, dragging her feet on the dirty concrete, sweeping for unseen hazards with her bare toes, her every nerve wound tight in anticipation of another cruel steel trap snapping closed around them. The agonizing memory of the last one was still fresh in her terrified mind. It was so intensely real that she couldn't dismiss it as any kind of illusion or dream.

And she *really* didn't want to experience that again.

The source of the light was coming from another space, through an open doorway, from another room. And as she drew closer, she realized that it wasn't red like the glow of that awful sky. It was a dingy sort of yellowish white. Could it be her dropped flashlight?

She wanted to reach that light, but she didn't dare pick up her pace and risk getting hurt again. She set her jaw, wiped at those stubborn tears and urged her racing heart to calm down.

Her eyes had adjusted a little. She could see more of the space around her. There were wooden pillars farther out in the darkness, and bare joists above her head. Every surface was covered in a thick layer of dust, but she could see no cobwebs, no litter, no footprints or other indication that anyone had been here in a very long time.

When she at last reached the doorway, she pressed herself close to the wall and peered through it. There was a short hallway there, leading to a single flight of stairs. The light was coming from a dim, naked bulb over the landing at the top.

She was somewhere with electricity now?

Satisfied that there was nothing awful lurking there, she slipped through the doorway. It was a relief to be back in the light, able to see where she was placing her feet, and yet she found herself hesitating, reluctant to approach the steps. She felt so desperately exposed. She covered herself and listened for any noises from above.

Gnawing at her lower lip, uncertain, she started up the first few steps, grimacing at the pain in her knee, her eyes fixed on the landing ahead. There was another corridor leading to the left, she saw. A way out, perhaps? Or another of the Priestess' cruel traps?

It was so quiet. She couldn't hear the wind blowing anymore. The only sound was the hum of electricity from the bulb overhead and she couldn't decide if this silence made everything feel better or worse.

A hard shiver raced through her, like a cold and unexpected draft, bringing with it a strange and staggering certainty. She let out a startled gasp and turned around, her arms raised to defend herself from whatever was rushing toward her. In the process, a sharp pain shot through that injured knee, causing her to stumble and sit down hard on the dusty step.

Except there was nothing there.

She sat there, goosebumps on her skin, the hair on her arms standing on end. It reminded her of the feeling she had back at the wedding reception, after that first deceptive encounter with Hotdog Creep. And just like back there, the feeling was gone as quickly as it came over her.

But she wasn't eager to dismiss it this time. After all that had happened, she'd be a fool to dismiss anything. She lingered there, her wide eyes staring down those steps and into the darkness looming behind the open doorway.

Something *could* be down there. She couldn't see very much of that space while she was creeping through it. And there had been no shortage of frights since she set off on this decidedly *one-star* vacation. But if there was anything watching her from that darkness, it wasn't ready to show itself.

Covering herself again with one hand, she reached out and gripped the handrail with the other. With a grimace, she pulled herself to her feet and began backing up the stairs, her eyes fixed on that deceptive darkness, unwilling to trust it.

Nothing moved. There was still no sound but the electric hum of that old bulb.

But if she kept her gaze fixed behind her, what about the unknown space above? She glanced back at the landing behind her, half-expecting one of those shadowy things to be crouched there, just waiting for her to meet its blinding white eyes before ripping her face off for real this time.

But she was still alone in this creepy stairwell.

She wished she knew what awaited her up there. What was this place? How did she get here? She hadn't understood anything since the Murk snatched her away from Olivia and Wayne.

She limped up the rest of the steps and peered into the next corridor. She couldn't see how far it went. There weren't any more lights in there. And everything was pitch black. Was it nighttime? Or were there simply no windows in this place?

Or maybe the windows were all covered up...

Those graffiti-covered concrete walls flashed through her mind again. Gilbert House... That was something the others told her about, wasn't it? How the first-floor windows and doors were all bricked over in a desperate attempt to keep out the things they found in the world that awful building somehow pierced?

Was that where she was? Was she *inside* the nightmare this time? Trapped with the violent monster that murdered Olivia's old friends?

Again, she looked up at that one, humming bulb. No... That wasn't a part of it. They told her the building was pitch black inside. And why wouldn't it be? It didn't even exist, as far as the rest of the world knew. There wouldn't be any electricity there.

But that wasn't really Gilbert House before, either, she realized. That was just some kind of bizarre illusion. It had to be, or she'd be dead right now, torn to pieces by those shining-eyed demons.

The *real* Gilbert House was back in Briar Hills, on the far side of that great, black lake, beyond the edges of the Denselands and outside the impassible wall.

And yet... She lowered her gaze to the dark corridor stretched out before her again. This was real, too. As real as it needed to be. Real enough for her to feel the concrete beneath her bare feet. Real enough to feel her bones crushed in the jaws of a steel trap. Real enough to feel herself being disemboweled by the claws of those shining-eyed monsters.

She didn't want to go through any of that again.

She had to get out of here. But which way was out? Was it down that long, dark corridor? Or was it back the way she came? Or was there a way out at all? She still didn't know how she ended up here. What was real and what wasn't?

She stared into the darkness before her, still covering herself, her head tilted to one side. What was that noise she was hearing? It wasn't just the hum of the light bulb anymore. There was something else, too. A *different* sort of hum.

She took a tentative step forward, leaning into the darkness, squinting, trying to see what might be there.

Was something moving just beyond the bulb's meager reach? Or was that only her terrified imagination?

She took a step backward, her heart leaping.

That definitely wasn't her imagination. Something awful was moving in that darkness. She could almost see it.

The humming was getting louder and louder. Was that really the light bulb? Or had that noise been something else from the very beginning?

"Here they come," whispered the impostor in her ear.

A multitude of huge, deformed hands covered in festering sores lunged out of the darkness, clawing at the floor and walls.

Andrea didn't wait to see what kind of abomination was attached to those hands. She turned to flee back down the steps, but with a deafening pop, the lone light bulb blew, plunging her into perfect darkness.

Blind again, she missed the first step.

She fell.

She screamed.

And in the all-enveloping pitch black that consumed her, she felt every agonizing broken bone on her way to the bottom.

Chapter 48

Everett had been walking for what felt like hours and yet he hadn't gone anywhere.

It wasn't that he simply hadn't found anything in all the distance he'd traveled. And it wasn't that he'd only circled right back to where he started. He literally hadn't moved from this one spot. It was like being on a treadmill. He was still in the very same place he was when he entered this queer, empty dimension. Alice told him as much. Walking was only an illusion. The very concept of "traveling" didn't exist here. There was no need for it because there was nowhere to go. However *that* logic worked...

But he wasn't sure what else he was supposed to do. He hadn't come up with a plan yet for leaving a place where you couldn't go anywhere because there was nothing there—including doors—and no way to reach anything if it *were* there. It was a real head-scratcher. And it was even more boring than that endless Red Waste he found himself stuck in after losing track of Wayne and Olivia. He wished there was at least *something* here.

Not that he could see anything even if there was, he supposed...

He should probably just sit down and reserve his strength, but he could think better while walking. He wasn't good at sitting patiently. Sitting made him feel antsy. And what was the worst that could happen? It wasn't like he was in any danger of getting himself lost.

This was all delightfully *weird*...but it was still boring. He really wanted to get out of this place.

His thoughts kept returning to the dollhouse. That was a place of his own creation, his own subconscious imagination weaving things into reality. He couldn't help wondering if this place was the same, if he'd somehow conjured this empty world and trapped himself here, if he only needed to understand how to imagine himself back out of this situation.

(No.)

He glanced down at Alice. A mere force of habit, given that it was still utterly dark here and his eyes were useless. "I know." He didn't really think it would be anything so simple. And yet he tried it anyway, to *imagine* a way out. He imagined a light in this darkness, a beacon he could move toward, an exit sign of some sort, but this wasn't the same as the dollhouse. This was the wrong side of the void. They weren't all the way back to the City Beyond Memory, but they were no longer in that upside down world where everything, even reality and imagination, were inverted.

This was neither the world he knew *nor* another dollhouse. This was somewhere else entirely, something completely different. The solution wasn't going to be the same as it was on the other side.

The good news, however, was that they *were* on the correct side of the void. He was fairly sure getting past that was the hardest part of moving between the two. He'd somehow managed not to lose himself to that nothingness twice now, and his head was clear again. If there was a way out of this nowhere place and back to the City Beyond Memory, he'd find it. He was sure of it.

He stopped walking. He was missing something, he decided. Because if he couldn't go anywhere, then the fact was that he must already be where he needed to be.

That made sense. Right?

(Of course it didn't, but when had that ever stopped him?)

He stood there, staring blindly into the unending blackness, listening to the silence over the roar of his own pulse in his ears, feeling the hard concrete beneath the soles of his shoes and nothing more. It didn't even *smell* like anything here.

So what was he supposed to do?

"Think," he told himself. Don't be distracted by all the

questions and useless observations. There had to be *something* here, some little detail he was overlooking. If there were nothing at all, then how would this be any different from the void?

Very slowly, he turned around, straining to see something in the dark, to feel some presence, to hear some whisper of a sound...

He stopped.

Sound.

He turned back the other way, even more slowly, his eyes closed this time, shifting all his attention to his ears.

It wasn't a sound, per se... Rather, it was the sounds that were already there. The muted shuffling of his feet. His breath as he inhaled and exhaled. The constant droning of his blood pumping in his ears, a faint ring of tinnitus on one side. Even the soft rubbing of his clothes as he shifted his weight.

These were all the sounds he carried with him everywhere he went. So then...why did they seem to grow fainter when he faced this way?

(Hush.)

This word confused him for a moment. Hush? Images of quiet libraries and sleeping babies popped into his head, but that didn't make any sense. He was being as quiet as possible already.

He turned his head a little to one side, then the other. Those sounds inside his head changed with the direction.

She wasn't telling *him* to hush, she realized. She was referring to *this*. The way all the sound was hushed when he turned his ear in a certain direction. It was important. And it was incredibly subtle. It was no wonder he didn't notice it immediately.

He found the quietest point and focused his attention in that direction.

Except...that wasn't quite right either. It wasn't the direction that mattered. He'd already established that directions were meaningless here. No, this was something else. Something outside his limited range of understanding.

He stood there, motionless, listening, trying to grasp whatever it was he couldn't perceive. It wasn't easy. His brain was hardwired to operate within the physical laws of the world he was born to. Understanding an environment where basic rules such as direction, distance and time were inconsistent or altogether missing was tricky. He was going to have to use a framework of thinking that was entirely new to him.

He wouldn't even be capable of understanding this much if not for Alice, he was sure. She was feeding him what information she could, but there was only so much she could do for him. Ultimately, it was *he* who was going to have to take whatever step came next.

He focused on the sound, because that was the only thing that had given him any clues so far, his full attention aimed into the hushed zone he'd found, dialed in on just that one direction that wasn't a direction at all but something altogether different...he guessed...?

This was so confusing.

But slowly, he realized that he was tilting his head far to one side, as if trying to look at something sideways, despite the fact that he was still utterly blind and couldn't *see* anything at all. And what difference did it make to *listen* to something sideways?

Was he doing *anything* right?

Sideways...

He frowned. Why did that word sound so strangely right?

Sideways.

"I'm supposed to turn something sideways?" he asked, confused. There was nothing here except him and Alice. "Am I supposed to turn *myself* sideways?"

He frowned at the jumbled thoughts in his head.

"I'm trying," he informed her. "But I don't understand any of it. That doesn't sound like something a human can do."

But then again, a human wasn't supposed to be able to imagine a mysterious spiritual being into a sentient, telepathic doll, so what did he really know about what humans could and couldn't do? This wasn't his world so why would his world's rules apply?

At this point, he wasn't even sure if what he needed to do was sit down and think really hard or stop thinking altogether.

"Hm?" Again, he looked pointlessly down at the small form

cradled against his chest. "I *am* focusing on what's important. Getting back."

Another strange wave of half-imagined concepts and images blew through his mind like wind through a drafty house. It was too much at once. He couldn't quite grasp what she was saying. He let it circle around in his head for a moment, picking through the pieces, letting the important bits sink in.

"Oh…" he muttered. "You mean what's so important *about* getting back." Besides simply getting home, he supposed. "I mean, I have to get back to the others, right?" Wayne and Olivia. Violet. Andrea. And the others, too. The ones he hadn't met.

Was he supposed to be focusing on *them*?

Again, he turned his attention back to the hushed zone. He cleared his mind and listened to it.

Alice was right. Getting back was only the means to the end. What was important was his new friends. He needed to get back to them and make sure everyone was okay. Someone might need his help.

He took a step toward the hushed zone. It did nothing, of course. He didn't really move. It was more symbolic than anything. He took the step to help realign himself. It was like stepping out of his state of ignorance and into a new state of focus and determination.

He was going to go back.

He'd made up his mind, after all. And he could do anything he pleased when he made up his mind. Just look at how far he'd already come.

Except…nothing was happening.

"Oh yeah," he laughed. "I forgot. Gotta do it sideways."

What an utterly bizarre world he'd found. He didn't even understand what sideways meant in a place with no directions. Was sideways *not* a direction? Was he missing something?

Without thinking about it, he tipped his head to the side again, as if trying to look at a sideways picture.

Everything seemed to go a little wonky after that. He felt the world spinning and shrinking, wrapping itself around him, entombing him in this darkness while at the same time filling him with the intensely contradicting sensation of being set free. He didn't understand it. He couldn't even describe it. But it was strangely pleasant and refreshing, like waking up from a really great nap.

Then, just as quickly, he was falling through an endless darkness.

Chapter 49

Erin stared up into the branches overhead, her breath caught in her throat.

They were only crows. Crows were only birds. Birds were only animals. And yet for some reason the sight of them up there sent a chill racing through her body like nothing she'd ever experienced before.

Why were there so many? And why *here*? What could have drawn them to this place? And why were they all being so eerily *quiet*. She'd only heard the one caw that first drew her attention to them. Otherwise, they'd all been sitting there in silence, staring down at her from above.

Were *they* what she felt watching her this whole time?

She wanted to run back the way she came. She didn't want to walk under them all. But if she was right about the path Horatio laid out for her, could she afford to go back? Would she be able to go around?

She definitely didn't want to have to come back and do all of this from the beginning. These woods were creeping her out.

Slowly, she started forward, her arms raised, ready to defend herself in case they suddenly took flight and dived at her like in that old Alfred Hitchcock movie.

How quickly would they be able to peck out her eyes if they suddenly swarmed her? They were scavengers. They ate meat. Would so many of them be able to strip the flesh from her bones like a school of piranha? Had anything like that ever happened before?

But they didn't leave their perches. Some of them shuffled a little. Some of them fluffed their feathers. Some of them stretched their wings and then settled back in. But they all stayed in place. And they all remained unsettlingly quiet.

She was looking up at them, not where she was stepping. Inevitably, she tripped over something. With a painful cry, she fell forward and landed sprawled in the thick brush. Above her, the crows stirred. A few of them cried back at her, almost seeming to scold her. But not one of them took flight. They all stayed right where they were, watching her with their strange, beady eyes.

She lay there, gazing up at them, still expecting one to dive at her. When none did, she risked a look back to see what she'd tripped on.

A very old tombstone was jutting out of the tall grass.

A grave? She frowned at it, confused. Looking around, she realized that there was another a few feet away, mostly hidden in the brush. And another beyond that.

She stood up, distracted, and looked around. There were at least a dozen of them, she quickly saw. Probably more. They were difficult to make out. Only a few of them were still standing upright. Most were leaning. Many had fallen over completely. And none remained legible. Any names or dates had vanished with time. Each and every one was weatherworn and covered in moss.

Understanding dawned on her and for a moment she forgot about the crows above. "Forgotten Field of Buried Darkness," she whispered. This was, indeed, a field once upon a time. And it was most definitely forgotten, almost entirely reclaimed by the forest. No one had tended to it in many years. And what was buried beneath her feet right now...boxes filled with darkness...things that would never see the light of day again...

This was where she was meant to be. Another marker on Horatio's mysterious map.

Except...

Again, she peered up at those branches, at those silent corvids all peering back at her, watching, almost judging her.

What was the deal with them? There wasn't anything this spooky back at the sawmill. There were only those fleeting glimpses of shadowy somethings that she'd been seeing more and more often everywhere she went this past year. It was business as usual for her. So what made this cemetery different?

She couldn't stop thinking about how the last time she saw so many crows in one place was in Crump, where she found the Elysium Fog. Was there some kind of connection? Were they some kind of omen for spiritual places?

She was still looking up at them, still contemplating the mysterious feeling they instilled in her, when one let out a loud caw and the others followed suit. In just a few seconds, the quiet forest was filled with the dreadful racket of hundreds of screaming birds.

She covered her ears, amazed at how loud they were, and crouched down, still convinced that they were merely waiting for a chance to swoop down and draw blood.

But something wormed its way into her head, a rogue thought, a strangely intense feeling, like she was focused on the wrong thing. She was so fixated on the birds that she was missing something important.

She squeezed her eyes closed, confused. What was wrong with her? Mere crows filled her with fear and apprehension? Random thoughts and feelings kept popping into her head? Why did she feel so crazy?

And yet, when she dared a look behind her, she realized that she was no longer alone.

A woman was standing behind one of the tilted headstones.

She was very thin, with long, dark hair. She wore a black dress and her head was bowed, her face hidden in the shadows. She looked as if she were grieving a loved one. But who came to a cemetery like this to grieve? This wasn't the kind of cemetery where loved ones came to pay respects. This was the kind where the buried had been long forgotten.

Erin stared at the woman, an intense fear welling up inside her. She spent no time wondering how that woman arrived in that spot without her hearing her. She didn't rationalize any part of it. She knew instantly that she wasn't looking at a living human being. And she knew that she was in terrible danger at this moment.

She took a step backward as the crows continued screaming at her from above, not daring to take her eyes off the woman.

Why couldn't she see her face? Why was it so dark? The shade wasn't this deep before. The sky above was clear and blue through the swaying branches, and yet it was as if dark clouds had gathered overhead, plunging her into an early twilight.

Gooseflesh prickled up her arms. The temperature had dropped. A puff of steam escaped her mouth.

Her stomach was twisted into a nervous knot.

Careful not to trip again, and without taking her eyes off the woman, she began to back away.

The woman lifted her head slightly, following her with eyes still concealed in darkness, watching her every move.

Her breathing had gone ragged. Her body was trembling. She felt like she might throw up. She couldn't remember ever being this afraid in her life. Even meeting Horatio didn't feel like this. Because Horatio, in spite of his ominous message about her inevitable demise, intended her no harm. This woman...no, this *thing*...was different. She was *radiating* a foul aura, like something *evil* staring back at her.

Did the crows become agitated because this "woman" appeared? Or was she there the whole time and she simply didn't see her? Were they trying to warn her? Or had they somehow *summoned* the thing in the black dress?

She took another step backward, feeling her way around the trees and the stones.

The woman leaned forward and placed a shriveled hand on the tilted headstone.

She still could see no eyes in that unnatural darkness, but she found that she could somehow see a mouth. Thin, dry lips parted open, revealing gleaming white teeth that looked far too big to belong to any human.

She stumbled over a pine sapling and let out a startled gasp.

It was as if the woman were merely waiting for her to make a mistake. In an instant, she lurched forward, shifting from upright to all fours, revealing impossibly long limbs and a hideously distended face.

And she wasn't alone.

Dozens of them came crawling out of the darkened forest like a swarm of giant bugs, each one flashing a grin of enormous teeth.

Beneath that canopy of screaming crows, Erin turned and fled for her life.

Chapter 50

"Are you sure you know what you're doing?" grumbled Austin. It was irritating, lying here, helpless, waiting on this great oaf to finish plugging him into the stoneworks. He could have finished two more books in the time he'd already taken.

"Yep," was Corey's only response. To his credit, he didn't stop working. He didn't even waste time giving him a dirty look.

As far as humans went... Well, he wasn't anything remarkable, that was for sure. But then again...he supposed he could've been stuck with *worse*.

It wasn't really Corey's fault, after all, that this process took so long. It would have been finished in an instant if not for his unfortunate run-in with that unnatural abomination.

He never dreamed he'd be ambushed like that in the Faceless Ones' very stoneworks, forcing him to rely on a mere human in order to complete his mission. And he wasn't so completely disgusted with mankind that he wasn't aware that he was, as the human named Wayne so elegantly put it back at the thorn gate, being "kind of a dick." The truth was that this whole ordeal was frustrating. He was so close to completing his purpose, so close to returning to that blissful peace he awoke from centuries ago in the depths of the birthing chamber in that remote forest.

He'd done nothing but wait obediently for his time to come and yet it felt as if he were being punished. Had he done something to displease the Keeper? Had he failed some aspect of his mission that he wasn't aware of, perhaps? Was he never meant to develop such a negative view of the humans he was forced to live among for so long? Was he supposed to have engaged with them more? Had his fondness of their fiction caused him to miss something while his nose was buried in his books?

No. Those were all equally real possibilities, he understood. So great was the mind of the Keeper that he was capable of accounting even for the movements of his enemies, often turning their best attempts at betrayal and sabotage into just another spinning gear working for the cycle in his great machine. But none of those scenarios fit exactly right. Something deep down in his programming was telling him that this was always the way things were going to happen. Why else would the Faceless Ones even bother planting the seeds of stoneworks knowledge deep in their genetic code?

The two of them were always meant to meet. They were always meant to be here in this chamber at this moment.

And it wasn't his place to ask why.

He was only another tool for the Keeper's machine.

He was only the bootup disk.

Again, he turned and looked longingly at his books. He might not have time to finish a new one, and not finishing a book always felt wrong. Disrespectful. Even if it wasn't a good book, he always finished it. But he could re-read one that he'd already finished. He already knew how it ended, so it wouldn't matter if he ran out of time.

Corey's hands stopped moving. They did that now and then, Austin had noticed. He was always aware when it happened. Those were *his* internal parts he was handling, after all. It was usually because he became distracted by something he sensed within the stoneworks. It was rather infuriating, if he were being honest. Every moment he spent sitting there doing nothing was another moment of insufferable humiliation here on this floor. But he didn't want to engage in whatever passed for conversation with the oversized fool. Nothing he said ever seemed to do anything anyway. Nothing ever fazed the man. He'd just lie here, thinking about his books, ignoring him. Hopefully he'd start working again soon.

But instead of getting back to work, Corey asked a question that surprised him: "What's real?"

Austin turned and looked at him, puzzled. "What?"

He was staring down at the bloody strings in his hand, his great brow creased, a deep frown on his pudgy face. "What's really here? What can't I see?" Slowly, he turned his head and met his gaze. "I know I'm only seein' *some* of it. That's part of why everything's so weird here. But what am I missing?"

What was real? What was he missing? What bizarre questions. What did it matter? He was perfectly capable of completing his job regardless of how much or how little of the "real" he could see. He was only wasting time again, asking stupid questions, dragging out this humiliation.

"I can feel more than my senses can detect," pondered Corey. "Like something just beyond my line of sight or just out of range of my ears. It's there, right in front of me, but I can't figure out how to focus on it. And I can't stop thinking that if I *could* grasp it, I could do this a lot faster."

Austin stared at him for a moment, surprised. He could sense that? Humans were such odd creatures. He wasn't wrong. There *was* more than his natural senses would allow him to detect. There was *always* more. Everywhere. The universe was filled with more things that *couldn't* be detected by human senses than *could*. He'd always found it curious, in fact, that creatures in such high regard to the Keeper possessed such *limited* senses.

"It's *you*," he seemed to decide, his gaze sliding to his torn torso, to the piles of bloody strings still spilling out of his broken body. "You're not what you appear to be at all, are you?"

"Considering that I was created in a very different universe," he replied, "I very much doubt that I'd be exactly as I appear to you in yours."

His face still pinched into that deeply thoughtful frown, Corey nodded slowly. "Dif'rent physics…" he muttered.

Austin had never seen any universe other than this one. He only gained consciousness when he awoke here. Until then he was little more than a package waiting to be delivered. But he held a certain amount of knowledge about the universes that came before. Enough to ensure that he understood the cycle and his role in it all. He knew that things changed when old universes died and new ones were born. The rules that governed them became overwritten. Old concepts sometimes ceased to be and new ones replaced them. The entire process was nothing short of catastrophic, so explosively violent that the old universe came completely undone, essentially shattering like glass. Even time itself could be fractured in the resulting chaos, changing things in the past in unpredictable ways.

Corey's gaze shifted back to his face. He locked eyes with him. "What are you?" he asked. "Really?"

"Impatient," he replied. "Please get back to work."

Corey ignored him. He sat there, not moving, staring back at him, waiting for a proper response to the question he asked.

Austin sighed. "I can't explain something to you that you have no way of understanding. There are components of my body that exist outside the range of your human senses and beyond your ability to understand. I was made to blend in with your society and move about unnoticed to better be able to do the job I was given. So I can't answer your question. The best I can offer you is a metaphor. If you can imagine me as a marionette dancing on a stage, you might be able to comprehend a fraction of my whole. Everyone sees the puppet. You, with your uniquely ingrained knowledge, can glimpse the strings, telling you there's something more. But what you can't see is the puppeteer pulling those strings. The greater part of me is hidden, even from you."

Corey finally looked away. His gaze swept across the room as if trying to imagine another Austin, bigger and stranger and more complex, looming in the space around them, undetectable, but frightfully real. He nodded. "This part of you's an illusion," he seemed to decide. "Physical representation…"

"That's…one way to put it, I suppose." He wasn't exactly wrong. But it was grossly simplified.

Again, Corey looked down at the bloody strands he was holding. "Not really strings…" he decided. Then he looked at the contacts protruding from the wall, those deceptively simple stone spikes that were nothing less than what they appeared and yet at the same time nothing of the sort.

"There aren't any concepts in this universe to compare my

inner workings to," he explained. "You're better off trying to understand the various dimensions that make up reality as a whole. You're already aware of the fact that physical space can overlap, allowing multiple realities to occupy the same space."

"Portals," he replied, nodding. "Some inside, like pockets. Some outside, like the Wood."

Austin wasn't sure he fully understood what some of that nonsense was, but he pushed on anyway. "And all those realities exist simultaneously within one or more of the three separate core planes of existence."

"Natural, supernatural and unnatural," he deduced.

"Precisely. The realms of the Three Powers. But there also exists, within every reality, a *spectrum* in which everything in existence has its place. That's where much of the unexplainable is hidden, forever shifted from view, out of reach, unobtainable regardless of how curious you may be about it."

Again, he nodded as if there were any way he could fully understand such concepts.

"And finally, there's also the 'great coin.' Everything that exists has two sides. A heads and a tails. A sort of mirror reality that is bound to this one."

This seemed to give him pause. He frowned a little deeper and tilted his head a little to one side as he contemplated the concept.

"You humans—and the vast majority of things, really—exist exclusively on one side of the coin. You're never meant to see the other side, though it does, on rare occasions, happen that someone finds a way to slip through. I, on the other hand, exist on both sides at the same time. What you see of me is only a sliver of my whole."

Corey sat there for a few seconds, letting all of that sink in. Then, very slowly, he began to nod again. "Cool."

Austin blinked up at him, bemused. Cool? That was all he had to say about it?

He looked down at the strands in his bloody hands again, then up at the stone walls around them. "Same with this stuff," he deduced. "The temple stone. It exists across all those things, too, doesn't it?"

He raised an eyebrow, surprised. "It does. That material is a universal constant. It's part of what makes it able to retain past universes' properties and keep working as originally designed, regardless of what changes have taken place throughout the cycle."

Corey nodded again. "Makes sense."

Austin scowled at him. There was no way that made any sense at all to a mere human. And yet as he lay there watching, he turned away and went back to work, as if perfectly satisfied.

Humans were so strange.

And in all his many years, this might be the strangest one he'd ever encountered.

Chapter 51

Violet pounded on the lid, desperate, screaming for some-one—*anyone*—to *please* get her out of this box! She couldn't stand it. She was going to lose her mind in here!

You have to calm yourself.

But she couldn't calm herself. How did the other one ex-pect her to find any kind of calmness while she was *literally buried alive?* She already told her that she was powerless to help her in this world. Was she supposed to just lie here and get comfortable while she slowly and torturously suffocated?

She knew that screaming was only burning through the ox-ygen faster, but she couldn't help it. No one was coming for her. No one knew where she was. Even if they did, no one knew how to get here. This was an entirely different *universe* than the one everyone else was in. And yet she couldn't make herself stop screaming.

She was going to scream herself to death in this black, claustrophobic hell.

This was far worse than being eaten alive by those mutant boars or broken and battered by those hooved devils. Those end-ings were indescribably agonizing, but at least they were *fast.* How long was she going to suffer here? How long would it take her to die like this?

She was sobbing. Her knuckles and palms were raw and burning from battering them against the wood, as were her knees and feet. It felt as if her heart might explode inside her chest.

Endure.

Easy for *her* to say! Sentinels didn't have breathing holes! What the hell did *she* know about it?

Endure just a little longer.

"*Help me!*" she screamed. The other one took the wheel to help her escape the Not-Everett thing. She took the wheel to help her escape the storm drafts. Why the hell couldn't she do the same *now?* "*Please just get me out of here!*"

"No one's letting you out," said a voice in the darkness that made her screams catch in her throat.

"Who's there?" she gasped.

There was suddenly someone in the box with her. A body was pressing down on her, compressing her chest and belly, weighing her down, making it even harder to catch her breath.

"This is my world," said a woman's voice so close that she could feel the breath on her trembling lips. "You belong to me now."

Her world? Was this who the other one warned her about? The Priestess of Ruin herself?

A fresh wave of terror rushed through her, even more intense than before as an image materialized in her mind of not a flesh and blood woman lying atop her, but a rotting, oozing *corpse.*

"*Let me out!*" she cried.

"I'm going to play with you forever," said the corpse woman as a foul and putrid stench filled the box, choking her.

"*Somebody help me!*"

But no one was coming to help her.

As quickly as she appeared, the corpse woman vanished, leaving her alone in the suffocating darkness again.

She had only a moment to thrust her hands and feet out, confirming that nothing awful was sharing the cramped space with her.

Then there was an awful cracking sound and dirt began to trickle into the box, onto her terrified face.

Chapter 52

I'm broken…

The thought passed through the muddled madness inside Andrea's head as she lay alone in the cold darkness, throbbing daggers of pain digging into her body. Everything felt wrong. Her body felt twisted, every slightest movement was torture. She couldn't get up. She couldn't move. She couldn't scream. She couldn't even *breathe.* Every breath she tried to draw felt like an icepick in her breast and filled her mouth and nose with a dreadful, overwhelming taste and smell of blood.

Unable to see and overcome by fright, she'd fallen. She remembered the floor disappearing from under her. A terrible pain in her foot, only the first of many. The stairs rushing up to meet her… A dizzying blur of agonizing snaps.

How many bones did she break? How much damage had she suffered? Was she going to die here, all alone in this awful darkness? There was no one to help her… No one to even find her lifeless body…

She didn't want to die, but even worse, she didn't want to die lost in this nightmare place with no one else around. She wanted to be with her friends. She wanted to see her family again. She hated the idea of being all alone. She'd *always* been afraid of being all alone!

"Oh, sweetie," said a dreadfully familiar voice.

From somewhere in that awful darkness, she felt a hand on her face, caressing her cheek. It was warm and soft.

Stella…?

No… Not Stella. Not really.

"You *wish* you were all alone," she whispered, her lips and her breath brushing against her ear.

Andrea felt a strange, carnal sort of fear swell inside her fractured body. Her heart was pounding. The pain in her chest became a twisting, grinding agony. She wanted to run away, but she couldn't.

Because she was broken...

"Are we having fun yet?" asked the Priestess of Ruin.

Chapter 53

It felt strange, leading Nicole through the glass labyrinth by her hand, fussing over her like some lost and fragile child. This was the woman who saved her and Andrea from that insane cultist. The woman who kicked her through the gateway in that cursed hospital at the risk of her own life and soul. The woman who twice pulled her from the clutches of Gwilym Glum. She was one of the strongest and most capable women she'd ever met.

She couldn't understand it. How did *she* become the strong one? And was she really able to do this? She wasn't brave. She was no hero. She was still just a frightened little girl, far too intimidated by the world to be of any use to anyone.

But it wasn't as if she had a choice. She couldn't just leave her back there to fend for herself, alone and afraid and heartbroken. She didn't think she could do that to *anyone*, much less Nicole, to whom she owed so much. And neither could she simply stay with her. The longer she was here in this endless darkness, the more apparent it became that something was calling to her from the depths of the glass labyrinth.

But the glass labyrinth was different now. Something had changed.

She was frightened out of her mind the first time she was here, desperate to avoid the thing with too many mouths, so no one would blame her if she'd missed some little details about the space, but it was almost as if she were looking at it for the first time.

She cast her psychic gaze out around her, bemused at the sheer complexity of what she glimpsed there. These mysterious passages twisted and turned and split and merged, as confounding as one might expect a maze to be, but unlike the stone laby-rinth, *these* passages circled around and doubled back on them-selves without ever meeting, over and over again, not just left and right and forward and back and even up and down, but at every possible angle, with no rhyme or reason, following no logic whatsoever. It was like looking at an entire stack of maps all laid out on top of each other, each one bleeding through all the rest, blending together, seemingly taking up the same page. If they turned right up ahead, they'd circle right back around to this very same spot, but it wouldn't really be this same spot. It would be somewhere else. A different page in the stack. And in a different orientation. A different dimension, perhaps?

It was like the cracks in the glass, she realized. Distortions and refractions, false angles and split perceptions, a myriad of kaleidoscopic reflections splitting her psychic gaze into a multi-tude of directions all at once and with no frame of reference.

It was too much for her. It felt like a sensory overload, con-fusing her psychic eye until her brain couldn't tell the difference between a clear path and a dead end.

Was it different now because the monster was gone? Did its absence change some fundamental part of her ability to perceive it? Or was it the dark entity that shattered the wall and set the monster free? Did *she* do something to entangle the glass passag-es?

She was creeping forward, moving slowly, watching the path before her unravel in that strange and unnatural way that made no sense and followed no reason. Those dangerous voids still dotted the queer landscape, empty spaces in her psychic per-ception that represented something even that cursed part of her mind couldn't comprehend. Whatever they were, they loomed on all sides of them. And they weren't merely sitting there, either. Each one was somehow drifting about, flickering, moving inde-pendently of the rest of the space. Were they alive after all? Some kind of *creature* lurking in these confounding passageways? A sort of guard dog?

She couldn't find any logic in their movements, couldn't sense where they were going or where they were coming from.

And she couldn't predict when one might spring up right in front of her.

"Feels weird here," said Nicole in that same strangely timid voice she used when her sock fell down.

"Are you okay?" she worried, glancing back at her. The thought of her breaking down again was frightful, but far worse was the thought of something happening to her in this glass dimension that she dragged her into.

"I think so...?" She reached up and rubbed at her swollen eyes. "I don't know how to explain it. Just tired, maybe?"

"Maybe." But she very much doubted it. It was probably the glass labyrinth. She could only see the stone, after all, meaning that from her point of view, everything here was very small and very dark. And probably very three-dimensional. But the glass labyrinth was twisted in ways that were far stranger than the Denselands and Tristesse Lane. If any part of her brain were capable of understanding that—and she'd found that most people were able to sense *something* about the unnatural, even if they couldn't or wouldn't acknowledge it—then she was probably aware, if only on some subconscious level, that the path her feet were following didn't match the changes in directions they kept taking. Especially when the labyrinth rolled around them like a giant hamster ball.

She turned and looked forward again, distracted.

Twice now, she glimpsed something moving behind the distorted glass. Figures creeping through the darkness. She could tell somehow that she was glimpsing things in the other labyrinth, out in the surrounding stone, but those glimpses were too fleeting and too deformed to tell if they were someone she knew, or even whether they were man or beast. But a few times she'd heard the soft muttering of hushed conversation drifting through the glass, reminding her that they weren't really alone in this sprawling temple. And yet they might as well be on different planets, because no one could reach them here in the glass. No one was going to come to their rescue if she messed up.

She pushed onward, her psychic eye wide open, watching for the mysterious voids that still danced all around them, defying any kind of reason.

They seemed different now. Last time she understood that they were things to be avoided, dangers of some kind, but she never sensed that they were actively stalking her like some sort of creature. But something about the way their movements were mismatched to her fragile understanding of the glass labyrinth's layout felt oddly intentional.

What hadn't changed was that feeling of primal fear, as if some long-buried code in her very DNA was warning her to steer clear of them.

Now that the monster with too many heads was gone, were the real dangers free to play?

There was one above them, she realized, though it was unclear just how near or far it was. She focused her psychic eye on it as she crept forward, watching it.

For some reason, she found herself imagining some kind of *mirror*... But that didn't make sense. Why would a mirror frighten her so much?

She squinted up at it (old habits) and tried to piece together the information inside her brain.

No... Not that it *was* a mirror, she realized. That it *acted* something like a mirror. Not that it reflected light back at her in any way, but that it distorted the space around it, creating that perception of a void.

Nicole stopped walking, pulling her from her thoughts. She looked back, concerned, and found that she was staring off into the distance. "Is there something in here with us?"

Gina blinked at her, confused, her psychic eye darting back to that looming void overhead. She shouldn't be able to sense the same things she did. "Why?"

She was blinking, as if trying to clear her vision. "I don't know," she replied. "I just feel like..." But she trailed off and fell silent, the words abandoning her before they could pass her lips.

Something didn't feel right. She seemed off somehow, uncharacteristically frail. Was it just the lingering trauma from losing Keith, or was this place harming her in some way?

Maybe this was a bad idea. Maybe she should look for another crack. What if it wasn't safe for others to be here?

When she last exited this area, it took her to Nicole and Keith. If she found another crack, was it possible that it might take them near one of the others? Someone who could help her look after Nicole? Someone she'd be safe with while she finished whatever she needed to do in here?

It was worth a shot, wasn't it?

She just had to find one of those cracks.

But as she used her psychic eye to glance around, she realized that the void-thing had vanished from above them. She turned around, startled. When did that happen? She was keeping her psychic eye fixed on it, tracking it, yet it was just gone.

Where did it go?

She turned all the way around, the labyrinth rolling with her, twisting and coiling and balling itself up in every direction as she moved. But it seemed to have completely disappeared.

It was unsettling to lose track of one like that. She couldn't help thinking that they could just as easily appear as disappear.

"What's wrong?" worried Nicole.

"Nothing," she replied automatically. She couldn't count the times she'd forgotten herself in front of people and been asked that same question. She was so used to answering with that word and trying to pretend like nothing was there, even though there was almost always *something* there.

But this was different. This wasn't some stranger in a classroom or a store or an elevator who noticed her behaving strangely. This was Nicole. She didn't need to lie. She wasn't going to tell her she was weird or call her a freak or act like she was some kind of psychopath.

And yet, she couldn't look into that wounded face and tell her that there were things to be afraid of down here. She needed to take care of her. It was her turn to protect this woman.

But as she cast her psychic eye out again, searching for dangers, she realized that something was wrong.

The space around them was broken somehow.

She felt something like this before, too, back when she was still trying to escape the thing with too many heads. The space ahead of her was fractured and disjointed. She remembered distinctly feeling as if continuing might cause her to fall even deeper into the madness of the glass labyrinth, like standing on a sheet of thin ice…

And now they were right in the middle of that space.

"Oh no…" she sighed.

Then everything shattered.

Chapter 54

Wayne couldn't see or hear anything. The wind and rain and thunder and lightning had turned everything into a strobing and howling black and white blur punctuated with earth-shaking explosions and crackles of electricity. He crawled across the stone, splashing and shouting for Olivia, but he couldn't find her anywhere.

Where did she go? How could he have lost her?

He had to find her!

He didn't even know what happened. They were running through the storm, trying to reach the other side before they could be struck by lightning. Then she suddenly turned and shoved him backward. But it wasn't *her* that sent him flying backward like that. She couldn't muster that kind of force, even on an adrenaline high.

Something hit them. Something powerful.

It felt like a bomb went off. He was aware of landing hard on his back, of water rushing up his nose, of a strange stinging sensation running up and down his limbs. He didn't think it was lightning. He didn't know what being struck felt like, so maybe he was wrong, but it felt much more *physical*. More like being hit by a truck.

And Olivia was *between* him and whatever it was! Where did she go? Was she hurt?

He couldn't lose her!

He stumbled to his feet and forced his eyes open into the pounding rain, trying hard to see through the hazy chaos.

A bolt of lightning split the sky, silhouetting the strange, tiered structure looming ahead of him. It struck him as bizarre the first time he saw it. It didn't go with anything else here in this bleak, featureless world. It looked out of place. Like the sentinels had grown bored one day and decided to add a decoration to the top of one of their blocky creations. If it was always intended for them to pass this way, he'd reasoned, then perhaps they'd meant for it to act as a lightning rod, hopefully preventing them from being struck dead in this raging storm. But of course, he had no way to know the intentions of an ancient race of faceless, psychic giants. It could have a purpose far beyond his understanding.

And right now, he could care less about the structure. He was searching for his fiancée. She had to be here somewhere. But *where?*

Another lightning bolt exploded overhead, blinding him.

That structure… She wouldn't have gone *into* it, would she? He couldn't imagine her doing such a thing on purpose. It was far too dangerous. But if she were stumbling around blind…if she didn't realize which way she was going…

He splashed toward it, shielding his face, needing to be sure.

But something moved across his line of vision in the flickering light of the surrounding storm, startling him and freezing him in his tracks. An odd, rippling sort of shape seemed to flutter through the air in front of him. But there was nothing there. There was only stone and water everywhere he looked.

Was it only the wind and rain in his eyes?

It didn't matter. He had to look for Olivia. He had to find her. He had to make sure she wasn't hurt. That was the only thought in his panicked brain that mattered.

The wind shifted again and pummeled him from the front, blinding him, but he wouldn't be stopped. He stumbled forward again, his arms crossed in front of his face.

Was that her voice just now? A shout? A cry for help, perhaps?

Was he getting closer to her?

He peered between his upraised arms and again glimpsed that strange shimmer. Closer this time. As if the rain itself had begun to move of its own will.

What the hell *was* that?

And was it getting closer?

Again, he heard a cry carried on the wind. He was certain it was her voice this time! But which direction was it coming from? Where was she?

Then she was there. Familiar arms encircled him. A warm body pressed against his back. A wonderfully familiar voice cried out his name.

But he had no time to relish the sensation.

She yanked him backward with all her strength, surprising him. He stumbled, trying to maintain his balance, only to step on her foot in the process. Afraid of hurting her, he jerked his weight the other way, but lost his balance.

He fell backward, onto her. Cold water splashed up around them.

It was in that startling instant that lighting exploded overhead, lighting up the rooftop, and he saw that strange shimmer sweep through the air above him, barely missing him.

It was no shimmer, he realized. It was a void in the downpour, a shape only visible in the way it blocked the blowing rain.

That was what hit them, he realized.

And like a fool, he was stumbling straight toward it.

That structure…those columns… It was no decoration. It was a *cage*. And there was something terrible inside it.

(*Beware the prisoner.*)

Was that what the voice was talking about back there? Was *this* the "prisoner"?

Olivia was already getting to her feet, still tugging at him. What was he doing? He didn't have time to stop and try processing any of this weirdness. He'd found her. Or rather, *she'd* found *him*. He hadn't actually managed to be of any use, truthfully. But she was with him now and that was all that mattered. Now he had to focus on keeping her safe. And if he was going to do that, he needed to be moving. He shook it off and stood up, letting her lead him away.

She was shouting something at him, but he couldn't hear her over the storm. It was probably something along the lines of, "Come on!" or, "Hurry!" or maybe just, "Move your dumb ass!"

He doubted that she could see any better than him in this punishing rain. It was her psychic alarm. She must've sensed the danger they were heading toward. That was why she shoved him backward. And it was probably how she was able to find him first. It probably told her he was in danger.

This was all so blasted complicated!

Water splashed over them as something huge slammed against the stone behind them, wrenching a startled scream from Olivia.

Whatever was in that cage might be trapped inside it, but it had a long reach. And it wasn't going to let them go so easily.

He wanted to do something. He needed to protect her. But he couldn't even see! What was he supposed to do?

Meanwhile, she was clinging to his hand, pulling him along, steering him to the left now.

He felt an ominous crackle in the air around him. Everything felt charged. Then there was another blinding flash. Another deafening boom. The world seemed to tremble beneath their feet.

This was insane. Was this part of the Keeper's plan, too? A giant, invisible monster in a goddamned *hurricane*? Five years ago, during the hours that he spent as one of the dearly departed, everyone told him that the Keeper informed them that they would face the sentinel's "judgment," that what they did on that burning mountain would determine the future of all mankind. Was this like that, too? Was all of this just some sort of trial? Even though the little freak was supposed to already know everything that was going to happen?

Nothing about any of this made any sense.

Olivia stopped suddenly and threw her weight against him, knocking him back. A second later, something slammed into the water in front of them.

He wiped at his face and opened his eyes in time to see that strange, watery shimmer rising upward. For just an instant, he could almost see it. It was like a great, muscular tentacle, and yet nothing at all like the fabled images of monsters like the kraken or even Lovecraft's madness-inducing eldritch horror, Cthulhu.

Instead of great, toothy suction cups on the undersides, there were strange, squirming things protruding from every inch of it, like a great, slimy eel covered in thousands of bloodsucking leeches. (Though he couldn't for the life of him figure out why his mind would conjure something so skin-crawlingly vile to compare it to.)

Before he could process it any further, Olivia yanked hard on his hand, leading him forward again, faster now, struggling against the resistance of the water.

It didn't even feel cold, he realized. His brain was too distracted to notice the temperature. His adrenaline was pumping. And there was nothing he could do. He couldn't see. He couldn't hear. If not for Olivia, he'd have been crushed under one of those foul arms by now. He was little more than a burden for her to bear. If something happened to her on this rooftop, it would be his fault for slowing her down.

He caught a glimpse of something moving ahead of them in another flash of lightning. A familiar shimmer. A twist in the natural flow of the blowing rain. A void where there shouldn't be one.

What is that thing? he wondered.

Something strange happened then. As if in answer, everything seemed to slow down. The din of the storm faded into an eerie silence. Waterdrops slowed to a crawl.

He was aware of a great pain blossoming deep inside his head, like a tiny explosion in the middle of his brain, sending shockwaves outward.

Stone. Water. Air. And flesh. All of them turning together like gears inside a clock. Ticking. Spinning. Spiraling. Working.

He squeezed his eyes shut against the pain, yet he continued to see. In fact, he saw everything, in every direction at once.

The city. The storm. The labyrinth. And consciousness. A machine like nothing he'd ever imagined before, all of it perfectly aligned, perfectly synced, perfectly timed.

It was eerily familiar, this sensation of seeing in every direction while seeing nothing at all, of growing deaf to the cacophony of the world yet able to hear the whispers of the true universe lying just beneath it.

This was what it was like when he was dead.

But how was he able to see like this now? He couldn't have died again. Could he?

He turned his attention to the structure containing the "prisoner" and found that he could see it there. It was enormous...yet it was at the same time little more than a whisper of a thing... It had no color, and yet there was a bizarre quality that he could only describe as iridescent. It was like a drawing spread across the thinnest of tissue papers and then folded over and over, its lines overlapping in confounding ways that made it impossible to see what the original image was. It was horrific. Nightmarish, even. And yet there was something oddly beautiful about it. Something inside it possessed the most graceful sort of flutter that radiated from its very core, turning those deadly and grotesque arms into something that twinkled like Christmas lights in a snowstorm.

That creature... No. Not a creature at all. It wasn't alive. Nor was it a spirit. It was a part of the other world. An *unnatural entity*. Or, more precisely he somehow understood, a *fragment* of an unnatural entity. Just a portion of one, split apart from the rest of itself and imprisoned here. It was as much a part of the machine as he and Olivia were. All three of them, along with every atom of the stone and the water and the lightning and the wind, made up everything that the Keeper designed. And what was going on right now was no test, no trial. This wasn't simple survival. There was something about the three of them being in this place at the same time, something about the energy and the emotions and the will of each of them, that was integral to the inner workings of the sentinels' great and unfathomable machine.

But...*how* did he know this? How was he seeing what he was seeing right now?

His attention was drawn forward. The doorway. The open passage leading into the next tower. The exit Olivia was desperately guiding him toward while avoiding those great, slamming tentacles.

Someone was there, he realized. An impossibly tall form

stood in front of it, facing him. A feminine form, but with no hair, no eyes, no ears. With only a faint bump of a nose and a mere slit of a mouth.

The Sentinel Queen. Naked and strange, monstrous, yet strangely lovely. She was reaching toward him, beckoning him.

But the Sentinel Queen was dead. And this was the City Beyond Memory, on the other side of an impassible wall. Even her spirit shouldn't be here...

"Find me," her unnatural voice whispered into his brain.

Then, as quickly as it came upon him, it all vanished. Lightning flashed. Thunder crashed. The wind howled and the rain pelted him. The prisoner pounded the earth behind them, splashing water high into the air. Olivia cried out, terrified.

He stumbled a little at the abrupt change from slow motion to real time, but managed somehow to stay on his feet.

"What the hell was that?" he gasped, but the storm swept away his voice even as it passed his lips.

Olivia ran toward the doorway, letting her psychic mind guide her through the blinding storm. It was directly ahead of them. He glimpsed it in the strobe of the lightning. And there was no Sentinel Queen standing in front of it, living or spectral. Had he only imagined it? Was that all just some kind of bizarre hallucination?

They were almost there.

Olivia turned and grabbed his shirt with both fists, then yanked him downward. ("Get down!" he understood.)

He didn't hesitate. He threw himself to the ground atop her. An instant later, something dreadful swept through the air directly over them, missing them by bare inches.

He didn't have time to feel relieved. She was already shoving at him, shouting for him to get moving. He scrambled back to his feet. Before he could remember which way they were going, she had his hand and was pulling him forward again.

"Find me," he heard the Sentinel Queen say again as they splashed forward.

But how was he supposed to find someone who was dead? And in another universe?

No. There was no way the Sentinel Queen would still be calling out to him. It was a trick of some kind. Maybe the prisoner was getting into his head, trying to distract him. He should ignore it.

The doorway was right there. He could see it through the blowing rain now that they were closer to the wall and more shielded from the wind.

He tightened his grip on her hand and pushed himself to go faster.

Then they were in the next passage and the storm died to a bare whisper of its former fury around them.

Olivia didn't stop, however. She kept pushing forward, eager to be as far from that rooftop as possible.

And he didn't argue with her.

Chapter 55

The floor of the massive chamber sloped downward for several hundred feet, leading them deeper and deeper into the empty darkness. Brandy kept looking back the way they came, wondering how many levels they'd already descended.

Was this right? Were they supposed to be going down? She thought Gina said they needed to go up.

Ahead of them, a third sentinel emerged from the darkness, identical to the first two.

What was it with these guys? What were they trying to tell them?

"This feels kind of familiar," observed Albert.

"Does it?" She stared at the third sentinel as they approached it, those outstretched arms and that tiptoeing sort of stride. She was fairly sure she hadn't seen one posed like that before.

"Can't put my finger on it, though."

Again, she looked back over her shoulder. She hated the claustrophobic feel of those cramped passageways, but she found that she liked these huge, open spaces even less. There was something unsettling about not being able to see what was around them. Even the ceiling was lost in darkness. Anything could be lurking in here, just out of sight, watching their every move.

They walked past the sentinel. He was so ridiculously tall that they passed right under his outstretched arm. They didn't even have to duck.

She had to keep reminding herself that those things were real once. They weren't always just statues. They were a living race of beings, the ones responsible for building all these places, apparently. According to Lucianna they all died out, disappearing sometime around the last cycle. But until five years ago, there was still one out there. Or at least a hybrid of one.

The Sentinel Queen. Her bizarre physiology was proof enough that the sentinels were real. She had the same elongated form, the same lack of facial features, even the same oversized genitals (although female instead of male, obviously).

Albert said that Lucas Kneede murdered her last son, poisoned him somehow, which in turn for some reason caused her own time to run out, essentially killing her, too. He called her "the Mother" and it was almost as if she were somehow tied to that title, that she ceased to exist the moment she no longer had any children left.

It was all very sad. And she couldn't help wondering if things might've been different if Kneede hadn't interfered. Would she have somehow escaped the fall of the first temple? Would she still be helping them today if she were still out there?

"What's that?" asked Albert, snapping her back to attention. She was staring down at the sloped floor ahead of her, lost in thought, and her light was aimed there instead of illuminating where they were going.

She lifted the light to reveal two more statues, one on the left and one on the right. But they weren't sentinels. They were something far more crude. They looked less like perfectly carved figures than roughly shaped Playdough. "Those are like the ones back in Mysteria," she realized as they approached.

They looked like two cartoonish men with their backs turned to them, crouched down on all fours. They had no individual fingers or toes at the ends of their long arms and legs and their faces were comprised of only a single, gaping mouth, from which poured a very familiar brownish-yellow substance. It was drizzling from those lipless mouths and into a shallow groove on the floor that carried it away into the darkness ahead.

Albert knelt down beside the one on the right and examined it. He even reached out and dipped the tip of his finger into the flowing ooze, which seemed quite unnecessary to her, but whatever. "Ichor…"

Brandy wrinkled her nose at it. "Emphasis on the 'ick.' That stuff looks *so* nasty."

It was the stuff that appeared whenever he reached inside those statues with Yggdrasil's Seed and transported them to the Ruin. It was Kneede who first called it that and explained that it was some kind of pan-dimensional goop from "beyond the boundaries of all worlds." It was apparently what connected the different realities within the hotel, or something. And it was also covering the floor within the tunnel the carriage traveled through, suggesting that it probably also helped to transport them safely across the deadly Wood to the distant Denselands.

Did that mean there was another side to this place, too? And which side were they on? Back in Mysteria, ichor only flowed from the statues on the ruined side. Did that mean there was a *nice* version of this place they hadn't seen yet?

Not that it mattered, she supposed. They didn't have the key anymore. She lost the seed when they passed through that enormous wall.

Albert wiped his fingers on his shorts and examined the groove that the ichor was flowing through. Psychic or not, she knew him well enough by now to practically read his mind. Her own thoughts on that stuff were something along the lines of "ew gross" and that was pretty much it, but *he* wanted to know more. That was who he was. It was his nature to be curious. And right now he was wondering why it was here, what it was for and, most of all, where it was flowing.

He stood up and continued onward without speaking.

She didn't ask any questions. Nor did she protest. She didn't particularly want to have anything to do with that foul-looking stuff, but he wasn't wrong. They wouldn't escape this labyrinth by avoiding things like this. They needed to examine everything or they'd risk missing their chance to finish this awful business and go home.

Besides, according to Kneede, that stuff had something to do with transporting them to different places, meaning that—just maybe—it was their ticket to leaving this fucking labyrinth.

But she still didn't like it.

She glanced back once more, still paranoid about the darkness at their backs and all the imagined horrors that might be lurking unseen there, and followed after him, illuminating the way with the flashlight.

Ahead of them, those narrow grooves grew wider and deeper, despite the fact that there was only a drizzle of that sludge flowing through it. Were they going to encounter more of those freaky oozing statues?

But Albert stopped walking as the floor in front of them changed. The grooves yawned open, spreading out on either side of the path ahead of them, revealing a great pool of ichor waiting at the bottom of the slope. The path they were following continued several yards farther, creating a raised path, but then it, too, dipped beneath the surface. Everything beyond that, for as far as she could see, was submerged.

"That's a *lot* of ick…" she breathed.

"I knew I'd seen this stuff before," said Albert. "There was a room just like this in the first temple."

"Was there?" She didn't remember it.

"There were three rooms," he recalled. "One with this stuff. One with water. And one with mud."

"Oh yeah!" The mud chamber. "That was *really* fucking gross." They'd had to wade through that foul, stinking sludge butt naked. It was awful. She had that stuff *everywhere*. "I never saw the other two rooms," she realized. She and Nicole sat down and took a break while Albert and Wayne examined the three choices laid before them. But she remembered them talking about it. "That was *this* stuff?"

"It's also why those sentinels seemed familiar," he added, gesturing forward.

She shined her light out into the room ahead of them. There was a fourth statue standing out in the sludge, just within the beam's reach, submerged to its thighs in ichor.

"They're posed differently, but they're just like the ones that were 'walking' off into each of those rooms. They were telling us that we were supposed to go one of those ways, but not *which* way."

She nodded. She remembered now. It wasn't anything the sentinels showed them that made them choose the mud. It was all the dirt inside the box. Albert realized that everything was so clean in the temple, yet the box's contents were filthy, meaning that someone had included a hunk of dried mud that had broken apart while he was still trying to figure out how to open it. And now that she was thinking about it, that weird pose they were all making... It sort of looked like they were wading through deep water, treading along the bottom on their toes like that, using their arms to stay afloat.

Or something considerably *ickier* than water...

She tipped her head to one side as she considered the sentinel. "But these guys are facing the wrong way, aren't they?"

"I'm thinking it still means the same thing. There's only one choice this time."

She made a face at this. "What do you mean, 'one choice'? There's no way I'm going in there!"

He turned and looked at her. "Seriously?"

"*Yes*, seriously. What the fuck?"

"This is *way* less gross than that mud."

"I'm not doing *that* again, either."

"It doesn't even smell like anything."

"I don't care! We don't even really know what that stuff is! Last time you touched it, we ended up in that nightmare hotel! What if it sends us somewhere a hundred times worse this time?"

"What if it sends us right where we're supposed to be?"

"I'm not touching that shit!"

Albert stared at her for a moment, but said nothing more. He simply turned and looked out over the sludge-filled chamber.

She hated when he did that. He wasn't going to start a fight with her over something like this. He knew he was asking a lot. But he wasn't turning back, either, meaning he really felt like they should be continuing forward. Now he was just lingering there, trying to decide what to do, probably contemplating whether he should leave her here and check it out himself, which also wasn't happening. They only had one light, after all, and the last thing she wanted was for them to get separated again.

She knew she was being stubborn. And she also knew he was being very patient with her. He never raised his voice. He was speaking calmly the whole time. She was the one who was getting riled up.

How did *she* always end up being the bad guy in these situations?

He sighed and looked back the way they came. "Sentinels..." he muttered. "If anything's going to show us how to get out of here, it's them. That's their whole job."

She wanted to tell him that *these* sentinels were *morons* if they thought she was just going to follow them out into that gross sludge, but she bit her tongue. He wasn't wrong, after all. And she could almost read his thoughts. They hadn't seen a sentinel since the anxiety room. Did she really want to risk going back and having to deal with one of those instead, just because she was squeamish about a little goo?

"Wait..." said Albert, his eyes narrowing as he stared into the gloom behind her. "What's—" He stumbled backward, a look of surprise on his face, and she twirled to shine the light at whatever he was looking at.

But there was nothing there.

When she turned to ask him what was wrong, it was just in time to see him knocked off his feet and shoved backward into the ichor.

Chapter 56

Everett realized that he wasn't, in fact, falling. It was more like *flying*. Because there was no "down" in this directionless world. And there was nothing for him to land on. He wasn't traveling in the same sense that he was used to moving. This was *sideways* traveling. But not sideways as in *laterally*, like some kind of crab. Not sideways *through* space, but *between* it, like when he fell through the cracks in the nightmarish upside-down city to land in that glittering forest. He was speeding through some kind of pathway, passing through the gossamer fabrics that divided worlds such as these.

It wasn't something he should have been capable of doing, he realized. As a mere human, he should have been trapped in that nowhere place forever, unable to go anywhere, languishing until he eventually dropped dead. Either he possessed abilities he wasn't aware of or—far more likely—this was all Alice. She was lending him some of her mysterious spiritual power, making the impossible possible.

It was a completely different sensation from being adrift in the void. This was an exhilarating feeling, like being on a rollercoaster. And while it was kind of hard to think clearly while hurtling through not-space at what felt like warp-speed, he wasn't completely lost in himself like he was in that dreadful emptiness. He remained aware of who he was and what he wanted, with no real danger of losing his grip on his goal. And he was most certainly moving toward that goal.

It was there. He could feel it. The City Beyond Memory, looming ahead of him. He couldn't see it. He couldn't tell how far away it was or how soon he'd reach it, but he knew it was there. He was racing toward it. It was only a matter of time. Then he'd be able to search for his friends.

But a fresh wave of invading thoughts distracted him from this experience. He blinked into the darkness as he struggled to piece it together. "What decision?" he asked.

But Alice didn't explain it to him. She merely left him with that one thought weighing on his brain.

He had a decision to make.

But…what kind of decision? Concerning what? What were his choices? Was this path he was speeding along going to diverge? Was he going to have to choose the right way on the fly?

That didn't seem right. He'd already determined that he was heading straight for it. In fact, he could almost see it there ahead of him. A great, sprawling labyrinth blooming from the haze inside his mind. Was it even bigger than he remembered? It was entirely contained within those gigantic stone walls and yet it seemed to go on forever. Not merely outward, and not even merely upward through those countless stone towers, but far deeper into the earth than he ever imagined.

Wait… How was he supposed to find *anyone* in a place that size?

It was like being dropped in the middle of a vast wilderness with no instructions. He could wander for *weeks* and never encounter another soul in a place that size. Maybe even *years*.

But almost as quickly as the thought crossed his mind, Alice urged him to look closer.

Even from this distance, he could sense them. A mere handful of areas within the endless stone passageways that seemed almost to glow, as if through thermal goggles.

Those were the places where people were!

He couldn't tell who was who. He couldn't even tell how many people were in each spot. But he knew all the places where people were. All the other travelers like him. Wayne and Olivia were down there somewhere. And Andrea and Violet. And the people who arrived here with each of them, too. And that weird Austin guy from the train. They were all down there. He could see those particular locations. And by focusing his attention on any one of them, he could be sure he landed close by. He wouldn't have to be alone anymore!

(Decision.)

Right... He'd forgotten. He still had a decision to make. And now he understood what it was Alice wanted him to decide. He needed to choose which of those human presences he wanted to land near.

Did it really matter, though? Everyone he'd met so far was so nice. And even if he found someone new, it was going to be a friend of someone he *did* know. It was a total win-win. Wasn't it?

But Alice's message wormed itself through his brain. A dire warning. Not all was well in the labyrinth. More than one of them were in danger.

It was a sobering realization. He cleared his head and looked again. He could see them all, but they weren't all the same. Not everyone was actually *in* the city. Some of them had somehow slipped outside the stone, just as he'd done. And they didn't have magical, self-aware dolls to help them get back.

Two in particular seemed to be glowing especially bright.

Something bad was happening down there. They needed his help.

That was where he needed to be!

Except...he couldn't choose both of them. How was he supposed to decide? Who should he choose? He didn't even know who they were! If he could tell that one was Wayne and one was Olivia, for example, he'd choose Olivia in a heartbeat. Wayne would be angry with him if he didn't. And he was much more confident that Wayne could hold his own. But it was going to be a shot in the dark. What if he chose wrong? What if someone died because he messed up?

Time was running out. He was approaching the boundary of the city.

He'd forgotten that he was still blind and deaf in this nowhere nothingness. So intensely was he focused on the dilemma in front of him that he was all but convinced that he was looking at the City Beyond Memory with his own eyes and listening to the screaming of the wind and the thunder as he plummeted toward the storm.

What did he do?

It was one or the other. The two brightest burning presences.

He forced himself to stop thinking. He closed his eyes and pushed everything from his mind.

Just like that, he was lost again in silent, windless darkness, adrift in a peaceful emptiness.

That was better.

This was what he needed.

Now there were only the two choices.

He could sense familiar faces. Kind words. Gentle souls. He knew both of them. He'd met them. That much became clear. He was about to be reunited with someone he'd traveled with.

But who?

He reached out with his hand, letting it guide him.

"This one."

Chapter 57

The awful thing didn't wander off. Nor did it exactly just disappear. Erin couldn't really explain it, but it just sort of…wasn't there anymore. There was no transition that she could recall between then and now, and yet she was sure she didn't black out or anything. It was as if the very concept of chronology had taken a vacation from these corridors, erasing all notion of before and after.

Was that a ghost thing, she wondered. Or just a thing with scary, incomprehensible murk monsters?

The true universe was so confusing.

And it didn't end with that monster, either. Even when she was scared out of her mind, she couldn't stop thinking for some reason about Breastbroke. Those strange, overgrown acres of wilderness where shadowy things prowled just beyond her vision and crows gathered in mass murders and unimaginable secrets lay hidden for ages untold.

And those awful things in the forgotten cemetery…

God, what a fright!

But it wasn't just that she was remembering those places. That day felt weirdly connected to this moment. It made no sense, but ever since she manifested in this corridor, it felt almost as if she'd been shifting back and forth between that day and this one.

It sounded ridiculous, of course. That all happened more than two years ago. And yet the memory felt so fresh. Did it have something to do with this human body she made for herself? Time wasn't constant when it came to the Denselands *or* to the dead. Maybe there was a similar effect with consciousness. Maybe her very memories had been somehow compacted.

But she could only make wild guesses. She wasn't smart enough to understand this kind of weirdness.

Slowly, still terrified that the thing might not really be gone, she turned and looked behind her. It was pointless, of course. There was nothing to see. It was still pitch black in this passage. But at the same time, she could somehow sense those darkling shapes wafting around her, drifting through the darkness, brushing past her in that dreamlike way.

The thing was gone, wandered off to some other murky area.

She took a shaky breath and tried to remember if it was the first one or if she'd been breathing this whole time. (Ordinary things like breathing shouldn't feel so strange.) Then she continued forward, still trembling with that desperate fear that she felt so strongly, both just now and two years ago.

It was such an eerie parallel, this identical, dreadful terror, the sensation that she was standing before something truly evil.

Was that all this was? A reminder?

No. She could actually *feel* the scratches in her arms and legs where those thorns clawed at her. There was a pain in her shin where she tripped over that stone. Her legs were aching from trekking through that overgrown wilderness in spite of the fact that she'd been standing still this whole time.

She could almost *smell* the forest around her.

The deafening sound of those crows cawing… Was that only inside her head? Or was it actually echoing through this empty corridor?

"I'll see you again," whispered a strangely familiar voice from behind her, making her jump. But there was no one there.

Was it only a memory of the events that occurred in that forest that day?

A dreadful feeling was bubbling up deep inside her. Something that was supposed to stay forgotten was worming its way upward. Her head was filled with the chaotic cawing of crows and a desperate need to run. It wasn't safe here. They were right behind her!

She wasn't going to make it!

Chapter 58

Violet couldn't breathe.

Her head was pounding. Her chest ached for air. Her throat was raw from screaming. And she was utterly exhausted.

How long had it been? Hours? Days?

The box was almost filled up with dirt, slowly covering her. It was in her mouth and nose. It burned her eyes. She kept squirming, shaking it off, clearing it away, but it was only slipping down, filling the space beneath her, until her face was pressed against the lid and there was nowhere left to go.

Worst of all, she could feel things crawling around in the dirt, making her skin crawl. Would she linger long enough before suffocating to feel the bugs begin to feast on her body?

This was so much worse than the devils and the boar-things, an entirely new kind of suffering that just went on and on and on until she felt as if she might go mad.

And what was going to happen when she finally died in this awful place? Would she just wake up in another nightmare? Again and again? Forever?

You've endured, whispered the other one. It was the first she'd spoken in what felt like a very long time. Violet had begun to believe that she'd abandoned her as a lost cause.

She tried to ask what she was talking about, but opening her mouth only let in more dirt.

She'd endured? Endured *what?* Everyone's worst nightmare? She was dying in here! She'd endured *nothing!*

And yet, she was beginning to realize that something had changed.

The stagnant air had thinned. She felt as if a great weight

were being lifted. Her body shivered as something shifted around her, something not quite physical, but not quite mental, either. Something that was both within her and without. Something that filled her mind with a strange, dizzying sensation.

Then the earth seemed to move beneath her. The dirt began to slide away, draining from around her like water down a drain.

Was she *sinking?*

She reached out with her aching hands, but felt no wood. Her fingers only sank into the shifting soil, as if she were sliding down an empty hole, being slowly swallowed by the earth

She let out a weary, strangled cry, afraid of whatever new hell she was descending into.

She was moving faster now, not just sinking but sliding. *Falling.* Deeper and deeper into the earth, caught in a landslide of shifting soil, faster and faster.

She wanted to scream, but her face was covered in dirt. She couldn't even breathe.

What was happening now?

Then everything changed again. The dirt was falling away from her. Fresh air filled her lungs.

"There you are!"

She blinked hard, trying to clear the dirt from her eyes, but someone was already wiping it away for her, gentle hands brushing her face, a puff of cool breath blowing over her, clearing away the remaining particles. "What's happening?" she sputtered, the taste of it still strong on her tongue.

"Take it easy. I've got you."

Finally, she looked up to find a familiar face beaming at her with that big, goofy grin. "Everett...?"

He was kneeling down, holding her against him, supporting her.

"Sorry I took so long. I got a little lost."

She reached up with her dirty fingers and touched his face. Those big, excited eyes. That messy hair. There was no sign of that stretched mask covering something dark and melty and horrible. The hands gripping her didn't bubble or drip or smoke. And his voice didn't have an unnatural gurgle hidden beneath it.

"It's you…" she gasped, fresh tears welling up in her eyes.

He looked confused, but he kept grinning. "Yep. It's me. Who else would it be?"

She hooked her fingers around the back of his neck and thrust herself at him, kissing him.

Chapter 59

Corey let out a great gasp and toppled backward onto the stone floor.

An intense surge of energy had just flashed through the contacts, up his arm and seemingly right into his very brain.

Violet!

He had no idea what just happened, but she was there! For the first time since they were separated, he could feel her distinct presence!

It was her and someone he didn't recognize. The twelfth party member. The one Olivia called Everett, he deduced. They were both still safe. And they were together! Violet wasn't alone out there.

Thank God!

He closed his eyes and lay there, feeling his heart racing with relief. He'd begun to fear the worst.

"What can possibly be wrong with you?" grumbled Austin.

"Taking a break," He replied. "Piss off."

"Why do you need a break? You've barely been working."

He didn't open his eyes. He didn't sit up. He didn't even look at him. He merely lifted one bloodstained hand and gave him the finger.

"Childish," Austin muttered in response.

Corey ignored him. He couldn't be happier that Violet was still safe. But he also couldn't ignore the other side of the coin.

If Violet and Everett were safe...then the one Gina and Nicole were grieving was either Andrea or Keith.

He didn't like that.

No one would blame him for feeling relieved that Violet

was still out there somewhere, but he naturally felt a great sense of guilt over that relief. He remembered meeting Andrea back in All Trails Crossing, when she fell out of the sky, a random stranger with unnatural, bright red hair and all those piercings, but a sweet and cheerful and chatty personality. And he remembered meeting Keith, too, back at the thorn gate, traveling with Wayne and Olivia, all busted up and bloody but still pushing onward in spite of it. And he didn't take any of Austin's nonsense when he was being rude to Olivia.

He wouldn't want to choose between them. He wanted them both to come back safe.

But he never had a choice in any of this. Not from the beginning.

He opened his eyes and stared up at the stone ceiling. He didn't really know anything. Maybe he was wrong somehow and things weren't as they seemed. Maybe Andrea and Keith were both fine and Albert and Brandy's creepy cat lady lied to them about two of them not making it out alive.

Or maybe he wasn't really feeling what he thought he was feeling. Maybe being able to sense everyone else's emotions was merely some kind of hallucination. What did he really know?

Maybe everything wasn't all it seemed to be. Maybe *nothing* was what it seemed to be.

(*I can't explain something to you that you have no way of understanding.*)

He turned and looked at Austin. He stared at him for a moment, letting these new thoughts swirl around in his brain, piecing together something new.

The way he perceived the workings of this stone temple as some kind of ancient supercomputer... If his brain could take concepts like those and simplify them into something he was capable of understanding, then it stood to reason that it was a universal trait for humans, and not limited to the things hidden within these stone walls. Perhaps the more complex something was, the more his brain automatically simplified it for him.

And Austin was *highly* complex...

(*There are components of my body that exist outside the range of your human senses and beyond your ability to understand.*)

He lifted the strands he was holding between his bloodied fingers and looked closely at them. An artificial human being powered entirely by these *strings*…

(*If you can imagine me as a marionette dancing on a stage, you might be able to comprehend a fraction of my whole. Everyone sees the puppet. You, with your uniquely ingrained knowledge, can glimpse the strings, telling you there's something more. But what you can't see is the puppeteer pulling those strings. The greater part of me is hidden, even from you.*)

He'd dismissed it as lost physics or even as some kind of nanotechnology, too small for him to see. But what if it was even stranger than that? What if he simply couldn't perceive what the real workings inside that bisected body looked like?

And if he couldn't even perceive his actual form…was it possible he couldn't perceive *anything*? Was everything he witnessed in this place a mere construct of his brain, masking whatever was really here?

He turned his gaze back to Austin as a new thought popped into his head. What if the entire reason their brains translated these things wasn't simply for comprehension, but for *protection*? What if seeing and hearing such things would prove so utterly alien that it could drive a person mad? Not unlike all those Lovecraft stories about eldritch horrors? In that light, Austin would be something far scarier than any kind of lost technology.

"Do you intend on being useless all day?" snapped Austin.

He didn't reply. He didn't even stop staring at him. He sat there a moment, letting those fascinating thoughts simmer.

"Get to work," he grumbled.

Corey reached out and tugged at one of the strings. Immediately, Austin's dead arm jerked back, smacking his forehead.

"That was immature."

With a satisfied smirk, he turned and stared up at the ceiling again. But his mind kept churning through these fascinating thoughts.

Perceptions versus reality… What was his human brain preventing him from seeing? What secrets of the universe might be right in front of him if only he could comprehend it all?

But even if nothing else was as he perceived it, he found himself certain that he wasn't imagining being able to feel the presences of his companions out there. It wasn't just an illusion when he felt Violet return to the labyrinth.

She was there.

And she was safe. For now.

He should get back to work and see what else the strings revealed to him.

But not just yet. He was going to lie here a minute or two more, pondering these fascinating thoughts and basking in the relief of knowing that Violet was still out there somewhere. And in the knowledge that he was annoying the rude artificial man. He was especially enjoying that little detail.

Chapter 60

Nicole couldn't remember where she was. Everything was all jumbled together. The wedding. Hotdog Creep. Tristesse Lane. It was all mixed up and blurred like the lingering images of fitful dreams in the morning. Andrea. And Gina. Where were they? And Brandy and Albert? And Keith?

Keith!

She blinked hard, confused. But when she opened her eyes, nothing she saw made any sense.

She was standing before an enormous black gate, staring through long-rusted bars at a long, earthen path leading to an ominous structure jutting high into a sky that was somehow both pitch-black and aglow with strange light.

She was naked and she was covered in black filth. The air was heavy and sickly and foul. And she was weary and weak. Her body ached. Her mouth was parched. How long had it been since she ate or drank anything? How long since she rested?

Behind her stretched a black eternity, a hellish sea of foul sludge churning with things too monstrous to call monsters.

Memories flashed through her mind. Nightmares too numerous to count. Horrors too terrible to recall.

No...

Not here...

Not again...

She couldn't bear to do it again!

She wanted to scream, but the noxious air prevented her from filling her lungs enough without choking her. She could only manage a sickly cough that burned her throat and sent bolts of pain shooting through her ribs.

"I'm here. I've got you."

She struggled to catch her breath, confused.

"Please be okay," worried Gina.

Nicole blinked back her tears and coughed again. The burning in her throat and lungs was gone. She was sitting slumped on the floor and Gina was clinging to her, keeping her from falling over. "What happened?" she gasped, looking down at herself. She was no longer naked or covered in that foul, black filth, although she still had those gross black smears from the exploding monster with all those heads. And for some reason her bra had come undone and was half-off. Her legs and feet were sore from so much walking, but that overwhelming weariness was gone. She couldn't even remember why she felt so weary... What was she doing back there? And where was that place? Why did it fill her with such overwhelming emotions?

"You passed out. When I tried to wake you up, it was like you started choking."

She rubbed at her irritated throat, the memory of that burning cough still lingering there. "Passed out?" She tried to remember what happened before that but everything was a blur. She remembered feeling worn out. She remembered feeling as if they weren't alone in here. And she felt as if she could almost remember Gina letting out a startled, "Oh no!" before everything faded into that nightmare...

"The glass broke," explained Gina, as if that made any sense whatsoever. There *was* no glass. Everything was still plain gray stone. Their surroundings still looked the same to her. "It was like falling through a rotten floor, except...without the falling. Or the floor."

Her head was spinning. She couldn't even begin to unpack that.

"Basically, we've slipped deeper into the glass labyrinth. I'm not sure yet if we're closer to where we need to be or farther from it. But I'm sure that it's probably going to get more dangerous now."

"Okay," she sighed, rubbing at her weary eyes. There didn't seem to be anything else *to* say. It wasn't as if she had the option of quitting. And it didn't seem like she was ever going to understand all this weirdness.

And what was with that dream just now? Something about a gate? It was already fading from her memory, leaving nothing but a lingering feeling of imposing dread. And even that was quickly melting away.

Another forgotten nightmare brought on by the terrors of five years ago? Like the ones she had about that fucking meadow?

"Can you get up?" asked Gina.

She nodded. "I'm good. Sorry to worry you."

"Don't be sorry. I don't mind."

Together, they rose to their feet. She felt a little unsteady for a moment, but Gina held tight to her arm, determined to look after her. She pressed her hip against the wall to steady herself and fixed her bra. "Any idea where we go from here?"

"No." She turned and looked at the wall in front of them. Nicole pointed her flashlight there, a mere reflex, before realizing that she wasn't looking *at* the wall, but rather *through* it, at whatever was beyond it. "But I didn't really know where we were going before, either, so…"

"Right. Fucking labyrinths."

"My first priority is to keep us away from anything that feels dangerous. But I still let us fall through the cracks back there. I'm sorry."

"Not your fault. You keep having to worry about me."

"It's fine."

"It's *not* fine," insisted Nicole. "This shit is *dangerous*."

"It's fine," she said again. "Really." She glanced back at her, an embarrassed expression eclipsing her usually sleepy features. "It helps. I feel like I can be a little braver if it means protecting you like you've protected me."

Nicole stared at her for a moment, surprised. "Okay," she replied at last, unsure what else to say. This woman was something else. She seemed so meek and timid, but she wasn't sure she'd ever met someone so strong. She just kept pushing through it all.

Gina turned and faced the darkness of the passage ahead of them. "This way," she decided. She gave her hand a gentle tug and they both started walking.

She felt safe with Gina, she realized. She wanted to stay with her. She didn't want to get lost in any more of those scary dreams.

But she realized that the dream was already forgotten. All that was left was a fleeting déjà vu sort of feeling...something only vaguely familiar...something that may or may not have once been a memory...

Chapter 61

"That was *awful!*" gasped Olivia. She was having trouble catching her breath and her heart wouldn't stop pounding. She couldn't tell whether her body was trembling more from the cold or from the terror of the ordeal they'd just endured.

"Yeah," agreed Wayne, sounding just as breathless as she was. He hadn't taken his eyes off the path behind them since they entered the passage. "But you did awesome out there. Saved my ass. *Lots* of times."

She was happy of that, of course. She couldn't bear the thought of anything happening to him. But she honestly had no idea how she managed to do anything. She could barely see her hands in front of her face in that tempest. Her psychic alarm simply started screaming at her and she reacted out of blind terror. Every move she made was a fear reflex against a new feeling of startling panic. She didn't know where she was or what she was doing at any given time. It felt like she was in one of those horror movies where the monsters just kept popping up at every turn and the panicked heroine just kept screaming and fleeing blindly in some other direction, overturning trashcans and bookshelves to slow down her pursuers until, at some point, she somehow simply managed to stumble out of danger for a moment.

She *never* wanted to experience anything like that ever again!

The passage leading away from that storm-drenched rooftop was very much like the one that led them to it in the first place, so much in fact that she kept worrying that she'd become turned around and gone back the way they came by mistake in spite of her psychic brain prodding her along. It was even curving like the other one, but to the right, exactly as if they were going back the way they came. But somehow she didn't think that was the case. She couldn't tell by looking, but it *felt* like they were still moving forward.

"You okay?" asked Wayne once he'd caught his breath and was thoroughly convinced that the thing outside wasn't going to come slithering through the passage behind them. "It didn't hurt you, did it?"

"I'll be fine," she assured him, though she *did* get thrown around a good amount. She was already pretty sore, but now her whole body was aching. The first attack hit her across the back and that was definitely going to bruise. She *always* bruised. And that was more than a little bump. It sent her rolling across the flooded rooftop. She was lucky she didn't crack any bones.

She *really* hoped all these marks were healed up before their wedding. She didn't want a single reminder of this awful journey in any of her precious photographs.

"What *was* that thing?" she asked, looking back over her shoulder. "I never really saw it."

"I'm pretty sure it was invisible. I could only see where it was blocking the rain."

"Seriously? An *invisible monster*?"

"I know, right?"

"How's *that* fair?"

"Well, it was mostly trapped in that big cage, so I guess that was *something*."

Cage? She recalled that stone structure in the middle of the rooftop back there. Was that what that was? And it was "mostly" trapped in there? So…that was just the thing reaching out and slapping at them? "I *hate* this place," she groaned.

Wayne chuckled a little at this. It was a comforting sound, that familiar chuckle. It reminded her of home. Cozy evenings snuggled up on the couch. Delicious meals shared at the table. Blissful nights snoozing in his arms.

She wanted so badly to go home. But with every step she took on this insane journey, she was finding it harder to believe that she was ever going to see home again.

Beneath her, the floor began sloping upward again. Just like in the last passage, the water receded and dry stone appeared from the constant gloom ahead. An improvement, certainly, but it did little to improve her *mood*. She was still soaked to the bone, after all. And there were plenty of horrors outside of the temple's waters to worry about.

The constant splashing of her footsteps was now replaced with the squelches and squeaks of her soaked shoes. They were going to attract every monster in the labyrinth. She was sure of it.

"I saw the Sentinel Queen back there," said Wayne.

So abrupt and bizarre was this casual reveal that she stopped walking and forgot entirely about the monsters. She turned and looked up at him, convinced that she must've misheard him. "What?"

"Yeah, I know. Not saying it was her. I was hit with some kind of weird, like…" He shook his head, struggling to find the right words to describe it. "I don't know. A vision, maybe? I don't think it was just a hallucination. It felt like someone was trying to communicate with me. I don't know how much of it was real, but for a few seconds, it felt like I could almost remember when I was dead."

She stared at him, letting this process. "So… Now I have to worry about the ghost of your ex, too?"

This caught *him* off guard. His face seemed to pucker. "What? No! How does—? Why would you call her that?"

"You told me you slept with her."

"I did *not!* She…" His face turned even more sour. She could almost see him struggling to avoid the word "raped." He didn't like that word, she knew. And understandably so. It was an icky word. And it wasn't quite how it happened. "Seduced" was a better word, but he didn't like that, either. One suggested that he was a helpless victim and the other that he was simply coerced. "She's *dead*," he argued instead. "She can't really be here. It was just some kind of illusion."

"*Erin's* dead. And *she's* most definitely here."

"That's different!"

"How's that different?"

"I don't know! But it is!"

She giggled. She couldn't help it. She didn't have Brandy's talent for keeping a straight face, even when she wasn't exhausted and shivering. "Relax. I'm just teasing you. I know what happened with her."

"It wasn't like I *wanted* to."

"We weren't even dating yet when that happened."

"Still…" he muttered.

"It's none of my business what kind of freaky women you were into back then."

"I wasn't 'into' her at all!"

"You're so cute when you're flustered," she informed him.

"No I'm not," he grumbled, making her giggle again.

She shined her light into the unknown ahead of them. It was only a brief distraction, but she already felt better. She didn't think anyone else in the world could be capable of making her feel better in a place like this. She always felt so *comfortable* around him. Even in a place like this, just being near him was so *natural*. That said, she had no intention of pushing the matter. It was something of a sore subject for him. And it wasn't really about the Sentinel Queen. It went farther back than that.

Once upon a time, he had another girlfriend, his high school sweetheart. But he made a mistake and it all fell apart.

She remembered when all this started up again, way back in Dunnen, when her psychic alarm went off for the first time since the Temple of the Blind and she made him turn off the road they were on, steering him down Main Street instead. That felt like so long ago. How many days had it been since that moment? But she recalled the way his gaze lingered on the family restaurant as they drove past. The one Gail used to work at.

He told her all about it, of course. He kept no secrets from her. He said that cheating never once even crossed his mind. And yet somehow he ended up in the arms of someone else. A girl named Claire, who was dating a friend of his at the time, even. For years he put up walls, refusing to get close to anyone, afraid that he'd only end up ruining everything again. He went through most of his college life avoiding people, scared to get close to anyone.

And that was also the reason he was so shaken by what happened with the Sentinel Queen that night. For the second time in his life, he lost control of his senses to a woman he had no particular romantic connection with. It reinforced his fear that he couldn't trust himself, that he was just some kind of heartless monster with no self-control.

He was even afraid of getting too close to *her* when they first came back from the temple. He kept asking if she was sure she really wanted to spend her time with someone like him, no matter how many times she told him she'd made up her mind. For a while, she was afraid he'd push her away, but somehow she broke through his defenses and made him hers.

But in spite of his past, she simply couldn't believe that he'd ever be untrue to her.

She knew it, deep in her heart.

No one could convince her otherwise.

And it remained true now. She trusted him with all her heart.

"She wasn't real," he said, though she couldn't tell if he was saying these words to reassure her or himself. "I can't say why, but I'm sure of it. That whole...*vision* or whatever it was... I think the point was for me to understand that everything in this temple is connected somehow. Every passage, every room, every wall, every monster. And every one of us. That was what I was thinking when it was happening. And maybe seeing her there like I did meant that even the first temple is somehow still connected, too, even though it's gone."

Everything connected... Every piece. Every detail. Something about that struck her as profoundly true, though she wasn't sure she was capable of fully understanding what it meant. Connected how? And why? For what purpose?

Ahead of them, the floor leveled out and then an intersection emerged from the darkness. The path they were on split, forking not into two, but *five*. She didn't remember seeing anything like this while making their way down to that dangerous rooftop, meaning this couldn't be the way they came. That was a relief. It would've been so easy to get turned around in the storm. And she didn't care at all for the thought of having to go back out in that dreadful weather.

She started on the right, shining her light down one passage, then the next, trying to feel which way was best, but Wayne pointed his light at the leftmost path before she'd finished examining the second one.

"There," he said. "That voice again."

"What'd it say?" She added her flashlight to his, turning her attention in that direction. She didn't feel any of that pervasive dread at the thought of going that way, which was always a good sign.

"Too faint to hear. But I could tell it was coming from that way."

She stood there a moment longer, visualizing walking down that passageway, making sure no unpleasant feelings wormed their way into her mind. "Okay," she said at last. "Let's try it."

"I hope this is what we're supposed to do," he sighed as they started walking again.

Her too. But at this point, she was finding herself more and more curious about just who this mysterious voice that only her fiancé could hear belonged to.

(*I saw the Sentinel Queen back there.*)

Was it possible for her to still be out there somewhere? In some form or another? Or was something deceiving him?

She tightened her grip on his arm and continued onward, wondering what more the labyrinth intended to throw at them.

Chapter 62

"Wait…" Albert squinted into the darkness. At first, he dismissed it as nothing more than the previous sentinel statue, but they'd walked farther than that. Something *else* was standing in the darkness, something that wasn't there before. "What's—"

The thing in the darkness rushed at him. A gray, featureless shape that was neither a sentinel nor those crude, ichor-spewing abominations, but something nightmarishly in-between. He stumbled backward, startled, as it sprinted into the light, revealing skin like wax paper stretched over lumpy bones and hair like mats of spiderwebs trailing behind it. It had no eyes or nose or ears. Instead, its face was taken up by a single gaping mouth filled with black, oozing teeth.

He managed enough lucidity in that moment to fear for Brandy, who was standing closer to the monster, but it ignored her and rushed straight at him, thrusting its bony hands into his chest and knocking him backward.

An instant later, he felt his bare back splash into the viscous ichor pool.

He heard Brandy cry out for him, but he was too dazed and panicked to respond. He struggled to sit up and scoot away, ready to fight the monstrous thing that was hovering over him.

But the wax paper monster was gone.

Dolly stood there instead, her blue eyes gleaming with evil delight. "Boo," she whispered. Then, with a deeply unpleasant giggle, she grasped his shoulders and shoved him down beneath the surface of the ichor, where darkness devoured everything.

Chapter 63

Brandy rushed after Albert, screaming for him, terrified. She didn't understand what happened. It looked as if something had attacked him, but there was nothing there. It was as if he simply became startled and threw himself backward into the ichor.

As she splashed into the crude pool, she saw him sit up and scurry backward, deeper into the chamber, away from her. Then he suddenly vanished beneath the surface as if something had grabbed him.

What was going on? Was he hurt? Was it another of those psychic predators?

Still clutching her flashlight, she waded out to where he vanished and then dropped to her hands and knees, searching for him.

Where'd he go? She couldn't see a thing through the ichor. It was too thick and murky. But it was barely knee-deep. She should be able to feel him down there somewhere. He was literally *right here*!

She crawled forward, splashing, crying out for him.

The feel of the ichor against her skin was cold and slimy and nauseating. It made her skin crawl. But none of that mattered right now. She had to find him. She had to get him out of there. They weren't supposed to get separated. She shouldn't have let go of his hand.

She didn't even understand what happened. What attacked him? And how could they defend themselves against it?

The pool was deeper the farther out she went. It was splashing up around her chin and her mouth, threatening to dirty her glasses, rendering her blind on top of everything else. She scrambled to her feet, but slipped and sat down hard in the foul ooze. She let out a frustrated cry and tried again.

"*Albert?*"

She plunged her arms into the ichor and felt something. A bit of cloth? His shorts? But when she lifted it out, she found that it was only one of his socks.

She cursed and threw it aside.

"*Albert?*" she cried again. Where was he? He couldn't have just disappeared.

Except, *of course* he could have. Wasn't that what just *kept* happening? Nicole disappeared. Gina disappeared. Andrea disappeared.

But not Albert. She couldn't stand the thought of it. She had to find him. She had to get him back!

She turned all the way around, searching for any sign of movement in the dull glow of the dirty flashlight.

Was it her fault? Did this happen because she was being a baby about entering this pool? They'd been clinging to each other for hours, determined not to let something exactly like this happen again, but she let go of him and let him get ahead of her, all because she didn't want to go near the ichor.

She let out a frustrated cry and splashed farther out into the pool. She called out his name, desperate to hear his voice again. But the chamber was silent.

No... He couldn't be gone! He was here somewhere! She just had to find him!

But...how long had he been under there now? Was he going to drown?

She was panicking. She couldn't breathe. Her heart was pounding and tears were welling up in her eyes.

She had to find him.

She had to...

Chapter 64

"You save a girl from being buried alive, she's apt to kiss you," said Violet as she shook the dirt from her hair, a grotesque reminder of the horror she'd just endured. "That's how it is. Don't read too much into it."

"Yeah," said Everett, nodding. He still looked dazed. "Totally."

Somehow, they were back inside the labyrinth. The *real* labyrinth, not the fake one with the bloody sky looming overhead and gruesome death lurking around every corner. They were in a small, square room with three passageways leading away from the middle of two of the walls and a single sentinel statue standing against the fourth in that stiff, default pose.

"Doesn't mean we're a couple or anything."

"Okay. Sure."

She probably shouldn't have done that. He was so young. There were *ten years* between them! And he was clearly inexperienced with that sort of thing. She didn't want to toy with his feelings or anything. She'd never been that kind of girl. In fact, she'd never really had much interest in dating at all. Most of the boys who came around bored her. But she couldn't help herself. It just sort of happened. She was so relieved to be out of that damned box. And so happy to find her way back to him and know that he was still safe. She was so worried about him out there on his own somewhere.

And she wasn't exactly in her right mind in that moment, either... Being buried alive was kind of a big deal.

It was strange. All that had happened, all the trauma she'd endured, and yet within minutes it had faded like the images from a bad dream. All the time she spent under that sickly sky felt like fleeting moments, completely disassociated with this present reality.

She felt as if she should be curled up on the floor, sobbing uncontrollably, and yet she found herself right back where she left off, as if nothing had happened.

Was that simply the nature of the Ruin? Just as death couldn't take her in there, neither could the trauma? Or was something else at work, taking all that awfulness and pushing it down, protecting her? Was the other one capable of doing such a thing for her?

She gave her hair a final shake and then reached up under her shirt, trying to wipe the grime out from under her bra. "By the way," she added, glancing over at him. "What's with the doll?"

He had the little thing tucked in the crook of one arm, casually carrying it around like a little girl in an old Norman Rockwell piece, as if it were the most normal thing in the world. It was a pretty little thing, dressed in a little white and yellow dress, well loved, with messy golden hair. But where the hell did he even *find* a doll out here in the literal middle of nowhere? And why would he be carrying it around with him?

Distracted by the fact that she was rummaging around in her boobs—a fact that was clear by the light flush across his cheeks—he needed a few seconds to process that question, but finally he blinked and stood up straighter, averting his eyes. "This is Alice," he replied, as if it having a name weren't every bit as weird as carrying around a doll in the first place. "She's, um…" He glanced down at her. "It's kind of a long story?" He scratched awkwardly at the back of his head. "She's a spirit."

"So…you brought a haunted doll?"

"No. She's not a ghost. She's a different kind of spirit. And she's not haunting the doll. She *is* the doll. This is her. I…kinda made her?"

Violet blinked at him, as if she could somehow reboot her brain like that and make more sense of him.

"I rescued her and now she's here. She's the reason I was

able to find you."

She withdrew her hands from her shirt and pointed at the doll. "Just for the record," she informed him, "that's probably not gonna help you score more kisses. From, like, *anybody*. Just in general."

"Oh," he replied, as if that were news to him. "Sorry?"

"It's fine," she sighed, reaching behind her and tugging at her shorts. "Ugh. I got dirt in my butt crack."

Everett cleared his throat and looked away, making a show of examining the nearest passage leading out of the room.

"So you're saying that thing's alive?"

"More or less," he replied. "I mean, she's a spirit, so she's not really *alive* so much as..."

"Dead?"

"*Aware.*"

"Gotcha." She dusted herself off and looked down at her filthy socks. Her feet still hurt from running across that rocky forest floor. And she was still covered in scrapes and bruises. But the more serious injuries had vanished as if imagined. "Well, thank you, Alice, for saving my ass, because it really sucked in there."

"She says you're welcome. And she's glad you're okay."

"That is...so sweet and creepy at the same time..." She turned her attention to the lone sentinel standing against the wall. God, those things were freaky. They never looked that big in those dreams, but then again, she supposed she was seeing them through the "eyes" of the other one that whole time, so that she was essentially their size. That empty face was especially creepy now that she knew it wasn't just some kind of metaphor, that the sentinels really were utterly faceless. But what kept drawing her gaze every time she looked over there, absurdly enough, was that enormous penis.

That was just wrong. It was ridiculous. She didn't want to believe it was real, but like those blank faces, she'd seen them for herself—in a manner of speaking—swinging freely in the wind as those monstrous freaks strolled past and scurried up sheer walls.

She was pretty sure that she'd rather be back inside that

grave than inside the other one if one of these guys showed up wanting to mate.

She pushed the unpleasant thought from her head and focused on the thing's pose, instead. "Albert told us that these guys sometimes gave clues about which way we're supposed to go."

"Albert…" replied Everett, nodding.

"Right. You don't know him do you?"

"I mean, I know *who* he is. You guys have all talked about him. But I haven't met him. He's the, like, guy with all the ideas or whatever, right?"

"Something like that." She studied the statue's pose. Its details. Hands and feet and chest and…other things… "But this guy doesn't seem to be saying anything." She glanced around the otherwise empty room. "I wonder what he's doing here, then?"

This wasn't the same place she was in *before* the Ruin captured her. And it didn't look familiar in that strange, dreamlike way the other one had of showing her which way to go. How far off course had she been sent? Was it even possible to get back to where they needed to be now?

Everett pointed at the passage leading from the wall to the left of the sentinel. "Alice says we should go that way."

She frowned at him.

"I know. I heard how it sounded, too."

"That's good."

"I trust her."

"If you say so." She turned and faced him, curious. "What happened to you, anyway? Where'd you go?"

"It's a really…*weird* story."

She nodded, her gaze drifting back to the doll. "I'll bet."

"It was nuts. Someone called 'the Priestess of Ruin' sent me to some kind of crazy flipside version of everything."

This surprised her. The Priestess of Ruin? She remembered her bragging about having two "little birdies" trapped. "Was the sky all red and freaky looking?" she asked.

"What? No. It was more like…" He crumpled up his face as he thought back over the time between now and when they were separated. "It was a *lot* of stuff…but no red skies. At least, I don't think so. I was trapped in a dollhouse through most of it."

"Dollhouse…" she repeated, staring at the little doll again. "Makes sense," she lied.

"Like I said. Weird."

She pondered this for a moment. Albert and Brandy described stumbling into a ruined world with a red sky back when they were still looking for the carriage house under the hotel, but did not all parts of the Ruin have that same bloody sky? Or was the Priestess referring to someone else?

She wanted to hear what he went through, wanted to compare it to what she experienced, but when she looked up, he was staring at the floor with a deeply concerned look on his face. "You okay?"

"It's just…" He shook his head. "I had to make a decision back there," he explained. "I'm glad I found you, but I can't stop wondering about the path I didn't take."

She stared at him for a moment, letting this sink in. Another path. Did he mean another person? Another prisoner of the Ruin? "You're saying someone else might have needed saved, too?"

"I think so," he replied. "I was sure I felt two different people. But I couldn't tell who was who."

(*Two little birdies caught in my cage…*)

"Can we get there?" she asked, her heart leaping at the thought of someone else still caught in that hellish trap.

But he was shaking his head. "No. It was one or the other. I can't get back to that place now."

"Oh shit…" She was so relieved to be rescued, but she didn't like the idea that her brave young hero had to choose her over someone else. She couldn't help feeling guilty.

"It's…" He looked down at the strange little doll in the crook of his elbow. "I made the right decision," he decided. "I know that. I was supposed to save you." He looked up and met her gaze. "I know that much. I was always going to make the decision I did." Then his eyes wandered across the room, as if staring out into the mysterious vastness of the labyrinth. "I just really hope everyone else is okay."

"Yeah," she sighed. "Me too."

"By the way, what happened to your shoes?"

She glanced down at her dirty socks, distracted. "I don't want to talk about it."

"Okay."

Chapter 65

"Are we having fun yet?"

Andrea took a great, shuddering gulp of air and cried out in pain.

Except…the pain was gone. She was gasping for breath, her heart racing, tears streaming from her eyes, but the agony that had racked her body had entirely vanished, just like with the steel trap and those monsters' claws.

She was back in those crumbling walls again, hanging like some sacrificial virgin by those chains beneath that blood-tinted sky.

Was that other place just some kind of nightmare? Was this her actual surroundings? What was real and what wasn't? Was that *voice* she heard real? It *sounded* real. It wasn't inside her head. It sounded as if Stella, herself, had spoken right into her ear.

(*Are we having fun yet?*)

No. She most certainly wasn't.

She looked up at the chains wrapped around her arms and tried to wriggle free of them, but they wouldn't budge. She was stuck here, unable to free herself, defend herself or even cover herself.

She gave them one final shake and huffed, frustrated. The motion sent a dull pain through her wounded knee. Once again, that one seemed to remain perfectly real for some reason.

"Oh, look at you," laughed Stella's mocking voice, "getting all *mad*."

She looked up to see a shadow sliding across the graffitied concrete. Except it couldn't have been a shadow because it had no body with which to throw a shadow. It was a twisting, lumpy sort of shape that was neither human nor beast and filled her belly with a boiling sense of utter dread.

Again, she yanked at the chains, but they refused to yield. "Let me go!" she shouted, trying not to sound as frightened as she felt and almost certainly failing miserably. The tears still streaming down her face were probably a dead giveaway.

The shadow seemed to dance across the wall. With nothing to cast it, it reminded her of Peter Pan's shadow in that old Disney movie. That scene had always felt a little unsettling to her somehow, the way that living, disembodied shadow was both playful and somehow subtly sinister, like if it ever truly got away it might commit terrible atrocities.

Or maybe she just had a morbid imagination as a kid...

What was this thing? Ada said it was something "far stronger than a mere spirit" and that it might have been watching her since the first doorway.

(*It seems to attract unwanted things. And it delights in your misfortune.*)

Erin described it as something neither living nor dead. Ancient. Primitive. And dangerous.

(*And it's particularly focused on* you *for some reason.*)

"What do you want with me?" she demanded.

She thought she managed to sound a bit more threatening with this, but the ancient, primitive, dangerous thing responded only with one of Stella's far-too-familiar energetic laughs.

"Why do you sound like *her*?" she shouted.

"*That's* an easy one," said the shadowy impostor-thing as it detached itself from the wall and bubbled toward her. It didn't move like the black blobs in the murk passages. It wasn't as dark. She could see through it. But then those strange shadows peeled open somehow and out stepped a very familiar shape. Those long, reddish-brown curls and thick eyebrows. That slight overbite. That somewhat bigger than average forehead. And all those freckles. "It's because I *am* her."

Andrea stared down at her friend, confused. It no longer simply *sounded* like Stella. It *looked* just like her, too. Every detail was unnervingly familiar. Right down to her abundance of jewelry, including her favorite ring with the large, iridescent white stone. But for some unfathomable reason that was *all* she was wearing.

"Surprised?"

"*Yeah.* Why are *you* naked?"

Stella spread her arms as if to show off her already exposed figure and grinned, utterly unashamed. "It's not a real party unless you lose your clothes, don't you think?"

Andrea's head was spinning. What was going on? Why was this thing going so far to pretend to be her friend?

"Besides," she added, stepping closer and flashing her that mischievous grin she knew too well, "it's customary to disrobe when confronting the Faceless Ones' trials. Didn't anyone tell you that the first time?"

"What would I care what the sentinels thought was *customary*?"

"True enough, I suppose. But sometimes there are reasons for customs to start."

She shook her head and yanked at the chains, rattling them. She had no interest in discussing the sentinels and their stupid rules. "Let me down!"

Stella stepped up to her, still grinning. "You don't like it up there?"

"*Why would I like it?*"

"Why *wouldn't* you?" she countered. She reached up and slid her hand up the inside of her thigh, startling a yelp out of her. "Who doesn't like a little bondage action now and again?"

"*Stop that!*" She tried to twist her body around, but the bindings wouldn't let her. "Who are you?" she shouted. This made no sense. It was some kind of trick. "Why are you pretending to be Stella?"

"I'm the same Stella you've known all these years," she replied, smiling up at her, clearly enjoying this strange game. "I don't know why you're acting so surprised. I never lied to you. Don't you remember? I told you *so many times* I was a goddess of chaos."

"You...?" She frowned, distracted. That silly thing she was

always going around telling people? But that was just nonsense. Something she spouted to justify her childish love for mischief and drama.

Wasn't it?

And yet, didn't Ada say that the thing causing all their trouble had been watching her since she returned from the first temple? She met Stella less than a year after that, when she began her freshman year at Briar Hills University. How easy would it have been for something like that to insert itself into her college life?

"It's a lot to handle, isn't it?" she asked.

"You're saying you're a real goddess? Like an *actual goddess*?"

"Of course."

"And you look like *that*?"

Stella scowled. "What do you mean, like this? What did you expect a goddess to look like?"

"I don't know. Cate Blanchett? Gal Gadot?"

She managed to look offended. "Unrealistic beauty standards much?"

Andrea wrinkled her nose at her. "You just said you were a *literal goddess*."

"You can't believe everything you see on those old Greek statues, you know. That's all photoshopped."

"What...?" This was too much. Her head was spinning. And these chains were hurting worse the longer she hung here. She pulled at them again, rattling them, but it was a futile effort. "I don't understand any of this. You sent me to that dead spirit highway and left me there to die!"

"True," said Stella. "But you *didn't* die, did you? You found your way out. Just like the Keeper planned. No harm no foul."

"You sold out my friends to Glum!"

"And *they* found *their* way out, too," she replied. "They made it to one of the gates just like you did. Again, the Keeper's designs remain infallible. That clever little shit."

Andrea stared down at her, distracted. Nicole and Gina were safe? Erin told her as much, but she wasn't convinced that she'd tell her the truth if they were in danger. Olivia and Wayne confirmed that Keith made it inside the city, and she trusted them wholeheartedly. But could she trust *anything* this woman said? If she was telling the truth now, then it meant she'd been lying to her since they day they met. She *said* she never lied, she said that silly line about being a goddess of chaos so many times, but it was still a lie. She wouldn't be convinced otherwise.

And the very thought made her mad. She struggled against the chains again, rattling them. There was something off about them, she realized, something about the way they clung to her. They didn't feel real. It was almost as if they had a will of their own. The longer she was up here the more apparent it became. Despite the fact that they were heavy chains, they didn't feel like they were pulling down on her. It felt as if they were choosing to cling to her over obeying the pull of gravity. Except…what kind of logic was *that*?

"You can glare at me all you want," huffed Stella, "but don't act like *you've* never lied to *me*. What's the difference between me not telling you about me and you not telling me about you?"

Andrea blinked at her, confused. "What?" That was quite the mouthful, but she understood well enough what she was accusing her of. "That's *not* the same thing and you know it!"

Stella only shrugged and stood there with that silly smirk on her face.

She growled, frustrated. This woman knew damned well that she couldn't have told her about the temple and Gilbert House even if she wanted to. She was just trying to get under her skin. This was classic Stella she was dealing with, looking to stir up trouble wherever she could. She was getting really tired of these games. And she was positively *sick* of being bound here. "Let me down, already!"

Stella rolled her eyes. "Fine." Then, as she turned away, the unbreakable chains holding her simply seemed to melt into nothing, dropping her without any warning at all.

She uttered a surprised yelp and then thumped onto the hard, unforgiving ground on her belly with a breathless "Oof!"

"Better?"

"What the hell?" she snapped, pushing herself up onto all fours, only to cringe at the pain in her wounded knee again.

Then she realized that not all the chains had disappeared. There was still one connected to a stake driven deep into the earth in front of her. The other end was attached to an iron collar clamped around her neck. She sat up and yanked at it, but it wouldn't budge. "Seriously?"

"Don't like that either?" Stella turned back and leaned toward her, her larger-than-average breasts hanging down in front of her face. "What *are* you into, then?" she asked, reaching out and plucking a clump of dirt from her hair. "Besides mud wrestling, I mean."

"I did *not!*" she snapped, flushing a little. How could *Stella* be a goddess? Shouldn't goddesses be old and wise? She was *way* too immature to be any kind of deity!

Stella laughed, those plump breasts jiggling obscenely before her eyes.

"Put some clothes on!" she shouted, yanking at the chain again. "And give back *mine*, too!"

She stood up straight again, still laughing.

"Let me *go!*"

Then, without warning, the chain and collar were gone. Her weight shifted and she stumbled backward, striking the back of her head against the concrete. "Ouchie…" she grumbled. She looked down at herself, expecting to find that she was wearing shackles around her ankles this time, or maybe stuck waist deep in quicksand or maybe just strapped to a tree or something, but there were no more bindings. It was only *her* standing there, naked and bruised, but free. She covered herself and shot her "friend" a dirty look. "Are you done?"

"I'm just making a point," said Stella.

"What, that you're a bully?"

"That you can't get away, of course." She pointed at the wall behind her.

Andrea turned around to find that it was gone. Instead, she was looking out through iron bars, as if she were locked up inside a jail cell, looking out over the blood-tinged landscape of the Ruin. And when she turned around again, confused, she found that those bars were all around her.

It wasn't a cell at all, but a *cage*.

"Trapped little birdy," giggled Stella.

"Let me out!" she shouted, grasping at the cold bars.

"It won't make any difference if I do. You'd still be trapped. In a cage. In chains. In the City Beyond Memory. In the Denselands. Even in what you call the 'real world.' You can't leave unless someone lets you. It's all the same prison. The only difference is the size of your cell."

"I don't care!"

"Really?"

The bars melted away like the chains. In an instant, she was standing in the middle of a long-dead forest, surrounded by the skeletons of once towering trees. She turned and looked around, confused.

"The *illusion* of being trapped changes," said Stella. "Sometimes, it even resembles freedom. But the fact is that you've *never* been free. Someone has *always* had you by the scruff of your neck, telling you where to go, what to do, *who you are*. Sometimes Glum. Sometimes Hochog. *Me*, of course." She turned and met her gaze. "And especially *the Keeper*."

Andrea stared back at her. This was all so confusing. She was still trying to wrap her head around the fact that Stella Umbertan was an actual goddess of chaos. She certainly didn't have the bandwidth to process some deep, philosophical speech about how life is just a giant prison. "You sound like that Hotdog creep," she informed her. "Are you going to tell me the whole universe is a colossal mistake, too?"

She shrugged. "Maybe it is. Who knows? Goar Nangup was here in the beginning, after all. Before there was anything anywhere. And I'd wager he'll be here long after everything's gone."

Andrea couldn't help feeling a chill wash over her at the very mention of the madman's so-called god. She didn't want to think too much about that, so instead she asked, "What about you? Were *you* here in the beginning?"

With a strange sort of twinkle in her eye, Stella flashed her an unsettlingly sinister sort of grin, like nothing she ever saw cross her face before. She leaned closer and replied in a dramatic whisper, *"Even longer."*

Andrea took an involuntary step backward. "What *are* you?"

Her face melted back into that familiar, obnoxious grin so quickly that she could almost believe she only imagined the frightening expression she was wearing a moment ago. She even reached up and ran a hand through her long curls, a gesture that was as familiar as her voice. "You don't think I'll reveal all my secrets *that* easily, do you?"

She wrinkled her nose at Stella's naked chest. "You're revealing *everything else*, aren't you?"

Chapter 66

They were right behind her!

Erin tore through the brush and the briars, ignoring the slapping branches and the swarming bugs and the cobwebs and those awful, shrieking crows.

She wasn't going to make it!

She could see them on either side of her, grotesque, twisted things with long, bony limbs scurrying through the brush on all fours, far too fast and agile for those lunky, awkward movements.

And those *teeth*! Why would anything have teeth like that? It was the creepiest thing she'd ever seen, neither human nor beast. They weren't fangs or tusks. They were huge and blocky and far too numerous to fit inside their mouths, giving each of them a freaky, oversized grin like some kind of exaggerated, clownish mask. It didn't seem possible for any living thing to possess so many teeth.

But that was exactly it, wasn't it? Some part of her understood that these weren't living things at all. They were spirits. Ghosts. Phantoms. And they were *powerful* ones.

(*On the other side of the veil, things sometimes change.*)

In her state of panic, she barely registered this strange thought. It seemed to come from nowhere. It wasn't a memory, per se. She didn't think anyone had ever said those words to her. She didn't hear it in a movie. It seemed to be her own thoughts, from her own experiences. Except that didn't make any sense. Why would she know something like that? This was the first she was seeing of such things.

It was nothing. Random words flashing through her panicked mind, of no importance whatsoever in this desperate moment. Because right now the only thing that mattered was escaping these monstrosities.

But she didn't know how to get away. She was in the middle of this forest. There were no buildings to hide in. There was no one to help her. She was running *away* from her car. At this rate, even if she somehow survived these things, she was going to end up hopelessly lost.

One of the monstrous, grinning horrors leapt at her. An old man in a dirty suit with a sagging belly and the same shadowed eyes and nightmare grin. She screamed and jumped backward, avoiding its twisted, grasping hands by mere inches. She staggered a few steps, off balance, then changed direction and sprinted away.

How did she end up in this mess? It was only by chance that she even came to this area. She was planning to head north again, making her way back toward Indianapolis and Chicago, where she always knew how to find reliable work and a comfortable place to stay for a few days or even weeks. Just like that fateful day last year, she simply caught sight of a potential job on a bulletin board and decided to check it out.

Did Horatio know she'd make her way here, even when she had no idea where she was going? Were these mysterious clues nothing more than a clever trick to draw her to the right place at the right time? And for that matter, was it possible that her being in this area on this day was the only reason he chose her? If she'd never come here, would someone else have been chosen instead? Would she still be living her perfectly uneventful life, blissfully ignorant of all these frightful things?

Again, one of the grinning creatures lashed out at her. A younger man this time, thinner, fitter, but with the same hideous and impossible grin stretching his lips apart. Again, she changed direction, dodged another leaning headstone and ducked under a low branch.

There were too many of them. She couldn't avoid them forever.

What were they? Why were they here? And why were they

so pissed off at her? She didn't do anything! She was just following Horatio's stupid directions!

Something struck her back and she stumbled forward with a startled cry, somehow managing not to fall. But before she could regain her stride, something else hit her from the side, sending her tumbling into a thicket of prickly bushes.

She rolled onto her belly, desperate to get to her feet and run, but one of the grinning freaks already had hold of her ankle, pulling on her, dragging her backward through the thickets. She clenched her fists around whatever branches she could find, ignoring the gouging thorns that bit into her flesh in the process.

She looked up to see several more crawling toward her, those hellish, grinning faces down at her own level, pushing through the weeds and the brush like serpents slithering through the grass. The sight made her heart stutter in her chest. But she couldn't seem to kick herself free of the thing's grip.

This was a real mess she'd found herself in. What would happen if she died before retrieving the thorn? Was it possible to fail so completely? But she couldn't think of any way out of this mess. They were too fast. The terrain was too wild. She couldn't keep running forever.

Would it matter, she somehow managed to wonder. Horatio told her this job he gave her was crucial, that she was the only one who could do it, but was he telling her the truth? Or would he just go out and find another pawn if she got herself killed out here?

She rolled onto her back and kicked at the thing gripping her ankle, her hands raised to defend against the others as they gathered around her with their enormous, gnashing teeth and those eerily long limbs.

But as she looked around, she realized that something strange was happening.

By now these things should have been piling on top of her like a pack of wolves taking down a deer, but the others had all scurried off in other directions. The one pulling on her leg was the only one still focused on her. It yanked at her with both its gnarled hands while baring those awful, inhuman teeth at her.

She thrust her foot up, driving her heel into that twisted face, and wrenched herself free.

The monster let out a furious snarl that was lost beneath the din of those screaming birds and it thrust its distorted arms out at her, swinging wildly.

She scooted backward, dodging them, and scrambled to her feet, ready to defend herself from whichever monster leapt at her next.

But the forgotten cemetery was a scene of utter chaos.

Those monstrous things were thrashing about, swinging their arms, snarling in hideous voices that were drowned away by the cawing of those crows. They almost looked as if they were in pain.

Even the one that had just attacked her was twisting around as if struggling with some invisible assailant.

Erin backed away, confused. Was it the crows? Were they doing something? Were they helping her?

(...*not what they appear to be...*)

She frowned and looked up into those branches, confused. What was that memory just now? Was it something Horatio told her?

A better question, she realized, was why the hell was she just standing around? She turned and ran, determined to be well away from this overgrown patch of wild nightmares before these things came to their senses and remembered that they were trying to eat her.

But...was she still going the right way? She couldn't remember which direction was back! Was she already lost?

One of the things leapt out and grabbed her shirt, startling a scream from her. She jumped back, yanking herself free, then turned and fled.

It didn't matter how lost she ended up. That was a problem for later. Right now, she needed to get out of here!

The brush was thicker in this direction. She felt things tearing at her shirt and her arms. A sharp pain drew itself across her thigh. Something jabbed her in the belly. She couldn't run properly here, but she could hear something tearing after her and didn't dare turn back.

Maybe denser foliage meant she was near the edge of the cemetery. Would these things be able to follow her off the property? Did things like this have rules they had to follow? It seemed almost silly to think about, but at this point, she'd grasp at any straw she could find.

Something prickly slapped her in the face and she lifted her arm to shield herself.

Then something caught her foot, tripping her. She fell. Suddenly she was tumbling down a steep incline, the world spinning around her.

She screamed.

Then the ground disappeared beneath her. She was falling.

She had time to suck in a startled breath, a single gasp, then she struck the ground again with a thump that sent a pain through the back of her shoulder and knocked the breath out of her.

She rolled once more, then slid to a stop.

She lay there, dazed, listening to the cacophony of caws, her body racked with pain.

Did she hurt herself? Had she broken something? How bad was it?

She blinked through a curtain of tears and stared up the hill she'd just careened down, expecting those monsters to be descending on her already, eager to take advantage of her clumsiness, but there wasn't one to be seen.

Did she dare to hope she'd stumbled out of danger?

She closed her eyes again, still struggling to catch her breath. That really hurt...

All she wanted was to lie here until the pain went away, but she couldn't let herself be careless. Just because those things hadn't already attacked her again didn't mean they were gone for good.

And yet, was it her imagination, or were those crows beginning to quiet down?

Slowly, she sat up, groaning. Her arms and legs seemed to be working fine. No bones were broken, she didn't think. But she was a total mess. Her palms and elbows were bloody, as were her knees. She was covered in scratches. And was her nose bleeding?

That was just great. How was she supposed to perform looking like this? Everyone was going to think she let some gorilla of a boyfriend wail on her every night. As if she wouldn't put a creep like that in the ER faster than the neighbors could call 911. She wouldn't tolerate someone like that, not just for herself, but for any woman who might happen along afterward. But it wasn't exactly a good look for her potential employers...

She cursed under her breath and rubbed at her aching head. That wasn't exactly her top priority.

Those crows had definitely calmed. It sounded like only a handful of them were still carrying on. And the lighting had changed, too. It was bright and sunny again, no longer dark and dreary as if a storm were moving in. And still there was no sign of those things...

What was that all about, anyway? What were they? Why did they attack her? Had she done something wrong?

She sat there, panting, trying to catch her breath, and stared across the strangely tranquil gully stretched out before her. There was a row of low bluffs over there, carved from the hillside from the same ages of runoffs that created the narrow valley. It was the same kind of bluffs on this side that she tumbled over, the reason for that painful fall.

She only dropped two or three feet, but it still hurt...

She wasn't used to this sort of abuse.

As the cawing of the crows died away completely, leaving the forest in an eerie silence all around her, she blinked at the landscape before her, distracted. The section of bluff across from her had an unusual shape to it. There were five chunks of rock protruding from the earth, almost like the fingers of an enormous stone hand peeking out.

(*...beneath the Slumbering Giant's Palm...*)

Wait... She'd found it? Was this where she was supposed to be?

If she'd found the last of Horatio's idiotic clues, then she was almost done. All she had to do was figure out where the thorn was from here.

But she was so tired from that last scare...

She closed her eyes and took a calming breath. She just needed a moment.

But for some reason, she found her head filled with images of a stone corridor stretching through an endless darkness in a vast and very distant labyrinth...

Chapter 67

Austin watched Corey work, his pudgy hands moving rhythmically, connecting him, piece by piece, to the terminal's contacts. It seemed like such a slow process. But he reminded himself that this was a mere human doing this job, and as far as humans went, he was moving fairly fast. If he'd been stuck here with anyone else, they wouldn't have even known where anything went. He would've been stuck talking them through the process, and that would've taken *far* too long. He very much doubted it would even be possible.

Still, he couldn't help being impatient.

He just wanted to finally finish his job. Was that so much to ask?

Frustrated, he turned his attention outward. Being even partially wired into the stoneworks allowed him to become one with it. The more plugged-in he was, the more he found himself aware of the goings on elsewhere in the labyrinth. And the more aware he became, the more he found that it wasn't just Corey who was taking his sweet time doing his job. All of them seemed to be simply stumbling around like drunken monkeys. One of them had already managed to get himself killed, even.

At this rate, he might just end up stuck here forever.

And yet, that wasn't to say that they weren't making progress. Things were happening out there. Two of the emotional locks had been opened. They'd managed to access the supernatural and unnatural portions of the labyrinth. And, far more impressive, the thing that attacked him when he first arrived in this terminal was gone. A tremendous expulsion of unnatural power had slain it completely. It was as if it had somehow imploded upon itself, which was strange. He wasn't sure *how* they managed it, but he didn't have to worry about it coming back to interfere with his upload again, and that was at least one bit of good news.

But there were still several intruders prowling the stone-works, any one of which might pose a significant problem. He might have been concerned if not for his knowledge of the Keeper's tenacious mechanizations, his endless backup plans. Everything always happened as the Keeper intended it, after all. One way or another, he always prevailed.

Perhaps that was why he could afford to trust such important business to mere humans. But it was still beyond him why he seemed to value these creatures so much. As far as he was concerned, their flaws far outweighed their merits. He couldn't see what—

He stared at his spilled books, his thoughts broken, distracted. What was that just now? It felt like something happened while he was—

He watched Corey as he wound another of the bloody strings into place. When did he turn to look at him? He was turned the other way, looking at his bag and his strewn boo—

Corey was lifting another string from the coil on the floor next to him, his attention focused on the task before him. But when did he finish connecting the previous strand? When did he reach down for the next? He never looked away, and yet he seemed to have missed—

He was staring at his own raised hand, at the "blood" staining his fingers, a complex fluid that looked just like what flowed through human veins, but was no such thing. But he couldn't for the life of him remember lifting that hand or shifting his gaze to—

He blinked up at the ceiling, confused. What a bizarre experience. This wasn't something that had ever happened before. It was as if time were skipping ahead on him, a few seconds or minutes at a time. Had something gone wrong with his artificial brain? A malfunction in his memory? Had he been damaged worse than he thought by the shapeless, ambushing monster? He didn't think it was Corey. He would've noticed if he'd made a mistake plugging him into the stoneworks.

Whatever it was, it seemed to have passed. Those strange, rapid-fire moments of broken time had stopped as quickly as they started. And Corey didn't seem to have noticed it at all. He was still happily working, oblivious of whatever oddity just occurred behind his back.

He wouldn't mention it to him, of course. He needed to be working on what he was doing, not getting distracted. And what would he do anyway? Even with his head full of the Faceless Ones' blueprints, it was very doubtful that there was anything he'd be able to do about it.

Yet now that the strange sensation had passed, he found himself convinced that something was different than it was before. He could feel something new rippling through the stone. It was like a vibration, one that started deep inside him and radiated outward, a subtle tremor, an echo, reverberating, ringing throughout his very being like the great tolling of a deafening bell, coursing through his artificial consciousness. The feeling was both profound and ominous, igniting in him an unfamiliar cascade of sensations, sparks of brand-new awareness, foreign and yet innately recognizable, filling him with a strange mix of excitement and dread that he'd never experienced before.

He turned his head and watched Corey work again. Still, it wasn't him. He didn't do anything. Nor did he seem to have noticed it. He was entirely preoccupied with the task before him, as he was supposed to be.

No, this sensation came from somewhere much farther away, from another part of the Faceless Ones' labyrinth, perhaps even from *outside* the labyrinth. There were plenty of those, after all. Little bits and pieces that extended outward from it, like burrowing roots, snaking their way into dark and strange dimensions beyond what normal humans could typically find.

Something had changed.

There was a shift in perception, an expansion of awareness, a transformation of all that defined his existence. For the first time in all his torturous years wandering the earth, he felt curious. He felt intrigued. He felt *surprised*. And even stranger, he felt *vulnerable.*

Had something profound happened?

Had some part of the machine perhaps failed?

No. Impossible. The Keeper's mechanizations were infallible.

And yet he found himself quite certain that something was now profoundly different than it was before, something with enough significance to perhaps even alter the outcome of the long-foreseen and meticulously detailed events taking place around him.

He found himself thinking for some reason that something had just *revealed* itself... But he didn't understand what that something was or in what way it was revealed or to whom.

He lifted his gaze to the center of the terminal's ceiling, to those thin, stone rods protruding downward. Such a simple design once, in a long-forgotten universe, reduced to a thing beyond myth over unthinkable stretches of agonizing time. And yet, through the miracle of the Faceless Ones' primordial stone, they still functioned, even in a universe devoid of the very thing they were designed to collect and redirect.

The Keeper thought of everything.

Therefore, the Faceless Ones prepared for everything.

And yet he was increasingly certain that something *new* was looming on the distant horizon. Was it possible that there was something the Keeper *didn't* anticipate?

Or was he simply more broken than he realized? Maybe his body was malfunctioning and his reasoning was being affected.

He supposed it wasn't worth thinking too much about. After all, he only had to function a little while longer. Once he was finally plugged into the machine, his purpose would be done. Whatever came next wouldn't matter. And whether he reached that point damaged or not was irrelevant.

And he probably *was* damaged, he supposed. He *had* been torn in half, after all.

Chapter 68

The glass labyrinth had changed again, Gina realized. Except, perhaps it was more accurate to say that the glass labyrinth was *still changing*. Because with each step she took it seemed to shift and twist and remake itself, revealing more empty and distorted passages waiting just beyond the warped walls, passages with no beginnings or ends, passages with no ways in or out, passages that were turned around and inverted in maddening ways that made them impossible to walk through even if she knew how to enter them. Passages that weren't passages at all and yet somehow could be nothing else.

It was deathly silent here. She hadn't heard any voices or glimpsed any shadowy figures since landing in these depths, which was a little unnerving in spite of the fact that it made little difference either way. The stone and the glass were entirely separate things. Even when she stood with her hands pressed to the wall and stared at Violet right on the other side, they were nowhere near each other. It was only an illusion, a fleeting glimpse of the other side, a clue, perhaps, that she hadn't really gone anywhere, that she was still on the very fringe of the glass labyrinth, that for all her running and turning and rolling, she'd only barely scratched the surface of this unnatural realm.

And if that were true, then perhaps it was no accident that she fell through the cracks back there... Maybe that was exactly what she was meant to do.

She closed her eyes and cast her psychic gaze across her surroundings again. She was aware of the passage she was walking through. She was aware of those other, *impossible* passages knotted and tangled up all around her. And she was very much aware of Nicole following at her heels, still clinging tightly to her hand. With her inner eye, she could see every part of her at once, from her dirty socks to her night tree tattoo to the blood pumping through her veins. This deep inside the glass labyrinth, there was something about her presence that made her stand out, like a shining beacon in the dark. The longer they traveled together, the more apparent it was.

Perhaps it had something to do with the fact that she was the only other thing in this surreal glass dimension that was real.

Yes… That felt significant. She grasped at this thought and opened her eyes.

This wasn't real. There was no glass. It was only a mental perception of the perceived transparency of these particular surroundings as her brain understood it. She'd already come to this conclusion. And yet she now realized that she was still thinking of it as a glass labyrinth.

It was no wonder she couldn't grasp the truth of it all.

She needed to *unsee* the glass.

But how did she do that?

"It feels weird here," said Nicole. It was the first words she'd spoken in a while. And she still sounded strangely meek, like a lost and frightened child. "Like we're not supposed to be here or something."

"That's not surprising," said Gina. "This isn't someplace you could get to without me."

"That could be it."

"Or it could just be how this place is. It's not part of the natural or supernatural worlds. People are either alive or they're dead. That's all. There's nothing else. They belong to those two worlds. The unnatural is something completely other, somewhere we don't belong, full of things we can't understand. So you're right. We're not supposed to be here."

"That's unsettling as fuck," she muttered.

"Sorry."

"Don't be," Nicole insisted. "But why are *you* the only one who can see all this stuff? That sounds like literally the *worst*."

"Sometimes," she replied. But that was a lie. It was *always* the worst. She'd been asking that question her whole life. Ada called it the "unnatural" but to her it was as common as the air she breathed. It had always been one nightmare after another, surrounding her everywhere she went, watching her with strange eyes from every shadow, peeking in her windows, stalking her down every hallway. It wasn't fair, being so different, seeing things no one else was meant to see.

Gina stopped walking.

The unnatural... An entire reality outside the range of her human comprehension...

Was that it? Was that the answer to understanding these queer surroundings? Was she trying too hard to forcefully wrap her human consciousness around an inhuman concept?

"What's wrong?" whispered Nicole. She was shining her light around, worried that she'd sensed something dangerous nearby.

"Just thinking," she replied, giving her hand a reassuring squeeze.

All her life, she'd been shutting out these unnatural things, ignoring them, hiding from them, pretending they didn't exist. Until Cakwetak. When she started working at that terrible tower, it was more important than ever to pretend like she couldn't see those things, but she no longer had the luxury of ignoring them. She was basically a spy. While she went about her daily job, completing projects for the company's clients, she was secretly using her psychic abilities to survey the building around her. She learned the secret to riding the elevator past the fifth floor. She studied the layouts of the hidden upper levels. She memorized the routines and patterns of the unnatural things that prowled those areas. And when the time came, she acted as a guide, sneaking the Keeper's chosen seekers safely through that nightmare to Janon Tane's office door.

In many ways, this job had been much more difficult. She was never physically attacked in Cakwetak. She never dealt with monsters. Tane never tortured her the way Glum did. He never sent a monster with too many heads to murder her. She never had to deal with insane cultist stranglers with mind-manipulating powers. She quietly did her job, pretending not to notice all the horrible things inside that building, from the atrocities that took place on the upper floors all the way down to the abomination dressed up like a receptionist, and nothing ever bothered her. But at least this time she didn't have to pretend anything. She embraced her psychic eye and let it lead her. She wasn't even carrying a flashlight because she didn't need to see her physical surroundings when she could psychically see *everything*.

"That's it," she muttered to herself.

Nicole leaned closer, trying to hear what she was saying. "What's up?"

She glanced back at her, her mind still racing. "Is it okay if I hold the flashlight for a little while?"

"Of course," she replied, holding it out for her. She didn't hesitate. She didn't ask why. She didn't even think about it. Even though she knew perfectly well that she didn't *need* a light, that she could see better in perfect darkness than anyone else could see in broad daylight.

Because she trusted her.

Because they were in this together. Until the end.

She took the flashlight and shined it into the passage ahead of her. This was one of those "missing the forest for the trees" kind of situations, she finally understood. She was trying so hard to see the truth that she was being overwhelmed with input. She'd completely tuned out everything her human eyes were seeing in order to focus on the psychic data.

And she'd missed something.

She crept forward, studying the space ahead of her, the stone walls on either side, the surfaces above and below. She could still see all that other stuff. It wasn't something she could turn off. But she needed to ignore it. She needed to force it back down, the way she used to do when she was growing up and desperate to hide these horrific abilities.

The path split ahead of her, forking left and right. But the confounding twists and turns revealed by her inner gaze made it hard to notice. The rightmost path was eclipsed by an undulating vortex of knotted space.

Had she been going in circles this whole time?

Aiming the light in this direction and staring hard into the halo it cast, she crept onward, following it.

She thought she recalled Andrea mentioning that her friends had psychic abilities that were neither too weak nor too strong, a perfect balance of sorts, allowing them just the right amount of foresight to navigate the first temple. This was like that. She couldn't have entered the glass labyrinth without these hateful abilities, and yet she couldn't find what she was here to find with those abilities alone.

Was this why she was the way she was? All those years she spent growing up, sobbing into her pillow, all alone in her room, asking why she was such a monster? Was this the answer?

Was she ever anything more than the Keeper's toy?

"Feels different again," whispered Nicole.

"Something's changing," she agreed. She aimed the light at the ceiling above them. No longer was it the same smooth and featureless stone. There was a line running down the middle of it directly overhead.

"What's up with that?"

It was a good question. None of the temple's other surfaces looked like that. Everything was either perfectly flat and smooth or impossibly detailed statues. She aimed the light farther ahead. The line curved back and forth, slowly, subtly at first, but more as they crept forward. Soon there were two lines. Then three.

"We're close to something," she realized.

"Good something? Or bad something?"

Gina kept walking. "We'll find out soon enough."

Chapter 69

Wayne stopped and looked back the way they came. Again, that strange feeling of something having changed filled him. He couldn't put his finger on what was triggering it. There was no specific detail, no shift in the atmosphere, no temperature variation, not even a subtle sense of that weird vertigo he felt when they used the thorn. So what was it? Was it only his imagination? Olivia didn't seem to notice anything and *she* was the psychic one.

"What is it?" she whispered.

"Just nerves," he assured her. He didn't know how to describe it anyway. There was no sense giving her more things to worry about when he didn't know whether it was real or even if it was something to be concerned about. He continued forward, pushing ever onward into that mysterious darkness.

He couldn't stop thinking about the Sentinel Queen. That vision of her standing in front of the door, as if showing them the way forward... He saw her so clearly. Every grotesque detail of her unnatural body, from those long, creepy fingers to those strange, upturned breasts to her obscenely long labia dangling between her thighs. And of course that empty, nearly featureless face...

She wasn't human, after all. She was one of *them*. The sentinels depicted in all those bizarre statues. Monstrous, towering beings without faces.

And yet there was something strangely alluring about her. He remembered standing before her for the first time and feeling his body attempting to react to her, as if he were instead standing in front of the most gorgeous woman he'd ever met. It was a crude reaction to her psychic stimulus. She, herself, described it as being "in heat" and yearning to be a mother again before her time ran out. The same reason she did what she did to him in the first segment of that terrifying road.

(Before you go, I have something to give you. A gift from me.)

The memory of that dizzying moment was always unpleasant. She never gave him any choice in the matter. She simply took him. She filled his head with confusing thoughts and stripped him of all control over himself. It was *terrifying.*

And it wasn't the first time it had happened...

But he didn't want to think about Claire. He hated thinking about Claire. Even after all these years, he still harbored so many emotions about her and that hot, summer day.

His arm kept brushing against the wall, so he steered himself back toward the middle, but he only bumped into Olivia, making them both stumble a little.

He stopped, confused. She was pressed against him, blinking up at him. She, too, was against the wall. There was nowhere for her to go.

"What's happening?" she asked. "Why're the walls closing in?"

He reached over her and pressed his hand against the wall behind her. They were able to walk side-by-side without any trouble this whole time, but now there wasn't room for them both. It was like the passage was shrinking. His first thought was that the walls might literally be closing in on them, slowly coming together like some cruel, ancient boobytrap from an Indiana Jones movie.

But the walls weren't moving. The passage was simply very gradually growing narrower.

The first temple had areas like this, places where the passages were smaller, making them proceed single-file or hunched over or both. And of course there was that one passage that shrank so much he practically got his fat ass stuck in it.

He looked up at the stone above him, but the ceiling didn't seem to be closing in. It was still the same height. If that had been getting lower, too, he probably would've noticed it much sooner. He didn't have nearly as much clearance overhead as Olivia did, after all.

"I don't like this," groaned Olivia.

He didn't either. He was in no mood to get himself stuck on top of everything else he'd been through. "We'll have to go one at a time," he reasoned. "You want to go in front? Or in back?"

She pouted up at him. She didn't want to do either. She wanted to keep clinging to his arm like this. It was comforting for her. And he didn't blame her. It had been so easy for everyone to become separated from them. Everett, Corey, Keith and Andrea had all vanished in the blink of an eye while they weren't looking. All it took was a second.

She let go of his arm and reached around him, then she pressed her face against his chest.

He put his arms around her and held her. This was fine. They could both use a moment. It had been a long, emotional journey.

He looked forward and then he looked backward. Darkness on both sides. Nothing more. It felt like that was all it had been. How many hours had passed? And there was always something new and unpleasant just around the next corner, it seemed.

A shrinking passageway...

Was this why he felt that odd sense of something changing before? Did he subconsciously notice the shrinking dimensions of the passage ahead without understanding exactly what it was? Or was it the other way around? Was whatever he felt back there responsible for changing the path before them? Anything was possible in a temple, it seemed, so why not?

Olivia lifted her face and looked up at him. Then she pushed those pretty lips out at him, that familiar and ever-so-adorable "kiss me" face.

He leaned down and kissed her. It was what she needed right now. And it was what he needed, too, he realized. This felt so nice, so perfectly *normal.*

He loved her so much.

And she was so warm...

Maybe they could just stay like this for a while. That would be nice. He squeezed her a little tighter, held her a little closer, savored the taste of those beautiful lips.

On second thought, maybe some cramped passageways might make for a nice change of pace. He could use a beautiful distraction.

And yet, as he held her against him, kissing her, he heard that mysterious whisper calling out to him again, a voice too faint to catch the words it was speaking, but loud enough to be sure it wasn't merely his imagination.

It wasn't Erin. He found himself certain of that now. But who was it? Could Olivia have been right? Was it possible that the Sentinel Queen's restless spirit was somehow here with them, too?

He pushed all these spiraling thoughts from his head and focused on what was right in front of his face.

Olivia. His beautiful fiancée. His lovely bride-to-be.

She was all he wanted to think about, after all. She was everything that really mattered and she always would be.

And yet he was suddenly struck by a strange certainty.

Something was wrong.

This wasn't Olivia he was kissing. It was the Sentinel Queen again. He felt the strange, featureless contours of that alien face pressed against his. No lips. No nose. No eyelashes. No hair. She was crouched over him, those long, monstrous fingers groping at him like they did that night…

He let out a gasp and pulled away, startled.

But when his eyes flew open, it was only Olivia there, staring up at him, those pretty brown eyes wide open, those perfect plump lips still puckered, frozen with surprise.

"What's wrong?"

It was a good question. Only his imagination? Was he just tired?

His heart was suddenly pounding. What was wrong with him?

"Wayne?"

"I'm fine," he sighed, trying to calm his racing pulse. "Just a weird feeling for a second there." He shined his light forward again. "I heard the voice again," he added. Maybe that had something to do with it somehow.

He took a breath, then turned his gaze back on his fiancée.

God, she was beautiful.

"Jumpy, I guess," he assured her. Then he kissed her again.

That was Olivia's kiss. He knew it like he knew the inside of his own head. Why would he mistake it for something like the long-dead Sentinel Queen? She didn't even have lips!

He needed to get his head in the game. How was he supposed to protect her if he was letting his imagination get the best of him?

Chapter 70

Brandy sat at the edge of the foul pool, sobbing, her shivering body covered in cold, oozing ichor.

Albert was gone. She couldn't find him anywhere.

Had something unseen dragged him out into the chamber and drowned him there?

No. She couldn't believe that. This wasn't water or mud or quicksand. It was *ichor*. This was the stuff that showed up every time they were sent to that poisoned alternate world back in the Lucianna Mysteria, the stuff that filled those creepy statues with the hollow heads. Kneede told them that it had pandimensional properties. If that were true, then it probably just sent him somewhere else.

Right?

But where? And how did she get to him?

She kept trying to feel him, like she did when she was all alone in the Denselands, but she couldn't get control of herself. She was too scared and cold and miserable. She couldn't even stop crying, much less concentrate. It was about as far as she could get from the proper mindset for sex magic. Even if he was out there somewhere, trying to find her, she wasn't going to be able to connect with him.

This was so frustrating!

It was that witch. She was sure of it. What else was there that only *he* would've seen. She ambushed him while he was distracted, took advantage of their argument.

That *bitch*.

She still couldn't understand why she was trying to sabotage them. Would ending the cycle somehow set her free from the pervert's contract and also save her from whatever hell she was too terrified of to leave him?

She hated that woman. She just wanted to wrap her hands around that dainty little neck and strangle the evil bitch. But she wasn't even here. She was only in her husband's head for some fucked-up reason.

She sniffled and looked down at her soiled hands. Ichor... Why did it have to be *this* shit? It was *so* gross. It looked like something someone very sick might vomit up.

She took a deep, shuddering breath and let it out again. She needed to get ahold of herself. It was a *good* thing this stuff was ichor. It meant that there was a good chance her husband wasn't dead, but merely displaced. She needed to shake it off and find him.

She was stronger than this.

But the truth was that she was terrified that maybe he *wasn't* out there somewhere, that she wouldn't be able to find him...because he wasn't anywhere to be found...

Stop it, she snapped at herself. That was no way to think.

She could do this.

She closed her eyes and forced herself to focus on his face. That was all that mattered. Those familiar features. And it was so easy. She'd stared into those dark eyes so many times that she could picture them the instant she closed her own. Whenever he wasn't with her and she was missing him, she could see him so clearly in her fantasies. She could see him right now, as clear as a photograph in front of her face. But that wasn't him. Not yet. That was nothing more than a placeholder. She needed to do more than just *picture* him. She needed to *feel* him. She needed to reach out and touch him.

But she was so cold and uncomfortable.

She realized that she was clenching her teeth and forced herself to stop. Her whole body felt tight. She was on edge and afraid to loosen up.

This was so *hard*.

Where are you? she cried out at him inside her head.

But of course he didn't answer. Why would he? She was so

utterly unfocused that she could barely hear her *own* thoughts, much less hope for *him* to hear them.

She cursed as a fresh wave of frustrated tears welled up in her eyes.

Come on! She needed to get this right. What if he was in danger right now? The longer it took, the more likely she was to lose him.

"Stupid fucking *sex* magic," she grumbled. Why did it have to be the pervert's magic? If it was only about emotion, why didn't the Keeper have them learn how to harness their *fear*? There was plenty of *that* shit in this fucking place.

(*Negative emotions are the most difficult to control. Fear, anger and sadness are too invasive. They can too easily overwhelm the mind, making it impossible to focus properly.*)

Oh, right… The pervert *did* say that, didn't he?

Fucking creep.

"Ugh!" She blinked back her tears and steeled her resolve. She had to make this work. And that meant she was going to have to find the right mindset in spite of her discomfort and fear.

But how did she accomplish that? It wasn't like she could just flip a switch.

Well…not *always*.

She needed to forget what was going on around her and focus entirely on her feelings for her husband.

She stared at the sentinel standing out in the ichor, her thoughts churning. The sight of it there reminded her of those other statues, the ones in the sex room. If she focused on those for a while, maybe those invasive feelings would seep into her. Sometimes it worked like that. But down here, she felt like thinking too much about an emotion room might have the reverse effect, making it even harder to focus.

She needed to utilize her *own* sexuality somehow.

Was it possible to do something to *trick* her body into reacting?

She pulled her knees up against her chest and hugged them. Six years ago, she was blindsided by the sex room and flung into wild, untethered lust with a man she barely knew, then found herself naked in those dark corridors with him, suffering all the humiliation, shame and vulnerability that came with it. *Five* years ago, she returned to that place, thinking she was armed with enough knowledge to avoid such discomfort, only to be faced with the decision of either watching her beloved Albert continue into the darkness without her, never knowing if he'd ever return, or disrobing once again, this time in front of Nicole *and* a man she didn't even know.

Someone else might have come back from that sort of thing traumatized, but all those experiences only changed her life for the better. She met her future husband, they *both* grew closer than ever to her best friend and she returned home with three very precious, brand-new friends she *always* felt completely comfortable around.

All of that from one crazed, frantic fuck in a freaky statue room.

So why did this whole sex magic thing piss her off so much? She was *already* so promiscuous with Albert. Wasn't being able to make *actual fucking magic* while doing it just a really awesome bonus?

She sighed. It wasn't as if she hadn't *enjoyed* those magic-making sessions. She simply hated how that creepy pervert seemed to have taken complete control of their very *sex life*. It felt so...*gross*.

She let go of her knees and cursed under her breath. The pervert wasn't worth the effort it was taking to hate his guts. He certainly wasn't a good enough reason to make her hesitant to do what she needed to do to find her husband.

This had nothing to do with that creep. It was between her and Albert.

She shined her light around one last time, then set it aside. She stripped off Albert's tee shirt and placed it next to the light. Then she removed her shorts and added them to the pile.

This felt so wrong... But hopefully that was precisely what would make it work. A hard break between the cold reality of the temple and the warm comfort of fantasy.

She lay back on the hard stone and closed her eyes. She

rested her arms at her sides and spread her knees, forcing herself to open up, a symbolic sort of offering to her displaced lover.

This would be *so* embarrassing if anyone could see her, but at this point, she'd just be happy to no longer be alone, which probably meant that there was exactly zero chance of someone happening to walk into this room while she was like this.

At least the ichor had washed away most of the blood. There were only a few smears and streaks left. If someone *were* to see her, at least she wouldn't look like a sex addict *and* a total psychopath…

She took several calming breaths and waited for her frightened heart to quit pounding so hard.

Except she already felt it pounding with a different sensation. These past six years with Albert had trained her body to react when she offered herself to him. Even—it seemed—when he wasn't even present. A familiar sort of exhilaration was slowly filling her, that lovely warmth spreading deep inside her belly, calming those intrusive shivers.

Yes. This could work. It was almost a Pavlovian reaction, like salivating at the sound of a beeping microwave. Her body reacted on its own, expecting him. At this rate, she'd find him in no time.

But she couldn't let herself get distracted. She forced herself to relax and focused on his face, imagining him right in front of her.

I'm here, she thought, willing the words into the universe around her. *Come get me.*

There was something surprisingly erotic about the sound of those words inside her head. It gave her heart a sudden palpitation. It felt so…*naughty.* So seductive.

Albert was out there somewhere. She had to believe that. And how could he resist her like this? How could he not come racing back to her?

She took another calming breath, her eyes still closed, and focused on that part of her down there between her open legs, exposed and waiting, anticipating her lover's touch. She pictured him kneeling over her, his body reacting to her, and hers shuddered with a sudden and intense yearning for him.

But her imagination was only going to get her so far, she realized. She needed to bring herself closer to that feeling of being with him.

It was embarrassing…mortifying even…but it wasn't as if she hadn't done this sort of thing before. Albert couldn't *always* be around, after all. Sometimes she couldn't wait. She did what she needed to do. She did it a *lot*, in fact. She was quite good at it, in her humble opinion. But this wasn't exactly her safe and comfy bedroom she was about to do this in…

No. She couldn't think about where she was. Where didn't matter. She was alone. And she had a purpose.

She pressed her hands to her bare hips and slowly slid them up her lean belly. The ichor had left her skin oily and slick. The stuff was gross…but the feeling wasn't entirely unpleasant, she had to admit. She could make herself imagine that it was only lotion. Sunscreen and sweat had felt like that a lot while they were still on their honeymoon, and *that* was a lovely thought. She could work with that.

She cupped her hands over her pert breasts, squeezing them, imagining that it was Albert's touch she was feeling, that he was kneading them in that gentle but firm way that he had, lightly pinching and tugging at her excited nipples.

God, she loved when he did that…

She could feel her temperature rising. She was no longer shivering, but instead *quivering*. Her body shuddered with hungry yearning.

"Albert…" she whispered into the silence of the dark and empty chamber around her. She squeezed her thighs together against a trembling wave of pleasure and bit her lip, a soft moan escaping her.

She wanted him back. Right now. She *needed* him. She couldn't stand being apart from him.

But he still wasn't there. She needed to take it farther.

She tugged more firmly at her left nipple as her right hand crept back down her slick belly, past the silver stud in her navel and down to that aching part of her below.

A different kind of shiver raced through her body as her finger slipped over that sensitive place. Intense. Ecstatic. *Electric.* She gasped and twitched. An obscene sort of groan forced its way up from somewhere deep inside her.

"Oh, fuck..." she breathed. Her hands were moving faster now, more aggressively. Her hips seemed to move on their own, meeting the rhythm. She was breathing hard, her breasts heaving, sweat beading on her skin.

This was it. This was the intense feeling she needed. If what she did back in that psychic monster's lair allowed them to reach across unfathomable distances and embrace, then *this* should send him speeding toward her like a runaway rocket. How could he resist her?

Vaguely, she was aware that she probably looked like a total freak, lying there on the stone floor, all alone, her bare flesh covered in slimy ichor, panting like an animal while pleasuring herself. But she didn't care. That didn't matter. Only Albert mattered.

"Where are you?" she gasped. "I need you..." She let out a great, sultry moan that echoed off the stone walls around her. "I need you so fucking bad right now..."

Brandy...

She felt her heart leap. Albert! He was there! She'd found him!

Thank God!

But she couldn't let herself get too excited. If she lost her concentration, she'd lose him again. She forced herself to keep moving, to keep that electric feeling coursing through her nerves. Not *too* much, not enough to expend all that energy and waste it, but just enough to keep it flowing until she had him firmly in her grasp.

Again, she pictured his face. His eyes. His hair. His lips. She pictured his body. His chest. His arms. His waist. She pictured him grasping her knees and spreading her thighs apart. She pictured that special part of him moving toward her, hard and strong and ready to fill her aching depths.

"Albert..." she sighed.

Brandy...

It was working. He was there with her. She could feel him leaning over her. But if she opened her eyes now, he'd be gone. She needed just a little while longer.

She made herself slow down. She raised her arms and laid them on the floor above her head, her thighs still spread. *Take me,* her body said. *I'm yours. I give myself to you.*

A shivery sensation crept up her thigh. Ghostly fingers caressed her.

So close... Almost there...

She had to be careful. It would be so easy to lose him after getting this far. But she could do this. This was Albert. His mere presence had always soothed her when she had a troubled mind. She could use that. She could be both calm and excited at once. Because he was her perfect fit.

She took a slow, deep breath and focused on his voice, on hearing him over the pounding of her own heart. *Where are you?* she asked him as she imagined reaching out for him. If they could connect, maybe she could bring him back to her, like when they both traveled to Nicole's location out in the Denselands.

But he didn't answer her. Instead, she felt his fingers close around hers. His hand was so warm...his skin so soft...so *real...* It made her heart skip a beat.

Not yet. He was so close, but somehow she knew he wasn't quite there yet. She needed to stay focused. She didn't want to lose him.

Come back to me, she begged, her body trembling with desperate anticipation. *Please...*

Then his body was pressed against hers.

He was kissing her.

She wanted him so badly and he was *right here.* Those were his lips pressed to hers. Her body was quivering with anticipation. She reached up with her free hand, wanting to embrace him, but she didn't quite dare. She was afraid she'd try to touch him and find that he still wasn't there.

His other hand closed around her tender breast and she let out a surprised gasp.

Now!

She gripped his hand tighter and threw her other arm around him. Then she wrapped her legs around him, encircling him, *capturing* him as they kissed. She'd drag him back to her if that's what it took. And she wouldn't let go. Not ever again!

Wait... Something about this felt wrong.

No... *Everything* about this felt wrong!

This wasn't Albert! It didn't even *feel* like him anymore. This was someone smaller, someone lighter.

It wasn't even a *man*!

Teeth chomped down on her lower lip, wrenching a surprised scream from her.

"He's *mine* now, bitch!" growled Dolly.

At the same time, a sharp pain shot across her left breast.

She sat up with a terrified scream, her fists swinging, trying to fight off the foul witch...but she was alone in the ichor chamber.

She leapt to her feet and grabbed her light, shining it back and forth, searching her surroundings, but there was no one else there.

Gasping for breath, her heart pounding, she wiped at her bleeding mouth, cursing.

The bitch *bit her*? She spat on the floor, eager to rid herself of the taste of both the blood and that woman's lips. How utterly revolting!

Then she looked down at her burning breast. Five bloody scratches were drawn across it.

Teeth *and* claws.

"*Fucking cunt!*" she shouted.

Chapter 71

It felt a little strange, holding Violet's hand again. And a little awkward, if Everett were being honest. That wasn't just a peck she gave him back there. That was a full-blown kiss. The kind they showed in movies. He wasn't expecting that. He was pretty sure he even felt her tongue for a second or two there.

(*Doesn't mean we're a couple or anything.*)

Right. Of course it didn't. It was like she said. Just an impulse. A spur of the moment kind of thing. She was frightened and alone and in trouble. He didn't even do anything all that special, he didn't think. He was pretty sure Alice had more to do with rescuing her than he did. But she was probably confused and in some state of shock at that moment.

It didn't mean anything. Except, "Hey thanks!" maybe… Something like that…

So why was he having so much trouble forgetting about it?

He should be focusing on the path ahead of them. The Priestess of Ruin might still be lurking nearby.

He glanced down at Alice. That wasn't just a random bit of common sense, he understood. It was what she was telling him. Get his head in the game before he ended up banished back to the void and poor Violet ended up in another coffin.

"I still can't believe she tried to bury you alive," he said, pretending not to be obsessing over that kiss. "That's messed up."

"No shit. And she didn't *try* to do anything. She *did* it. I'm probably gonna have nightmares about that for the rest of my life."

"I'm sorry I didn't get back sooner."

She glanced back at him, a bewildered sort of expression on

her dirty face. "Forget that. I'm just glad you came back at all."

He supposed she was probably right. Saving her sooner would definitely have been better, but that really seemed like one of those "better late than never" situations.

She kept pushing forward, pulling him along, not daring to stop or even slow down. Likely out of fear that the monstrous Priestess of Ruin would snatch her away again. He certainly couldn't blame her.

"Why don't you tell me about that dollhouse?" she suggested, sounding eager for anything to help get her mind off the inside of that grave.

"It's kind of hard to explain. From what the Eeshee and the puzzle box told me way back in the Denselands, there's some kind of...flipside? To everything? And that's where I was? Like we're all on one side of the paper and if you flip it over, that's where I was for a while? Does that make sense?"

"Nope."

"Yeah, it didn't really make sense hearing myself say it, either." He kept looking down at her hand. She had such pretty hands, so small and soft, like a child's. She didn't have fancy nails like Olivia and Andrea. They were short and painted a simple black that was mostly scuffed off now. And she wasn't wearing any rings or bracelets. Only a watch. Just that and that strange blue shard of glass that hung around her neck. "I guess that was kind of the flipside of this labyrinth," he continued, half-convinced that she must've noticed him gawking at her hand like a weirdo. "Everything was reversed, but not, like, *physically*. More like...*conceptually*."

"How does *that* work?"

"Reality became fluid and imagination became tangible, I guess?"

"Huh..."

"Yeah. Like I said. Weird." Maybe it would be better if he started back at the beginning. Floating around in that void. Or would that only make things *more* confusing?

But before he could speak again, a strange sound erupted from somewhere up ahead. Violet stopped and clenched his hand hard enough to make him wince. He mouthed the word "ow" but didn't dare say it loud enough for her to hear him. Instead, he managed to keep his voice even and whisper, "What was that?" instead.

"Hound," she whispered back.

A hound? Didn't Wayne say something about a creature he called a hound while they were still on the train? Something about monstrous, four-legged beasts covered in slashing razors? Was he remembering that right? Because that didn't sound like a real thing.

Violet was sweeping her light across the floor in front of them, he realized, which was somewhat confusing, since the sound seemed to come from somewhere farther ahead of them. Were they smaller than he was led to believe?

"Not in *this* passage," she muttered to herself. "I think we're safe for now."

"How can you tell?"

"Hounds scratch up the floor in passages they can get into." Already, she was moving again, though slower now, creeping on her toes. She didn't exactly look confident. "No scratches, no hounds."

"Okay," was all he could think to say to that. Good safety tip, he supposed. Don't wander down any passageways with scratched floors. Although he wasn't sure what kept them corralled to specific corridors…

"I ran into some of those things earlier. They're like something straight out of hell."

"You actually saw them?"

"Like a demonic cross between a lawn mower, Freddy Kreuger and a pissed-off chihuahua."

"Oh…" He wasn't sure how to picture that, so he dismissed it and simply reported, "Alice says there's a safe path ahead. We're still going the right way."

She didn't respond to this. Instead, he saw her glance back at the little doll, uncertainty painted across her pretty face. He didn't exactly blame her.

It was getting easier to communicate with Alice, but no less strange. If anything, it was even weirder that he understood her. Not because she was a talking doll, but precisely because she *didn't* speak. There were no words. She had no voice. The information simply popped into his head as if it were his own thoughts and ideas. He wasn't even sure how it was that he knew when she was talking and when he simply thought of something on his own. He simply just knew.

He was glad it was Violet he found when he returned. She seemed pretty chill, overall. He suspected that Wayne might have taken one look at his little dolly companion and forbid him from tagging along. It seemed like the sort of thing he might draw the line at.

Ahead of them, the path split. A second passage branched off to the right. The noise was coming from that way.

Alice let him know that straight was, indeed, the wiser of the choices, but Violet was already pulling him forward, continuing on without stopping for any doll advice, so he decided not to mention it.

Instead, he looked back at the passage they were passing, curious. Was that really some sort of creature making that noise? It sounded more *machine* than beast. He kind of wanted to see one... But he chose to keep that to himself, too.

The sound faded back into silence again. It happened quickly. Violet was moving a little faster now that they were past the dangerous passage, but they still weren't moving all that fast. The sound should have receded slowly, meaning that whatever was making it must have sped off in some other direction.

How many monster-infested passageways might they have walked right past in this darkness *without* hearing that sound, he couldn't help wondering. Was it only dumb luck that they didn't stumble into one of those as soon as they arrived here?

They continued forward for several minutes without speaking. Everett, for one, kept thinking about the hounds. He wanted to ask her to describe them for him, but he didn't feel like that would be a very good idea. It seemed like something she was eager to forget about for a while. But he was so *curious*.

"What's that?" she whispered, distracting him from his

thoughts. She was shining her light up ahead. The passage seemed to open up into another chamber.

She didn't ask the question because she couldn't tell it was a room of some sort. As soon as he looked up, he saw it, too. There was something off about the floor in there. It was darker than it should've been.

They were going to need to be careful.

He frowned and looked down at Alice. There was no specific reason to think that they needed to be careful. Other than the fact that this whole labyrinth was full of dangers and so they should *always* be careful, that was. But this wasn't just a casual "don't let your guard down" kind of warning. She was telling him to be careful. And she was saying it for a reason.

Violet was moving slowly again, creeping toward the room ahead. She was perched on her toes, the muscles in her calves tight and ready to spring into a dead sprint, even without a psychic doll's ominous warning ringing inside her head, so he didn't bother passing the message along. Instead, he focused on those alien thoughts inside his own head, trying to piece together the unintelligible tangle of half-comprehensible ideas she was using to communicate what they needed to do.

The first thing he was aware of—beyond that they needed to be careful—was another confirmation that this was the correct way. This was important, he realized. Because there were dangers here. It would be easy to turn back and avoid it, but that would be a mistake. Either there was no other way through here or turning back would take too long for them to finish whatever they were here to do. Or perhaps turning around would prove to be even more perilous than whatever stood in their path now.

Violet crept to the end of the passage and shined her light into the space waiting for them. "What the hell is *this?*" she whispered.

It was a good question. The space was enormous. And it wasn't like any other chamber he'd seen here. There was no floor or ceiling that he could see. Instead, he was looking out at what he could only describe as a rough conglomeration of stone columns and archways and openings laid out in every direction, creating a pattern like a bizarre cross between a sort of insectile honeycomb and porous volcanic rocks. It was literally a room full of *holes*, as if the only purpose the stone provided was merely to separate the space into as many openings as possible. The way back was an ordinary corridor consisting of smooth, straight surfaces and right angles, but everything in front of them was rough and raw. It was like no other part of the labyrinth that he'd seen. In fact, it looked like something that might've been more at home in that twisted nightmare skyline he glimpsed on the other side of the void.

She shined her light through several stone holes, revealing nothing but more of the same behind each one, then turned and looked at him. He wasn't sure what she wanted him to say. Alice already told him not to turn back. All he could do was feign confidence and nod encouragingly.

"Okay," she sighed, turning her attention back to the tangles of stone and shadow standing before them. "But I have a bad feeling I'm not going to like this area."

Chapter 72

Andrea stared at the scene before her, so familiar and yet so alien. She grew up in that house. She played in those rooms, in this yard. She laughed and cried and loved inside those walls. But just like her own apartment, it lay in ruins beneath that sickly crimson sky, shattered fragments of her past strewn about her feet. "What is this place?" she asked, not sure if she really wanted to hear the answer.

"It's sort of like the Wood," explained Stella. "Everywhere and nowhere all at once, ever present but very rarely reachable. Some people call it 'the Ruin,' but the *place* doesn't really have a name. The Ruin is what we call the inevitable chaos that radiates from reality, a sort of natural biproduct of existence, the tendency for everything to drift apart and do its own thing. This world acts as a sort of insulation layer for living worlds, absorbing the Ruin and keeping it from unraveling the Keeper's meticulous design."

"I don't understand any of what you just said."

Stella laughed that strangely familiar laugh and casually brushed her hand through her hair again, as if they were back in their favorite coffee shop, chatting over lattes instead of standing here naked, staring at the ruins of her childhood home under an apocalypse sky at the center of an uncrossable forest. But she wasn't trying to be funny. She felt like her life had been turned upside down. Psychic psychopath wedding crashers. Towering horse-legged monstrosities. Barely-theres and sentient streets. Gouging stations and man-eating fish people. And now she was supposed to just accept that troublesome Stella wasn't just spouting nonsense when she called herself a *goddess of chaos*? It was all so much. Was anything ever going to be normal again?

"This isn't real," said Andrea.

"It tends to mirror the spaces closest to it, but it can also present itself as places familiar to those who enter it."

"So…it's like those pocket dimensions Gina told us about. It's just…*mimicry.*"

"It is," said Stella. "This isn't your world. It's still there. Your parents are safe."

"Thank God…"

"But don't think for a second that this isn't real, too." She turned and faced her, her hands on her hips, still not bothering to hide herself, and looked out into the forest behind them. "There are things out here that will happily eat you alive."

Andrea turned to follow her gaze and found that something tall and shadowy was wandering through the skeletal trunks in the distance as if summoned. Her heart leapt at the sight and she crowded a little closer to Stella without thinking about it. For a moment, all her poor brain was capable of registering was that there was another monster over there and she didn't want to experience her guts being ripped out again.

But that thing wasn't what she saw outside her apartment. It was something different. Something much taller and stranger.

"What are they?" she whispered.

"The short answer is that they're souls corrupted by the Ruin," she replied, not bothering to lower her voice at all. A benefit of being a god, she supposed. What was there to fear when you were already the scariest monster in the room? "But it's far more complicated than that."

"I'll take your word for it…" She watched the strange creature as it wandered through the blood-tinged wasteland. It was too far away to see clearly, but it definitely wasn't even close to being human. It was taller than many of the dead trees. Its arms dragged the ground as it walked. Its feet were huge and covered in strange, dangling things that resembled roots more than toes. And it looked for some reason as if its head were facing the wrong direction.

Stella walked away and Andrea turned to follow her, but she

stumbled as another bizarre wave of vertigo washed over her. She closed her eyes, nauseous, and focused on steadying herself. "Why does that keep happening?"

"That's your physical body reacting to various changes in your environment," she explained. "Happens when I move things."

"Move things?" When she opened her eyes again, she realized that everything was different again. They were suddenly back at the clubhouse where Brandy and Albert were married. She was staring out over the lake, but the water had all dried up. Only the lakebed remained, a dead expanse of dusty, cracked earth.

She turned around, her heart leaping, her arms crossed over her naked body, her brain insisting that this was a public place, that there must be countless people here, all of them staring at her.

But there was no one. They remained alone in this nightmare world.

"You're the one doing this?" She recalled stumbling around in the ruins of her and Nicole's apartment. She felt that same disoriented dizziness then, too, making it impossible to walk. It was around the same time she knelt on that nail and stepped on something sharp. Was that why those particular injuries didn't go away with all the others? Something about being moved around within the Ruin?

"I can do whatever I want here," replied Stella. She glanced back at her with that grin that used to be obnoxious but was quickly beginning to look blatantly sinister. "This is my world. I'm the Priestess of Ruin."

"I thought you were the 'goddess of chaos.'"

"Same thing."

"You're so *weird!*"

"You know you love me."

"I used to…" she muttered, feeling a sickly sort of pang deep in her heart. "Is Stella even your real name?"

"Oh I've had *so* many names," she sighed as she turned to face her again.

"Okay… So which is your *real* one? Who were you born as?"

"I don't have one. I wasn't really born. In the beginning, everything was…" She pursed her lips and gazed up at the red sky, pondering it for a moment. "…*yet to be*," she finished. "Including concepts like names."

"That's kind of freaky…"

"For longer than I was ever anyone else, I was Tia. Some of the Old Ones still call me that sometimes. You can, too, if you want. But you can also just keep calling me Stella. It's not like I really lied when I told you it was my name. It's what I chose to be called the day we met."

This was all so *weird*. She had so many questions. "Old Ones?" she asked first.

"Others who've been around for a long time. Remnants. Gods. Things like that."

Andrea looked out over the dry lakebed, her head still spinning. "What is it you're *doing*? Ada said you were the reason all that awful stuff happened to us while we were trying to get to Cedric's Cove."

"That's true. I was the one who convinced Glum to kidnap you. I was the one who sent the horsemen to run you off the road. And I was the one who kept letting Goar Nangup's psychotic little pet know where to find you."

"Oh my god!"

"And that's just what I did to *you*. I sabotaged the gatekeepers of the stone and shadow roads. I sent terrible things to ambush your friends. I'll even take credit for sending the monster that killed the troublemaking bimbo with the sunflowers." She pointed out over the dry lake. "Right over there."

This sent a fresh chill down her spine. She killed Erin, too? "*Why?*"

"Shits and giggles?" she replied with that increasingly nasty grin.

"*Seriously?*"

"No. Not seriously. I had my reasons. But it *was* entertaining watching you all struggle."

Andrea groaned. "You don't make any sense. How are you a chaos goddess if you're the one *behind everything*? That's not chaos. It sounds to me like you're a total control freak."

Stella laughed. "Well, nothing is ever really black and white, is it? Sometimes the best tool for creating chaos is the very order that seeks to suppress it."

Andrea frowned. "Huh?"

Again, she laughed. "Let's just say that sometimes you have to play your enemy's games to have any chance of beating them."

"That answers *nothing*! Why would you do all those things? Why...?" She shook her head, bewildered. "Why bother pretending to be that ghost girl back in that creepy hospital if you were just going to strand me in that dead spirit highway?"

"I didn't. Ghost Girl was real."

"What?"

"Yeah. She was a little *too* helpful. So I sent her away."

"How? *Where*?"

"Somewhere she couldn't be a bothersome little brat," was her only reply. "I wouldn't worry about her."

She stood there, her hands still crossed over her body, trying to process all of this. Ghost Girl was real? The one who led her to the exit in that creepy hospital and then saved her from Hotdog in Cedric's Cove? And for all that, Stella just...*sent her away*? And then she pretended to be her just to screw with her? What happened to her? Was she okay? Was she gone forever?

None of it made any sense. *Was* there any sense to be made? Or was this woman simply *insane*? What kind of monster was she? Had she been friends with some kind of *she-devil* all this time?

"And as for *why*..." Stella continued, "...you couldn't comprehend the entirety of it. Everything's a lot more complicated than what can be perceived by a human being like you. Kind of like making a movie. All you see on the screen is two people having an intense conversation alone in a room. But in reality, they're standing on a set, surrounded by cameras, lights and an entire crew of people. Reality is a lot like that. Humans are extremely limited to what they can perceive and understand. But the short answer to your question is that I want to break the Keeper's machine."

Andrea stared at her as she processed this. "Again..." she said after a moment, "...*why*? I get that Hotdog's creepy god wants the worlds to end because he's trapped underneath it or something. That *kind of* makes some sort of sense, I guess. But what do *you* get out of it?"

"I told you," she said as she turned and walked across the dead lawn. "I'm the Priestess of Ruin. The chaos goddess. The primordial personification of anarchy and bedlam. The more unraveled everything becomes, the stronger I am."

Andrea followed after her, frustrated. "But if you let the world end, wouldn't that mean no more chaos?"

Stella stopped walking and turned to face her again, a surprising smile spread across her face. "Clever girl. That's true. But what if I don't *end* it all? What if I break the machine *just enough* to make a real mess of the *next* world?"

"What?"

"It's happened before. And it was *gloriously chaotic.*"

"That's just..." She shook her head, bewildered. "...*crazy*!" She couldn't even imagine what a world like that would look like. It sounded horrible. "Why?" she asked again.

"Because I'm *bored*!" shouted Stella, startling her. "The worlds the Keeper creates...one after another...they just keep getting smaller and smaller. We keep *losing* things. No one believes in anything anymore. We're locked into this rigid framework of logic that prevents people from doing all the amazing things they used to be able to do. No one sails the stars anymore. No one manifests their imagination. No one tames the elements. I mean, just fucking look how little *magic* is left in the world today!"

Andrea stared at her, her eyes wide with surprised wonder. She remembered Gina telling her that she'd heard magic was real once. That felt like so long ago...

"People used to do amazing things. They used to *live thousands of years*. They used to *summon gods into existence*. They used to *transcend realities*. But not anymore." She fixed Andrea with those dark eyes, her grin gone. She looked neither sinister nor mischievous. She looked strangely sorrowful, as if her heart truly ached for all these lost things. "The Keeper took all that away from you. All in the name of patching up a flawed system that's eventually going to fail anyway. It's like slapping duct tape on a sinking ship, delaying the inevitable, buying time but preventing nothing."

Andrea felt so confused. The Keeper did all those things? He took away their magic? What did that mean? What kinds of worlds had they left behind?

"I'm not going to let him take away anything else. I'm going to break his machine. I'm going to break the cycle. I'm going to make him start over."

"And how would you even do that?" she countered. "You just said back there that the Keeper planned for everything. That includes you, too, doesn't it?"

"True. There aren't many in existence who could beat him. But I *have* bested him a few times. I know a thing or two about his mind. I know that his machinations contain a few precious constants. Take even one of those away, and the whole system crashes."

"And you think you know where one of those is?" Because it sounded to her like a case of a needle in a haystack on a cosmic level. People just kept talking about how the Keeper could see everything coming, that nothing ever happened that he didn't plan for, that his designs were utterly and completely infallible.

Stella took a step toward her, that mischievous smirk returning to her face and making her look strangely sinister again. "I don't *think* anything. I *know*."

Andrea took a step backward, the hairs on the back of her neck standing up, and bumped into something. She turned to see what was there, only to find herself back in the crumbling walls of Gilbert House.

"All I have to do is remove *you* from the equation," said Stella. She lifted her hand, revealing fingers that had stretched into hooked knives. "And it'll all...fall...down."

Chapter 73

Erin was standing in the pitch-black corridor, deep within the City Beyond Memory, surrounded by shifting, darkling murk.

But at the same time, Erin was sitting on the dirty forest floor, covered in scratches, bruised and bleeding and out of breath, staring at the stone Giant's hand reaching out of the earth.

She could feel the smooth stone floor beneath her feet.

She could smell the forest around her.

It was cool and stale.

It was hot and humid.

It was eerily silent.

The air was filled with all the symphonies of nature.

Was she going mad? She pressed her hands against her face, struggling to clear her muddled thoughts.

Why was she back there? That was months ago! And it wasn't something she wanted to go through again! If she were going to get thrown back into her past, why couldn't it be a pleasant memory? It would be so nice to be learning to play her guitar again with Paxton. They'd lost touch ages ago. She missed her. Or that music festival she went to when she was twenty-one? That was fun. Or why not that weekend she spent with that handsome drummer she met in Milwaukee? *That* was a memory she'd gladly relive a few times. (*So* hot!) But no, she was stuck in that Kentucky wilderness, risking her life for an ancient-ass cosmic key that was just going to eventually get her killed anyway!

This didn't make any sense. Why was she reliving *that* day in her head? Wasn't there something she was supposed to do here in the present? Somewhere at the far end of this black passage?

There was something on the far side that she needed to find…
Something important…

She needed to focus.

She took a deep breath and lowered her hands, her useless eyes still closed against the darkness, and reached for the wall again.

But the wall wasn't there.

Confused, she opened her eyes.

She was standing in that forest from last year, staring at the stone bluffs that resembled a buried giant's protruding hand…

Why was she back here again? What was happening?

Except…hadn't she been here this whole time?

She blinked down at herself, at the bleeding scratches on her legs and arms, at the burrs tangled in her socks and laces. At the dirt on her scraped knees.

What was she thinking about just now? Something about a dark passageway? What did that mean?

Was she so tired that she simply nodded off and started dreaming for a second there?

She pushed the crazy notion from her mind and stood up. The heat must be getting to her. All that running. The trauma of that awful fright those things in the forgotten cemetery gave her.

She just needed to focus.

And yet, as she crossed the dry streambed to the other side of the gully, she looked back over her shoulder.

She still felt as if someone were watching her…

Chapter 74

That was odd...

Corey looked down at his hands, at the bloody strings he was holding. Something was off, but he couldn't quite put his finger on where the problem was. An error in his understanding? A typo in the sentinels' coding? No. That didn't feel right. The sentinels were as unerring as the Keeper. Was it something *he* was doing wrong? A fault in his understanding? A hole in the translation? Some small detail that he'd overlooked?

He wanted to take *this* string... He reached out and held it toward one of the sharp contacts. It should go *there*. Precisely at the base, right where it met the wall. And yet that wasn't right. Something was amiss.

Except it should be utterly impossible for him to make a mistake. Everything he needed was right there inside his brain, all neatly tucked away and waiting for this moment. That was how it had been since he arrived here. Why would anything change now?

He could feel the wrongness in the energy as he held is hand out like that. It was like a mild electrical current flowing through him, except it felt...*sideways?* He frowned. He didn't understand what that meant, but it was the only way he could think to describe it. It was just sideways.

Again, he lowered his hand and stared at the contact as he tried to wrap his head around what he was doing wrong.

"Why did you stop again?" asked Austin.

"Just thinkin'," he replied without hesitating. Maybe he made a mistake with one of the surrounding contacts?

No. Again, that didn't feel right. Each one of them had fit

perfectly so far. There was a very faint yet very distinct signature to each one, almost like a gentle, magnetic tug at his fingers, pulling the string toward it, as if the two *yearned* to be joined. This was the first one that didn't feel like that.

Because it was wrong.

But it wasn't supposed to be wrong. It shouldn't be possible for him to do anything wrong. The genetic programing in his brain should have been perfect.

"I don't have time for you to sit around 'thinking.' Please do your job."

Corey ignored him. He stared at the stone spike. Something to do with that, perhaps? A malfunction in the device?

Again, that felt wrong.

Maybe it was something much simpler. He looked down at all the wires still coiled up beside him on the floor. A problem with the *order*, perhaps? Something else that needed connected before this one could be attached?

He should have expected something like this from the start. After all, he was dealing with incredibly advanced and incredibly *ancient* technology. *Not* encountering some kind of trouble should have been more unlikely.

But the more he thought about it, the more convinced he was that this wasn't an error with the machine. And he didn't make a mistake. Something else was going on here. Something he couldn't quite grasp.

If the problem wasn't with him and wasn't with the machine... He looked back at Austin, his thoughts churning. "How well can you self-diagnose your damaged body?"

"What are you babbling about?" he asked without looking at him.

"Are you aware of all the parts of you that got broke?" he clarified. "When you got your ass tore off?"

Now he turned his head, glaring at him. "Yes, I'm very much aware of my present condition," he snapped.

"No blind spots?" he pressed. "Nothing busted in there where I can't reach?"

"Quit fooling around and get back to work."

He looked down at the string again. If he attempted to go ahead and attach it, ignoring that bizarre "sideways" electrical current that hummed at his approaching fingers, it might shed some light on what was wrong. If he sent the equivalent of a short back through the strings and into Austin's body, he might be able to identify any problems and tell him what he did wrong. And it might be amusing to watch what the stoneworks equivalent of a short circuit might do to the rude little robot man. Two birds with one stone. But somehow he didn't think that would be a good idea. He could do far more than blow a proverbial fuse. He could damage something important, delaying his work here, which might put the others in danger. Or he could *break* something, making it impossible for him to finish at all.

No. Better to set this one aside and keep working. See if he came across any more like it.

He placed it on the floor, separate from the others, just in case, and then plucked another from the coil and continued his work.

But as he wrapped the next string around the stone contact, he found himself frowning at his bloodstained fingers.

He was missing something, he realized.

If he could only grasp the full picture, he might just be able to see it.

Except...what did that mean? The full picture? Wasn't he already carrying around an entire advanced civilization's blueprint collection in his genetic memory?

He pushed on as he pondered these new revelations.

Maybe it would come to him once he'd made some more progress.

But somewhere deep down, he couldn't help feeling that this was entirely wrong, that this problem simply shouldn't exist. And it felt *bad*.

Something was wrong.

And he didn't know if he could fix it.

Chapter 75

Nicole dragged the fingers of her free hand along the ridges in the wall as she walked. That single line along the ceiling had spread to every surface, creating a strange pattern of twists and curls and squiggles. "They sort of look like *brains*," she realized. "In an abstract sort of way, I guess…"

She hadn't seen any other surfaces like this. The only carvings she'd ever seen besides the statues were the archways leading in and out of the City of the Blind, which were covered in tiny likenesses of people that might have been from the emotion rooms. Everything else was smooth and clean and perfectly flat.

Gina was still holding the flashlight, still sweeping it across these new surfaces. "I don't know how to describe it, but there's some kind of purpose to it. It makes me think of a circuit board for some reason, but I know it's not the same thing."

A circuit board? She glanced back over her shoulder, considering it. She didn't know anything about electronics, but she was fairly certain there was no kind of electricity flowing through these walls. She wondered what Albert would make of it. Would he have any theories about how a temple of stone could be like a circuit board?

She wondered how he and Brandy were doing out there. Gina said they were still together last she saw them. Were they *still* together? Were they able to find anyone else between then and now? Andrea, perhaps?

She hoped they were all still safe. She couldn't handle any more bad news.

Gina stopped walking.

Ahead of them, the passage ended. There was a round room

waiting there, about twenty feet in diameter. Was that what they were looking for? Their destination?

But there was nothing inside the room. It was entirely empty.

"Can you see it?" asked Gina, her voice hushed.

She glanced down at her, confused. "See what?" she whispered.

She didn't reply. She merely nodded, as if she already knew what her reply was going to be.

Nicole squinted into the gloomy space, as if perhaps she'd simply missed something, but it looked the same as the passage they were standing in. It had the same brain-like patterns etched into the walls, ceiling and floor. "What do *you* see?"

"Mirrors," she muttered.

"What?" She felt a strange jolt of fear pass through her at the mention of the word, though she couldn't understand why. What could be so frightening about mirrors? She used them every day. And besides, there weren't any mirrors in that room. There was only that same dull, gray stone as every other surface in this fucking hell maze.

Gina started forward again, slower now, creeping toward the opening ahead of them, but she stopped short of entering the room.

"What does that mean?" she pressed. "I don't understand you. Is it safe?"

But she only shook her head. She didn't seem to understand it either. She wasn't being secretive, Nicole knew. She simply didn't have the answers. And blurting out questions wasn't helping. She clenched her jaw against the urge and forced herself to relax. She needed to let her think. This was probably a psychic thing, something a normie like her wouldn't understand even if someone *could* explain it to her.

Besides, the feeling was already gone. The thought of mirrors didn't frighten her. Why did she feel so startled for a second there? Was she just tired.

She looked around as they crept closer to the room. An empty space deep in a temple with no apparent purpose that made her psychic friends stop and look as though they'd seen a ghost... Was it another space like the one that killed Beverly Bridger? Or something similar to that? Something only someone like Gina could see?

No. Even as weary and emotionally drained as she was, that didn't feel right. This was something else, something to do with the "glass" Gina was talking about.

She reached up and wiped at her nose with her hand. She'd been sniffling since that last crying fit. Hopefully she hadn't made herself sick running around wet and half-naked down here in this darkness. This was already the absolute worst. How much more miserable could she be?

Then again, she probably shouldn't be complaining. At least she was still alive.

"I'm getting mixed signals from this room," said Gina. "It's dangerous here, but it's also where we're supposed to be. We have to be careful."

Nicole nodded. "Okay. Just tell me what to do."

Gina squeezed her hand. "Don't let go of me. No matter what happens."

She wanted to ask what it was she thought might happen, but decided against it. She was supposed to be asking less questions and letting her work. And besides that, she wasn't sure she wanted to know. Something about the way she was standing there, hesitant to enter, was frightening enough. The longer they stood here, the more ominous that room seemed to her.

"Mirrors..." muttered Gina, talking to herself again. "But not mirrors. Not light. Not reflections. More like how magicians use them. Optical illusions. Forced perception. Tricks of the mind." She stared into that empty space, thoughtful. "Deceptions..."

Nicole squinted at the room in front of them. Optical illusions? Was there something hidden there? Something right in front of her face that she simply couldn't see? Was that another thing they had to be wary of?

She found herself imagining some horrible monster crouched in the middle of that carved floor, perfectly camouflaged, just waiting for them to get a little closer so it could lash out and gulp them down. The thought was somewhat silly, she thought, almost cartoonish, given how many things she'd encountered that were far more terrifying than some fairy tale invisible ogre, and yet it sent a subtle shiver through her body anyway.

"Holes…" Gina muttered on. "Gaps… Different from the cracks that let me move back and forth…"

She nodded again, as if she understood any of that.

"Those were just doorways. This is like a freeway interchange."

Nicole was aware that she wasn't at the top of her game right now, but she really wasn't able to make sense of any of this. Holes and gaps and cracks and doorways and freeways? It was just an empty room. There weren't even any other passages leading away from it. It was a dead end.

Except it obviously wasn't.

"What's in there?" she dared ask, unsure if she really wanted to hear the answer.

"Decisions," replied Gina. "Lots of them."

And yet she could see exactly *none* of them…

"There are so many ways we can go from here," she went on. "So many places we could end up. One wrong step and we could go somewhere impossible to come back from."

Nicole didn't ask any more questions. She very much doubted that anything more she had to say on the subject would be less terrifying than all the things that were racing through her mind. She merely nodded again and kept her mouth closed.

"Don't let go of me," she warned again, squeezing her hand for emphasis. "I don't know what might happen. We can't risk getting separated."

Nicole wrapped both her arms around Gina's and gripped her tightly. "I trust you."

She glanced up at her, clearly uneasy about the task before them, but managed a brave nod. Then she crept forward, into the mysterious, empty room.

Chapter 76

Olivia didn't care for this new area of the labyrinth.

Her back was pressed to one wall, sidling along the narrow passage while the other wall crowded against her front, so close that her heavy breasts grazed it whenever she drew a breath.

Wayne was beside her, leading the way, wagering that there were probably fewer dangers behind them in this darkness than ahead of them, and she hadn't dared let go of his hand even in this tight spot where losing him seemed downright impossible. It certainly didn't appear that he was going anywhere too quickly. He was bigger than her, after all, his belly sliding along the surface much the same way her boobs kept doing, and so did the toes of his shoes with each step he took, threatening to trip him.

For a while, they were able to continue walking normally, if not side-by-side where she could properly cling to his arm as she pleased, but the walls kept closing in. It seemed to have stopped shrinking some time ago, but if it started getting smaller again, she wasn't sure how much farther they could continue.

Someone as small as Andrea could probably slip through here without a problem, she was sure, but for a plus-size like herself, it was becoming pretty claustrophobic. She really hoped they reached the end soon. The idea of finding another nasty surprise while caught in a tight spot like this was more than a little unnerving.

Thankfully, she hadn't felt anything from her psychic alarm since escaping the invisible thing on the storm-drenched rooftop. But she'd still rather not be squished in this little space like a waffle. It was much nicer when she was just squished up against Wayne. She could've stayed there for hours, she thought, just enjoying his kisses and imagining that they were somewhere safe and warm.

She just wanted to go home and be with him. It felt like forever since she saw her own bedroom.

"There's an opening up ahead," reported Wayne.

"Thank goodness. I'm starting to feel like a sardine."

"Let's save any thanks until we see what's up there."

He had a point. Just because her psychic alarm wasn't going off didn't mean they hadn't arrived somewhere even more unpleasant than this cramped passage.

It was a slow process, sidling through this crack of a corridor. It took several minutes to reach the end of the passage. And somehow, knowing they were nearing the end made that claustrophobic feeling even worse. Her body seemed to grow impatient. Even though she was sure the walls weren't any closer together, it felt harder to breathe. She wanted out of here *now*.

"Almost there," promised Wayne. He must have been able to hear her breathing getting heavier. He'd always had a knack for noticing little details like that. He always knew when she was feeling uncomfortable or unhappy.

She closed her eyes and willed herself to stay calm just a little while longer.

"What the hell is *this*?" he growled, making her heart sink a little.

What indeed? What was he looking at? She couldn't see around him!

"Careful," he warned as he slipped out of the narrow gap, still clinging to her hand.

As soon as he was out of the way, she saw it. The chamber waiting there was unlike any they'd encountered before. It was the same smooth, gray stone as every other chamber of the labyrinth, but it was shaped like an upside-down cone, open above them but tapering almost to a point beneath them, the whole space roughly three stories tall. There was a narrow pathway spiraling around it, providing a way up and down, and all along that pathway were several dozen more passages leading out from the chamber in every direction. But these passages weren't all the same. There was a variety of shapes, each and every one of them unnervingly small. To leave through any one of them, they were going to have to either sidle through it like they did the one that brought them here or crawl through on their bellies.

None of them looked big enough to be at all comfortable.

"They're just making fun of me at this point," she decided, annoyed. "Seriously, every other girl here is *way* skinnier than me, why am *I* the one who finds this spot? It's like they're *trying* to bump off the fat girl."

"Don't do that," said Wayne. "You know I hate hearing you talk about yourself like that."

She made a face at him, the one that said, "It's my body, I'll talk about it however I want," but he wasn't looking at her. He was shining his light from one passage to the next, trying to decide where they should go from here.

He wasn't wrong, she knew. Body positivity was important. And she also knew there was a difference between being overweight and simply being curvy. Like her mother and her sister, it was just simply the way she was built. Wide hips. Large bust. Round butt. Strong thighs. Her legs had a certain muscle tone to them. She wasn't rocking a six-pack by any means, but her belly also was neither saggy nor bulging. She was very healthy. She was just sort of...well-rounded, maybe? But when your best friends were skinny little things like Andrea and Brandy or the very model of fitness like Nicole, it was sometimes hard not to think of yourself as the chubby one. And it wasn't like she said it to put herself down. The fact was that it wasn't Albert and Brandy or Andrea and Nicole who found themselves in the itty-bitty part of the labyrinth. It just seemed sort of intentional, was all.

"Feel anything?" asked Wayne.

"What?" She blinked up at him, distracted.

He glanced down at her and gestured at his head. "Any clues from the upstairs navigational department?"

"Oh..." She turned her light out over the room in front of them. Not only was it an unhealthy habit referring to herself by phrases like "fat girl" and "the chubby one," it had the added inconvenience of making Wayne argue the matter with her, which always made her a little bit giddy and distracted... Again, probably not the healthiest mindset, but she couldn't help it. She liked hearing him tell her how perfect he thought she was.

But now wasn't the time to be distracted by flattery. She had a gift. And she was supposed to be using that gift to scout a safe way forward. Except, she'd never encountered *this* many passages before... She didn't know where to begin.

She shined her light at one, then the next, moving her way along the room, trying to take her time in spite of the fact that she just wanted to find the right one and get out of this maze of cramped spaces. But nothing was coming to her.

Even focusing on the path behind her didn't give her any real sense of dread beyond a subtle and unnecessary feeling that she probably didn't want to go back to that stormy rooftop.

Was this psychic thing even working properly? She still didn't know how trustworthy it was, what dangers she may remain blind to, what monstrous things might be able to hide themselves from her...

"This is hard," she said as she turned her attention to the higher passages.

"Take your time."

Easy for him to say. He wasn't the one responsible for keeping them both out of trouble. It was unnerving worrying about what might go wrong if she missed something.

But as she peered into one passage after another, she continued to feel nothing at all.

"Maybe there's not a wrong way," he reasoned after a moment.

"Or not a *right* way," she countered. If she'd already made a mistake before they arrived here...and if it was too late to turn back... But then again, she supposed if that were the case, she should have been able to feel it. That was how it worked, wasn't it? It was a psychic alarm, not a compass.

Was it just that it really didn't matter which way they went?

"What about that voice you were hearing?" she asked.

He was making his way slowly up the spiraling pathway, his light aimed up at the stone ceiling, gently pulling her along as she continued to cling to his arm. "Every now and then I can still hear it, but it's too soft. I can't hear where it's coming from."

In other words, they weren't getting any help from *anywhere*. Perfect.

He stopped walking, a puzzled expression on his face as he stared up at the highest passages. Then he lowered his light and stared down at the floor of the room below them. "I'm not sure what to do. Picking one at random doesn't seem like a good idea, but I'm not sure what *else* to do at this point."

She ducked down and shined her light as far into the passage behind them as it would reach. Something tickled at the back of her mind, a subtle warning, perhaps? A sign of danger? But it was weak. Hardly an imminent doom. And as she squinted into the darkness, she thought she could see why. The passage was even narrower farther back. An uncomfortable crawl, for sure, even more claustrophobic than the one they just exited from. But probably not impossible.

She was starting to think that maybe he was right. There was no right or wrong way. They might just have to pick one.

But when she stood up again, she found that he was still staring down at the bottom of the cone-shaped space before them, a strangely thoughtful expression on his face. "You okay?"

"Hm?" he asked, distracted. Then he blinked and glanced at her, but only briefly. His eyes were quickly drawn back to the bottom. "Sorry. I just feel like..." He trailed off. Then he shook his head. "Something about that looks really familiar for some reason."

She looked down at the very bottom of the chamber, at the point where his light was aimed. It didn't look familiar to her. It was just a little patch of stone and the beginning of this spiraling ramp they were standing on. There weren't even any passages at the very bottom. It was too small an area.

But Wayne tightened his grip on her hand and started down the ramp, leading the way.

Curious, and with no ideas of her own to speak of, she focused on keeping up and not stepping too close to the edge of the path.

"Remember Nora's Lilac Grove?"

"Nora's what?" she asked, confused. Then she remembered. "Oh, you mean that weird trailer park place?" God, but that felt like so long ago…

"Remember what we remembered when we got there?"

"What?" Remember what they remembered? Was he feeling okay?

"Our *dreams*," he stressed.

"Oh!" She *did* remember, she realized. As they drove through that labyrinth of mobile homes of all sizes and shapes and ages, she began to realize that it all looked weirdly familiar. She remembered distinctly feeling as if she'd seen that old, burnt-out husk of a trailer and those faraway power lines before. Although she'd forgotten all about them as quickly as she'd awakened, she'd been having dreams about that place for a while. They only came back to her when she saw those things with her own eyes and realized that they were familiar. "Wait… Is this room like that? You dreamt about it?"

"I'm not sure if it was a dream, exactly, but I had a serious case of déjà vu when I looked down from up there. I *know* I've seen this *somewhere* before. I just don't know where."

They circled around the loops of spiraling pathway, all the way to the bottom of the room.

"I think there might be something down here."

"I don't see anything," she said as they approached the base of the ramp. There wasn't anything *to* see. There was nothing down here. It was just an empty space. But she was starting to feel something. An uneasiness. A tensing of her muscles. Like watching a suspenseful movie and hearing the music ramp up. Was something going to happen?

"I don't either," he agreed. "But there must be *something*. It's the only thing that—"

But he wouldn't have a chance to finish that thought. He stepped off the platform and onto the floor of the cone-shaped room, and then the floor simply seemed to vanish.

Still clinging to each other, they fell.

Chapter 77

Brandy trudged through the filthy ichor chamber, hugging herself against the cold, sniffling back tears.

Albert wanted to go this way, to see what the sentinels were trying to show him, and he was usually right about such things, so that was what she decided to do. Besides, she was already covered in this shit. What did it matter now?

But it felt so awful, pushing on without him.

That fucking witch...

Her lip was still throbbing, the taste of blood lingering on her tongue. And those scratch marks on her breast wouldn't stop burning.

It didn't help that she wasn't wearing a bra. Albert's over-sized tee shirt was soaked with heavy ichor and kept rubbing against the scratches. Especially the middle one that cut right across her areola, nicking her sensitive nipple. That one was particularly painful.

Where did the bitch even come from? She was sure she was connecting with Albert. It sounded like him. It *felt* like him. Right up until it wasn't. Was she just pretending to be him to get as close to her as possible, the better to attack her? Or did she really find him and she somehow swapped places with him when she let her guard down?

It made her stomach turn thinking about that foul woman kissing her.

She didn't think she'd ever wanted to gouge someone's eyes out as badly as she did right now.

She shined her light behind her, still paranoid about the darkness back there, especially now that she was alone. She hadn't made it very far yet. She could still just make out the partially submerged sentinel, its bare ass shining in the gloom.

The ichor was still getting deeper. It was past her belly button now. Once it reached her chest, those scratches were probably going to hurt even worse. She *really* hoped she didn't end up having to swim in this stuff. Was it even possible to do that? Or would she only sink in something so dense? She wasn't sure how that sort of thing worked.

What a miserable ordeal.

She kept going over what happened back there in her head, trying to understand what went wrong. First, there was the way Albert disappeared. She couldn't push that awful look of surprise on his face from her mind. And the way he simply toppled backward into the ichor... It really looked as if something had physically attacked him. It even looked like he was pulled under. Dolly was supposed to be inside his head, wasn't she? And yet Albert told her that she was the one who broke their flashlight back in the anxiety room, trying to prevent her from reading the pervert's book. How could she only be inside his head but *also* be capable of affecting things around him?

And then there was what happened with that spell. Why did the sex magic connect her to Dolly instead of Albert? Did being inside his head mean that she was able to intercept them whenever she wanted? How were they supposed to deal with something like that? She was *cheating!*

"Bitch!" she grumbled again. "Fucking *whore!*"

And another thing! Didn't the pervert say she wasn't allowed to attack them? Something about their contract forbidding her from doing them any harm? What happened to *that?*

She wanted to sit down somewhere and cry. It was all just too much. She couldn't handle this, not all on her own. But a bigger part of her refused to give that conniving little slut the satisfaction, so she trudged onward, deeper and deeper into the disgusting, viscous ooze.

It felt so gross...

It was oozing up the legs of her shorts and into every crevice of her body. It felt so slimy and cold against her skin.

Albert was right, though. No matter how she looked at it, this was better than that reeking muck they were all forced to wade through last time. That stuff smelled like the foulest swamp mud, mixed with garbage and shit and any number of dead things. It was just as cold as this, and just as slimy feeling in places, but it was also gritty and lumpy and squelched hideously between her toes. And worst of all was how she remembered it *burning* in all her scrapes and scratches. In contrast, this stuff was odorless and had only *one* grotesque texture. It looked and felt a lot like clean motor oil, she realized, slick and smooth and thick. And it didn't sting in any of her scratches, not even when it climbed up under her shirt to the claw marks that sadistic hussy left on her poor tit. It was the weighted-down tee shirt that was irritating her there. If anything, the cold was actually sort of numbing…

She trudged onward, frustrated and alone, angry and afraid.

It was up to her shoulders now. She crept forward on her toes, her arms out at her sides, paddling gently to keep herself upright and prevent her head from dipping below the surface.

It occurred to her that she'd now assumed the same pose as the sentinels that led her here. Those clever, giant, horse-hung freaks. Albert would call it proof that she was doing what they meant for her to do. He was usually right, after all. Especially about this sort of thing.

She should've just listened to him.

If she hadn't been so squeamish about entering the ichor, would he still be here with her? Was letting go of his hand and throwing a childish fit about not wanting to wade through the gross goo the only reason that spooky bitch was able to get her claws into him? She felt so *stupid*. After what happened with the psychic predator, she should have known better.

Wherever he was, she hoped he was safe. But she kept glancing at the flashlight clutched in her hand. It was the only one they had, meaning wherever he was, he was in the dark. And it wasn't even theirs, she recalled. They lost both of theirs when they were separated from Violet and Corey. This was Nicole's, meaning that neither she nor Albert had a means of illuminating their way through this darkness. Nor did Gina. Would they really be all right in a place like this without any light?

It wasn't even doing her any good right now, ironically. There was nothing in this room to see but an endless lake of ichor. The walls and ceiling were well beyond its reach. There were no support beams to be seen. There weren't even any more sentinels. She was feeling her way along the submerged floor with her toes. Being blind wouldn't make any difference at this point.

At least the ichor wasn't getting any deeper. As long as she stayed on her toes, she could keep her chin out of it.

God, but it felt so gross...

She looked behind her again. The sentinel was well out of sight by now, too. There was literally nothing to use for bearings. It was going to be almost impossible to keep to a straight line. If this room was too big, she might never find her way to the other side.

She fixed her attention straight ahead, trying her best to stay on course.

Except...

She stopped and stood there a moment, perched on her toes, frowning into the darkness ahead of her.

Was she facing forward? It was very possible she'd already veered off course a little, the way she kept looking back like that, but she was sure she was moving at least *mostly* in a single direction. Yet she suddenly didn't feel so sure anymore...

She shook it off and continued creeping forward. It was only her imagination. Just a bit of paranoia, born from the realization of how easy it would be to get turned around if she wasn't careful. But she hadn't been here long enough to get herself turned in a completely wrong direction.

So why did it feel like she was going the wrong way?

Again, she stopped. She shined her light back and forth, squinting in every direction.

Was she going *this* way? Or was it more *that* way?

All this stress was getting to her, she realized. She was tired and frustrated, her head full of worries and doubts. She just needed to trust herself and keep going. The sooner she crossed this awful room the better.

And yet she found herself wondering for some reason if this was even the same chamber she was just in, as if *that* made any sense. Of course it was the same chamber. Where else would she be? It wasn't as if she'd walked through a doorway without knowing it.

Was it only her imagination?

This stuff didn't smell like anything, but was it giving off some kind of odorless fumes that were beginning to mess with her head? That was an unpleasant thought. How would she protect herself from something like that?

Her shoe slid a little on the stone floor, startling her out of her strange thoughts as she slipped down to the top of her neck.

She had to be careful. This stuff was slimy. And the last thing she wanted was her entire face covered in it.

She pushed onward, her attention focused on her footing this time. But still she couldn't shake that feeling like she was only getting herself hopelessly lost.

She tugged at Albert's shirt, pulling it away from the tender scratches on her chest. It felt like it was getting twisted around her.

"Albert..." she sighed. "Where are you?"

Chapter 78

"Where am I?" muttered Albert.

He was in a daze, his head spinning, struggling to grasp this bizarre new situation he'd found himself in.

He was standing alone in an unfamiliar kitchen, surrounded by immaculately clean countertops and modern appliances. There was a single light on over the stove, but everything else was dark. It appeared to be the middle of the night and he could hear the faint sound of rain pattering on the windowpanes.

None of this made any sense, of course. After all, he was fairly sure he was just being drowned in a pool of foul, slimy ichor by Shanzer's nasty little witch.

He didn't remember going for a snack break.

There was no sign of Dolly. Did that really happen? Or was it only some kind of bizarre illusion? And how'd he end up here, in some random kitchen? Why the hell did stuff like this keep happening to him?

More importantly, where was Brandy? Was she somewhere in this house with him? Or was she still back in that ichor chamber, with no idea where he'd gone? He needed to find her. He swore he wouldn't let anything separate them again. But he wasn't even sure where to begin looking for her. He didn't understand where he was or how he came to be here.

He wanted to call out her name, but he didn't quite dare. He still didn't know anything about this place. Something was telling him that it would be a mistake to announce his presence.

He looked down at himself, confused. There was slimy ichor smeared on his skin, but he wasn't covered in it like he should've been. His shorts were wet and stained and his hair was tacky with it, but it wasn't dripping off his body. The blood was gone, too, seemingly washed away when he went under. Had he already dripped dry? How long ago did that awful encounter happen? How much time had he lost?

He was still half-naked. His shirt and shoes were still gone. And so was one of his socks now. Did he lose that while struggling to fight off Dolly? He couldn't *remember* struggling. He recalled her pushing him under…then *nothing*. He was just standing here in this kitchen he'd never seen before in his life.

It was a really *nice* kitchen. Much fancier than his and Brandy's apartment kitchen. It reminded him of his aunt and uncle's house in the city, but this wasn't theirs. His first thought was that maybe he was dreaming again. The cat lady and her creepy voices. But there were no cats here. None that he could see, anyway. And that place had either looked like his own home or like that shadowy, dust-covered room with the old lady who looked somewhat less than alive.

He turned around, scanning the space, half-expecting to see feline eyes staring at him from every surface. But the more he looked, the more details popped up. There were fresh apples and oranges in a basket on the counter. There was a single dirty fork and a coffee mug in the sink, waiting to be washed. The light was glowing on the dishwasher, announcing that the contents were clean and ready to be put away. There were small, potted plants in the window above the sink, one of which looked a little withered. And there was an opened envelope and someone's reading glasses sitting on the island.

If this was a dream, it was the most vivid one he'd ever had.

He walked across the room, through the dining area and out into the spacious living room. Everything remained completely unfamiliar, and yet the details were incredible. There were rugs on the floor, decorations on the walls and books on the shelves. There were even framed portraits hanging up, filled with smiling faces that he also had never seen before.

It looked just like some random people's house.

But why would he be in a stranger's house?

Again, he looked back across the gloomy space, the hairs on

the back of his neck prickling. If this wasn't another of the cat lady's creepy dreams, then Dolly must've brought him here. But why? What was she up to?

He realized that he was clenching his fists and forced himself to relax. It was agitating being away from Brandy again. He didn't like being alone. And he liked the idea of leaving *her* alone even less.

His gaze fell on the door. What would happen if he simply tried to leave? Would he even be able to? Already, he found himself convinced that it wouldn't work like that. Either the front door would lead somewhere impossible, like right back into the kitchen or maybe to an entirely different house, or it simply wouldn't open, like the doors in Shanzer's sleezy manor.

Still, he'd feel pretty stupid if he ignored it and it actually turned out to be the way back to Brandy. That was the sort of thing that would be just his luck, after all.

He walked toward the door, only to freeze mid-step when the silence was broken by a strangled cry from elsewhere in the house.

He turned back, sweeping the ceiling with his eyes. That came from upstairs. Was someone in trouble? It sounded like a woman. Was it Brandy? Was that witch hurting her?

He forced himself to remain calm. He didn't hear it very well. He had no idea if it was really her. It could be someone else. Maybe it was Gina. Or Nicole. They had no idea where either of them went. Maybe Dolly trapped one of them here, too. And what about Andrea or Olivia? Violet? They were all sealed up inside the impassible wall, so it wouldn't make sense for it to be anyone else. But then again, that was assuming any of this was remotely real.

(Boo.)

He shuddered at the memory of that damned witch hovering over him in that ichor pit, grinning that wicked grin, giggling that sadistic giggle.

He turned his attention to the stairs. He couldn't help wanting to race up them, itching to find the source of that cry. Something in the back of his awful mind kept insisting that was Brandy's voice, that she was being harmed up there, that he needed to hurry. But what if that was exactly what Dolly wanted him to do?

He needed to stay logical about this.

If this *was* her doing, then he very much doubted there'd be any way out. Confronting her might be the only answer. And if this *wasn't* her for some reason, then he should probably check on whoever just cried out upstairs. Just in case.

Although he *really* wasn't happy about it…

There was a luxurious fireplace on one wall, its oversized interior dark and cold. He snatched up the iron poker from its stand and gripped it tight, making a mental note that weapons weren't usually this easy to find, meaning it was probably going to prove to be useless. Then he crossed the room and squinted up into the ominous darkness atop the steps.

There was a window up there, and a faint light somewhere beyond. A streetlight, maybe? Or a security light of some sort? It offered little in the way of illumination, instead only highlighting the raindrops pouring down the glass.

He started up the steps, all too aware of his mismatched feet, one stockinged and one bare. It made no difference, really. A single sock wasn't going to affect his ability to walk or run, and yet wasn't it odd how strange it felt wearing only one? He'd probably end up tossing it away soon. But for now, he needed to keep his attention fixed on his surroundings. If Dolly was here somewhere, then he couldn't afford to let himself get distracted. He wouldn't let her catch him off guard again.

He stopped and listened. Was that footsteps he just heard? Or only his imagination and the sound of the rain?

In his head, he could almost hear the witch's nasty, evil giggle as she watched him from whatever shadows she was lurking in.

He pushed on, determined. He needed to be careful, but he couldn't afford to take his time. What if Brandy was in danger? What if she needed him to save her? These were the questions that wouldn't stop needling him.

He reached the top and turned the corner, only to find himself looking down a long, dark hallway. *Too* long and dark, he felt.

It was like looking down a hotel hallway. Was this house even this big? The first and second floor didn't seem to match.

The only light was coming from under a closed door about halfway down it on the left. While he stood watching, he saw a shadow crawl from one side to the other.

Someone was in there.

Brandy? Dolly? Or someone else entirely?

Again, someone cried out. A soft voice, feminine, muffled, desperate. It was still impossible to identify and yet his brain insisted that it was Brandy's voice, forcing him forward, pushing him toward that door.

He gripped the poker in both hands, ready to defend himself from whatever he found up here.

His heart was thundering. He might as well be back in that awful anxiety room, working himself into a full-blown attack.

He felt something cold and sticky beneath his bare foot. When he looked down, his sole was stained a dark color.

It was only now that he saw the stains on the carpet and walls.

Blood.

It was splattered everywhere.

A desperate panic began to well up inside him. What was happening up here? Whose blood was that? His gaze fell on the wall next to him, where a smeared handprint stared back at him.

Gilbert House's blood-spattered walls flashed into his mind. The horrific scene he found behind one door. The hideously brutalized remains of poor Trish...

Was this going to be like that? Were there things behind these doors that he'd never be able to unsee?

His thoughts rushed back to Brandy. Where did she go? Was she somewhere safe? Or could this blood...?

He couldn't take it anymore.

He rushed forward and threw open the door.

Chapter 79

Violet didn't like this place. Why was it so different from the rest of the temple? She could feel the raw, uneven stone pressing up against her bruised soles through her filthy socks, threatening to trip her or stub a toe with every step she took in this endlessly oppressive darkness. She ducked under a low arch and inched around a tight corner past a gaping hole on the floor. She shined her light down it as she passed. It seemed to plunge forever into the darkness, branching off in countless other directions along the way. In this chamber, they were constantly just one wrong step from a deadly fall. It certainly wasn't the sort of place she wanted to find herself in need of a fast retreat.

"Why is this even here?" she wondered aloud. "What's the point?"

"There's not really a single answer," replied Everett. "The simplest way to put it is that this whole labyrinth is a series of trials and tests, making sure we have what it takes as a species to keep moving onward, I guess. But it's a lot more than that. There are things involved that we're not capable of understanding. Things about the sentinels. Things about the Keeper. And things about the technology and materials they used. And then there's our inherent limitations in perceiving the world around us. That more than anything, I think. We only ever see a small percent of what's really there. And even a lot of what we *do* see isn't what it appears to be. I imagine we'd be a little bit like a germ crawling through the inner workings of a cell phone, too small to see anything with any clarity and no way to comprehend what any of those components..." He was looking around as he spoke, taking it all in, but he trailed off as he finally realized that she'd stopped walking and was staring at him. "...do anyway," he finished, looking embarrassed.

"Did your doll tell you all that?"

"Kind of. Some of it. More or less. Some of it I already kind of knew. Or...suspected, I guess. I don't really *know* that much."

She turned her attention forward again and scanned the options in front of her. She could go through the opening to the right and from there either continue forward or climb down into a lower area. Or she could climb *up* and into an opening above her, continuing forward from there. Or she could go left and around, roughly back the way they came, with several more paths splitting off along the way. Choosing felt rather meaningless, if she were being honest. There were too many choices, too many openings, too many holes in the stone. And no matter which she picked, everything would look completely different within a few steps and she'd be faced with all the options all over again.

It reminded her for some reason of the tokkatok nest she and Corey stumbled into in Minnesota that frigid January. She wasn't entirely sure why. That was dirt, not stone. And the holes those creatures bore were each separate tunnels that all branched out from a central shaft in an organized manner. They weren't jumbled up and overlapping like these. Most of these didn't even go anywhere. And yet she found her thoughts drawn back to those horrible creatures again and again as she pushed deeper into this labyrinth of holes, making her feel more uneasy with each passing minute.

Was that what this was? Some kind of hive? A home for something terrible built right into the temple as some kind of trial?

She needed to stay calm. There was no sign of anything living down here. If she let her imagination get away from her, she might frighten herself. And if she let herself be frightened, she could easily get careless. She shined her light down another gaping hole beside her and saw that it was a forty foot drop. Carelessness wouldn't be her friend in a place like this.

The worst part was that this place didn't look familiar to her at all. Did the other one ever bring her here? How lost was she?

And for that matter, where *was* the other one. She hadn't heard a peep out of her since Everett rescued her. Was she simply conserving her strength again? Or was it possible that the Priestess of Ruin did something to her?

Are you there? she tried. But there was no answer.

"Alice says we should be moving upward," reported Everett. "Like, *always* upward."

She shined her light up into the openings above them. The strange little doll wanted them to climb?

"I mean, it kind of makes sense. We're trying to get to the *top* of the city, right? The top of the tallest tower?"

(*The other side of the colors.*)

She frowned as the other one's words drifted back to her, an image of that world's impossibly colorful sky hanging overhead in those bizarre dream-visions.

The Oblivion Door.

She stood there a moment, trying to determine whether that was her own thoughts or a confirmation from the other one from somewhere inside her. It was so difficult to tell the difference when they were both the same voice.

"So I guess we should be climbing," reasoned Everett. He stood behind her, still holding her hand, his neck craned, squinting up into the gloom hanging overhead. "Looks kind of dangerous," he observed. "Are you comfortable with it?"

She glanced back at him. He was so sweet and considerate. "Don't worry about me," she assured him, recalling all the trees she played in growing up, always swift and graceful and fearless. Not only did she love it, but it was one of the few things she could do better than Corey. He was strong enough to climb, but his excessive weight and bulk had always slowed him down. And he was always good at knowing his limits, so he'd either stay on the ground or keep to the lowest branches, content to simply watch her from below. The memory made her smile a little. "I can climb."

"Good," he replied, nodding. "Me too."

She glanced down at their hands. The problem wasn't going to be the climbing, it was that they weren't going to be able to stay connected like this while they did it. And the thought of getting separated again, even just losing each other in this confounding room, made her feel sick. She didn't want to risk being left all alone again.

"We'll stay close together," he promised, clearly reading the concern on her face. "Help each other. Watch each other's backs."

"Okay," she replied. But she didn't like it. She held on for a moment longer before reluctantly letting go of his hand.

"Alice says the Priestess of Ruin isn't here right now. She says she's...preoccupied with something. I think..."

(*Two little birdies caught in my cage...*)

She felt a shiver race through her as those awful words surfaced again in her mind.

No. She couldn't be distracted by that ancient bitch and her mind games. She needed to focus on the task in front of her.

The stone was considerably rougher than most tree barks. There was no shortage of hand- and footholds. She felt her way up the stone wall, carefully choosing the best of them, and scurried up over the first ledge. Then she immediately turned and shined her light down for Everett, who wasted no time copying her movements.

The flashlight was a bit of a hinderance, slowing her down a little. She might have to tuck it into one of her pockets to free up both hands. Or maybe clench it between her teeth. But only if it became really necessary. It would be extremely bad if she were to drop it down one of those bottomless-looking holes. And she liked being able to aim it wherever she pleased. All those surrounding holes made her nervous. She was convinced there'd be something in here somewhere. And the less she could see, the more likely it would be to leap out and surprise her at any given second.

Everett didn't have a flashlight to worry about. Instead, he was still carrying that creepy, golden-haired doll, which appeared even more awkward. Especially since he was being weirdly careful with it, almost as if he were carrying a kitten instead of a queer little toy.

In spite of his strange burden, however, he seemed to manage his way up over the ledge easily enough, then perched there and grinned at her, perfectly pleased with himself.

She shined the light upward again. She couldn't see how far up it went. There were too many openings overlapping, each one a different size, a different angle, a different shape.

This might take a while.

And she had a feeling she was going to *really* start missing her boots in the near future.

Chapter 80

"You think *I'm* that important?" scoffed Andrea. She stared at those five gleaming blades moving toward her. It was such a strange thing to look at. She couldn't quite tell where the weapons ended and where Tia began. Her entire hand had become some kind of mechanical-looking collection of glistening shapes that seemed to fuse in and out of the flesh of her outstretched arm. She couldn't wrap her head around it. And the fact that she was terrified out of her mind didn't help. She was doing her best to remain calm, but her heart was pounding and she was quickly losing the battle against a fresh wave of tears. "There's no way. I don't even know what that little creep wants me to do. He doesn't tell me anything!"

"There's not a doubt in my mind," replied Stella.

No. Not Stella. *Tia.* Stella didn't exist. She was a lie from the very beginning. There was only the monster standing before her. She wouldn't think of this horrific *bitch* as Stella anymore. She didn't deserve that name.

"I mean, it *is* possible he's foreseen my interference and placed you in my path as a decoy. Maybe he *wants* me to kill you, hoping to keep my attention away from someone else. He's done it before. He's a wicked little bastard like that sometimes. Cold-blooded. Heartless. *Ruthless.* So maybe you're right." Her eyes flashed with evil delight and she leaned closer, pressing those dagger-like nails against her throat. "One way to find out, isn't there?"

Andrea squeezed her eyes closed. She could already feel the tears sliding down her cheeks again. She couldn't help it. She was so scared. And she felt so *used*. How could she have thought that this…*thing*…was ever her friend?

"No," sighed Tia, withdrawing her deadly nails a little. "I've already accounted for that possibility. If you were only a distraction to keep me from killing some *other* chosen soul, things would have gone very differently after I brought you here."

She blinked back those stubborn tears and stared at her. Since she brought her here? "All that stuff I went through?" she whimpered. The wreckage of her apartment. The roofing nail and the glass. Those monsters and the steel trap. The night tree? That was all some kind of sick test? To see if the Keeper would keep finding a way to save her? "You were trying to kill me?"

"Not *kill* you," corrected Tia. "Not *yet*. It wasn't that you *survived*. Existence in the Ruin is more fluid than solid, ever shifting, ever slipping through the rocks and gaps. It takes a lot to kill a person in such a place. The momentum of life tends to keep it in place, sending it slipping through the streams, drifting from one to another." She leaned forward, those tragically familiar eyes locked on hers. "No. It's that you're still here." She reached up and tapped Andrea's temple with one of those sharp nails. It felt like being pricked with a needle. "Up *there*."

Andrea reached up and rubbed at the spot, confused. "What?"

"After all that you've been through, you should be a drooling sack of raving madness by now." She flashed her a strangely insane-looking grin. "But look at you! You're still completely and utterly *you*."

She shook her head. "So, you were trying to *drive me crazy?*"

Tia didn't respond aloud. She flashed her a wide, toothy smile and opened her eyes wide while mouthing an excited "Yeah!" as if immensely proud of herself. It was such a painfully familiar response that it hurt her heart to see it again.

Why did it have to be Stella?

She felt so *betrayed*.

"But you're *not* crazy."

Andrea wrinkled her nose at her. "I was friends with *you* wasn't I?"

Tia pushed her mouth to one side and tilted her head as if

to say, "Fair point."

Really? That was why she was subjected to all that horror? This self-proclaimed "Priestess" was a certifiable lunatic.

"You're not even really traumatized," she added. "That's the real proof that you're one of his crucial ingredients."

"I'm not," she insisted, rolling her eyes for emphasis. Those experiences were terrifying, but after all she'd been through already, how was a few near-death hallucinations supposed to drive her to madness?

Tia leaned toward her, staring intensely into her eyes. "You don't even remember most of it, do you?"

"Remember *what*?" And yet, there was something so utterly and horribly *true* about that question that it sent a chill crawling down her naked back. Like flashes of a forgotten dream, brief, fragmented recollections flickered through her mind. Pain. Screaming. Blood. Burning flesh. Things so terrible that it felt as if her very brain were being ripped in half. Not just a few times, but over and over and over again, for endless hours. "Wait..." she breathed, a dreadful understanding creeping up from her deepest nightmares. "How long...have I been here...?"

"Time doesn't really work like that here, sweetie," replied Tia.

Time works funny in places like those, she recalled Gina telling them.

"Days or years or decades..." she went on. "All the same here."

Years? *Decades*? Was it possible? Had she been living through one deathly nightmare after another, again and again and again, trapped in an endless loop of horror and suffering?

"I lost my other little plaything pretty quickly," she said. "But *you* I've been playing with for a *long* time."

"Your other...what?" Was she saying that she was torturing someone else here in the Ruin, too? One of her friends? But what did she mean she *lost* her? Her heart leapt with fresh fear.

But the woman stuck her lip out in a childish pout and crossed her arms, pushing up those obscene breasts in the process. "Someone swept in and took her away before I could really gauge her importance to the Keeper."

So…someone saved her? She wasn't killed or driven mad? That was a relief. One less thing for her to worry about, at least.

"But I didn't really need you both," Tia decided, "so that's fine. I only need one of you. And trust me, you're the real deal. There's only one way you're still you right now. It's because the Keeper *needs* you."

"I'm telling you, you're wasting your time," Andrea insisted, trying hard to sound confident despite being frightened out of her mind.

"The Keeper of Minds," whispered Tia. She was suddenly pressed up against her, pushing her against the wall, those larger-than-necessary breasts mashed against her, her lips brushing her earrings as she spoke. "The Keeper of Wills. The Keeper of Fates."

Andrea never even saw her move, and yet she was right here, far too close for comfort. And she couldn't get away! Her bejeweled hands were pressed against the concrete on either side of her, keeping her in place. She tried to push her, but it was like pushing against the trunk of a tree. She wouldn't budge.

"Do you get it now?" she asked. "He decides what you can and can't do. He decides it all. He can put things in your brain, make it possible to do things you couldn't do otherwise."

"Get off me," she grunted, still trying to push her away. This was getting *way* too personal. They were *naked!* And she was absolutely *not* into lying psychopaths who pretended to be people's friends for *four stupid years!*

"And he can take things away whenever he wants, too." Finally, she leaned back and met her eyes. "Such as dangerous memories that might break a fragile little mind like a twig."

Dangerous memories… She frowned at this. Was that what happened to her? Was the Keeper really able to simply take away traumatizing memories to protect her sanity? Had he somehow rewired her brain to make her able to do the things she did? She remembered Albert saying that they never really did anything five years ago, that all they did was follow the Keeper's script. But was the truth even stranger? Were they all somehow *brainwashed* into being the exact people to do the job he wanted them to do?

"Don't think for a second that he's above fucking with people's minds," Tia warned her with a nasty sort of smirk. "Would you like to hear some of the terrible things that he let happen to the people he *didn't* need anymore?"

"No," she replied. "Will you get your udders off me already?"

Tia gave a far too familiar bark of a laugh, then turned and walked away.

Andrea crossed her arms over her own chest, a shudder of revulsion passing through her at the memory of the feel of her naked skin pressed against hers. That was another Stella thing, though, testing personal boundaries. Making people uncomfortable. Seeing how far she could take things before someone lost their temper. Another pang of regret echoed through her heart.

"There are always sacrifices in the Keeper's plans," said Tia. She was standing a few paces away, her back turned, staring up at that bloody sky with her hands on her hips, looking unnecessarily comfortable in her birthday suit. "It was true five years ago. And it's true now." She looked back over her shoulder. "But then, you don't know about that, do you?"

Andrea stared at her, confused. "Don't know about *what*?"

She made such an exaggerated pout at her that there was no chance it was sincere. "One of your friends has already paid the Keeper's price."

"What're you talking about?" She stepped forward, but something grabbed her from behind. The world seemed to turn sideways and she was lifted off her feet. Her eyes wouldn't focus. Her stomach gave an unsettling lurch. Then she was hanging again, cold links of steel wrapped around her bare body.

She squeezed her eyes closed, willing her swimming head to clear.

"That cute boat captain you set sail with. What was his name?"

"Keith?" She blinked, confused. She felt so weird. Her stomach was all knotted up and burning. She felt as if she were going to be sick.

"Yeah, him." She was standing the same distance away, but she was facing her again now, grinning that obnoxious grin. "He's dead. Sorry to say."

Keith was... *What?* She struggled against the chains, blinking back tears. She felt so disoriented. Why was she chained up again? When did that happen? Too much was going on all at once. She couldn't keep up with it all. "No..." She looked up to see that the crumbling walls of Gilbert House were gone. Stretched out before her was a lifeless expanse of flat earth, dotted with the skeletal trunks of long-dead trees. "You're lying."

"Why would I lie to you? It makes you so mad."

She looked up at the chains. She was dangling from the remains of some kind of rusty steel structure. "He can't be..."

"Oh, he most definitely is. Died right in Nikki's arms. *So* tragic."

She was shaking her head. No. That was a lie. It had to be. She wouldn't believe it. She was trying to get inside her head, to freak her out. That was what she'd been doing this whole time, after all, spouting lies and toying with her emotions. All that business about everyone being dead already...

"Believe what you want. I'll spare you the gory details, let you pretend that he went painlessly."

"Bitch," she groaned.

"The *biggest* bitch!"

"What is *wrong* with you?" she shouted.

Tia laughed. "Oh, sweetie..." She stepped forward, her familiar eyes gleaming with sadistic madness in the bloody light of that crimson sky. "I wouldn't know where to begin."

Andrea refused to play her games. She turned her attention to the chains, instead, struggling against them. "Let me down!"

Without warning, the chains went slack. She fell forward with a startled shriek, then yelped as she was yanked to a stop again. The next thing she knew, she was leaning far forward, suspended almost horizontally over the ground.

And Tia was standing directly below her, staring right up into her startled eyes.

"My point is that bad shit's gonna happen. You can't stop

it. Even if I let you succeed and make your way home, you'll just end up with your heart broken and your sleep full of nightmares. Nothing's going to change that. That's just the way the world is." She reached up and closed her hand around her throat. "Because that's the way the Keeper *made* it."

"So you're just going to make it worse?" Andrea challenged. Tia's grip was unnaturally strong, like a machine. It didn't even feel like human fingers. There was no softness to them. No warmth. And yet she remained able to speak. She wasn't strangling her. She was only holding her there, keeping her from struggling.

Her eyes widened in a clear, "Duh!" sort of expression. "That's kind of my thing, sweetie." She drew closer. Andrea couldn't tell if her freckled face was rising toward her or if she were being pulled downward despite the chains. It was disorienting. Something about this environment was messing with her head, making everything feel wonky. "I'm going to see just how infallible the Keeper's plans can be. Can he plan around something as unpredictable as me?"

No... Not something about this environment. It was something about *her*. Tia. This self-proclaimed goddess of chaos. It was almost as if reality itself was breaking around her.

Tia let go of her throat and dragged her fingers down her chest and across her exposed nipple.

"Don't touch me you weirdo! What the hell?"

Tia laughed. "But you're so wonderfully vulnerable like this. I just want to *violate* you."

"Are you bipolar or something?"

Again, she laughed, but she wasn't joking. First she tortured her. Then she admitted to trying to drive her mad. Then she blatantly dropped that whole, "your friend is dead" bomb on her. Then she got all pissy and preachy about the Keeper. *Again.* And now she was threatening to molest her? Mood swings much?

"You're so much fun to hang out with," she sighed. She lifted her hand, revealing that her nails had once again turned into those dreadful hooked knives. "It's almost a shame it's over."

Chapter 81

"Beneath the slumbering giant's palm…" muttered Erin.

She stepped up to the stone bluff and looked it over. There was a gap beneath it, just as Horatio's ridiculous clue suggested, tight and dark. She knelt down and peered into that darkness. It went back pretty far. Even in broad daylight, she couldn't see all the way to the back. Was there some kind of marker hidden in there? Something buried?

She knew she was supposed to locate something called "Yggdrasil's thorn," and that it was some kind of key…but beyond that, she didn't really know what it was. Was it a literal key? Like a skeleton key? Or more like something out of an old action adventure movie, where the key was some kind of magical, glowing stone or something? Or might it even be some kind of high-tech, alien device? She was still in the dark as to what, exactly, this thing was supposed to unlock.

She withdrew her cell phone and used its light to see what was there. But her heart sank a little when it illuminated a narrow opening hidden in the cracks of the rock. A cave? Really? She wasn't a fan of claustrophobic spaces. Or of bats. Or anything else related to caves.

But then again, she supposed it made sense. The thorn was ancient as hell, wasn't it? That was the impression she was given when Horatio told her about it. Or at least, it was part of what she thought she knew about the thing when that conversation was over. She still couldn't really remember what he actually said to her… But if it really was that old, then what better place to hide something for that long than to tuck it away inside a hard-to-find cave somewhere?

Still, she wasn't exactly happy about what she was going to have to do next.

She looked around, confirming that none of those ghoul-things had appeared again. If that was what happened just because she stumbled across that cemetery, what kinds of frightful things were waiting for her inside some dark, moldy cave?

Even if there weren't any monsters in there, wasn't it a bad idea in general to go poking around in caves? There could be anything living in places like these.

She groaned. She didn't want to do this. But she also didn't ever want to do any of that other stuff again, either.

Cursing under her breath, she crawled into the gap and wriggled her way toward the opening.

There had better not be any snakes in here.

But she could already see that there were spiderwebs. And where there were spiderwebs there were spiders. And where there were spiders, there were other tasty creepy crawly things for them to eat.

Luckily, she'd never been all that frightened of bugs. But it was still fairly icky. She tried to reach out and rake the space clean with her hands as she went, but still they managed to cling to her hair and face.

It was a tight squeeze, barely big enough to fit her shoulders through, but she could see fairly quickly that it opened up farther back. As long as she could keep dragging herself forward on her belly, she could count on it eventually getting easier.

But if she managed to get herself stuck down here, she was screwed. No one on earth knew where she'd gone, after all. It would be a very long, very agonizing way to die. And it seemed unlikely that anyone would ever find her body...

She couldn't think about that, though. If she let herself begin panicking, she'd almost certainly get herself stuck. She concentrated on her breathing, instead. Nice and steady. Shallow. Slow. There was plenty of room. She cleared her mind and focused entirely on moving forward.

It only took a few minutes to reach the first chamber, but it was long enough to confirm that she was never going to take up spelunking as a hobby.

The space was now big enough for her to continue on her hands and knees rather than her belly. It was an improvement, to be sure. It was even wide enough for her to turn around in if she needed to. But it was still much too small for her liking. And it was uncomfortable on her skinned palms and knees. She'd much rather be able to stand up. She didn't like the idea of not being able to run away at full speed if everything went south down here...

If something like those cemetery things appeared again, she wasn't going to have an easy escape.

She crawled forward, her light illuminating the way, her eyes peeled for signs of any dangerous creatures. She couldn't see to the end of the chamber, which was rather unnerving. But at least it wasn't wet and muddy. And for some reason, there weren't any spiderwebs in this part of the cave. In fact, she didn't see any bugs whatsoever. It was as if they just stopped somewhere between here and the opening and refused to go any farther.

What a ridiculous thought... Why would *bugs* of all things refuse to go somewhere? They wouldn't even stop crawling into the globes of her apartment's light fixtures and baking themselves under the bulbs.

The passage stretched farther into the hillside. It was sloping downward now, descending deeper into the earth, and the dirt covering the floor was thinning, giving way to raw stone, which was even more unpleasant against her bleeding hands and knees.

Again, she wished she'd at least packed some jeans on this trip.

Minutes passed and no end came into sight. It was getting steeper now. She couldn't help wondering what she'd do if she found herself somewhere she couldn't climb back up. But at the same time, she noticed that the space was getting taller. It was opening up a little, something positive for her to focus on.

But a few minutes later, the end of the chamber came into view and the floor ahead of her simply turned straight down.

A vertical shaft? How was she supposed to navigate something like that?

Confused, she crawled up to the edge and shined her light down the hole.

It was only about a six foot drop, but everything down there was different. Gone was the raw cavern walls. Instead, there was a perfectly flat, smooth floor.

"What the hell?" she muttered. That wasn't natural. Had she discovered some kind of hidden bunker?

Careful not to turn an ankle and strand herself in this weird, underground place, she dropped down and shined her light forward, discovering a small, perfectly square tunnel stretching away into the darkness.

Immediately, something about it struck her as familiar.

Had she been somewhere like this before?

(*This club exists at a point in space and time where the natural and supernatural worlds overlap.*)

She frowned at a flicker of a memory somewhere deep down in the depths of her mind. A vast forest full of black trees? Was that something she saw in a movie once?

(*You've reached the very heart of the Denselands.*)

Was she supposed to be somewhere else right now? It felt like there was something she was forgetting… Something to do with stone just like this?

(*A place where the weight of countless worlds is constantly crushing down on the impenetrable walls of the City Beyond Memory.*)

This stone…

Why did this look so familiar?

She squeezed her eyes closed and pressed her palm to one wall. She wasn't sure *why* she did it. It simply felt right somehow. It felt *familiar*. Smooth and cool to the touch, without a trace of dust or grime, as immaculate as the day it was constructed…

A passage that cut through the deepest heart of the murk…

There was something she needed to find… Something important… Something *crucial*… And this was the only passage that would take her where she needed to be. But there were dangerous things in this darkness, things that drifted like seaweed in the depths, but in shadow rather than water…

She opened her eyes, expecting only darkness, but somehow she was able to see.

Right… She had her cell phone light. Why did she think she was stuck in the dark?

What was that she remembered just now? *Was* it a memory? It was familiar, but she was sure she'd never been inside a passage like this one before. Was it something from a dream, perhaps?

Everything was so *strange*. What sort of world did she stumble into that day she visited the Elysium Fog?

She turned her attention to the corridor ahead of her. This place was creepy. Eager to find the thorn and get back out of here, she started forward.

Maybe things would make more sense once she had it.

Chapter 82

"I think I'm starting to understand it now," said Corey.

Austin glanced over at him, annoyed. He wanted to chat again?

"How you said you ain't what you appear to be. It's more than just a disguise, ain't it? Everything about you is so completely alien that we can't help translating everything about you into something recognizable."

"That's pretty much the gist of it, yes," he huffed. He wanted to tell him to shut up and get back to work, but the fact was that he hadn't stopped working. His hands were moving, making progress even as he ran his mouth.

"Makes me wonder what else in the world is like you. What have I come across in my life that I never thought anything 'bout but would've been completely crazy if I'd been able to see what was really there?"

"You'd be surprised," he replied. The fact was that there were things like that everywhere in the world. It was less common to stumble across a squirrel in a park than to find yourself within sight of something that didn't belong in the reality the human brain accepted.

"Even the vegetable trick wasn't what it seemed, was it?"

He scowled. "I'm still angry about that."

Corey chuckled. "I didn't actually make you talk in vegetables. I reverted you to some kind of sentinel machine code, didn't I? Whatever was coming out of your mouth wouldn't just be foreign, it'd be impossible for our brains to comprehend. It probably wasn't even words. Just...*raw data* or somethin', so we just heard you naming vegetables instead."

"Human brains are foolish. You never know what nonsense they'll choose to believe over the truth when it's outside their narrow field of understanding."

"I can't help wonderin' what things my brain's makin' me miss out on. But I kinda like all the made-up things it comes up with, too. I mean, how cool is it that we can craft our own realities instead of just seein' empty static when somethin' doesn't compute?"

"Whatever strikes your fancy, I suppose." He wished the man would just focus on his work. He'd stopped again. It was so frustrating when he did that. This was taking far too much time as it was. He wanted to shout at him to get back to work. Wasn't being bisected and left on the floor punishment enough? Why should he have to listen to this nonsense on top of that?

"Hm," grunted Corey. "No matter how I look at it..." he muttered.

What was he going on about now?

"Somethin' don't feel—"

"—that don't belong here."

Austin frowned and looked over at him again. What happened? Why did he just—

"—not matching up," said Corey.

"What?"

He turned and looked at him, holding up one of the bloody strands. "I know. Strange right?"

"What's strange?" he asked, confused. What was the oaf going on ab—

"—sure you're not broken somewhere?" asked Corey. He was suddenly leaning over him, frowning.

Austin blinked up at him, bewildered, as a strange feeling washed over him. It was as if the entire chamber were being tilted to one side, his weight shifting, making him feel as if he were about to fall in spite of the fact that he was already lying on the floor. Nothing was moving. And Corey didn't seem to feel the same thing. He was only sitting there, unfazed, watching him, meaning that it was something contained within him.

It wasn't something he'd ever experienced before, and yet

he found that he knew what it was. He'd read about it in his books, something humans experienced. It was vertigo. But why would *he* suddenly experience it? His body and mind were artificial. His sense of balance was fused into his very coding. It couldn't be disrupted.

It was still happening, even. It was such a surreal sensation. Was it some kind of unexpected reaction to something Corey did? Had he made a mistake somewhere?

No. That wasn't right.

Everything began to waver before his eyes, as if the entire world had begun to *melt*. Shapes and colors ran together.

Even stranger, he began to feel something impossible on his skin. A sensation like long, cold fingers gripping his body. Not merely the parts of him that still worked, but his nonfunctioning arm and lower back, even his *legs*...which, of course, were over *there*...

In all his many, many years, he'd never experienced any of these things. He wasn't mortal. He didn't get sick. He couldn't be poisoned. Drugs didn't work on him. He couldn't even get drunk (which he'd found unfortunate on quite a few occasions).

But the strangest sensation of all wasn't the vertigo or the hallucinations or even those phantom fingers. It was the sudden and alien feeling of *dread* that suddenly overwhelmed him. He'd never felt fear before. Unable to die, he'd never had any need of such an emotion. And there was no need for it *now*, as far as he was able to discern through the melting colors and those clawing fingers that couldn't be real. And yet he found himself gripped by a sudden and unexplainable terror that made no less sense than if he'd suddenly sprouted wings and a tail.

He squeezed his eyes shut, trying to force back all these strange feelings, and in the shallow darkness, he realized that there was a sound bombarding his ears, a strange sort of screaming, like the wailing of a wind, but filled with unnatural voices.

"What's going on?" asked Corey, still leaning over him.

Austin stared up into that melting face, his head churning with that alien fear. "Sabotage..." he breathed. Someone had done something. His programming was damaged.

He frowned that deep, thoughtful frown again. "What, like a computer virus or somethin'?"

A computer virus? Sure. Why not? Everything else was reduced to some stupid analogy, why not this, too?

And he wasn't entirely wrong, he was forced to admit. Something was eating away at him inside, corrupting his memory and corroding his core data. It wasn't so unlike contracting a computer virus. Something invasive and purposeful was eating its way through him.

Was this a part of the Keeper's plan, too? Was he doomed from the very beginning to come this far, to travel so long, only to fail this close to his goal? It seemed almost too ironic to be real...

"Hold on," said Corey, turning back to the strands piled around him. "We'll figure it out."

Right. They'd figure it out. He couldn't even see what he was really working on because his brain was rewriting everything to fit into its narrow capacity for understanding, but he was going to "figure out" how to remove it by dredging through his fake guts some more?

Humans were so frustratingly stupid.

But he didn't have time to tell him so. The world seemed to roll all the way over and everything ran together, plunging him into a confounding state of illogical data that might have been what these creatures referred to in his books as "absolute madness."

Chapter 83

Gina's heart was pounding. It felt as if she were creeping through a minefield. One wrong step could send them plummeting through an endless series of non-realities, each one more nightmarish than the last, with no hope of ever finding a way back.

The space here wasn't merely crinkled. It was folded over on itself so many times that she couldn't fully distinguish beginnings from ends, an unsolvable knot of unnatural dimensions and broken consciousness.

It wasn't going to be a matter of avoiding all of the holes in front of her. That wasn't going to be an option. It was about choosing the *right* path, the one that would take her where she needed to be without tearing her mind or body in half in the process. (And the less she thought about *that*, the better.)

"You should close your eyes," she realized.

"Okay," replied Nicole. She didn't hesitate. She didn't ask why. She told her she trusted her and she did. And that was good. She didn't want to explain that whatever was going to happen in this place would probably contradict her natural inclinations and her survival instincts might work against her, making her hesitate at the worst possible moment or, even worse, cause her to let go of her hand or even try to run away. If they were separated this deep inside the glass, she doubted she'd ever be able to find her again. She'd be lost forever.

There was no guarantee that wouldn't happen anyway. She didn't know what was in store for them here or how jarring it might be. If she were startled, she might still do something rash before she had time to think. But this was probably the best chance they had of getting through without any hiccups.

"And don't let go," she reminded her.

"I won't," Nicole promised, squeezing her hand for emphasis.

She felt like a liar, pretending to know what she was doing, pretending this was no big deal, like she was taking advantage of that trust. After all, what did she really know about any of this? She could barely even *see* what was waiting for them here. The very existence of these invisible, overlapping doorways was like an intrusive thought made manifest. It just popped into her head as she approached. Simply perceiving them was an exhausting task.

It was sort of like those stereogram pictures, the ones that revealed a secret image when you focused your eyes just right on them. If you looked right at the page, it was only nonsense. Repeating patterns, not unlike those etchings in the stone surfaces. And if she focused too far away, everything was blurry, warped like the images she saw through the glass labyrinth. This was the mistake she was making before. She was focusing entirely on the glass and leaving herself blind to the stone. When she realized this, she tried following the stone and ignoring the glass. But there was a point *between* the two that she needed to find. A sort of sweet spot. A goldilocks zone between the natural and the unnatural. That was where the path lay. That was where she'd find what she was looking for.

Her heart still racing, she crept forward, her eyes fiercely focused on those swirling patterns in the stone while her thoughts remained fixed on those unseen gaps within the room, feeling them, studying them, searching for the right path, careful to not step too close to the others. Many of them were drifting around, making it more difficult to keep track of them all.

The frightening truth was that it shouldn't have been possible for her to tell a right way from all the wrongs. It wasn't as if she'd ever encountered anything like this before. And yet she *could* see it. It was there. And the reason she could see it was that she could sense that awful unnatural energy flowing out of all the other places like a putrid and stagnant miasma. Deeper in the unnatural realm of this temple were things so terrible that she could almost smell them with her human nose. The very thought of getting too close to one of them made her knees tremble.

And yet she didn't dare let the fear show. As bad as this was, Nicole had been through so much worse. She needed to stay brave for her. After all the kindness she'd shown, after saving her life *multiple* times, this was the very least she could do for her in return.

But it was so hard to keep being brave. Especially here.

She focused hard on the path in front of her, careful that her rubbery legs didn't trip her up and send them both tumbling through some maddening hell, and let those awful energies circle through her psychic mind, sorting them out, one by one, peeling them back until only the correct one loomed in front of her.

But was it the correct one? She could feel the same dreadful energy emanating from there, too. It wasn't different from the others. It was merely the weakest of them all, the lesser of all the evils, the best of the worst case scenarios.

She didn't think about it. She didn't dare. She was already too far into the room. Those other paths had drifted around them, blocking the way back. If she lingered, they'd only end up falling into one of the other ones.

Still gripping Nicole's hand, she stepped forward and into the unknown.

Chapter 84

Brandy couldn't stand it anymore. She steadied herself on her toes and stripped off Albert's tee shirt. It smeared the ichor over her face in the process, but that didn't seem to matter. First of all, she'd already slipped and splashed the gross stuff all the way to her forehead several times now. Her glasses were already streaked with it. And secondly, it felt as if the stupid thing was strangling her. What was wrong with it?

She wiped away the oily goo and held the shirt up in front of her with one hand while she shined her light over it with the other. Why was it twisted around like that? Did she do that when she took it off? She thought she pulled it straight up and over. But was it even possible to get it twisted like that while wearing it?

Ichor was much thicker than mere water. It felt like some kind of oil. Did the drag of wading through something so dense and viscous pull on the fabric or something?

Her thoughts flashed back to that nasty little witch. Was she still able to toy with her somehow, even when she wasn't attempting a psychic connection with Albert? Was this supposed to be some kind of prank? A distraction?

A fresh wave of frustration washed over her and she felt a wild urge to simply throw the shirt aside, forgetting about it. But of course she'd only regret that. Instead, she clutched it against her bare chest, reminding herself that it was Albert's. And right now it was all she had of him.

Again, she shined her light around the empty chamber. It felt even bigger from down here, just inches above the surface of the ichor, as if she'd shrunk down to the size of a mouse in this already vast space.

And she was only growing colder the longer she remained submerged in it like this. She was shivering. She could feel her lips trembling. This was becoming as miserable as those frigid pools of water back in the first temple.

She wished she could catch just a glimpse of another light in this endless darkness. Being alone was the absolute worst. She hated it. And she was worried sick about all her friends.

She wanted so badly to try finding Albert again, but even if she wasn't concentrating on not drowning in this giant oil vat, she was sure the witch would only be waiting for her again. Next time, she might not bother with biting and clawing. She might just gouge out her eyes or rip out her throat. She couldn't go plunging carelessly into that spell while that murderous little bitch was haunting her husband's mind. She didn't know enough to keep them both safe.

Still clutching his shirt against her stinging breast with her free hand, she continued onward, tiptoeing across the oily floor.

At least, she *thought* this was still forward. She still hadn't been able to shake that feeling like this wasn't even the same chamber she started in. With every cautious step she took, she felt more lost.

At least holding Albert's shirt like this was considerably more comfortable than wearing it. Not only couldn't it twist itself up around her anymore, it also acted as a cushion against those nasty scratches.

"Fucking bitch..." she growled again. Just thinking about that woman pissed her off. She absolutely *hated* the idea of her being with her husband somewhere in this darkness. Lucianna was right. She was a psychopath. She wished she'd said yes to the pervert and shredded whatever contract was keeping her from her well-deserved date with hell.

God, she hoped he stayed safe out there, wherever he was...

She wondered if there might be a solution in his book?

Not that it mattered. It was with him, wherever he'd gone. But as long as he still had it, maybe *he* could find a way to evict

Dolly from his consciousness, making it safe for them to bond again.

But then again, Dolly already knew he had it. She broke their flashlight once in an attempt to keep her from reading it. She probably wouldn't allow him the chance to use it.

Besides, would he even be able to find her if she wasn't actively searching for him at the same time? Last time it took both of them.

She still didn't understand how all this magic bullshit worked. The pervert's lessons were hardly all-inclusive. As far as teachers went, he wasn't the absolute worst. They'd made it this far, after all. She was still alive. But he wasn't the best by any means, either. (And as far as human beings went, he was garbage.)

Again, she stopped and shined her light around. Why did it feel like she'd turned toward the right? She was sure she was doing her best to continue straight ahead through the darkness. Veering off course in this great expanse of nothingness was probably inevitable, given that there were no visible points of reference to keep her on course, but for some reason, she felt as if she could almost remember consciously making a slight turn a few minutes ago. But that wasn't something she would've done. That would only be a good way to ensure she lost her way in here.

What a bizarre thing to think, that she'd simply ignored every instinct and intentionally steered herself astray. Was it only her imagination playing tricks on her? Or was it something in her subconscious mind trying to tell her that she was drifting off course and attempting to make her correct it? Or might it be that hateful witch again, screwing with her head, trying to make her lose her way?

Fantastic. She couldn't even tell the bad guys from her own brain in this place. She was *so* fucked.

Confused and frustrated, she closed her eyes and trudged onward for a moment in peaceful darkness, ignoring those strange urges to veer left, at least for the moment. Maybe she should simply trust her instincts. She was supposed to be psychic after all. Maybe she knew more than she realized. But she wasn't certain, not by any means, and simple logic was telling her that she could end up far more lost if she began overcorrecting.

As she pushed onward without looking, she found that she could feel the weirdness of this chamber much stronger like this. It felt as if the gravity in the room were somehow amiss, pulling everything in unnatural directions, distorting the very layout of the space around her.

Again, she wondered if it was only her imagination, but it left such a strangely compelling feeling in her mind. She found herself imagining that there were no walls or ceiling in this chamber at all, but merely a floor that circled all the way around her, the ichor clinging to it like algae to the inside of a submerged pipe.

She knew that the Keeper's temples were otherworldly, full of mind-altering statues and frightful monsters, but this image in her head was pure fantasy. It had to be.

It wasn't the room at all, she began to realize. It was the ichor and its strange properties. Her mind was doing its best to understand what she was feeling. That was all.

This seemed important somehow. It felt like something she needed to remember.

She opened her eyes and glanced around again, but still there was nothing but ichor and darkness wherever she looked.

Ichor… She wished that old jerk never called it that. Something about the word just made this stuff feel even more gross. Wasn't that the word they used in Greek Mythology for whatever substance those old gods had instead of blood? Was she remembering that right? No wonder the word sounded so…*icky*…

Sighing, she took Albert's shirt, wrapped it around her chest and knotted it in the front, turning it into a makeshift bra. That should stay put a little better.

Again, she crept forward through the viscous ooze. But with each step she felt more and more as if she'd become turned around in this darkness.

Something wasn't right. She was suddenly very convinced that she should've found her way across this foul pool by now.

She'd made a mistake. She turned around, confused. Her heart was beating faster and faster. A strange panic was swiftly washing over her. She should've listened to her instincts sooner.

Was the ichor getting *colder*? She was shivering so hard she was having trouble catching her breath.

This was bad. Which way was she supposed to go? She needed Albert and his psychic maps.

She turned around again. How many times was that? Which direction was she facing before? If she wasn't already lost, she was now!

She took another step and felt her foot slide along the slick floor.

The ichor was getting deeper?

She tried to back up, but she couldn't get a grip on the stone. It was too slippery. She was gliding slowly along the bottom, deeper into the ick. The surface climbed up her neck and chin. She lifted her face upward and tried to paddle, but she was still sinking.

Something had changed. Was there a *current*? Was she being pulled forward? Was she being dragged *under*?

Why was this so hard? She felt as if she were struggling to wake up in the morning. Everything was fuzzy and sluggish. Her body seemed to be moving in slow motion.

Her mouth and nose dipped beneath the surface and she couldn't seem to push herself back up. It was as if the ichor were weighing her down.

Where'd the floor go? It was right there a moment ago! Why couldn't she feel it anymore? Had she slipped over a submerged ledge or something? She was sinking! She needed help! She was going to drown in this disgusting goo!

But help wasn't coming.

She closed her eyes as she dipped beneath the surface. It felt as if the ichor were *alive*. It slithered up her face. It oozed into her ears and pulled at her hair.

She wanted to scream but didn't dare give up her breath.

Impossibly, the floor seemed to have completely vanished. She was sinking deeper and deeper, descending into a suffocating blackness that wouldn't even allow her to kick her legs in a futile attempt to swim back up.

She clutched desperately at her glasses with one hand and clenched the other around her flashlight. She couldn't lose either of them or she'd be left blind. And yet, would it even matter? Did she have any chance of surviving this dreadful predicament?

She felt the world fading away from her. She was going to black out. And then she'd never wake up.

Albert... she thought as the world floated away from her. *I'm sorry...*

Chapter 85

Albert stared in horror at the scene before him.

There was blood everywhere, splashed on every wall, across every surface. It dripped from the ceiling and lampshade. It was smeared across the desk and the dresser. It was soaked into the neatly tucked bedspread and matching curtains. It pooled on the floor.

There were bloody handprints everywhere.

In the middle of the crimson mess were two people. A young man, barely more than a teenager, lay naked on the floor, his body flayed open and half-butchered, his lifeless eyes staring upward. A young woman of about the same age, also naked, also covered in blood, was sitting astride him, a bloody pair of sewing shears in one hand and something bloody and dripping in the other. They both had the same kind of hair, his stubbornly deductive brain informed him as if he could possibly want to know such a thing, dark blond and thick and wavy, suggesting that they were closely related. Siblings. Perhaps even twins, given their ages. And yet she was carving him to pieces before his very eyes, removing handfuls of flesh from him, bit by bloody bit, dropping them into a pile on the floor next to them.

Then, as he stood watching, she pulled out another piece, something long and slimy with gore, and forced it into her own mouth as she uttered one of those strangled cries that lured him to this nightmare.

What the hell was happening here? What had he stumbled onto? And how? Where did these two people come from? Did they arrive here with Olivia and Wayne? Questions poured through his terrified mind too quickly to contemplate the answer to any of them.

And as he stood there, the woman slowly turned and looked at him. Her gore-smeared face was drawn tight, her eyes wide, almost bulging, tears streaming down her cheeks and blood dripping down her chin. She looked horrified, almost mad, and yet her hands never stopped their gruesome work.

He took an involuntary step backward at the sight of those crazed eyes, at the desperate misery painted across her blood-soaked face.

"Help me…" she croaked at him, her voice barely escaping her trembling lips. "Please… Make me stop…"

Make her stop? What was that supposed to mean? He didn't dare get any closer. In fact, he took another step backward.

But he bumped into something. Long, slender hands reached around him, clutching at his bare chest. The sensation was familiar. How many times had Brandy reached around him just like this. She even dragged her fingernails across his skin like this. But he knew immediately that this wasn't Brandy. He didn't even have to look down at those black nails.

"Do you want to play with my toys, too?" Dolly whispered into his ear.

He twirled around, his heart leaping, and backed away from her, the fireplace poker raised in a desperate threat.

She was standing just outside the doorway, fully dressed for a change in a frilly black dress with a corset top and a short, poofy sort of gothic princess skirt and fishnet stockings. Gone was the bored, expressionless face of Shanzer's enslaved servant. Her features were lit up, her painted-black lips spread into an elated grin and her eyes gleaming with wicked delight.

Now there was a madwoman on either side of him. There was no way out!

Still gripping the poker with both hands, he turned and backed toward the corner of the room where he could put his back against the wall and keep eyes on them both.

But the bloody one made no move to get up and pursue him. She went on with her grisly deed as if she were on a schedule, choking back sobs as she pulled chunk after dripping chunk from the dead man's viscera.

Dolly stepped through the doorway, still smiling that evil smile, looking not at all wary of the makeshift weapon he held. She had her arms crossed behind her back, looking bizarrely casual for someone leaving bloody footprints in her wake. "I'll let you play. If that's what you want."

"Why would I want anything to do with…?" His gaze flashed over to the insane scene taking place in the middle of the room.

She tipped her head to one side, those long, black pigtails swinging innocently, as if she simply couldn't understand what he could possibly mean, as if the horror show before them were as G-rated as a pretend tea party.

He squeezed his eyes closed and forced his mind to clear. He couldn't let himself be distracted by her. Nothing here made any sense. That was what he needed to be focused on. This place wasn't real. It was like that room Shanzer locked them in when he was being attacked by the psychic predator. "This is all in my head, isn't it?" he said, opening his eyes and meeting her wicked gaze. "You're not really here."

She withdrew one dainty hand from behind her back and pressed her index finger against her lower lip, making a show of pondering the matter. "That *is* a reasonable conclusion," she decided. "And you're not entirely wrong. The disgusting pig gave me a window into your mind and a part of me stayed when we disconnected." That unpleasant grin spread even wider. "He doesn't know, of course." She shifted her finger, making a "shh" gesture, and giggled again.

A part of her stayed? And now he was stuck with this psychopath running around inside his brain, creating disturbing scenes like this one?

Again, she crossed her arms behind her back and took two dainty steps toward him, crossing one foot in front of the other as if putting on a show for him. Then she stopped and tipped her head the other way.

The bloody woman let out another desperate sob, pleading for the terror to stop.

Dolly ignored her. She never took her eyes off him. "But just because we're in *your* head doesn't mean *I'm* not real."

Albert blinked, confused. He was suddenly standing over the bloody woman, staring down at her, watching her cut apart the corpse she was sitting on. This close, he could see the hitching sobs that were shaking her body and hear the whimpering in her raspy breathing.

How did he get over here? He didn't want to be this close. He wanted nothing to do with whatever was going on here!

And where did his poker go? Did he drop it somewhere? It was all he had to defend himself with!

"It doesn't mean *this* isn't real, either," whispered Dolly, her lips brushing against his ear.

He cried out, startled, but found that he couldn't run away. He couldn't move at all. He was standing there, his body frozen, unable to do more than make his fingers and arms twitch a little.

"We may be in your head," she whispered, "but I'm in control now."

He felt her tongue flick against his earlobe and a shudder of revulsion raced through his paralyzed body.

"It's *you* who's in *my mind* now."

He watched as the woman pulled another piece from the man's butchered insides and stuffed it into her mouth. Again, she cried out, a great, tortured sob. Why was she doing that? What the hell was wrong with her?

"You're so lucky," whispered Dolly. "This is one of my most precious memories. I wouldn't share this with just anyone."

Again, he blinked. Again, everything changed. He was still standing over the bloody woman, but his hands were wrapped around her throat. He could feel his muscles trembling with effort. His teeth were clenched. Her bulging, terrified eyes were staring up at him, begging him. Why was he doing this? He didn't want to do this! But he couldn't stop! His body was moving on its own!

"Do you like my toy? Isn't she pretty?"

Her eyes were rolling up into her head. He was killing her. She was going to die right there in his bloodstained hands! And he couldn't make himself stop!

"I can make her do anything I want," Dolly went on. "I can make *you* do anything I want. And there's nothing you can do to stop me."

"Let me go," he grunted. "I don't want this."

Again, he blinked. Again, everything changed. The bloody woman and the butchered corpse were gone. Instead, it was Dolly kneeling before him with his hands around her throat. He was still straining, his body trembling with unwanted effort, but she didn't have the same terrified look as the bloody woman. Her eyes weren't bulging. Her face wasn't turning purple. She hadn't even stopped smiling.

"We're going to have so much fun together," she informed him.

"Let go!" he growled.

But she ignored him. "We're going to play and play and play." That smile spread and her lips parted, flashing him her teeth. For some reason, they were bloody. "For as long as your fragile little mind can last."

Chapter 86

How long had they been climbing? Violet hadn't been able to trust her watch since she left the Lucianna Mysteria. She couldn't remember the last time she bothered glancing at it. But her arms and legs were sore from climbing and her fingers and toes were burning from gripping the rough stone.

It would be just her luck to end up with blisters.

She pulled herself up over the next ledge and then settled herself and shined her light down for Everett again.

They'd come a long way already. If one of them should slip and fall, they might only drop a few feet and be fine, but if they were unlucky it could be a long, hard fall all the way to whatever was waiting at the bottom of this strange chamber.

Maybe it was time to take a little break. Rest would do them good. There was still no end in sight above them, after all. Pushing themselves too hard would only wear them out and leave them more likely to make a mistake.

God, she hoped they didn't have to climb this stuff all the way to the top of one of those towers. That sounded like worse torture than the Ruin right now. But just like when searching for portals with Corey, looking too far ahead rarely did her any good. Anything could happen in these worlds, she'd discovered. There was simply no way to plan for everything. Something unexpected was bound to come up.

And as she watched Everett struggle up the stone, creepy little doll clutched in the crook of his elbow, something new caught her eye. She blinked at the space in front of her, confused. A strange sort of lustrous shimmer swept across the gloom. For a moment, she couldn't wrap her head around it. But then she realized that she was looking at some kind of... *thread?* It was whisper-thin, like a fishing line, running diagonally across the empty space in front of her face, almost invisible except for that little reflection from her light that slid back and forth when she moved.

She leaned closer as Everett hiked his leg up over the stone and pulled himself the rest of the way up. It was strangely pretty. Prismatic. A myriad of colors flashed across her vision as she aimed the flashlight back and forth along the gossamer strand.

She reached out, curious.

"Don't touch that!" gasped Everett.

She snatched her hand back, startled, and looked at him. He was staring at her with wide, frightened eyes.

"What is it?" she asked, her voice withdrawn to a whisper by her racing heart, half-convinced that something awful was listening.

He shook his head. "I don't know. But Alice says it's dangerous."

Dangerous? But it appeared so delicate. What would've happened if he hadn't stopped her? Would it have hurt her?

She glanced around at the dark openings in the stone all around them. Suddenly she was imagining some kind of monstrous spider lurking in one of those many dark places, just waiting for someone to send even the slightest tremble down its web.

The very thought made her skin crawl.

"I don't..." He pursed his face as he struggled to comprehend whatever the strange little doll was telling him. "I can't really wrap my head around what she's calling it. Something like...'grandmother'? Or maybe it's more like...'*gray* mother'?" He shook his head. "It's not literal. That's just what the word sounds like in my head. It's another language or something. Like, it's not *anyone's* mother."

That was good, because what was in *her* head after hearing him call it that was a horrifying image of an ancient, corpse-skinned woman with spider legs and toxic venom dripping from her fangs. (The product of far too many late night horror movie marathons with Corey, she was sure.)

She shined her light back and forth, trying to glimpse where the lustrous gossamer strand began and ended, and whether there were more of them, but it was difficult to see in the ever-present gloom. If they were supposed to keep moving upward, then this particular strand wouldn't be an issue, but there were bound to be more. Not for the first time, she wished she had Corey's powerful light instead of this small one. But she wasn't entirely sure it would have made a difference. It was such a fine strand, so difficult to see, even up close.

She studied the space above her for a moment, searching hard for any faint glimpse of that gossamer shimmer. Then she began climbing again, eager to get far away from the one she'd already found.

"It's really, *really* old," said Everett, relaying what the doll was telling him. "The graymother, or whatever it's really called. Like, it was *already* super old when this place was being built. *That* kind of old."

Violet recalled the dreamlike visions of great stone slabs stacked for miles beneath that strangely colorful sky and felt a shiver at the idea that anything could be even older than that. What had they gotten themselves into? What manner of horror had they stumbled upon?

"I'm not really getting, like, an *evil* vibe from what Alice is telling me. But she's giving me these feelings of something *really dangerous*. Does that make sense?"

"Less demon from hell and more angry honey badger," she replied.

"Yeah! That's a good one!"

"Still sounds like somewhere we probably shouldn't be."

"It does, but she says this is the way we have to go."

"Of course it is..." she muttered. Why would there be a path *around* a deadly, ancient entity in a labyrinth the size of a major metropolitan city?

She grimaced at the pain in her sore fingers as she pulled herself upward. In her rush to continue climbing and get away from that mystery strand, she forgot about needing a break. Hopefully her fear of this chamber didn't push her beyond her limits. If they were to suddenly find themselves forced to climb for their very lives, she wasn't convinced that her muscles wouldn't give out, dooming her to an unceremonious fall.

"Does 'Alice' have any advice on *avoiding* this 'graymother' thing?" she asked as she hoisted herself up onto the next ledge. "Or are we just supposed to keep climbing until we find the top of this place?"

"I don't know if avoiding it is really possible," he replied. "We just go as fast as we can. That's pretty much the whole plan."

She cursed under her breath. That was a *terrible* plan. What were they supposed to do if it showed up? They couldn't exactly fight something in a place like this. And there was literally nowhere to run in here.

"The graymother isn't a physical being or a spirit or even a god," he explained, clearly repeating what the doll was telling him. "It's something entirely *other.*"

Still crouching atop the rough stone ledge, she shined her light into the empty spaces around her. There were more iridescent shimmers up here, revealing several more of those nearly invisible filaments. "What does that mean? What's something *other?*"

"I don't know. Just what it sounds like, I guess. Something *other* than everything else that exists. A one-of-a-kind presence, unlike anything that ever came before or after."

"That doesn't really explain anything," she informed him, shining the light upward now, checking the space above her.

"I know it doesn't." He clambered up over the ledge and crouched beside her. "It's not supposed to. I'm literally telling you that it *can't* be explained."

"Oh..." Slowly, she stood up, still scanning the space around her for those tiny threads.

"It's not something that's going to come out and eat us or tear us to pieces or beat us to death," he promised, "but it's still extremely dangerous. It'll harm us in ways I can't understand, much less describe."

"You're not making me feel any better." She reached up

and grasped a protrusion of stone, testing it, but she didn't like the grip. There appeared to be a better one a little higher.

"Sorry."

"It's fine," she assured him, reaching farther up. "I'm just a little freaked out, is all I—*ow!*"

She snatched her hand back, confused. There was a sharp pain and a strange sort of jolt, almost as if she'd been electrocuted.

And now her middle finger was bleeding.

"I told you to watch out!" gasped Everett, grabbing at her hand and looking at it.

"I didn't see anything!" She shined the light up at the wall. This time, she glimpsed it. A shimmer of iridescent light zipping past. It was no wonder she missed it. It was almost right up against the stone. "Shit!" She looked down at her finger again. There was so much blood! "How the hell did it *cut* me?"

Everett rummaged through one of his pockets as she looked closer. She could see the skin gaping where she touched the thread. It looked as if she'd sliced the pad of her finger with a very sharp knife. But she barely touched it! "The graymother's strands aren't a part of this or any reality," he explained as he withdrew a small, plastic case. Inside was an assortment of adhesive bandages. He picked through them for a moment, selected the best one for the job and unwrapped it. "It's unbreakable and immovable, but it's also hundreds of times finer than the edge of a razor blade."

"You could've explained that sooner," she grumbled. It was starting to hurt now. A dull, deep sort of ache. That wasn't going to make climbing up these rocks any easier...

"I didn't know. Alice didn't explain it to *me* until just now. I'm not sure she knew it until you actually touched it." He wiped away the excess blood with the tail of his shirt and then pressed the bandage over the cut. It was a fingertip bandage, ideal for the injury. The kid was better prepared than she was, that was for sure.

Well, she did wonder what would've happened if he hadn't stopped her from touching that first one. Now she knew, she supposed. If she'd tried to grab onto it, instead of just nicking it... What an awful thought! Maybe this was the universe's way of telling her to listen to him and his creepy little friend.

"Right now," he went on, "we have a bigger problem."

"What kind of problem?" But the words hadn't fully passed her lips when she felt it for herself. Something in the atmosphere had changed. The air here was growing thick and heavy. She could feel the temperature dropping, but not with her skin. The cold was spreading *within* her, an invasive sensation, seeping deep into her bones, her sinews, her marrow, as if her *soul* were icing over.

"Not good," muttered Everett.

Clutching at her bandaged finger, she stared wide-eyed into the gloom below them, her heart pounding. A strange hush had fallen over the chamber, but at the same time it felt alive with noise. The air buzzed faintly with strange vibrations that seemed to hover just beyond the range of her hearing, like barely perceived voices crying out in a disjointed symphony of haunting whispers in languages long dead and festering.

It was coming. She could sense it absolutely and undoubtedly. And yet it was a slippery sensation. It felt strangely there and not there at the same time, a mere *suggestion* of an approaching presence, like a weight pressing down at the very edges of her perception.

He wasn't exaggerating when he told her he couldn't explain it. This feeling wasn't like some monstrous beast bearing down on them. Nor was it like some kind of terrifying phantom approaching. This was something entirely different, something that defied understanding.

And it would be on them soon.

"We really need to get out of here," advised Everett. His voice was oddly calm, and yet she could hear an edge to the words, an underlying panic that she didn't care for. The kid was so *eager* to experience every dreadful thing they encountered. Why did he suddenly sound frightened?

Dazed, she looked up into the darkness above. The strand that bit her finger prevented them going up that way, but there was another opening to the right, and no sign of that dangerous shimmer. But for a moment, her legs wouldn't move. Those strands were almost invisible, and yet little more than a careless touch was all it took to bite so deeply into her unsuspecting finger. What would happen if she tried to move too quickly and placed her entire hand on one? Would it be sharp enough to sever her fingers? If she tripped over one, would it be enough to lose her whole foot? And what if she were to lose her footing altogether and fall?

She couldn't help imagining herself plummeting down through that darkness, strand after strand slipping effortlessly through her, slicing her to pieces...

"We have to go!" hissed Everett. "Now!"

Terrified out of her mind by both the horror approaching and the perils ahead, she forced herself to continue climbing.

Chapter 87

Erin screamed.

She couldn't help it. She didn't expect to run into a giant down here.

At the end of the narrow stone corridor was an even narrower opening, leading into a larger chamber beyond. Eager to find what was here and get out, she ducked through it without bothering to look and came face to face—sort of—with a ten-foot-tall humanoid creature.

The scream escaped her before she could realize that the creature was only made of stone. And no one would have blamed her. It was just standing there, as if waiting for her. It had freakishly long arms and legs, a giant Adam's apple and no facial features whatsoever.

Also, the thing was hung like a giraffe for some ungodly reason… Any woman in her right mind would've screamed.

But it was the incredible detail in the statue that really caught her by surprise. Every muscle, every crease, every *wrinkle*, carved so perfectly that her brain couldn't entirely accept that it was only cold, hard stone. She stood there a moment, her light fixed on it, taking it all in. It was so bizarre. It had no hair, no eyes, no mouth or nose or ears, only a smooth, featureless plane for a face, and yet it had cords in its long neck, protruding collarbones and a naval. It had nipples. It even had *fingerprints*. The details in that obscenely enormous penis alone was unbelievable. She couldn't help but reach out and touch the man's belly, convincing herself it wasn't really flesh simply mimicking stone.

It was turned slightly to one side, holding one hand out toward her, palm up, freakishly long fingers splayed, as if demanding some kind of tribute from her. The other hand was stretched out and pointing forward, into the waiting darkness.

A toll? Really?

She shined her light into the gloom ahead. There was a doorway there, she saw, with a set of stone steps leading down.

There was something strangely familiar about this place. That stone, in particular... She still felt as if she'd seen it somewhere before.

But where? *When?* She'd definitely never seen anything like this statue before.

Did Horatio say something about a place like this? She tried to remember back to that day, but the actual words he spoke to her were still buried in the haze of that moment. She still didn't understand what happened. It was as if she'd been drugged or something, but she knew it was nothing so mundane as that.

Afterward, she knew things. She knew of the existence of the thorn. She knew where to find it. (Or at least all that mysterious mumbo jumbo about iron gates and forgotten fields and giant hands that was supposed to point her to it, she guessed.) She knew that the world was far bigger and stranger than she'd ever suspected. She knew that monsters were real. And she knew that her days among the living were numbered. She didn't know what, precisely, the thorn looked like—and still didn't—but she knew that it was some kind of key to some extraordinary thing that was hidden somewhere far away. And she still had no idea exactly how or when she was going to die, but she knew that death wasn't really the end. Something came after. And what came after had something to do with Horatio's mysterious bar.

(*An anomalous wrinkle in the fabric of reality where it becomes possible for the physical and the spiritual to trade places.*)

But she definitely didn't remember anything about a bunch of stone rooms hidden under a Kentucky cave or a ten-foot-tall, faceless porn star statue demanding tips. She was fairly sure something like that would've come back to her by now.

And yet there were a few things, she was realizing, that she somehow understood anyway. She understood that this place, in spite of how clean it looked, was *extremely* old, as old as the world itself. Maybe even older somehow. She understood that this was no ordinary structure. It was a vault. And somewhere inside, the thorn was waiting for her. And finally, she understood that this guy wasn't demanding money.

He wanted her clothes. She was supposed to continue naked from here. (Although she couldn't for the life of her understand *why*.)

She stared at that outstretched hand, those half-curled fingers as long as her forearm.

Strange thoughts filled her mind. People she didn't know, but were just like her, she understood, trudging naked through a labyrinth of stone. Chamber after chamber bathed for eons in darkness, illuminated only briefly by their passing flashlights. Creatures like nothing she'd ever seen before. A towering pyramid with a bloody secret. And a burning mountain stretching high into an eternally black sky.

What...was that just now...? Those weren't *memories*. At least, they weren't *her* memories. Was it something Horatio showed her while she was in that mysterious haze that she couldn't remember? Who were those people? That place they were in looked the same as this one. She even recalled more freaky statues like this. But it was *enormous*. And that mountain... It didn't look like something from this world!

(*...all connected...round and round...past and present and future...*)

She squeezed her eyes closed and clenched her teeth, frustrated. Where were these thoughts coming from? What did they mean? What did Horatio say to her during that missing time in the Elysium Fog?

(*...many wheels turning...all parts of a great machine...an eternal clockwork engine of cosmic significance...*)

Somehow, she didn't feel like these were things Horatio explained to her. It was far stranger than that. She couldn't shake the feeling that she was explaining it to *herself*, as if some other version of her were speaking to her...

(*...past and present and future...*)

She could almost remember something... A lake? A pretty bridesmaid at a wedding? A black forest? A pale train rocketing through an unnatural darkness?

She opened her eyes again and found that she was standing in complete darkness, her hand pressed against the smooth stone wall while darkling shapes danced around her, seen but unseen.

"Past and future..." she whispered. She still didn't understand what was happening, how she could be both here and there, both now and then, but somehow it all made a little more sense than it did before.

There were two of her. One that was dead and one that was in a temporary imitation of the life she once had. But there was also a third. There was one of her that was still alive in the past that she was reliving so vividly that she thought it was the present. The stoneworks of the Faceless Ones—or the temples of the Sentinels, if one preferred—were anomalies in space and time that had the ability to transcend all concepts and rules. It was a singularity of sorts, where multiple points of a person's existence were able to connect, like looping a string back on itself. It was difficult to comprehend, and easy to become confused, but she was slowly talking herself through it, she thought.

This her—the *real* her in this true point in time—had a job to do here in the City Beyond Memory. She had something important to find, though she couldn't quite remember what that something was. *That* her was only a memory. She had a job to do in the past, inside the mysterious vault hidden in that remote Kentucky wilderness. She had to find and claim Yggdrasil's thorn, one of the Three Whispers, without which *this* her could never have entered this temple in the first place. *That* her didn't yet know of the events that would lead to *this* her, and yet she stood here now, in a position to communicate with that other version of herself. Because the two of them were connected.

What a strange dichotomy...

And what a curious predicament. It occurred to her now that she had the ability to affect the past in any way she chose.

What if she sent back a warning? What if she told that other her to flee that awful vault and never come back? Could she prevent her own death?

But then what? What consequences would there be for

something so drastic? Would something terrible happen? It wasn't as if she wandered out into the forest that morning on a lark. She did as Horatio instructed not because she somehow trusted him, but because of those awful things she started seeing, like the creeping, crawling things that stalked that beautiful wedding...

This was where she belonged, she realized.

Again, she closed her eyes and took a calming breath. "Do it," she breathed. "It's what you're meant to do."

(*Everything will be okay.*)

She frowned and opened her eyes. What was that just now? She shined her light around the small chamber, confused. For some reason she forgot she had her cell phone light with her. She thought she was wandering around in the dark.

Also, was she wearing something different? It seemed like she was wearing a dress rather than these shorts and tee shirt ...

And where did those strange thoughts come from?

Was this all Horatio? Did he fill her head with some sort of subliminal programming? Was she only doing all this because he brainwashed her somehow?

No. That didn't feel right at all. Horatio wasn't the villain. She could trust him.

Again, she looked at the statue's outstretched hand. *Do it,* she thought. *It's what you're meant to do.*

"Everything will be okay," she whispered.

Was she going crazy?

She sighed and stripped off her tee shirt. She wasn't sure why. She didn't know what being naked in this place would accomplish. It seemed to her that it would only make whatever was waiting at the bottom of those steps more frightening by leaving her more vulnerable. But somehow it seemed as if this was what she was supposed to do.

She hung the shirt on those outstretched fingers, then untied her shoes and placed them by its huge, freaky feet. She draped her socks over the upturned palm. Then she added her shorts and her bra and finally her panties.

She stood there in that stone chamber, staring at her

clothes, adorned in nothing but sunflowers.

"Everything will be okay," she said again.

Why did that phrase sound so true? How could she possibly know that everything would be okay? She wasn't that much of an optimist. And yet it really did feel like everything was going to be okay. She just had to do what she came here to do.

Alone and naked, she tightened her grip on her phone and set off down those stone steps, into the unknown depths of the vault.

Chapter 88

Wayne blinked up at the strange walls around him, confused. Where was he? This wasn't the conical chamber. Nor was it one of the temple's usual passageways. It was empty, stark and strangely sterile like all those labyrinth corridors, but everything else was different. That all-too-familiar gray stone, ever-present until now, was completely gone, replaced with something that looked more like polished white marble, but with a strange, translucent quality that cast a glowing halo around wherever he aimed his light. It was much larger than any of the temple corridors, at least thirty feet from the floor to the top of the arched ceiling, and there were evenly spaced depressions in the walls that looked like oval-shaped windows, but didn't open onto anything except more of that strange, translucent stone.

Olivia was still with him, thankfully. And she appeared unharmed from their fall. These were the most important things. They were still clinging to each other, holding on for dear life, determined to not be separated again, no matter where they might land or what fresh trouble they might fall into.

"Where are we?" she asked.

It was a good question. One he had no answer for. He shined his light back and forth, surprised at the increased reach these pale walls added compared to the temple's much darker gray. The smooth, white surfaces reflected his flashlight beam as much as it dispersed it, allowing him to see nearly the length of a football field in either direction. A welcome change, if more than a little peculiar.

But how did they get here? Didn't they fall through the floor back there? Did he remember that right? He was descending that spiraling ramp, making his way to the bottom of the chamber. But when he stepped onto the floor, his foot passed through it as if it were some kind of illusion. But there was no hole overhead for them to have fallen through to land here.

Except...*did* they really land here? He remembered falling. He remembered letting out a startled curse. He remembered Olivia screaming as the two of them dropped. And then...

He rubbed at his head, bemused. Then what? That was the weird part. He definitely recalled *falling*...but he didn't remember *landing*. The next thing he knew, the two of them were lying on this *other* floor, their arms wrapped around each other, dazed.

It almost felt as if he'd lost some time there...as if he'd missed something between then and now...

He stood up, his eyes peeled for any more surprises, and helped Olivia to her feet as well, careful not to let go of her for even a moment. He didn't trust this sudden change. This place didn't make sense. That same gray stone had been everywhere until now. In both this temple and the last one. The only places he hadn't been able to see it were places that were simply too big to see across with his light, places like that bizarre, alien ecosystem they found themselves flushed into. So what was *this* about? Had they somehow stumbled across an exit? Had they unwittingly reached the end of their journey?

Somehow he doubted it would be anything so nice.

Had they fallen through some kind of invisible hole in the ceiling? He couldn't reach that high to check whether his hand might pass right through the surface. All he could do was press his palm against the wall beside him, confirming that at least the walls were solid. It was smooth and cool to the touch, exactly as it looked like it should feel.

"This is weird, right?" said Olivia, those gorgeous brown eyes staring down the pale corridor stretched out before them. "It's not just me?"

"It's not just you," he assured her. "Are you feeling anything? Does it feel safe in here?"

She squinted as she searched those still-unfamiliar feelings inside her. "I think so. I'm not feeling any, like, *panic* or *dread* or anything. But…" She turned and squinted in the other direction, confused. "I don't know… I feel *something*… I can't put my finger on it."

He didn't press the matter. If she could put whatever was in her head into words she would have done it. She wasn't holding anything back. He was better off focusing on figuring out which direction they should go from here. They both looked the same for as far as he could see.

"Here."

He turned and shined his light the other way. He was sure he didn't imagine that. It was the clearest he'd heard the voice yet. It was a female voice. And it sounded young. A little girl? It reminded him of his youngest sister, Wendy, when she was little. But then again, all children sort of sounded to him like Wendy. He didn't exactly spend a lot of time around kids, so maybe that was simply his best frame of reference.

Either that, or something was imitating Wendy's voice on purpose… Some kind of trick? A means of slipping past his defenses?

But that didn't feel right. There was something oddly familiar about the voice, something beyond merely reminding him of his baby sister. He couldn't help feeling as if he *knew* this voice somehow.

"Which way?" asked Olivia, meaning she clearly hadn't heard it. And yet he knew he didn't imagine it. Would he have been able to tell that it came from this way if it had only been a voice in his head?

Again, why was *he* the one hearing it? Did it have something to do with having been dead? Was it some kind of spirit trying to communicate with him?

But again, why wouldn't Andrea have been able to hear it? It was speaking to him while she was still with them. And *she* was the one who was supposed to be able to hear ghosts. It made no sense!

He tightened his grip on Olivia's arm and started walking, following the mysterious voice. He was well aware that it might be a mistake. He had no way to be sure that this unknown speaker didn't mean them any harm. It could be a trap. It could very well be that chaotic presence Maeve warned them about, the thing Andrea called the Priestess of Ruin. But he followed it anyway. A part of it was simple curiosity, of course. He wanted to know *why* he was hearing the voice and no one else could. He wanted to know who—or what—was speaking to him. But he also couldn't help feeling that he couldn't ignore it forever. If he tried, it would only keep calling out to him. Perhaps it was better to just see what the unknown caller wanted from him and get it over with.

Besides, he had no idea how to go back the way they came.

"You're almost here," sighed the voice.

Was that supposed to make him feel better? Because there was still something dreadfully ominous about a mysterious voice luring him to some unknown destination deep inside a temple, of all things. Especially a voice that no one else was able to hear.

"Still not feeling anything?" he asked.

"Nothing I can describe," she replied, looking up at him. "I'm getting these weird, like, mixed feelings that I can't really explain. Like...*lots* of feelings. It's weird."

He met her gaze and frowned. What did that mean? Was it that whatever was waiting for them up ahead was something her psychic mind couldn't process for some reason? Or was it more sinister than that? Was something interfering with her somehow, scrambling the feelings her brain used to sense danger?

Not wanting to frighten her, he kept his questions to himself and focused on the path before them. But he couldn't stop thinking about what Andrea said back there.

(*She's, like, some kind of ancient god or something.*)

A supernatural entity, strong enough to challenge even the Keeper's perfect plans?

(*I sense a chaotic energy hovering over you, interfering.*)

Maybe this was a mistake. Had he unwittingly placed his beautiful fiancée in harm's way?

Ahead of them, the white passage opened up into an empty chamber roughly the size of their entire apartment. It was round and domed, made of the same translucent white stone. As they drew closer, he saw that there were six more passages leading out of it, each one identical to the one they were in now.

Another labyrinth? More impossible choices?

"Keep going," whispered the voice. Once again, it felt so strangely familiar, as if it had been speaking to him for months.

Again, he wondered if this voice could be something from his time while he was dead? One of the many things he'd forgotten as soon as he sucked in a new breath?

They stepped out into the open space and shined their lights around, taking it all in.

It was all so *different* from the rest of the temple. To Wayne, it all looked like something from a fairy tale. A mysterious, far-off palace from the pages of *Arabian Nights*, perhaps. A castle of frosted crystals, like a white version of the Emerald City from *The Wonderful Wizard of Oz*. The only thing the two had in common was a complete and utter lack of any kind of furnishings.

"Find me," whispered that voice again. It sounded close enough to be right in his ear, but at the same time seemed to be coming from one of the passageways to his left.

Beside him, Olivia shuddered and pressed herself closer to him. "I just felt a *really* big chill just now. I don't know why."

He glanced down at her again. Was it only a coincidence that she shivered exactly when the voice called to him? Or had she sensed something dangerous at that moment? And if so, was it a warning? A subtler version of the crippling panic that her psychic alarm typically overwhelmed her with?

He didn't like this. There were too many unknowns. And yet somehow he felt that turning back would accomplish nothing. They weren't inside the temple anymore. He was suddenly very sure of that. This was somewhere different. Something brought them here. And there was little reason to think that they'd simply be allowed to leave.

Olivia shook her head. It was a slow gesture, uncertain, uneasy. "I just... I don't understand what I'm feeling. It's not a psychic alarm, exactly. I don't feel like we're in any danger right now. But I feel *really* uneasy about being here, like it's going to lead somewhere I don't want to go."

"I'm here," breathed that mysterious voice. It was definitely drawing him toward that passage. And it sounded strangely excited, almost impatient.

He stepped closer to it, shining his light into it, illuminating the white surfaces. It wasn't as long as the last one. He could see a door, large and heavy, like the sort of thing you might find barring the way in some medieval castle, constructed from a thick, dark wood that he couldn't identify. But in stark contrast, the handle was strangely ornate. Silvery and shiny. Almost delicate.

The temple never had any doors. Unless you counted those seals that barred that nightmare tunnel. But those didn't even look like doors, much less like this.

"I feel sick," groaned Olivia.

He looked down at her again, concerned. "Do we need to turn back? Try to find a way out?"

But she shook her head again. She was staring at that mysterious door, her expression pinched. "No. I think we have to keep going forward. I feel like whatever's right in front of us is something we need to find. It's something *else* that's making me feel sick. Something farther away." She looked up at him. "Something that comes later, I think."

He stared into her eyes, uncertain. So…not the gallows, themselves, he supposed. Just the death march leading to them.

Again, he turned his gaze on that door. He took a breath, steeled his nerves, tightened his grip on Olivia's arm and started walking. It was time to get this over with.

"Please," sighed that soft, girlish voice. Did he know this voice from his dreams? Was that it? Like that conical stone chamber or Nora's Lilac Grove? "I've been waiting so long for you to come."

He frowned. What did that mean? Who was this? Did she know him?

He stepped up to the door and grasped the shiny handle.

"I'm finally going to meet you."

He glanced down at Olivia. She looked terrified, but she gave him a confident nod. She was ready for whatever was on the other side.

He didn't give himself a chance to change his mind. He pulled open the door. It looked heavy, but it moved smoothly. A warm glow poured out as it opened, the light radiating from a large fireplace directly across from the door, illuminating a room that was—for the first time in any temple—fully furnished. There was a low table on the right, with brightly colored cushions arranged around it and a bowl of fresh fruit sitting on it. There was a basin protruding from the wall behind the table with a constant stream of clean water pouring into it. There were stoneware cups and dishes on the fireplace mantle and a number of thick, warm rugs strewn across the bare stone floor. There were shelves on one wall with folded clothes and some personal hygiene products. The whole place sort of reminded him of his old dorm room... But what drew his attention was the large, four-poster canopy bed on the left side of the room, covered in warm blankets and at least a dozen pillows and stuffed animals.

A little girl was sitting in the middle of all that softness, her small legs curled beneath her, wearing a pretty, blue dress. She had long, dark hair tied back into a simple ponytail and was clutching a little stuffed panda. She appeared to be about six or seven years old.

It was pretty much the very *last* thing he expected to find waiting for him in this bizarre place, in spite of the fact that the voice had sounded like that of a little girl. It simply made much more sense that the girlish qualities would be a trick of some sort than that there'd actually be a little girl waiting here in her own private suite in a mysterious marble palace.

He felt as if he were losing his mind.

The girl gave them a big, bright smile. "I knew you'd find me," she said. Her eyes were wide and bright, but pale in color and strangely distant, almost dreamy.

He remembered thinking for a moment that the voice calling to him sounded like Wendy, and looking upon her now, he found that she sort of resembled her, too.

But Olivia saw something different. "She looks like *you*," she whispered.

The little girl hugged the stuffed panda, that smile growing only wider, and said, "Hello, Daddy."

Chapter 89

Andrea was again staring at those awful daggers where there should have been only fingers. She still couldn't fully grasp what she was looking at. They weren't blades. Nor were they claws. Something about them seemed to defy her brain, much like the murk, she realized. She wasn't capable of understanding whatever Tia really was. "Stop it," she gasped. "You can't do this."

"I can do anything I want," Tia informed her. "Chaos goddess, remember?"

She shook her head, fresh tears welling up in her eyes.

"Nothing personal. Just a means to an end."

Nothing personal? Really? This woman was promising to *murder* her! How was that *ever* not personal? "You can't," she said again, her voice cracking. "I have to finish what I started. My friends. They need me." Erin told her that none of them would ever be able to make it home without her. She wouldn't just be killing *her*.

"Sorry," said Tia, sounding not sorry at all. "Once you're gone, it'll all be over. A little snip-snip. A *tiny* bit of excruciating pain. Then it'll be done. The Keeper's tower of terrors comes tumbling down and nothing can start it up again."

"That doesn't make any sense!" shouted Andrea. "The Keeper plans for everything! You said so yourself! Do you really think he hasn't planned for *you*?"

"Of course he has," she laughed. "I'm sure of it."

"Then *why*? It won't make any difference! Everything is going to happen his way no matter what any of us do!"

"Oh there will be a difference," countered Tia. Her eyes and her grin had both gone wide. She looked positively crazed. "He's not the only one capable of anticipating every outcome. I've got that son of a bitch by his balls this time. He's out of tricks. No sleight of hand. No trump card. No castling. If he's going to beat me, then he's going to have to do something that even *I* can't predict."

Andrea stared down at her. The longer she spoke, the more worked up she was getting. Now she was practically panting, those obscene breasts heaving. There was sweat beading on her face.

"*That's* what this is about," she plowed on. "Not complete domination. I don't care about the end of the cycle. What turns me on is the thought of making a total fucking *mess* out of it! I'll take his machine apart, piece by piece, until even *he* can't fix it." She let out an animal-like squeal of glee at the idea, a sound that was almost *perverse*. "I'm going to force his hand. I'm going to see what he's really willing to do to protect his precious cycle. And I promise you it will be *gloriously* profound!" She gnawed at her lower lip and shivered with perverse delight. "I'm getting wet just thinking about it!" she declared.

"Ew!"

"Wanna see?"

"*No!*" She squeezed her eyes closed and turned away. "God! Stop it! Why are you like this?"

"Because it's fun!"

"Fun?" She glared down at her. "*You're threatening to kill me!*"

She gave her head an uncertain wobble. "No... 'Threat' sort of implies that I might not do it. I'm definitely going to kill you." She leaned forward and whispered, "That's kind of the important part, remember?"

"How can you be so cruel?"

"Easier than you might think." Again, she reached out with those awful blades.

A tear streaked down each side of Andrea's face. She couldn't free herself. And no one was coming to her rescue this time. She couldn't think of any way out of this. And it seemed so grossly unfair. Again, she wondered why it had to be Stella. Why did it have to be someone she thought she trusted? That was the worst part of it. "I was your friend..."

"Gods don't have friends, sweetie. Sometimes they have *pets*. And sometimes they have *cattle*. Just dumb animals waiting to be put to good use."

"That's all I ever was to you?"

She lowered her hand, those awful blades glinting in the blood-red light of that evil sky. "For what it's worth, I *did* enjoy the time we spent together. You've been one of my *favorite* pets, for sure. I think I might actually miss you a little. But let's be realistic here. Whether you die now or eighty years from now really isn't going to make a difference to me. One blink of an eye or two. Live long enough and time eventually loses its meaning. I've literally sat and watched centuries slide past. You're a speck of dust in the cosmos and barely a tick in the endless passage of time."

Andrea stared into those remorseless eyes, letting all of that sink in. "It's true..." she realized. "You're not even a little bit human, are you?"

Tia stared at her for a moment, seemingly surprised. "No," she replied, as if it were the stupidest question she'd ever heard. "I'm not."

She closed her eyes as another tear slid down her face. A lie. Just another false friend who turned away from her. She never cared. She never even had a heart. Or even a shred of humanity. Not from the very beginning.

She felt the tips of those blades press against her throat and squeezed her eyes tighter. She didn't want to hurt anymore. Was there pain in the murk? Was there suffering? Was there fear? There was no heaven, she knew that. Not out here in the middle of the endless Wood. Not beneath that poisoned sky. She'd already learned that awful truth. There were no spirit highways out here. All that awaited her was a lonesome and empty eternity.

As she hung there, waiting for the inevitable end, an image materialized in her mind. A great, coiled shape in the darkness. She wasn't sure what made her think of it, but it reminded her of a snake.

She didn't like snakes. That wasn't what she wanted to see

in her last moments of life.

But the image was persistent. It grew clearer and clearer. She could see the individual scales glinting even in the darkness, a faintly iridescent sheen sliding over them.

A head rose up from the center of those coils, enormous yellow eyes staring back at her, as clear as if she were looking at them in broad daylight.

Was this giant snake *Tia*? Was this her true form? A fitting shape for a sneaky, deceitful bitch. Or was it only her imagination manifesting a warning about the nature of her real enemy? A metaphor for the betrayal that was waiting for her from the start?

Real or imagined, that terrible serpent opened its mouth with a chilling hiss, its gleaming fangs dripping venom.

"Goodbye," said Tia.

Then the serpent struck.

Chapter 90

This was bad.

Corey scanned the multitude of strings stretched between the stone contacts and Austin's bisected torso, trying to understand what was happening. But while he possessed that strange, automatic understanding of what he was supposed to do to complete the job he was apparently sent here for, he lacked any real comprehension about the sentinel's technology or even most of the concepts on which it functioned.

He might as well be standing in the engine room of a futuristic alien spacecraft holding a wrench and a hammer.

He was here to sort the strings and wrap them around stone spikes. How the hell was he supposed to diagnose and repair some kind of sentinel technology computer virus?

Meanwhile, Austin had become unresponsive. His remaining working parts had gone rigid, his muscles taut. The veins on his neck were popping. One eye was half-closed while the other was wide-open and practically bulging. His mouth was stretched open in a frightful sort of silent scream and his functioning hand had clenched into a fist. He sort of looked like he'd had a stroke, really. But robots didn't have those, as far as he knew. And he certainly wasn't dead. He kept making a strange sort of clicking noise in his throat and now and then that bulging eye would twitch in one direction or another as if aware before fixing on the ceiling again.

As much as he wasn't missing being complained at, he understood that in order to complete his task, he needed the stuck-up machine functional.

He looked down at the strands coiled on the floor around

him. More and more of them were giving him that feeling of *wrongness* when he touched them, telling him that something bad would happen if he connected it to the contact spike.

"Virus…" he muttered thoughtfully to himself. He used the phrase when Austin started acting weird, but computer lingo was nothing more than a metaphor he was using to help him wrap his head around the sentinels' creations. Because what little he understood about it all was much more like using a computer than fixing a machine. He'd even compared that fake blood to some kind of liquid hard drive. But this wasn't a computer. It was something altogether different from anything he'd ever encountered before, different from anything *anyone* had ever encountered before. So would concepts like computer viruses even work? Or was it possible that this was something closer to a *biological virus*?

There was a fairly terrifying thought. Computers he could understand. Modern medicine, not so much. And would it remain limited to only infecting Austin? Or was he in danger, too?

And now that he was thinking about it, didn't Albert and Brandy say something about it being some kind of "infection" that plagued the Lucianna Mysteria while they were searching for the carriage house?

Was *that thing* one of the intruders that slipped through the gates when they all entered the City Beyond Memory? Was he dealing with some kind of sentient *disease* with the ability to sabotage even the Keeper's meticulous designs?

Austin kept saying that the Keeper didn't make mistakes, that he had everything figured out to the most miniscule detail. But was that really true? Could even a being such as that plan for *everything*?

But pessimism rarely solved any problems. Right now he needed to assume that there was a solution and focus on finding it. But where did he even begin?

He scanned the floor around him, looking over all those bloody strings that weren't really strings at all. They were something entirely different, something he shouldn't be able to pick up and hold in his hands or even see. There was nothing he'd ever encountered or imagined in his life that was exactly like it. Austin and all his marvelous bits and pieces might have been the only instance in all the universes that ever existed of such technology, after all. But if he were to loosely compare it to *anything* he could understand, he would probably describe them as computer programs. Lines of intricate coding, each one with a specific purpose, designed to work together in a hyper-complex algorithm hundreds of thousands of times more advanced than any concept of artificial intelligence.

And one by one, each and every one of them were failing.

Austin was dying. And he was taking with him the only means of unlocking the Oblivion Door.

And if they failed to open that door, then none of them were ever going to make it home.

He couldn't let that happen. He had to fix this.

He thought back on the journey that brought him here. Following the flow of that strange "energy" through the stone corridors to reach this room. The gate that would only be opened with Olivia's thorn. The control panels outside the wall. The mysterious carriage that brought him here with Violet and Albert and Brandy.

But none of that was what he was looking for.

The answer went much farther back than that.

(*I remember this place.*)

All the way back to that mysterious cave, deep inside where they first encountered the temple stone.

(*It's a safe place.*)

He'd forgotten about that place for so long. Only after he interacted with that first control panel did he finally begin to remember it. And even then it had come back to him so gradually that he couldn't quite recall when it was there. But looking back now, it was as fresh in his mind as it was while he was down there, as if it had been preserved inside his brain somehow.

He was able to reach inside the stone then, too. Just as he did at those hidden passages leading here. It wasn't a freak accident. He knew precisely what he was doing. He *remembered* it, as if he'd seen it all before somewhere. For poor Violet, it was as if he'd just performed some kind of intricate magic trick, but to him, it was as simple and as normal as breathing.

(*How'd you do that?*)

(*Dunno.*)

How did he already know that place? How could he be so sure that it was safe there? Why did he *know* anything? It wasn't that he'd been there before, he now realized. It was because he already possessed the knowledge necessary to do this job. He was born with it. Interacting with the temple stone, even just *touching* it, was enough to access the information hidden inside his brain.

(*It's like a machine. All connected together.*)

(*It's a bunch of rocks.*)

(*It's not.*)

He understood it, even back then. He had all the knowledge he was ever going to need about the stoneworks and the sentinels' technology.

He frowned. He had everything he needed then. And he had everything he needed *now*.

Again, he scanned the strings and those stone spikes.

Yes. He had the knowledge he needed. But like in that mysterious chamber twenty years ago, he wasn't going to be able to explain it, not even to himself. It was just something he was going to have to do.

He plucked three strands from the floor and two more from the sharp stone contacts and gripped them all in one hand. Then he picked up two more strands, eyeballed them for a moment, uncertain, then placed them inside his mouth and bit down on them. (It wasn't blood, after all. It only *looked* like blood.) Finally, he leaned forward and reached all the way inside Austin's torso with his free hand.

It was like the stone back then. And it was like those hidden doorways in the labyrinth. He needed to reach inside, between the molecules, as he'd thought of it. Except instead of stone, he needed to reach inside Austin, through the walls of his chest cavity, into a space that was neither within him nor without.

This was why he couldn't think about it. It made no sense.

He just had to do it.

"I got ya, buddy," he grunted as he felt his fingers slip through the impossible space inside the inside of him, like when it felt as if he were reaching between the very molecules of the stone.

A bizarre sensation seemed to trickle up his arm and into his body, sending jolts of strangely sour energy pulsing through his veins and into his clenched teeth. It was almost like being electrocuted, but nothing so pleasant. His legs became engulfed in a pins-and-needles sensation, his eyeballs began jittering back and forth on their own, his hair felt like it was standing on end and he suddenly and loudly passed gas as the world around him seemed to swirl into a churning gray cloud.

Then things started getting weird.

About the author

Brian Harmon is an independent author of horror fiction, suspense and dark adventure. He grew up in rural Missouri and now lives in Southern Wisconsin with his wife, Guinevere, and their three children.

For more about Brian Harmon and his work, visit
www.BrianHarmonBooks.com